The Works of George Eliot
IN TWELVE VOLUMES

Daniel Deronda

Part I

ILLUSTRATED

NEW YORK
P. F. COLLIER & SON

9

Elliot

CONTENTS.

DANIEL DERONDA.

BOOK I.—THE SPOILED CHILD.

CHAPTER I.

Men can do nothing without the make-believe of a beginning. Even Science, the strict measurer, is obliged to start with a make-believe unit, and must fix on a point in the stars' unceasing journey when his sidereal clock shall pretend that time is at Nought. His less accurate grandmother Poetry has always been understood to start in the middle; but on reflection it appears that her proceeding is not very different from his; since Science, too, reckons backward as well as forward, divides his unit into billions, and with his clock-finger at Nought really sets off *in medias res*. No retrospect will take us to the true beginning; and whether our prologue be in heaven or on earth, it is but a fraction of that all-presupposing fact with which our story sets out.

WAS she beautiful or not beautiful? and what was the secret of form or expression which gave the dynamic quality to her glance? Was the good or the evil genius dominant in those beams? Probably the evil; else why was the effect that of unrest rather than of undisturbed charm? Why was the wish to look again felt as coercion, and not as a longing in which the whole being consents?

She who raised these questions in Daniel Deronda's mind was occupied in gambling: not in the open air under a southern sky, tossing coppers on a ruined wall, with rags about her limbs; but in one of those splendid resorts which the enlightenment of ages has prepared for the same species of pleasure at a heavy cost of gilt mouldings, dark-toned color, and chubby nudities, all correspondingly heavy—forming a suitable condenser for human breath belonging, in great part, to the highest fashion, and not easily procurable to be breathed in elsewhere in the like proportion, at least by persons of little fashion.

It was near four o'clock on a September day, so that the

108

atmosphere was well brewed to a visible haze. There was deep stillness, broken only by a light rattle, a light chink, a small sweeping sound, and an occasional monotone in French, such as might be expected to issue from an ingeniously constructed automaton. Round two long tables were gathered two serried crowds of human beings, all save one having their faces and attention bent on the tables. The one exception was a melancholy little boy, with his knees and calves simply in their natural clothing of epidermis, but for the rest of his person in a fancy dress. He alone had his face turned toward the doorway, and fixing on it the blank gaze of a bedizened child stationed as a masquerading advertisement on the platform of an itinerant show, stood close behind a lady deeply engaged at the roulette-table.

About this table fifty or sixty persons were assembled, many in the outer rows, where there was occasionally a deposit of new-comers, being mere spectators; only that one of them, usually a woman, might now and then be observed putting down a five-franc with a simpering air, just to see what the passion of gambling really was. Those who were taking their pleasure at a higher strength, and were absorbed in play, showed very distant varieties of European type: Livonian and Spanish, Græco-Italian and miscellaneous German, English aristocratic and English plebeian. Here certainly was a striking admission of human equality. The white bejewelled fingers of an English countess were very near touching a bony, yellow, crab-like hand stretching a bared wrist to clutch a heap of coin—a hand easy to sort with the square, gaunt face, deep-set eyes, grizzled eyebrows, and ill-combed scanty hair which seemed a slight metamorphosis of the vulture. And where else would her ladyship have graciously consented to sit by that dry-lipped feminine figure prematurely old, withered after short bloom like her artificial flowers, holding a shabby velvet reticule before her, and occasionally putting in her mouth the point with which she pricked her card? There too, very near the fair countess, was a respectable London tradesman, blond and soft-handed, his sleek hair scrupulously parted behind and before, conscious of circulars addressed to the nobility and gentry, whose distinguished patronage enabled him to take his holidays fashionably, and to a certain extent in their distinguished company. Not his the gambler's passion that nullifies appetite, but a well-fed leisure which, in the intervals of winning money in business and spending it showily, sees no better resource than winning money in play and spending it yet more showily—reflecting always that Providence had never manifested any disapprobation of his amusement, and dispassionate enough to leave off if the sweetness of winning much and seeing others lose had turned to the sourness of losing much and seeing others win. For the vice of gambling lay in losing money at it. In his bearing there might be something of the tradesman, but in his pleasures he was fit to rank with the owners of the oldest titles. Standing close to his chair was a handsome Italian, calm, statuesque, reaching across him to place the first pile of napoleons from a new bagful just brought him by an envoy with a scrolled mustache. The pile was in half a minute pushed over to an old bewigged woman with eye-glasses pinching her nose. There was a slight gleam, a faint mumbling smile about the lips of the old woman; but the statuesque Italian remained impassive, and—probably secure in an infallible system which placed his foot on the neck of chance—immediately prepared a new pile. So did a man with the air of an emaciated beau or worn-out libertine, who looked at life through one eye-glass, and held out his hand tremulously when he asked for change. It could surely be no severity of system, but rather some dream of white crows, or the induction that the eighth of the month was lucky, which inspired the fierce yet tottering impulsiveness of his play.

But, while every single player differed markedly from every other, there was a certain uniform negativeness of expression which had the effect of a mask—as if they had all eaten of some root that for the time compelled the brains of each to the same narrow monotony of action.

Deronda's first thought when his eyes fell on this scene of dull, gas-poisoned absorption, was that the gambling of Spanish shepherd-boys had seemed to him more enviable:—so far Rousseau might be justified in maintaining that art and science had done a poor service to mankind. But suddenly he felt the moment become dramatic. His attention was arrested by a young lady who, standing at an angle not far from him, was the last to whom his eyes travelled. She was bending and speaking English to a middle-aged lady seated at play beside her; but the next instant she returned to her play, and showed the full height of a graceful figure, with a face which might possibly be looked at without admiration, but could hardly be passed with indifference.

The inward debate which she raised in Deronda gave to his eyes a growing expression of scrutiny, tending farther and farther away from the glow of mingled undefined sensibilities forming admiration. At one moment they followed the movements of the figure, of the arms and hands, as this problematic sylph bent forward to deposit her stake with an air of firm choice; and the next they returned to the face which, at present unaffected by beholders, was directed steadily toward the game. The sylph was a winner; and as her taper fingers, delicately gloved in pale-gray, were adjusting the coins which had been pushed toward her in order to pass them back again to the winning point, she looked round her with a survey too markedly cold and neutral not to have in it a little of that nature which we call art concealing an inward exultation.

But in the course of that survey her eyes met Deronda's, and instead of averting them as she would have desired to do, she was unpleasantly conscious that they were arrested—how long? The darting sense that he was measuring her and looking down on her as an inferior, that he was of different quality from the human dross around her, that he felt himself in a region outside and above her, and was examining her as a specimen of a lower order, roused a tingling resentment which stretched the moment with conflict. It did not bring the blood to her cheeks, but it sent it away from her lips. She controlled herself by the help of an inward defiance, and without other sign of emotion than this lip-paleness turned to her play. But Deronda's gaze seemed to have acted as an evil eye. Her stake was gone. No matter; she had been winning ever since she took to roulette with a few napoleons at command, and had a considerable reserve. She had begun to believe in her luck, others had begun to believe in it: she had visions of being followed by a *cortège* who would worship her as a goddess of luck and watch her play as a directing augury. Such things had been known of male gamblers; why should not a woman have a like supremacy? Her friend and chaperon, who had not wished her to play at first, was beginning to approve, only administering the prudent advice to stop at the right moment and carry money back to England—advice to which Gwendolen had replied that she cared for the excitement of play, not the winnings. On that supposition the present moment ought to have made the flood-tide in her eager experience of gambling. Yet, when her next stake was swept away, she felt the orbits of her eyes getting hot, and the certainty she had (without looking) of that man still watching her was something like a pressure which begins to be torturing. The more reason to her why she should not flinch, but go on playing as if she were indifferent to loss or gain. Her friend touched her elbow and proposed that they should quit the table. For reply, Gwendolen put ten louis on the same spot: she was in that mood of defiance in which the mind loses sight of any end beyond the satisfaction of enraged resistance, and with the puerile stupidity of a dominant impulse includes luck among its objects of defiance. Since she was not winning strikingly, the next best thing was to lose strikingly. She controlled her muscles, and showed no tremor of mouth or hands. Each time her stake was swept off she doubled it. Many were now watching her, but the sole observation she was conscious of was Deronda's, who, though she never looked toward him, she was sure had not moved away. Such a drama takes no long while to play out: development and catastrophe can often be measured by nothing clumsier than the moment-hand. "Faites votre jeu, mesdames et messieurs," said the automatic voice of destiny from between the mustache and imperial of the croupier: and Gwendolen's arm was stretched to deposit her last poor heap of napoleons. "Le jeu ne va plus," said destiny. And in five seconds Gwendolen turned from the table, but turned resolutely with her face toward Deronda and looked at him. There was a smile of irony in his eyes as their glances met; but it was at least better that he should have kept his attention fixed on her than that he should have disregarded her as one of an insect swarm who had no individual physiognomy. Besides, in spite of his superciliousness and irony, it was difficult to believe that he did not admire her spirit as well as her person: he was young, handsome, distinguished in appearance—not one of those ridiculous and dowdy Philistines who thought it incumbent on them to blight the gaming-table with a sour look of protest as they passed by it. The general conviction that we are admirable does not easily give way before a single negative; rather, when any of Vanity's large family, male or female, find their performance received coldly, they are apt to believe that a little more of it will win over the unaccountable dissident. In Gwendolen's habits of mind it had been taken for granted that she knew what was admirable and that she herself was admired. This basis of her thinking had received a disagreeable concussion, and reeled a little, but was not easily to be overthrown.

In the evening the same room was more stiflingly heated, was brilliant with gas and with the costumes of ladies who floated their trains along it or were seated on the ottomans.

The Nereid in sea-green robes and silver ornaments, with a pale sea-green feather fastened in silver falling backward over her green hat and light-brown hair, was Gwendolen Harleth. She was under the wing, or rather soared by the shoulder, of the lady who had sat by her at the roulette-table; and with them was a gentleman with a white mustache and clipped hair: solid-browed, stiff, and German. They were walking about or standing to chat with acquaintances, and Gwendolen was much observed by the seated groups.

"A striking girl—that Miss Harleth—unlike others."

"Yes, she has got herself up as a sort of serpent now—all green and silver, and winds her neck about a little more than usual."

"Oh, she must always be doing something extraordinary. She is that kind of girl, I fancy. Do you think her pretty, Mr. Vandernoodt?"

"Very. A man might risk hanging for her—I mean, a fool might."

"You like a *nez retroussé*, then, and long narrow eyes?"

"When they go with such an *ensemble*."

"The *ensemble du serpent?*"

"If you will. Woman was tempted by a serpent: why not man?"

"She is certainly very graceful; but she wants a tinge of color in her cheeks. It is a sort of Lamia beauty she has."

"On the contrary, I think her complexion one of her chief charms. It is a warm paleness: it looks thoroughly healthy. And that delicate nose with its gradual little upward curve is distracting. And then her mouth—there never was a prettier mouth, the lips curled backward so finely, eh, Mackworth?"

"Think so? I cannot endure that sort of mouth. It looks so self-complacent, as if it knew its own beauty—the curves are too immovable. I like a mouth that trembles more."

"For my part, I think her odious," said a dowager. "It is wonderful what unpleasant girls get into vogue. Who are these Langens? Does anybody know them?"

"They are quite *comme il faut*. I have dined with them several times at the *Russie*. The baroness is English. Miss Harleth calls her cousin. The girl herself is thoroughly well bred, and as clever as possible."

"Dear me! And the baron?"

"A very good furniture picture."

"Your baroness is always at the roulette-table," said Mackworth. "I fancy she has taught the girl to gamble."

"Oh, the old woman plays a very sober game; drops a tenfranc piece here and there. The girl is more headlong. But it is only a freak."

"I hear she has lost all her winnings to-day. Are they rich? Who knows?"

"Ah, who knows? Who knows that about anybody?" said Mr. Vandernoodt, moving off to join the Langens.

The remark that Gwendolen wound her neck about more than usual this evening was true. But it was not that she might carry out the serpent idea more completely: it was that she watched for any chance of seeing Deronda, so that she might inquire about this stranger, under whose measuring gaze she was still wincing. At last her opportunity came.

"Mr. Vandernoodt, you know everybody," said Gwendolen, not too eagerly, rather with a certain languor of utterance which she sometimes gave to her clear soprano. "Who is that near the door?"

"There are half a dozen near the door. Do you mean that old Adonis in the George the Fourth wig?"

"No, no; the dark-haired young man on the right with the dreadful expression."

"Dreadful, do you call it? I think he is an uncommonly fine fellow."

"But who is he?"

"He is lately come to our hotel with Sir Hugo Mallinger."

"Sir Hugo Mallinger?"

"Yes. Do you know him?"

"No." (Gwendolen colored slightly.) "He has a place near us, but he never comes to it. What did you say was the name of that gentleman near the door?"

"Deronda—Mr. Deronda."

"What a delightful name! Is he an Englishman?"

"Yes. He is reported to be rather closely related to the baronet. You are interested in him?"

"Yes. I think he is not like young men in general."

"And you don't admire young men in general?"

"Not in the least. I always know what they will say. I can't at all guess what this Mr. Deronda would say. What *does* he say?"

"Nothing, chiefly. I sat with his party for a good hour last night on the terrace, and he never spoke—and was not smoking either. He looked bored."

"Another reason why I should like to know him. I am always bored."

"I should think he would be charmed to have an introduction. Shall I bring it about? Will you allow it, baroness?"

"Why not?—since he is related to Sir Hugo Mallinger. It is a new *rôle* of yours, Gwendolen, to be always bored," continued Madame von Langen, when Mr. Vandernoodt had moved away. "Until now you have always seemed eager about something from morning till night."

"That is just because I am bored to death. If I am to

leave off play I must break my arm or my collar-bone. I must make something happen; unless you will go into Switzerland and take me up the Matterhorn."

"Perhaps this Mr. Deronda's acquaintance will do instead of the Matterhorn."

"Perhaps."

But Gwendolen did not make Deronda's acquaintance on this occasion. Mr. Vandernoodt did not succeed in bringing him up to her that evening, and when she re-entered her own room she found a letter recalling her home.

CHAPTER II.

This man contrives a secret 'twixt us two,
That he may quell me with his meeting eyes
Like one who quells a lioness at bay.

THIS was the letter Gwendolen found on her table:

DEAREST CHILD.—I have been expecting to hear from you for a week. In your last you said the Langens thought of leaving Leubronn and going to Baden. How could you be so thoughtless as to leave me in uncertainty about your address? I am in the greatest anxiety lest this should not reach you. In any case, you were to come home at the end of September, and I must now entreat you to return as quickly as possible, for if you spent all your money it would be out of my power to send you any more, and you must not borrow of the Langens, for I could not repay them. This is the sad truth, my child—I wish I could prepare you for it better—but a dreadful calamity has befallen us all. You know nothing about business and will not understand it; but Grapnell & Co. have failed for a million, and we are totally ruined—your aunt Gascoigne as well as I, only that your uncle has his benefice, so that by putting down their carriage and getting interest for the boys, the family can go on. All the property our poor father saved for us goes to pay the liabilities. There is nothing I can call my own. It is better you should know this at once, though it rends my heart to have to tell it you. Of course we cannot help thinking what a pity it was that you went away just when you did. But I shall never reproach you, my dear child; I would save you from all trouble if I could. On your way home you will have time to prepare yourself for the change you will find. We shall perhaps leave Offendene at once, for we hope that Mr. Haynes, who wanted it before, may be ready to take it off my hands. Of course we cannot go to the rectory—there is not a corner there to spare. We must get some hut or other to shelter us, and we must live on your uncle Gascoigne's charity, until I see what else can be done. I shall not be able to pay the debts to the tradesmen besides the servants' wages. Summon up your fortitude, my dear child; we must resign ourselves to God's will. But it is hard to resign one's self to Mr. Lassman's wicked recklessness, which they say was the cause of the failure. Your poor sisters can only cry with me and give me no help. If you were once here, there might be a break in the cloud. I always feel it impossible that you can have been meant for poverty. If the Langens wish to remain abroad, perhaps you can put yourself under some one else's care for the journey. But come as soon as you can to your afflicted and loving mamma,

FANNY DAVILOW.

The first effect of this letter on Gwendolen was half stupefying. The implicit confidence that her destiny must be one of luxurious ease, where any trouble that occurred would be well clad and provided for, had been stronger in her own mind than in her mamma's, being fed there by her youthful blood and that sense of superior claims which made a large part of her consciousness. It was almost as difficult for her to believe suddenly that her position had become one of poverty and of humiliating dependence, as it would have been to get into the strong current of her blooming life the chill sense that her death would really come. She stood motionless for a few minutes, then tossed off her hat and automatically looked in the glass. The coils of her smooth light-brown hair were still in order perfect enough for a ball-room; and as on other nights, Gwendolen might have looked lingeringly at herself for pleasure (surely an allowable indulgence); but now she took no conscious note of her reflected beauty, and simply stared right before her as if she had been jarred by a hateful sound and was waiting for any sign of its cause. By and by she threw herself in the corner of the red velvet sofa, took up the letter again, and read it twice deliberately, letting it at last fall on the ground, while she rested her clasped hands on her lap and sat perfectly still, shedding no tears. Her impulse was to survey and resist the situation rather than to wail over it. There was no inward exclamation of "Poor mamma!" Her mamma had never seemed to get much enjoyment out of life, and if Gwendolen had been at this moment disposed to feel pity she would have bestowed it on herself—for was she not naturally and rightfully the chief object of her mamma's anxiety too? But it was anger, it was resistance, that possessed her; it was bitter vexation that she had lost her gains at roulette, whereas if her luck had continued through this one day she would have had a handsome sum to carry home, or she might have gone on playing and won enough to support them all. Even now was it not possible? She had only four napoleons left in her purse, but she possessed some ornaments which she could sell: a practice so common in stylish society at German baths that there was no need to be ashamed of it; and even if she had not received her mamma's letter, she would probably have decided to get money for an Etruscan necklace which she happened not to have been wearing since her arrival; nay, she might have done so with an agreeable sense that she was living with some intensity and escaping humdrum. With ten louis at her disposal and a return of her former luck, which seemed probable, what could she do better than go on playing for a few days? If her friends at home disapproved of the way in which she got the money, as they certainly would, still the money would be there. Gwendolen's imagination dwelt on this course and created agreeable consequences, but not with unbroken confidence and rising certainty as it would have done if she had been touched with the gambler's mania. She had gone to the roulette-table not because of passion, but in search of it: her mind was still sanely capable of picturing balanced probabilities; and while the chance of winning allured her, the chance of losing thrust itself on her with alternate strength, and made a vision from which her pride sank sensitively. For she was resolved not to tell the Langens that any misfortune had befallen her family, or to make herself in any way indebted to their compassion; and if she were to part with her jewelry to any observable extent, they would interfere by inquiries and remonstrances. The course that held the least risk of intolerable annoyance was to raise money on her necklace early in the morning, tell the Langens that her mamma desired her immediate return without giving a reason, and take the train for Brussels that evening. She had no maid with her, and the Langens might make difficulties about her returning alone, but her will was peremptory.

Instead of going to bed she made as brilliant a light as she could, and began to pack, working diligently, though all the while visited by the scenes that might take place on the coming day—now by the tiresome explanations and farewells, and the whirling journey toward a changed home, now by the alternative of staying just another day and standing again at the roulette-table. But always in this latter scene there was the presence of that Deronda, watching her with exasperating irony, and—the two keen experiences were inevitably revived together—beholding her again forsaken by luck. This importunate image certainly helped to sway her resolve on the side of immediate departure, and to urge her packing to the point which would make a change of mind inconvenient. It had struck twelve when she came into her room, and by the time she was assuring herself that she had left out only what was necessary, the faint dawn was stealing through the white blinds and dulling her candles. What was the use of going to bed? Her cold bath was refreshment enough, and she saw that a slight trace of fatigue about the eyes only made her look the more interesting. Before six o'clock she was completely equipped in her gray travelling dress even to her felt hat, for she meant to walk out as soon as she could count on seeing other ladies on their way to the springs. And happening to be seated sideways before the long strip of mirror between her two windows she turned to look at herself, leaning her elbow on the back of the chair in an attitude that might have been chosen for her portrait. It is possible to have a strong self-love without any self-satisfaction, rather with a self-discontent which is the more intense because one's own little core of egoistic sensibility is a supreme care; but Gwendolen knew nothing of such inward strife. She had a *naïve* delight in her fortunate self, which any but the harshest saintliness will have some indulgence for in a girl who had every day seen a pleasant reflection of that self in her friends' flattery as well as in the looking-glass. And even in this beginning of troubles, while for lack of anything else to do she sat gazing at her image in the growing light, her face gathered a complacency gradual as the cheerfulness of the morning. Her beautiful lips curled into a more and more decided smile, till at last she took off her hat, leaned forward, and kissed the cold glass hich had looked so warm. How could she believe in sorrow? If it attacked her, she felt the force to crush it, to defy it, or run away from it, as she had done already. Anything seemed more possible than that she could go on bearing miseries, great or small.

Madame von Langen never went out before breakfast, so that Gwendolen could safely end her early walk by talking her way homeward through the Obere Strasse in which was the needed shop, sure to be open after seven. At that hour any observers whom she minded would be either on their walks in the region of the springs, or would be still in their bedrooms; but certainly there was one grand hotel, the *Czarina*, from which eyes might follow her up to Mr. Wiener's door. This was a chance to be risked: might she not be going in to buy something which had struck her fancy? This implicit false-hood passed through her mind as she remembered that the *Czarina* was Deronda's hotel; but she was then already far up the Obere Strasse, and she walked on with her usual float-ing movement, every line in her figure and drapery falling in gentle curves attractive to all eyes except those which dis-cerned in them too close a resemblance to the serpent, and objected to the revival of serpent-worship. She looked neither to the right hand nor to the left, and transacted her business in the shop with a coolness which gave little Mr. Wiener nothing to remark except her proud grace of manner, and the superior size and quality of the three central turquoises in the necklace she offered him. They had belonged to a chain once her father's: but she had never known her father; and the necklace was in all respects the ornament she could most con-veniently part with. Who supposes that it is an impossible contradiction to be superstitious and rationalizing at the same time? Roulette encourages a romantic superstition as to the chances of the game, and the most prosaic rationalism as to human sentiments which stand in the way of raising needful money. Gwendolen's dominant regret was that after all she had only nine louis to add to the four in her purse: these Jew dealers were so unscrupulous in taking advantage of Christians unfortunate at play! But she was the Langens' guest in their hired apartment, and had nothing to pay there: thirteen louis would do more than take her home; even if she determined on risking three, the remaining ten would more than suffice, since she meant to travel right on, day and night. As she turned homeward, nay, entered and seated herself in the *salon* to await her friends and breakfast, she still wavered as to her immediate departure, or rather she had concluded to tell the Langens simply that she had had a letter from her mamma desiring her return, and to leave it still undecided when she should start. It was already the usual breakfast-time, and hearing some one enter as she was leaning back rather tired and hungry with her eyes shut, she rose expecting to see one or other of the Langens—the words which might determine her lingering at least another day, ready-formed to pass her lips. But it was the servant bringing in a small packet for Miss Harleth, which had at that moment been left at the door. Gwendolen took it in her hand and immediately hurried into her own room. She looked paler and more agitated than when she had first read her mamma's letter. Something—she never quite knew what—revealed to her before she opened the packet that it contained the necklace she had just parted with. Underneath the paper it was wrapped in a cambric handkerchief, and within this was a scrap of torn-off note-paper, on which was written with a pencil, in clear but rapid handwriting: "*A stranger who has found Miss Harleth's necklace returns it to her with the hope that she will not again risk the loss of it.*"

Gwendolen reddened with the vexation of wounded pride. A large corner of the handkerchief seemed to have been recklessly torn off to get rid of a mark; but she at once believed in the first image of "the stranger" that presented itself to her mind. It was Deronda; he must have seen her go into the shop; he must have gone in immediately after, and repurchased the necklace. He had taken an unpardonable liberty, and had dared to place her in a thoroughly hateful position. What could she do?—Not, assuredly, act on her conviction that it was he who had sent her the necklace and straightway send it back to him: that would be to face the possibility that she had been mistaken; nay, even if the "stranger" were he and no other, it would be something too gross for her to let him know that she had divined this, and to meet him again with that recognition in their minds. He knew very well that he was entangling her in helpless humiliation : it was another way of smiling at her ironically, and taking the air of a supercilious mentor. Gwendolen felt the bitter tears of mortification rising and rolling down her cheeks. No one had ever before dared to treat her with irony and contempt. One thing was clear : she must carry out her resolution to quit this place at once; it was impossible for her to reappear in the public *salon*, still less stand at the gaming-table with the risk of seeing Deronda. Now came an importunate knock at the door : breakfast was ready. Gwendolen with a passionate movement thrust necklace, cambric, scrap of paper, and all into her *nécessaire*, pressed her handkerchief against her face, and after pausing a minute or two to summon back her proud self-control, went to join her friends. Such signs of tears and fatigue as were left seemed accordant enough with the account she at once gave of her having been called home, for some reason which she feared might be a trouble of her mamma's; and of her having sat up to do her packing, instead of waiting for help from her friend's maid. There was much protestation, as she had expected, against her travelling alone, but she persisted in refusing any arrangements for companionship. She would be put into the ladies' compartment and go right on. She could rest exceedingly well in the train, and was afraid of nothing.

In this way it happened that Gwendolen never reappeared at the roulette-table, but that Thursday evening left Leubronn for Brussels, and on Saturday morning arrived at Offendene, the home to which she and her family were soon to say a last good-bye.

CHAPTER III.

"Let no flower of the spring pass by us : let us crown ourselves with rosebuds before they be withered."—BOOK OF WISDOM.

PITY that Offendene was not the home of Miss Harleth's childhood, or endeared to her by family memories! A human life, I think, should be well rooted in some spot of a native land, where it may get the love of tender kinship for the face of earth, for the labors men go forth to, for the sounds and

accents that haunt it, for whatever will give that early home
a familiar unmistakable difference amid the future widening
of knowledge: a spot where the definiteness of early memories
may be inwrought with affection, and kindly acquaintance
with all neighbors, even to the dogs and donkeys, may spread
not by sentimental effort and reflection, but as a sweet habit
of the blood. At five years old, mortals are not prepared to
be citizens of the world, to be stimulated by abstract nouns,
to soar above preference into impartiality; and that prejudice
in favor of milk with which we blindly begin, is a type of the
way body and soul must get nourished at least for a time.
The best introduction to astronomy is to think of the nightly
heavens as a little lot of stars belonging to one's own home-
stead.

But this blessed persistence in which affection can take root
had been wanting in Gwendolen's life. It was only a year
before her recall from Leubronn that Offendene had been
chosen as her mamma's home, simply for its nearness to
Pennicote Rectory, and that Mrs. Davilow, Gwendolen, and
her four half-sisters (the governess and the maid following in
another vehicle) had been driven along the avenue for the
first time, on a late October afternoon when the rooks were
cawing loudly above them, and the yellow elm-leaves were
whirling.

The season suited the aspect of the old oblong red-brick
house, rather too anxiously ornamented with stone at every
line, not excepting the double row of narrow windows and
the large square portico. The stone encouraged a greenish
lichen, the brick a powdery gray, so that though the building
was rigidly rectangular, there was no harshness in the physiognomy which it turned to the three avenues cut east, west, and
south in the hundred yards' breadth of old plantation encir-
cling the immediate grounds. One would have liked the house
to have been lifted on a knoll, so as to look beyond its own
little domain to the long thatched roofs of the distant villages,
the church towers, the scattered homesteads, the gradual rise
of surging woods, and the green breadths of undulating park
which made the beautiful face of the earth in that part of
Wessex. But though standing thus behind a screen amid flat

pastures, it had on one side a glimpse of the wider world in the lofty curves of the chalk downs—grand steadfast forms played over by the changing days.

The house was but just large enough to be called a mansion, and was moderately rented, having no manor attached to it, and being rather difficult to let with its sombre furniture and faded upholstery. But inside and outside it was what no beholder could suppose to be inhabited by retired tradespeople: a certainty which was worth many conveniences to tenants who not only had the taste that shrinks from new finery, but also were in that border-territory of rank where annexation is a burning topic: and to take up her abode in a house which had once sufficed for dowager countesses gave a perceptible tinge to Mrs. Davilow's satisfaction in having an establishment of her own. This, rather mysteriously to Gwendolen, appeared suddenly possible on the death of her stepfather, Captain Davilow, who had for the last nine years joined his family only in a brief and fitful manner, enough to reconcile them to his long absences; but she cared much more for the fact than for the explanation. All her prospects had become more agreeable in consequence. She had disliked their former way of life, roving from one foreign watering-place or Parisian apartment to another, always feeling new antipathies to new suites of hired furniture, and meeting new people under conditions which made her appear of little importance; and the variation of having passed two years at a showy school, where, on all occasions of display, she had been put foremost, had only deepened her sense that so exceptional a person as herself could hardly remain in ordinary circumstances or in a social position less than advantageous. Any fear of this latter evil was banished now that her mamma was to have an establishment; for on the point of birth Gwendolen was quite easy. She had no notion how her maternal grandfather got the fortune inherited by his two daughters; but he had been a West Indian—which seemed to exclude further question; and she knew that her father's family was so high as to take no notice of her mamma, who nevertheless preserved with much pride the miniature of a Lady Molly in that connection. She would probably have known much more about her father but for a little incident which happened when she was twelve years old. Mrs. Davilow had brought out, as she did only at wide intervals, various memorials of her first husband, and while showing his miniature to Gwendolen, recalled with a fervor which seemed to count on a peculiar filial sympathy, the fact that dear papa had died when his little daughter was in long clothes. Gwendolen, immediately thinking of the unlovable stepfather whom she had been acquainted with the greater part of her life while her frocks were short, said:

"Why did you marry again, mamma? It would have been nicer if you had not."

Mrs. Davilow colored deeply, a slight convulsive movement passed over her face, and straightway shutting up the memorials, she said, with a violence quite unusual in her:

"You have no feeling, child!"

Gwendolen, who was fond of her mamma, felt hurt and ashamed, and had never since dared to ask a question about her father.

This was not the only instance in which she had brought on herself the pain of some filial compunction. It was always arranged, when possible, that she should have a small bed in her mamma's room; for Mrs. Davilow's motherly tenderness clung chiefly to her eldest girl, who had been born in her happier time. One night under an attack of pain she found that the specific regularly placed by her bedside had been forgotten, and begged Gwendolen to get out of bed and reach it for her. That healthy young lady, snug and warm as a rosy infant in her little couch, objected to step out into the cold, and lying perfectly still, grumbled a refusal. Mrs. Davilow went without the medicine, and never reproached her daughter; but the next day Gwendolen was keenly conscious of what must be in her mamma's mind, and tried to make amends by caresses which cost her no effort. Having always been the pet and pride of the household, waited on by mother, sisters, governess, and maids, as if she had been a princess in exile, she naturally found it difficult to think her own pleasure less important than others made it, and when it was positively thwarted, felt an astonished resentment, apt, in her cruder days, to vent itself in one of those passionate acts which look like a contradiction of habitual tendencies. Though never even as a child thoughtlessly cruel—nay, delighting to rescue drowning insects and watch their recovery—there was a disagreeable silent remembrance of her having strangled her sister's canary-bird in a final fit of exasperation at its shrill singing which had again and again jarringly interrupted her own. She had taken pains to buy a white mouse for her sister in retribution, and though inwardly excusing herself on the ground of a peculiar sensitiveness which was a mark of her general superiority, the thought of that infelonious murder had always made her wince. Gwendolen's nature was not remorseless, but she liked to make her penances easy; and now that she was twenty and more, some of her native force had turned into a self-control by which she guarded herself from penitential humiliation. There was more show of fire and will in her than ever, but there was more calculation underneath it.

On this day of arrival at Offendene, which not even Mrs. Davilow had seen before—the place having been taken for her by her brother-in-law, Mr. Gascoigne—when all had got down from the carriage, and were standing under the porch in front of the open door, so that they could have both a general view of the place and a glimpse of the stone hall and staircase hung with sombre pictures, but enlivened by a bright wood fire, no one spoke: mamma, the four sisters, and the governess all looked at Gwendolen, as if their feelings depended entirely on her decision. Of the girls, from Alice in her sixteenth year to Isabel in her tenth, hardly anything could be said on a first view, but that they were girlish, and that their black dresses were getting shabby. Miss Merry was elderly and altogether neutral in expression. Mrs. Davilow's worn beauty seemed the more pathetic for the look of entire appeal which she cast at Gwendolen, who was glancing round at the house, the land-scape, and the entrance-hall with an air of rapid judgment. Imagine a young race-horse in the paddock among untrimmed ponies and patient hacks.

"Well, dear, what do you think of the place?" said Mrs. Davilow at last, in a gentle, deprecatory tone.

"I think it is charming," said Gwendolen, quickly. "A romantic place; anything delightful may happen in it; it would be a good background for anything. No one need be ashamed of living here."

"There is certainly nothing common about it."

"Oh, it would do for fallen royalty or any sort of grand poverty. We ought properly to have been living in splendor, and have come down to this. It would have been as romantic as could be. But I thought my uncle and aunt Gascoigne would be here to meet us, and my cousin Anna," added Gwendolen, her tone changed to sharp surprise.

"We are early," said Mrs. Davilow; and entering the hall, she said to the housekeeper who came forward: "You expect Mr. and Mrs. Gascoigne?"

"Yes, madam: they were here yesterday to give particular orders about the fires and the dinner. But as to fires, I've had 'em in all the rooms for the last week, and everything is well aired. I could wish some of the furniture paid better for all the cleaning it's had, but I *think* you'll see the brasses have been done justice to. I *think* when Mr. and Mrs. Gascoigne come, they'll tell you nothing has been neglected. They'll be here at five, for certain."

This satisfied Gwendolen, who was not prepared to have their arrival treated with indifference; and after tripping a little way up the matted stone staircase to take a survey there, she tripped down again, and followed by all the girls looked into each of the rooms opening from the hall—the dining-room, all dark oak and worn red satin damask, with a copy of snarling, worrying dogs from Snyders over the sideboard, and a Christ breaking bread over the mantelpiece; the library with a general aspect and smell of old brown leather; and lastly, the drawing-room, which was entered through a small antechamber crowded with venerable knick-knacks.

"Mamma, mamma, pray come here!" said Gwendolen, Mrs. Davilow having followed slowly in talk with the housekeeper. "Here is an organ. I will be Saint Cecilia: some one shall paint me as Saint Cecilia. Jocosa (this was her name for Miss Merry), let down my hair. See, mamma!"

She had thrown off her hat and gloves, and seated herself before the organ in an admirable pose, looking upward; while the submissive and sad Jocosa took out the one comb which fastened the coil of hair, and then shook out the mass till it fell in a smooth light-brown stream far below its owner's slim waist.

Mrs. Davilow smiled and said, "A charming picture, my dear!" not indifferent to the display of her pet, even in the presence of a housekeeper. Gwendolen rose and laughed with delight. All this seemed quite to the purpose on entering a new house which was so excellent a background.

"What a queer, quaint, picturesque room!" she went on, looking about her. "I like these old embroidered chairs, and the garlands on the wainscot, and the pictures that may be anything. That one with the ribs—nothing but ribs and darkness—I should think that is Spanish, mamma."

"Oh, *Gwendolen!*" said the small Isabel, in a tone of astonishment, while she held open a hinged panel of the wainscot at the other end of the room.

Every one, Gwendolen first, went to look. The opened panel had disclosed the picture of an upturned dead face, from which an obscure figure seemed to be fleeing with outstretched arms. "How horrible!" said Mrs. Davilow, with a look of mere disgust; but Gwendolen shuddered silently, and Isabel, a plain and altogether inconvenient child with an alarming memory, said:

"You will never stay in this room by yourself, Gwendolen."

"How dare you open things which were meant to be shut up, you perverse little creature?" said Gwendolen, in her angriest tone. Then snatching the panel out of the hand of the culprit, she closed it hastily, saying: "There is a lock—where is the key? Let the key be found, or else let one be made, and let nobody open it again; or rather, let the key be brought to me."

At this command to everybody in general, Gwendolen turned with a face which was flushed in reaction from her chill shudder, and said: "Let us go up to our own room, mamma."

The housekeeper on searching found the key in the drawer of the cabinet close by the panel, and presently handed it to Bugle, the lady's-maid, telling her significantly to give it to her Royal Highness.

"I don't know what you mean, Mrs. Startin," said Bugle, who had been busy upstairs during the scene in the drawing-room, and was rather offended at this irony in a new servant.

"I mean the young lady that's to command us all—and well worthy for looks and figure," replied Mrs. Startin in propitiation. "She'll know what key it is."

"If you have laid out what we want, go and see to the others, Bugle," Gwendolen had said, when she and Mrs. Davilow entered their black and yellow bedroom, where a pretty little white couch was prepared by the side of the black and yellow catafalque known as 'the best bed.' "I will help mamma."

But her first movement was to go to the tall mirror between the windows, which reflected herself and the room completely, while her mamma sat down and also looked at the reflection.

"That is a becoming glass, Gwendolen; or is it the black and gold color that sets you off?" said Mrs. Davilow, as Gwendolen stood obliquely with her three-quarter face turned toward the mirror, and her left hand brushing back the stream of hair.

"I should make a tolerable St. Cecilia with some white roses on my head," said Gwendolen—"only, how about my nose, mamma? I think saints' noses never in the least turn up. I wish you had given me your perfectly straight nose; it would have done for any sort of character—a nose of all work. Mine is only a happy nose; it would not do so well for tragedy."

"Oh, my dear, any nose will do to be miserable with in this world," said Mrs. Davilow, with a deep, weary sigh, throwing her black bonnet on the table, and resting her elbow near it.

"Now, mamma," said Gwendolen, in a strongly remonstrant tone, turning away from the glass with an air of vexation, "don't begin to be dull here. It spoils all my pleasure, and everything may be so happy now. What have you to be gloomy about now?"

"Nothing, dear," said Mrs. Davilow, seeming to rouse herself, and beginning to take off her dress. "It is always enough for me to see you happy."

"But you should be happy yourself," said Gwendolen, still discontentedly, though going to help her mamma with caressing touches. "Can nobody be happy after they are quite young? You have made me feel sometimes as if nothing were of any use. With the girls so troublesome, and Jocosa so dreadfully wooden and ugly, and everything makeshift about us, and you looking so dull—what was the use of my being anything? But now you *might* be happy."

"So I shall, dear," said Mrs. Davilow, patting the cheek that was bending near her.

"Yes, but really. Not with a sort of make-believe," said Gwendolen, with resolute perseverance. "See what a hand and arm!—much more beautiful than mine. Any one can see you were altogether more beautiful."

"No, no, dear; I was always heavier. Never half so charming as you are."

"Well, but what is the use of my being charming, if it is to end in my being dull and not minding anything? Is that what marriage always comes to?"

"No, child, certainly not. Marriage is the only happy state for a woman, as I trust you will prove."

"I will not put up with it if it is not a happy state. I am determined to be happy—at least not to go on muddling away my life as other people do, being and doing nothing remarkable. I have made up my mind not to let other people interfere with me as they have done. Here is some warm water ready for you, mamma," Gwendolen ended, proceeding to take off her own dress and then waiting to have her hair wound up by her mamma.

There was silence for a minute or two, till Mrs. Davilow said, while coiling the daughter's hair: "I am sure I have never crossed you, Gwendolen."

"You often want me to do what I don't like."

"You mean, to give Alice lessons?"

"Yes. And I have done it because you asked me. But I don't see why I should, else. It bores me to death, she is so slow. She has no ear for music, or language, or anything else. It would be much better for her to be ignorant, mamma: it is her *rôle*—she would do it well."

"That is a hard thing to say of your poor sister, Gwendolen, who is so good to you, and waits on you hand and foot."

"I don't see why it is hard to call things by their right

names, and put them in their proper places. The hardship is
for me to have to waste my time on her. Now let me fasten
up your hair, mamma."

"We must make haste; your uncle and aunt will be here
soon. For heaven's sake, don't be scornful to *them*, my dear
child! or to your cousin Anna, whom you will always be going
out with. Do promise me, Gwendolen. You know, you can't
expect Anna to be equal to you."

"I don't want her to be equal," said Gwendolen, with a
toss of her head and a smile; and the discussion ended there.

When Mr. and Mrs. Gascoigne and their daughter came,
Gwendolen, far from being scornful, behaved as prettily as
possible to them. She was introducing herself anew to relatives who had not seen her since the comparatively unfinished
age of sixteen, and she was anxious—no, not anxious, but resolved that they should admire her.

Mrs. Gascoigne bore a family likeness to her sister. But
she was darker and slighter, her face was unworn by grief,
her movements were less languid, her expression more alert
and critical as that of a rector's wife bound to exert a benefi-
cent authority. Their closest resemblance lay in a non-resist-
ant disposition, inclined to imitation and obedience; but this,
owing to the difference in their circumstances, had led them
to very different issues. The younger sister had been indis-
creet, or at least unfortunate in her marriages; the elder believed herself the most enviable of wives, and her pliancy had
ended in her sometimes taking shapes of surprising definiteness. Many of her opinions, such as those on church government and the character of Archbishop Laud, seemed too decided under every alteration to have been arrived at otherwise
than by a wifely receptiveness. And there was much to encourage trust in her husband's authority. He had some agreeable virtues, some striking advantages, and the failings that
were imputed to him all leaned toward the side of success.

One of his advantages was a fine person, which perhaps was
even more impressive at fifty-seven than it had been earlier in
life. There were no distinctively clerical lines in the face,
no official reserve or ostentatious benignity of expression, no
tricks of starchiness or of affected ease; in his Inverness cape

he could not have been identified except as a gentleman with handsome dark features, a nose which began with an intention to be aquiline but suddenly became straight, and iron-gray hair. Perhaps he owed this freedom from the sort of professional make-up which penetrates skin, tones, and gestures, and defies all drapery, to the fact that he had once been Captain Gaskin, having taken orders and a diphthong but shortly before his engagement to Miss Armyn. If any one had objected that his preparation for the clerical function was inadequate, his friends might have asked who made a better figure in it, who preached better, or had more authority in his parish? He had a native gift for administration, being tolerant both of opinions and conduct, because he felt himself able to overrule them, and was free from the irritations of conscious feebleness. He smiled pleasantly at the foible of a taste which he did not share—at floriculture or antiquarianism, for example, which were much in vogue among his fellow-clergymen in the diocese: for himself, he preferred following the history of a campaign, or divining from his knowledge of Nesselrode's motives what would have been his conduct if our cabinet had taken a different course. Mr. Gascoigne's tone of thinking, after some long-quieted fluctuations, had become ecclesiastical rather than theological; not the modern Anglican, but what he would have called sound English, free from nonsense: such as became a man who looked at a national religion by daylight, and saw it in its relations to other things. No clerical magistrate had greater weight at sessions, or less of mischievous impracticableness in relation to worldly affairs. Indeed, the worst imputation thrown out against him was worldliness: it could not be proved that he forsook the less fortunate, but it was not to be denied that the friendships he cultivated were of a kind likely to be useful to the father of six sons and two daughters; and bitter observers—for in Wessex, say ten years ago, there were persons whose bitterness may now seem incredible—remarked that the color of his opinions had changed in consistency with this principle of action. But cheerful, successful worldliness has a false air of being more selfish than the acrid, unsuccessful kind, whose secret history is summed up in the terrible words, "Sold, but not paid for."

Gwendolen wondered that she had not better remembered how very fine a man her uncle was; but at the age of sixteen she was a less capable and more indifferent judge. At present it was a matter of extreme interest to her that she was to have the near countenance of a dignified male relative, and that the family life would cease to be entirely, insipidly feminine. She did not intend that her uncle should control her, but she saw at once that it would be altogether agreeable to her that he should be proud of introducing her as his niece. And there was every sign of his being likely to feel that pride. He certainly looked at her with admiration as he said:

"You have outgrown Anna, my dear," putting his arm tenderly round his daughter, whose shy face was a tiny copy of his own, and drawing her forward. "She is not so old as you by a year, but her growing days are certainly over. I hope you will be excellent companions."

He did give a comparing glance at his daughter; but if he saw her inferiority, he might also see that Anna's timid appearance and miniature figure must appeal to a different taste from that which was attracted by Gwendolen, and that the girls could hardly be rivals. Gwendolen, at least, was aware of this, and kissed her cousin with real cordiality as well as grace, saying: "A companion is just what I want. I am so glad we are come to live here. And mamma will be much happier now she is near you, aunt."

The aunt trusted indeed that it would be so, and felt it a blessing that a suitable home had been vacant in their uncle's parish. Then, of course, notice had to be taken of the four other girls, whom Gwendolen had always felt to be superfluous: all of a girlish average that made four units utterly unimportant, and yet from her earliest days an obtrusive influential fact in her life. She was conscious of having been much kinder to them than could have been expected. And it was evident to her that her uncle and aunt also felt it a pity there were so many girls:—what rational person could feel otherwise, except poor mamma, who never would see how Alice set up her shoulders and lifted her eyebrows till she had no forehead left, how Bertha and Fanny whispered and tittered together about everything, or how Isabel was always listening and staring and forgetting where she was, and treading on the toes of her suffering elders?

"You have brothers, Anna," said Gwendolen, while the sisters were being noticed. "I think you are enviable there."

"Yes," said Anna, simply. "I am very fond of them; but of course their education is a great anxiety to papa. He used to say they made me a tomboy. I really was a great romp with Rex. I think you will like Rex. He will come home before Christmas."

"I remember I used to think you rather wild and shy; but it is difficult now to imagine you a romp," said Gwendolen, smiling.

"Of course, I am altered now; I am come out, and all that. But in reality I like to go blackberrying with Edwy and Lotta as well as ever. I am not very fond of going out; but I dare say I shall like it better now you will be often with me. I am not at all clever, and I never know what to say. It seems so useless to say what everybody knows, and I can think of nothing else, except what papa says."

"I shall like going out with you very much," said Gwendolen, well disposed toward this _naïve_ cousin. "Are you fond of riding?"

"Yes, but we have only one Shetland pony amongst us. Papa says he can't afford more, besides the carriage-horses and his own nag; he has so many expenses."

"I intend to have a horse, and ride a great deal now," said Gwendolen, in a tone of decision. "Is the society pleasant in this neighborhood?"

"Papa says it is, very. There are the clergymen all about, you know; and the Quallons, and the Arrowpoints, and Lord Brackenshaw, and Sir Hugo Mallinger's place, where there is nobody—that's very nice, because we make picnics there—and two or three families at Wanchester: oh, and old Mrs. Vulcany, at Nuttingwood, and——"

But Anna was relieved of this tax on her descriptive powers by the announcement of dinner, and Gwendolen's question was soon indirectly answered by her uncle, who dwelt much on the advantages he had secured for them in getting a place like Offendene. Except the rent, it involved no more expense than an ordinary house at Wanchester would have done.

"And it is always worth while to make a little sacrifice for a good style of house," said Mr. Gascoigne, in his easy, pleasantly confident tone, which made the world in general seem a very manageable place of residence; "especially where there is only a lady at the head. All the best people will call upon you; and you need give no expensive dinners. Of course, I have to spend a good deal in that way; it is a large item. But then I get my house for nothing. If I had to pay three hundred a year for my house I could not keep a table. My boys are too great a drain on me. You are better off than we are, in proportion; there is no great drain on you now, after your house and carriage."

"I assure you, Fanny, now that the children are growing up, I am obliged to cut and contrive," said Mrs. Gascoigne. "I am not a good manager by nature, but Henry has taught me. He is wonderful for making the best of everything; he allows himself no extras, and gets his curates for nothing. It is rather hard that he has not been made a prebendary or something, as others have been, considering the friends he has made, and the need there is for men of moderate opinions in all respects. If the Church is to keep its position, ability and character ought to tell."

"Oh, my dear Nancy, you forget the old story—thank Heaven, there are three hundred as good as I. And ultimately, we shall have no reason to complain, I am pretty sure. There could hardly be a more thorough friend than Lord Brackenshaw — your landlord, you know, Fanny. Lady Brackenshaw will call upon you. And I have spoken for Gwendolen to be a member of our Archery Club—the Brackenshaw Archery Club—the most select thing anywhere. That is, if she has no objection," added Mr. Gascoigne, looking at Gwendolen with pleasant irony.

"I should like it of all things," said Gwendolen. "There is nothing I enjoy more than taking aim—and hitting," she ended, with a pretty nod and smile.

"Our Anna, poor child, is too short-sighted for archery. But I consider myself a first-rate shot, and you shall practice

with me. I must make you an accomplished archer before our
great meeting in July. In fact, as to neighborhood, you could
hardly be better placed. There are the Arrowpoints—they
are some of our best people. Miss Arrowpoint is a delightful
girl—she has been presented at Court. They have a magnificent place—Quetcham Hall—worth seeing in point of art;
and their parties, to which you are sure to be invited, are the
best things of the sort we have. The archdeacon is intimate
there, and they have always a good kind of people staying in
the house. Mrs. Arrowpoint is peculiar, certainly; something
of a caricature, in fact; but well meaning. And Miss Arrowpoint is as nice as possible. It is not all young ladies who
have mothers as handsome and graceful as yours and Anna's."

Mrs. Davilow smiled faintly at this little compliment, but
the husband and wife looked affectionately at each other, and
Gwendolen thought: "My uncle and aunt, at least, are happy:
they are not dull and dismal." Altogether, she felt satisfied
with her prospects at Offendene, as a great improvement on
anything she had known. Even the cheap curates, she incidentally learned, were almost always young men of family,
and Mr. Middleton, the actual curate, was said to be quite an
acquisition: it was only a pity he was so soon to leave.

But there was one point which she was so anxious to gain
that she could not allow the evening to pass without taking
her measures toward securing it. Her mamma, she knew,
intended to submit entirely to her uncle's judgment with regard to expenditure; and the submission was not merely prudential, for Mrs. Davilow, conscious that she had always been
seen under a cloud as poor dear Fanny, who had made a sad
blunder with her second marriage, felt a hearty satisfaction in
being frankly and cordially identified with her sister's family,
and in having her affairs canvassed and managed with an
authority which presupposed a genuine interest. Thus the
question of a suitable saddle-horse, which had been sufficiently
discussed with mamma, had to be referred to Mr. Gascoigne;
and after Gwendolen had played on the piano, which had
been provided from Wanchester, had sung to her hearers' admiration, and had induced her uncle to join her in a duet—
what more softening influence than this on any uncle who

would have sung finely if his time had not been too much taken up by graver matters?—she seized the opportune moment for saying: "Mamma, you have not spoken to my uncle about my riding."

"Gwendolen desires above all things to have a horse to ride—a pretty, light, lady's horse," said Mrs. Davilow, looking at Mr. Gascoigne. "Do you think we can manage it?"

Mr. Gascoigne projected his lower lip and lifted his handsome eyebrows sarcastically at Gwendolen, who had seated herself with much grace on the elbow of her mamma's chair.

"We could lend her the pony sometimes," said Mrs. Gascoigne, watching her husband's face, and feeling quite ready to disapprove if he did.

"That might be inconveniencing others, aunt, and would be no pleasure to me. I cannot endure ponies," said Gwendolen. "I would rather give up some other indulgence and have a horse." (Was there ever a young lady or gentleman not ready to give up an unspecified indulgence for the sake of the favorite one specified?)

"She rides so well. She has had lessons, and the riding-master said she had so good a seat and hand she might be trusted with any mount," said Mrs. Davilow, who, even if she had not wished her darling to have the horse, would not have dared to be lukewarm in trying to get it for her.

"There is the price of the horse—a good sixty with the best chance, and then his keep," said Mr. Gascoigne, in a tone which, though demurring, betrayed the inward presence of something that favored the demand. "There are the carriage horses—already a heavy item. And remember what you ladies cost in toilet now."

"I really wear nothing but two black dresses," said Mrs. Davilow, hastily. "And the younger girls, of course, require no toilet at present. Besides, Gwendolen will save me so much by giving her sisters lessons." Here Mrs. Davilow's delicate cheek showed a rapid blush. "If it were not for that, I must really have a more expensive governess, and masters besides."

Gwendolen felt some anger with her mamma, but carefully concealed it.

"That is good—that is decidedly good," said Mr. Gascoigne, heartily, looking at his wife. And Gwendolen, who, it must be owned, was a deep young lady, suddenly moved away to the other end of the long drawing-room, and busied herself with arranging pieces of music.

"The dear child has had no indulgences, no pleasures," said Mrs. Davilow, in a pleading undertone. "I feel the expense is rather imprudent in this first year of our settling. But she really needs the exercise—she needs cheering. And if you were to see her on horseback, it *is* something splendid."

"It is what we could not afford for Anna," said Mrs. Gascoigne. "But she, dear child, would ride Lotta's donkey, and think it good enough." (Anna was absorbed in a game with Isabel, who had hunted out an old backgammon-board, and had begged to sit up an extra hour.)

"Certainly, a fine woman never looks better than on horseback," said Mr. Gascoigne. "And Gwendolen has the figure for it. I don't say the thing should not be considered."

"We might try it for a time, at all events. It can be given up, if necessary," said Mrs. Davilow.

"Well, I will consult Lord Brackenshaw's head groom. He is my *fidus Achates* in the horsey way."

"Thanks," said Mrs. Davilow, much relieved. "You are very kind."

"That he always is," said Mrs. Gascoigne. And later that night, when she and her husband were in private, she said:

"I thought you were almost too indulgent about the horse for Gwendolen. She ought not to claim so much more than your own daughter would think of. Especially before we see how Fanny manages on her income. And you really have enough to do without taking all this trouble on yourself."

"My dear Nancy, one must look at things from every point of view. This girl is really worth some expense; you don't often see her equal. She ought to make a first-rate marriage, and I should not be doing my duty if I spared my trouble in helping her forward. You know yourself she has been under a disadvantage with such a father-in-law, and a second family, keeping her always in the shade. I feel for the girl. And I should like your sister and her family now to have the

benefit of your having married rather a better specimen of
our kind than she did."

"Rather better! I should think so. However, it is for me
to be grateful that you will take so much on your shoulders
for the sake of my sister and her children. I am sure I would
not grudge anything to poor Fanny. But there is one thing I
have been thinking of, though you have never mentioned it."

"What is that?"

"The boys. I hope they will not be falling in love with
Gwendolen."

"Don't presuppose anything of the kind, my dear, and
there will be no danger. Rex will never be at home for long
together, and Warham is going to India. It is the wiser plan
to take it for granted that cousins will not fall in love. If
you begin with precautions, the affair will come in spite of
them. One must not undertake to act for Providence in these
matters, which can no more be held under the hand than a
brood of chickens. The boys will have nothing, and Gwendolen will have nothing. They can't marry. At the worst
there would only be a little crying, and you can't save boys
and girls from that."

Mrs. Gascoigne's mind was satisfied: if anything did happen, there was the comfort of feeling that her husband would
know what was to be done, and would have the energy to
do it.

CHAPTER IV.

"*Gorgibus.*— * * * Je te dis que le mariage est une chose sainte et sacrée, et
que c'est faire en honnêtes gens, que de débuter par là.

"*Madelon.*—Mon Dieu! que si tout le monde vous ressemblait, un roman serait
bientôt fini! La belle chose que ce serait, si d'abord Cyrus épousait Mandane, et
qu'Aronce de plain-pied fut marié a Clélie! * * * Laissez-nous faire a loisir le tissu
de notre roman, et n'en pressez pas tant la conclusion."

MOLIÈRE: *Les Précieuses Ridicules.*

IT would be a little hard to blame the rector of Pennicote
that in the course of looking at things from every point of
view, he looked at Gwendolen as a girl likely to make a brilliant marriage. Why should he be expected to differ from his
contemporaries in this matter, and wish his niece a worse end

of her charming maidenhood than they would approve as the best possible? It is rather to be set down to his credit that his feelings on the subject were entirely good-natured. And in considering the relation of means to ends, it would have been mere folly to have been guided by the exceptional and idyllic—to have recommended that Gwendolen should wear a gown as shabby as Griselda's in order that a marquis might fall in love with her, or to have insisted that since a fair maiden was to be sought, she should keep herself out of the way. Mr. Gascoigne's calculations were of the kind called rational, and he did not even think of getting a too frisky horse in order that Gwendolen might be threatened with an accident and be rescued by a man of property. He wished his niece well, and he meant her to be seen to advantage in the best society of the neighborhood.

Her uncle's intention fell in perfectly with Gwendolen's own wishes. But let no one suppose that she also contemplated a brilliant marriage as the direct end of her witching the world with her grace on horseback, or with any other accomplishment. That she was to be married some time or other she would have felt obliged to admit; and that her marriage would not be of a middling kind, such as most girls were contented with, she felt quietly, unargumentatively sure. But her thoughts never dwelt on marriage as the fulfilment of her ambition; the dramas in which she imagined herself a heroine were not wrought up to that close. To be very much sued or hopelessly sighed for as a bride was indeed an indispensable and agreeable guaranty of womanly power; but to become a wife and wear all the domestic fetters of that condition was, on the whole, a vexatious necessity. Her observation of matrimony had inclined her to think it rather a dreary state, in which a woman could not do what she liked, had more children than were desirable, was consequently dull, and became irrevocably immersed in humdrum. Of course marriage was social promotion; she could not look forward to a single life; but promotions have sometimes to be taken with bitter herbs—a peerage will not quite do instead of leadership to the man who meant to lead; and this delicate-limbed sylph of twenty meant to lead. For such passions dwell in femi-

nine breasts also. In Gwendolen's, however, they dwelt
among strictly feminine furniture, and had no disturbing reference to the advancement of learning or the balance of the
constitution; her knowledge being such as with no sort of
standing-room or length of lever could have been expected to
move the world. She meant to do what was pleasant to herself in a striking manner; or rather, whatever she could do so
as to strike others with admiration and get in that reflected
way a more ardent sense of living, seemed pleasant to her
fancy.

" Gwendolen will not rest without having the world at her
feet," said Miss Merry, the meek governess: hyperbolical
words which have long come to carry the most moderate
meanings; for who has not heard of private persons having
the world at their feet in the shape of some half-dozen items
of flattering regard generally known in a genteel suburb?
And words could hardly be too wide or vague to indicate the
prospect that made a hazy largeness about poor Gwendolen on
the heights of her young self-exultation. Other people allowed themselves to be made slaves of, and to have their lives
blown hither and thither like empty ships in which no will
was present. It was not to be so with her; she would no
longer be sacrificed to creatures worth less than herself, but
would make the very best of the chances that life offered her,
and conquer circumstance by her exceptional cleverness. Certainly, to be settled at Offendene, with the notice of Lady
Brackenshaw, the archery club, and invitations to dine with
the Arrowpoints, as the highest lights in her scenery, was not
a position that seemed to offer remarkable chances; but Gwendolen's confidence lay chiefly in herself. She felt well equipped
for the mastery of life. With regard to much in her lot hitherto, she held herself rather hardly dealt with; but as to her
"education," she would have admitted that it had left her
under no disadvantages. In the schoolroom her quick mind
had taken readily that strong starch of unexplained rules and
disconnected facts which saves ignorance from any painful
sense of limpness; and what remained of all things knowable,
she was conscious of being sufficiently acquainted with through
novels, plays, and poems. About her French and music, the

two justifying accomplishments of a young lady, she felt no ground for uneasiness; and when to all these qualifications, negative and positive, we add the spontaneoous sense of capability some happy persons are born with, so that any subject they turn their attention to impresses them with their own power of forming a correct judgment on it, who can wonder if Gwendolen felt ready to manage her own destiny?

There were many subjects in the world—perhaps the majority—in which she felt no interest, because they were stupid; for subjects are apt to appear stupid to the young as light seems dim to the old; but she would not have felt at all helpless in relation to them if they had turned up in conversation. It must be remembered that no one had disputed her power or her general superiority. As on the arrival at Offendene, so always, the first thought of those about her had been, what will Gwendolen think?—if the footman trod heavily in creaking boots, or if the laundress's work was unsatisfactory, the maid said, "This will never do for Miss Harleth"; if the wood smoked in the bedroom fireplace, Mrs. Davilow, whose own weak eyes suffered much from this inconvenience, spoke apologetically of it to Gwendolen. If, when they were under the stress of travelling, she did not appear at the breakfast table till every one else had finished, the only question was, how Gwendolen's coffee and toast should still be of the hottest and crispest; and when she appeared with her freshly brushed light-brown hair streaming backward and awaiting her mamma's hand to coil it up, her large brown eyes glancing bright as a wave-washed onyx from under their long lashes, it was always she herself who had to be tolerant—to beg that Alice who sat waiting on her would not stick up her shoulders in that frightful manner, and that Isabel, instead of pushing up to her and asking questions, would go away to Miss Merry.

Always she was the princess in exile, who in time of famine was to have her breakfast-roll made of the finest-bolted flour from the seven thin ears of wheat, and in a general decampment was to have her silver fork kept out of the baggage. How was this to be accounted for? The answer may seem to lie quite on the surface:—in her beauty, a certain unusualness about her, a decision of will which made itself felt in her graceful movements and clear unhesitating tones, so that if she came into the room on a rainy day when everybody else was flaccid and the use of things in general was not apparent to them, there seemed to be a sudden, sufficient reason for keeping up the forms of life; and even the waiters at hotels showed the more alacrity in doing away with crumbs and creases and dregs with struggling flies in them. This potent charm, added to the fact that she was the eldest daughter, toward whom her mamma had always been in an apologetic state of mind for the evils brought on her by a stepfather, may seem so full a reason for Gwendolen's domestic empire, that to look for any other would be to ask the reason of daylight when the sun is shining. But beware of arriving at conclusions without comparison. I remember having seen the same assiduous, apologetic attention awarded to persons who were not at all beautiful or unusual, whose firmness showed itself in no very graceful or euphonious way, and who were not eldest daughters with a tender, timid mother, compunctious at having subjected them to inconveniences. Some of them were a very common sort of men. And the only point of resemblance among them all was a strong determination to have what was pleasant, with a total fearlessness in making themselves disagreeable or dangerous when they did not get it. Who is so much cajoled and served with trembling by the weak females of a household as the unscrupulous male—capable, if he has not free way at home, of going and doing worse elsewhere? Hence I am forced to doubt whether even without her potent charm and peculiar filial position Gwendolen might not still have played the queen in exile, if only she had kept her inborn energy of egoistic desire, and her power of inspiring fear as to what she might say or do. However, she had the charm, and those who feared her were also fond of her; the fear and the fondness being perhaps both heightened by what may be called the iridescence of her character—the play of various, nay, contrary tendencies. For Macbeth's rhetoric about the impossibility of being many opposite things in the same moment, referred to the clumsy necessities of action and not to the subtler possibilities of feeling. We cannot speak a loyal word and be meanly silent; we cannot kill and

not kill in the same moment; but a moment is room wide enough
for the loyal and mean desire, for the outlash of a murderous
thought and the sharp backward stroke of repentance.

CHAPTER V.

"Her wit
Values itself so highly, that to her
All matter else seems weak."
—*Much Ado About Nothing.*

GWENDOLEN's reception in the neighborhood fulfilled her
uncle's expectations. From Brackenshaw Castle to the Firs
at Wanchester, where Mr. Quallon the banker kept a generous
house, she was welcomed with manifest admiration, and even
those ladies who did not quite like her, felt a comfort in having a new, striking girl to invite; for hostesses who entertain
much must make up their parties as ministers make up their
cabinets, on grounds other than personal liking. Then, in
order to have Gwendolen as a guest, it was not necessary to
ask any one who was disagreeable, for Mrs. Davilow always
made a quiet, picturesque figure as a chaperon, and Mr. Gascoigne was everywhere in request for his own sake.

Among the houses where Gwendolen was not quite liked,
and yet invited, was Quetcham Hall. One of her first invitations was to a large dinner-party there, which made a sort of
general introduction for her to the society of the neighborhood;
for in a select party of thirty and of well-composed proportions
as to age, few visitable families could be entirely left out. No
youthful figure there was comparable to Gwendolen's as she
passed through the long suite of rooms adorned with light and
flowers, and, visible at first as a slim figure floating along in
white drapery, approached through one wide doorway after
another into fuller illumination and definiteness. She had
never had that sort of promenade before, and she felt exultingly that it befitted her: any one looking at her for the first
time might have supposed that long galleries and lackeys had
always been a matter of course in her life; while her cousin
Anna, who was really more familiar with these things, felt

almost as much embarrassed as a rabbit suddenly deposited in that well-lit space.

" Who is that with Gascoigne? " said the archdeacon, neglecting a discussion of military manœuvres on which, as a clergyman, he was naturally appealed to. And his son, on the other side of the room—a hopeful young scholar, who had already suggested some " not less elegant than ingenious " emendations of Greek texts—said nearly at the same time: " By George! who is that girl with the awfully well-set head and jolly figure? "

But to a mind of general benevolence, wishing everybody to look well, it was rather exasperating to see how Gwendolen eclipsed others : how even the handsome Miss Lawe, explained to be the daughter of Lady Lawe, looked suddenly broad, heavy, and inanimate; and how Miss Arrowpoint, unfortunately also dressed in white, immediately resembled a *carte-de-visite* in which one would fancy the skirt alone to have been charged for. Since Miss Arrowpoint was generally liked for the amiable unpretending way in which she wore her fortunes, and made a softening screen for the oddities of her mother, there seemed to be some unfitness in Gwendolen's looking so much more like a person of social importance.

" She is not really so handsome if you come to examine her features," said Mrs. Arrowpoint, later in the evening, confidentially to Mrs. Vulcany. " It is a certain style she has, which produces a great effect at first, but afterward she is less agreeable."

In fact, Gwendolen, not intending it, but intending the contrary, had offended her hostess, who, though not a splenetic or vindictive woman, had her susceptibilities. Several conditions had met in the Lady of Quetcham which to the reasoners in that neighborhood seemed to have an essential connection with each other. It was occasionally recalled that she had been the heiress of a fortune gained by some moist or dry business in the city, in order fully to account for her having a squat figure, a harsh parrot-like voice, and a systematically high head-dress; and since these points made her externally rather ridiculous, it appeared to many only natural that she should have what are called literary tendencies. A little comparison would have shown that all these points are to be found apart; daughters of aldermen being often well grown and well featured, pretty women having sometimes harsh or husky voices, and the production of feeble literature being found compatible with the most diverse forms of *physique*, masculine as well as feminine.

Gwendolen, who had a keen sense of absurdity in others, but was kindly disposed toward any one who could make life agreeable to her, meant to win Mrs. Arrowpoint by giving her an interest and attention beyond what others were probably inclined to show. But self-confidence is apt to address itself to an imaginary dulness in others; as people who are well off speak in a cajoling tone to the poor, and those who are in the prime of life raise their voice and talk artificially to seniors, hastily conceiving them to be deaf and rather imbecile. Gwendolen, with all her cleverness and purpose to be agreeable, could not escape that form of stupidity: it followed in her mind, unreflectingly, that because Mrs. Arrowpoint was ridiculous she was also likely to be wanting in penetration, and she went through her little scenes without suspicion that the various shades of her behavior were all noted.

"You are fond of books as well as of music, riding, and archery, I hear," Mrs. Arrowpoint said, going to her for a *tête-à-tête* in the drawing-room after dinner. "Catherine will be very glad to have so sympathetic a neighbor." This little speech might have seemed the most graceful politeness, spoken in a low, melodious tone; but with a twang fatally loud, it gave Gwendolen a sense of exercising patronage when she answered, gracefully:

"It is I who am fortunate. Miss Arrowpoint will teach me what good music is. I shall be entirely a learner. I hear that she is a thorough musician."

"Catherine has certainly had every advantage. We have a first-rate musician in the house now—Herr Klesmer; perhaps you know all his compositions. You must allow me to introduce him to you. You sing, I believe. Catherine plays three instruments, but she does not sing. I hope you will let us hear you. I understand you are an accomplished singer."

"Oh, no!—' die Kraft ist schwach, allein die Lust ist gross,' as Mephistopheles says."

"Ah, you are a student of Goethe. Young ladies are so advanced now. I suppose you have read everything."

"No, really. I shall be so glad if you will tell me what to read. I have been looking into all the books in the library at Offendene, but there is nothing readable. The leaves all stick together and smell musty. I wish I could write books to amuse myself, as you can! How delightful it must be to write books after one's own taste instead of reading other people's! Home-made books must be so nice."

For an instant Mrs. Arrowpoint's glance was a little sharper, but the perilous resemblance to satire in the last sentence took the hue of girlish simplicity when Gwendolen added:

"I would give anything to write a book!"

"And why should you not?" said Mrs. Arrowpoint, encouragingly. "You have but to begin as I did. Pen, ink, and paper are at everybody's command. But I will send you all I have written with pleasure."

"Thanks. I shall be so glad to read your writings. Being acquainted with authors must give a peculiar understanding of their books: one would be able to tell then which parts were funny and which serious. I am sure I often laugh in the wrong place." Here Gwendolen herself became aware of danger, and added quickly—"In Shakespeare, you know, and other great writers that we can never see. But I always want to know more than there is in the books."

"If you are interested in any of my subjects I can lend you many extra sheets in manuscript," said Mrs. Arrowpoint— while Gwendolen felt herself painfully in the position of the young lady who professed to like potted sprats. "These are things I dare say I shall publish eventually: several friends have urged me to do so, and one doesn't like to be obstinate. My Tasso, for example—I could have made it twice the size."

"I dote on Tasso," said Gwendolen.

"Well, you shall have all my papers, if you like. So many, you know, have written about Tasso; but they are all wrong. As to the particular nature of his madness, and his feeling for Leonora, and the real cause of his imprisonment, and the character of Leonora, who, in my opinion, was a cold-hearted woman, else she would have married him in spite of her brother—they are all wrong. I differ from everybody."

"How very interesting!" said Gwendolen. "I like to differ from everybody. I think it is so stupid to agree. That is the worst of writing your opinions; you make people agree with you."

This speech renewed a slight suspicion in Mrs. Arrowpoint, and again her glance became for a moment examining. But Gwendolen looked very innocent, and continued with a docile air:

"I know nothing of Tasso except the *Gerusalemme Liberata*, which we read and learned by heart at school."

"Ah, his life is more interesting than his poetry. I have constructed the early part of his life as a sort of romance. When one thinks of his father Bernardo, and so on, there is so much that must be true."

"Imagination is often truer than fact," said Gwendolen, decisively, though she could no more have explained these glib words than if they had been Coptic or Etruscan. "I shall be so glad to learn all about Tasso—and his madness especially. I suppose poets are always a little mad."

"To be sure—'the poet's eye in a fine frenzy rolling'; and somebody says of Marlowe:

' For that fine madness still he did maintain,
Which always should possess the poet's brain. '"

"But it was not always found out, was it?" said Gwendolen, innocently. "I suppose some of them rolled their eyes in private. Mad people are often very cunning."

Again a shade flitted over Mrs. Arrowpoint's face; but the entrance of the gentlemen prevented any immediate mischief between her and this too quick young lady, who had over-acted her *naïveté*.

"Ah, here comes Herr Klesmer," said Mrs. Arrowpoint, rising; and presently bringing him to Gwendolen, she left them to a dialogue which was agreeable on both sides, Herr Klesmer being a felicitous combination of the German, the Sclave, and the Semite, with grand features, brown hair floating in artistic fashion, and brown eyes in spectacles. His English had little foreignness except its fluency; and his alarming cleverness was made less formidable just then by a certain softening air of silliness which will sometimes befall even Genius in the desire of being agreeable to Beauty.

Music was soon begun. Miss Arrowpoint and Herr Klesmer played a four-handed piece on two pianos, which convinced the company in general that it was long, and Gwendolen in particular that the neutral, placid-faced Miss Arrowpoint had a mastery of the instrument which put her own execution out of the question—though she was not discouraged as to her often-praised touch and style. After this every one became anxious to hear Gwendolen sing; especially Mr. Arrowpoint; as was natural in a host and a perfect gentleman, of whom no one had anything to say but that he had married Miss Cutler, and imported the best cigars; and he led her to the piano with easy politeness. Herr Klesmer closed the instrument in readiness for her, and smiled with pleasure at her approach; then placed himself at a distance of a few feet so that he could see her as she sang.

Gwendolen was not nervous: what she undertook to do she did without trembling, and singing was an enjoyment to her. Her voice was a moderately powerful soprano (some one had told her it was like Jenny Lind's), her ear good, and she was able to keep in tune, so that her singing gave pleasure to ordinary hearers, and she had been used to unmingled applause. She had the rare advantage of looking almost prettier when she was singing than at other times, and that Herr Klesmer was in front of her seemed not disagreeable. Her song, determined on beforehand, was a favorite aria of Bellini's, in which she felt quite sure of herself.

"Charming!" said Mr. Arrowpoint, who had remained near, and the word was echoed around without more insincerity than we recognize in a brotherly way as human. But Herr Klesmer stood like a statue—if a statue can be imagined in spectacles; at least, he was as mute as a statue. Gwendolen was pressed to keep her seat and double the general pleasure, and she did not wish to refuse; but before resolving to do so, she moved a little toward Herr Klesmer, saying with a look of smiling appeal: "It would be too cruel to a great musician. You cannot like to hear poor amateur singing."

"No, truly; but that makes nothing," said Herr Klesmer, suddenly speaking in an odious German fashion with staccato endings, quite unobservable in him before, and apparently depending on a change of mood, as Irishmen resume their strongest brogue when they are fervid or quarrelsome. "That makes nothing. It is always acceptable to see you sing."

Was there ever so unexpected an assertion of superiority? at least before the late Teutonic conquest? Gwendolen colored deeply, but, with her usual presence of mind, did not show an ungraceful resentment by moving away immediately; and Miss Arrowpoint, who had been near enough to overhear (and also to observe that Herr Klesmer's mode of looking at Gwendolen was more conspicuously admiring than was quite consistent with good taste), now with the utmost tact and kindness came close to her and said:

"Imagine what I have to go through with this professor! He can hardly tolerate anything we English do in music. We can only put up with his severity, and make use of it to find out the worst that can be said of us. It is a little comfort to know that; and one can bear it when every one else is admiring."

"I should be very much obliged to him for telling me the worst," said Gwendolen, recovering herself. "I dare say I have been extremely ill taught, in addition to having no talent —only liking for music." This was very well expressed, considering that it had never entered her mind before.

"Yes, it is true: you have not been well taught," said Herr Klesmer, quietly. Woman was dear to him, but music was dearer. "Still, you are not quite without gifts. You sing in tune, and you have a pretty fair organ. But you produce your notes badly; and that music which you sing is beneath you. It is a form of melody which expresses a puerile state of culture—a dandling, canting, seesaw kind of stuff—the passion and thought of people without any breadth of horizon. There is a sort of self-satisfied folly about every phrase of such melody; no cries of deep, mysterious passion—no conflict—no sense of the universal.   It makes men small as they listen to it.   Sing now something larger.   And I shall see."

"Oh, not now—by and by," said Gwendolen, with a sinking of heart at the sudden width of horizon opened round her small musical performance.   For a young lady desiring to lead, this first encounter in her campaign was startling.   But she was bent on not behaving foolishly, and Miss Arrowpoint helped her by saying:

"Yes, by and by.   I always require half an hour to get up my courage after being criticised by Herr Klesmer.   We will ask him to play to us now: he is bound to show what is good music."

To be quite safe on this point Herr Klesmer played a composition of his own, a fantasia called *Freudvoll, Leidvoll, Gedankenvoll*—an extensive commentary on some melodic ideas not too grossly evident; and he certainly fetched as much variety and depth of passion out of the piano as that moderately responsive instrument lends itself to, having an imperious magic in his fingers that seemed to send a nerve-thrill through ivory key and wooden hammer, and compel the strings to make a quivering lingering speech for him.   Gwendolen, in spite of her wounded egoism, had fulness of nature enough to feel the power of this playing, and it gradually turned her inward sob of mortification into an excitement which lifted her for the moment into a desperate indifference about her own doings, or at least a determination to get a superiority over them by laughing at them as if they belonged to somebody else.   Her eyes had become brighter, her cheeks slightly flushed, and her tongue ready for any mischievous remarks.

"I wish you would sing to us again, Miss Harleth," said young Clintock, the archdeacon's classical son, who had been so fortunate as to take her to dinner, and came up to renew conversation as soon as Herr Klesmer's performance was ended. "That is the style of music for me.   I never can make anything of this tip-top playing.   It is like a jar of leeches, when you can never tell either beginnings or endings.   I could listen to your singing all day."

"Yes, we should be glad of something popular now—another song from you would be a relaxation," said Mrs. Arrow-point, who had also come near with polite intentions.

" That must be because you are in a puerile state of culture, and have no breadth of horizon. I have just learned that. I have been taught how bad my taste is, and am feeling grow-ing pains. They are never pleasant," said Gwendolen, not taking any notice of Mrs. Arrowpoint, and looking up with a bright smile at young Clintock.

Mrs. Arrowpoint was not insensible to this rudeness, but merely said, " Well, we will not press anything disagreeably : " and as there was a perceptible outrush of imprisoned conver-sation just then, and a movement of guests seeking each other, she remained seated where she was, and looked round her with the relief of a hostess at finding she is not needed.

" I am glad you like this neighborhood," said young Clin-tock, well pleased with his station in front of Gwendolen.

" Exceedingly. There seems to be a little of everything and not much of anything."

" That is rather equivocal praise."

" Not with me. I like a little of everything; a little ab-surdity, for example, is very amusing. I am thankful for a few queer people; but much of them is a bore."

(Mrs. Arrowpoint, who was hearing this dialogue, perceived quite a new tone in Gwendolen's speech, and felt a revival of doubt as to her interest in Tasso's madness.)

" I think there should be more croquet, for one thing," said young Clintock; " I am usually away; but if I were more here I should go in for a croquet club. You are one of the archers, I think. But depend upon it, croquet is the game of the future. It wants writing up, though. One of our best men has written a poem on it, in four cantos;—as good as Pope. I want him to publish it. You never read anything better."

" I shall study croquet to-morrow. I shall take to it in-stead of singing."

" No, no, not that; but do take to croquet. I will send you Jenning's poem, if you like. I have a manuscript copy."

" Is he a great friend of yours?"

" Well, rather."

"Oh, if he is only rather, I think I will decline. Or, if

you send it me, will you promise not to catechise me upon it and ask me which part I like best? Because it is not so easy to know a poem without reading it as to know a sermon without listening."

"Decidedly," Mrs. Arrowpoint thought, "this girl is double and satirical. I shall be on my guard against her."

But Gwendolen, nevertheless, continued to receive polite attentions from the family at Quetcham, not merely because invitations have larger grounds than those of personal liking, but because the trying little scene at the piano had awakened a kindly solicitude toward her in the gentle mind of Miss Arrowpoint, who managed all the invitations and visits, her mother being otherwise occupied.

CHAPTER VI.

"Croyez vous m'avoir humiliée pour m'avoir appris que la terre tourne autour du soleil? Je vous jure que je ne m'en estime pas moins."—FONTENELLE: *Pluralité des Mondes.*

THAT lofty criticism had caused Gwendolen a new sort of pain. She would not have chosen to confess how unfortunate she thought herself in not having had Miss Arrowpoint's musical advantages, so as to be able to question Herr Klesmer's taste with the confidence of thorough knowledge; still less, to admit even to herself that Miss Arrowpoint each time they met raised an unwonted feeling of jealousy in her: not in the least because she was an heiress, but because it was really provoking that a girl whose appearance you could not characterize except by saying that her figure was slight and of middle stature, her features small, her eyes tolerable, and her complexion sallow, had nevertheless a certain mental superiority which could not be explained away—an exasperating thoroughness in her musical accomplishment, a fastidious discrimination in her general tastes, which made it impossible to force her admiration and kept you in awe of her standard. This insignificant-looking young lady of four-and-twenty, whom any one's eyes would have passed over negligently if she had not been Miss Arrowpoint, might be suspected of a secret opinion that Miss Harleth's acquirements were rather of a common order; and such an opinion was not made agreeable to think of by being always veiled under a perfect kindness of manner.

But Gwendolen did not like to dwell on facts which threw an unfavorable light on herself. The musical Magus who had so suddenly widened her horizon was not always on the scene; and his being constantly backward and forward between London and Quetcham soon began to be thought of as offering opportunities for converting him to a more admiring state of mind. Meanwhile, in the manifest pleasure her singing gave at Brackenshaw Castle, the Firs, and elsewhere, she recovered her equanimity, being disposed to think approval more trustworthy than objection, and not being one of the exceptional persons who have a parching thirst for a perfection undemanded by their neighbors. Perhaps it would have been rash to say then that she was at all exceptional inwardly, or that the unusual in her was more than her rare grace of movement and bearing, and a certain daring which gave piquancy to a very common egoistic ambition, such as exists under many clumsy exteriors and is taken no notice of. For I suppose that the set of the head does not really determine the hunger of the inner self for supremacy: it only makes a difference sometimes as to the way in which the supremacy is held attainable, and a little also to the degree in which it can be attained; especially when the hungry one is a girl, whose passion for doing what is remarkable has an ideal limit in consistency with the highest breeding and perfect freedom from the sordid need of income. Gwendolen was as inwardly rebellious against the restraints of family conditions, and as ready to look through obligations into her own fundamental want of feeling for them, as if she had been sustained by the boldest speculations; but she really had no such speculations, and would at once have marked herself off from any sort of theoretical or practically reforming women by satirizing them. She rejoiced to feel herself exceptional; but her horizon was that of the genteel romance where the heroine's soul poured out in her journal is full of vague power, originality, and general rebellion, while her life moves strictly in the sphere of fashion; and if she wanders into a swamp, the pathos lies partly, so to speak, in her having on her satin shoes. Here is a restraint which nature and society have provided on the pursuit of striking adventure; so that a soul burning with a sense of what the universe is not, and ready to take all exist-ence as fuel, is nevertheless held captive by the ordinary wire-work of social forms and does nothing particular.

This commonplace result was what Gwendolen found her-self threatened with even in the novelty of the first winter at Offendene. What she was clear upon was, that she did not wish to lead the same sort of life as ordinary young ladies did; but what she was not clear upon was, how she should set about leading any other, and what were the particular acts which she would assert her freedom by doing. Offendene re-mained a good background, if anything would happen there; but on the whole the neighborhood was in fault.

Beyond the effect of her beauty on a first presentation, there was not much excitement to be got out of her earliest invita-tions, and she came home after little sallies of satire and knowingness, such as had offended Mrs. Arrowpoint, to fill the intervening days with the most girlish devices. The strongest assertion she was able to make of her individual claims was to leave out Alice's lessons (on the principle that Alice was more likely to excel in ignorance), and to employ her with Miss Merry, and the maid who was understood to wait on all the ladies, in helping to arrange various dramatic costumes which Gwendolen pleased herself with having in readiness for some future occasions of acting in charades or theatrical pieces—occasions which she meant to bring about by force of will or contrivance. She had never acted—only made a figure in *tableaux vivans* at school; but she felt assured that she could act well, and having been once or twice to the Théâtre Fran-çais, and also heard her mamma speak of Rachel, her waking dreams and cogitations as to how she would manage her destiny sometimes turned on the question whether she would become an actress like Rachel, since she was more beautiful than that thin Jewess. Meanwhile the wet days before Christmas were passed pleasantly in the preparation of costumes, Greek, Oriental, and Composite, in which Gwendolen attitudinized and speechified before a domestic audience, including even the housekeeper, who was once pressed into it that she might swell the notes of applause; but having shown herself unworthy by observing that Miss Harleth looked far more like a queen in her own dress than in that baggy thing with her arms all bare, she was not invited a second time.

"Do I look as well as Rachel, mamma?" said Gwendolen, one day when she had been showing herself in her Greek dress to Anna, and going through scraps of scenes with much tragic intention.

"You have better arms than Rachel," said Mrs. Davilow; "your arms would do for anything, Gwen. But your voice is not so tragic as hers; it is not so deep."

"I can make it deeper, if I like," said Gwendolen, provisionally; then she added, with decision: "I think a higher voice is more tragic: it is more feminine; and the more feminine a woman is, the more tragic it seems when she does desperate actions."

"There may be something in that," said Mrs. Davilow, languidly. "But I don't know what good there is in making one's blood creep. And if there is anything horrible to be done, I should like it to be left to the men."

"Oh, mamma, you are so dreadfully prosaic! As if all the great poetic criminals were not women! I think the men are poor cautious creatures."

"Well, dear, and you—who are afraid to be alone in the night —I don't think you would be very bold in crime, thank God."

"I am not talking about reality, mamma," said Gwendolen, impatiently. Then, her mamma being called out of the room, she turned quickly to her cousin, as if taking an opportunity, and said: "Anna, do ask my uncle to let us get up some charades at the rectory. Mr. Middleton and Warham could act with us—just for practice. Mamma says it will not do to have Mr. Middleton consulting and rehearsing here. He is a stick, but we could give him suitable parts. Do ask, or else I will."

"Oh, not till Rex comes. He is so clever, and such a dear old thing, and he will act Napoleon looking over the sea. He looks just like Napoleon. Rex can do anything."

"I don't in the least believe in your Rex, Anna," said

Gwendolen, laughing at her. "He will turn out to be like those wretched blue and yellow water-colors of his which you hang up in your bedroom and worship."

"Very well, you will see," said Anna. "It is not that I know what is clever, but he has got a scholarship already, and papa says he will get a fellowship, and nobody is better at games. He is cleverer than Mr. Middleton, and everybody but you calls Mr. Middleton clever."

"So he may be in a dark-lantern sort of way. But he *is* a stick. If he had to say, ' Perdition catch my soul, but I do love her,' he would say it in just the same tone as, 'Here endeth the second lesson.' "

"Oh, Gwendolen!" said Anna, shocked at these promiscuous allusions. "And it very unkind of you to speak so of him, for he admires you very much. I heard Warham say one day to mamma, 'Middleton is regularly spoony upon Gwendolen.' She was very angry with him; but I know what it means. It is what they say at college for being in love."

"How can I help it?" said Gwendolen, rather contempt-uously. "Perdition catch my soul if I love *him*."

"No, of course; papa, I think, would not wish it. And he is to go away soon. But it makes me sorry when you ridi-cule him."

"What shall you do to me when I ridicule Rex?" said Gwendolen, wickedly.

"Now, Gwendolen, dear, you *will not?*" said Anna, her eyes filling with tears. "I could not bear it. But there really is nothing in him to ridicule. Only you may find out things. For no one ever thought of laughing at Mr. Middleton before you. Every one said he was nice-looking, and his manners perfect. I am sure I have always been frightened at him be-cause of his learning and his square-cut coat, and his being a nephew of the bishop's, and all that. But you will not ridi-cule Rex—promise me." Anna ended with a beseeching look which touched Gwendolen.

"You are a dear little coz," she said, just touching the tip of Anna's chin with her thumb and forefinger. "I don't ever want to do anything that will vex you. Especially if Rex is to make everything come off—charades and everything."

And when at last Rex was there, the animation he brought into the life at Offendene and the Rectory, and his ready partnership in Gwendolen's plans, left her no inclination for any ridicule that was not of an open and flattering kind, such as he himself enjoyed. He was a fine open-hearted youth, with a handsome face strongly resembling his father's and Anna's, but softer in expression than the one, and larger in scale than the other: a bright, healthy, loving nature, enjoying ordinary, innocent things so much that vice had no temptation for him, and what he knew of it lay too entirely in the outer courts and little-visited chambers of his mind for him to think of it with great repulsion. Vicious habits were with him "what some fellows did"—"stupid stuff" which he liked to keep aloof from. He returned Anna's affection as fully as could be expected of a brother whose pleasures apart from her were more than the sum total of hers; and he had never known a stronger love.

The cousins were continually together at the one house or the other—chiefly at Offendene, where there was more freedom, or rather where there was a more complete sway for Gwendolen; and whatever she wished became a ruling purpose for Rex. The charades came off according to her plans; and also some other little scenes not contemplated by her in which her acting was more impromptu. It was at Offendene that the charades and *tableaux* were rehearsed and presented, Mrs. Davilow seeing no objection even to Mr. Middleton's being invited to share in them, now that Rex too was there—especially as his services were indispensable; Warham, who was studying for India with a Wanchester "coach," having no time to spare, and being generally dismal under a cram of everything except the answers needed at the forthcoming examination, which might disclose the welfare of our Indian Empire to be somehow connected with a quotable knowledge of Browne's Pastorals.

Mr. Middleton was persuaded to play various grave parts, Gwendolen having flattered him on his enviable immobility of countenance; and at first a little pained and jealous at her comradeship with Rex, he presently drew encouragement from the thought that this sort of cousinly familiarity excluded any serious passion. Indeed, he occasionally felt that her more formal treatment of himself was such a sign of favor as to warrant his making advances before he left Pennicote, though he had intended to keep his feelings in reserve until his position should be more assured. Miss Gwendolen, quite aware that she was adored by this unexceptionable young clergyman with pale whiskers and square-cut collar, felt nothing more on the subject than that she had no objection to being adored: she turned her eyes on him with calm mercilessness, and caused him many mildly agitating hopes by seeming always to avoid dramatic contact with him—for all meanings, we know, depend on the key of interpretation.

Some persons might have thought beforehand that a young man of Anglican leanings, having a sense of sacredness much exercised on small things as well as great, rarely laughing save from politeness, and in general regarding the mention of spades by their naked names as rather coarse, would not have seen a fitting bride for himself in a girl who was daring in ridicule, and showed none of the special grace required in the clergyman's wife; or, that a young man informed by theological reading would have reflected that he was not likely to meet the taste of a lively, restless young lady like Miss Harleth. But are we always obliged to explain why the facts are not what some persons thought beforehand? The apology lies on their side, who had that erroneous way of thinking.

As for Rex, who would possibly have been sorry for poor Middleton if he had been aware of the excellent curate's inward conflict, he was too completely absorbed in a first passion to have observation for any person or thing. He did not observe Gwendolen; he only felt what she said or did, and the back of his head seemed to be a good organ of information as to whether she was in the room or out. Before the end of the first fortnight he was so deeply in love that it was impossible for him to think of his life except as bound up with Gwendolen's. He could see no obstacles, poor boy; his own love seemed a guaranty of hers, since it was one with the unperturbed delight in her image, so that he could no more dream of her giving him pain than an Egyptian could dream of snow. She sang and played to him whenever he liked, was always glad of his companionship in riding, though his borrowed steeds were often comic, was ready to join in any fun of his, and showed a right appreciation of Anna. No mark of sympathy seemed absent. That because Gwendolen was the most perfect creature in the world she was to make a grand match, had not occurred to him. He had no conceit—at least not more than goes to make up the necessary gum and consistence of a substantial personality: it was only that in the young bliss of loving he took Gwendolen's perfection as part of that good which had seemed one with life to him, being the outcome of a happy, well-embodied nature.

One incident which happened in the course of their dramatic attempts impressed Rex as a sign of her unusual sensibility. It showed an aspect of her nature which could not have been preconceived by any one who, like him, had only seen her habitual fearlessness in active exercises and her high spirits in society.

After a good deal of rehearsing it was resolved that a select party should be invited to Offendene to witness the performances which went with so much satisfaction to the actors. Anna had caused a pleasant surprise; nothing could be neater than the way in which she played her little parts; one would even have suspected her of hiding much sly observation under her simplicity. And Mr. Middleton answered very well by not trying to be comic. The main source of doubt and retardation had been Gwendolen's desire to appear in her Greek dress. No word for a charade would occur to her either waking or dreaming that suited her purpose of getting a statuesque pose in this favorite costume. To choose a motive from Racine was of no use, since Rex and the others could not declaim French verse, and improvised speeches would turn the scene into burlesque. Besides, Mr. Gascoigne prohibited the acting of scenes from plays: he usually protested against the notion that an amusement which was fitting for every one else was unfitting for a clergyman; but he would not in this matter overstep the line of decorum as drawn in that part of Wessex, which did not exclude his sanction of the young people's acting charades in his sister-in-law's house—a very different affair from private theatricals in the full sense of the word.

Everybody of course was concerned to satisfy this wish of Gwendolen's, and Rex proposed that they should wind up with a tableau in which the effect of her majesty would not be marred by any one's speech. This pleased her thoroughly, and the only question was the choice of the tableau.

"Something pleasant, children, I beseech you," said Mrs. Davilow; "I can't have any Greek wickedness."

"It is no worse than Christian wickedness, mamma," said Gwendolen, whose mention of Rachelesque heroines had called forth that remark.

"And less scandalous," said Rex. "Besides, one thinks of it as all gone by and done with. What do you say to Briseis being led away? I would be Achilles, and you would be looking round at me—after the print we have at the Rectory."

"That would be a good attitude for me," said Gwendolen, in a tone of acceptance. But afterward she said with decision: "No. It will not do. There must be three men in proper costume, else it will be ridiculous."

"I have it!" said Rex, after a little reflection. "Hermione as the statue in the Winter's Tale! I will be Leontes, and Miss Merry, Paulina, one on each side. Our dress won't signify," he went on laughingly; "it will be more Shakespearian and romantic if Leontes looks like Napoleon, and Paulina like a modern spinster."

And Hermione was chosen; all agreeing that age was of no consequence; but Gwendolen urged that instead of the mere tableau there should be just enough acting of the scene to introduce the striking up of the music as a signal for her to step down and advance; when Leontes, instead of embracing her, was to kneel and kiss the hem of her garment, and so the curtain was to fall. The antechamber with folding doors lent itself admirably to the purposes of a stage, and the whole of the establishment, with the addition of Jarrett the village carpenter, was absorbed in the preparations for an entertainment which, considering that it was an imitation of acting, was likely to be successful, since we know from ancient fable that an imitation may have more chance of success than the original.

Gwendolen was not without a special exultation in the prospect of this occasion, for she knew that Herr Klesmer was again at Quetcham, and she had taken care to include him among the invited.

Klesmer came. He was in one of his placid, silent moods, and sat in serene contemplation, replying to all appeals in benignant-sounding syllables more or less articulate—as taking up his cross meekly in a world overgrown with amateurs, or as careful how he moved his lion paws lest he should crush a rampant and vociferous mouse.

Everything indeed went off smoothly and according to expectation—all that was improvised and accidental being of a probable sort—until the incident occurred which showed Gwendolen in an unforeseen phase of emotion. How it came about was at first a mystery.

The tableau of Hermione was doubly striking from its dissimilarity with what had gone before: it was answering perfectly, and a murmur of applause had been gradually suppressed while Leontes gave his permission that Paulina should exercise her utmost art and make the statue move.

Hermione, her arm resting on a pillar, was elevated by about six inches, which she counted on as a means of showing her pretty foot and instep, when at the given signal she should advance and descend.

"Music, awake her, strike!" said Paulina (Mrs. Davilow, who, by special entreaty, had consented to take the part in a white burnous and hood).

Herr Klesmer, who had been good-natured enough to seat himself at the piano, struck a thunderous chord—but in the same instant, and before Hermione had put forth her foot, the movable panel, which was on a line with the piano, flew open on the right opposite the stage and disclosed the picture of the dead face and the fleeing figure, brought out in pale definiteness by the position of the wax-lights. Every one was startled, but all eyes in the act of turning toward the open panel were recalled by a piercing cry from Gwendolen, who stood without change of attitude, but with a change of expression that was terrifying in its terror. She looked like a statue into which a soul of Fear had entered: her pallid lips were parted; her eyes, usually narrowed under their long lashes, were dilated and fixed. Her mother, less surprised than alarmed, rushed toward her, and Rex, too, could not help going to her side. But the touch of her mother's arm had the effect of an electric charge; Gwendolen fell on her knees and put her hands before her face. She was still trembling, but mute, and it seemed that she had self-consciousness enough to aim at controlling her signs of terror, for she presently allowed herself to be raised from her kneeling posture and led away, while the company were relieving their minds by explanation.

"A magnificent bit of *plastik* that!" said Klesmer to Miss Arrowpoint. And a quick fire of undertoned question and answer went round.

"Was it part of the play?"

"Oh, no, surely not. Miss Harleth was too much affected. A sensitive creature!"

"Dear me! I was not aware that there was a painting behind that panel; were you?"

"No; how should I? Some eccentricity in one of the Earl's family long ago, I suppose."

"How very painful! Pray shut it up."

"Was the door locked? It is very mysterious. It must be the spirits."

"But there is no medium present."

"How do you know that? We must conclude that there is, when such things happen."

"Oh, the door was not locked; it was probably the sudden vibration from the piano that sent it open."

This conclusion came from Mr. Gascoigne, who begged Miss Merry if possible to get the key. But this readiness to explain the mystery was thought by Mrs. Vulcany unbecoming in a clergyman, and she observed in an undertone that Mr. Gascoigne was always a little too worldly for her taste. However, the key was produced, and the Rector turned it in the lock with an emphasis rather offensively rationalizing—as who should say, "It will not start open again"—putting the key in his pocket as a security.

However, Gwendolen soon reappeared, showing her usual spirits, and evidently determined to ignore as far as she could the striking change she had made in the part of Hermione.

But when Klesmer said to her, "We have to thank you for devising a perfect climax: you could not have chosen a finer bit of *plastik*," there was a flush of pleasure in her face. She liked to accept as a belief what was really no more than delicate feigning. He divined that the betrayal into a passion of fear had been mortifying to her, and wished her to understand that he took it for good acting. Gwendolen cherished the idea that now he was struck with her talent as well as her beauty, and her uneasiness about his opinion was half turned to complacency.

But too many were in the secret of what had been included in the rehearsals, and what had not, and no one besides Klesmer took the trouble to soothe Gwendolen's imagined mortification. The general sentiment was that the incident should be let drop.

There had really been a medium concerned in the starting open of the panel: one who had quitted the room in haste and crept to bed in much alarm of conscience. It was the small Isabel, whose intense curiosity, unsatisfied by the brief glimpse she had had of the strange picture on the day of arrival at Offendene, had kept her on the watch for an opportunity of finding out where Gwendolen had put the key, of stealing it from the discovered drawer when the rest of the family were out, and getting on a stool to unlock the panel. While she was indulging her thirst for knowledge in this way, a noise which she feared was an approaching footstep alarmed her: she closed the door and attempted hurriedly to lock it, but failing and not daring to linger, she withdrew the key and trusted that the panel would stick, as it seemed well inclined to do. In this confidence she had returned the key to its former place, stilling any anxiety by the thought that if the door were discovered to be unlocked nobody would know how the unlocking came about. The inconvenient Isabel, like other offenders, did not foresee her own impulse to confession, a fatality which came upon her the morning after the party, when Gwendolen said at the breakfast-table: "I know the door was locked before the housekeeper gave me the key, for I tried it myself afterward. Some one must have been to my drawer and taken the key."

It seemed to Isabel that Gwendolen's awful eyes had rested on her more than on the other sisters, and without any time for resolve, she said, with a trembling lip: "Please forgive me, Gwendolen."

The forgiveness was sooner bestowed than it would have been if Gwendolen had not desired to dismiss from her own and every one else's memory any case in which she had shown her susceptibility to terror. She wondered at herself in these occasional experiences, which seemed like a brief remembered madness, an unexplained exception from her normal life; and in this instance she felt a peculiar vexation that her helpless fear had shown itself, not, as usual, in solitude, but in well-lit company. Her ideal was to be daring in speech and reckless in braving dangers, both moral and physical; and though her practice fell far behind her ideal, this shortcoming seemed to be due to the pettiness of circumstances, the narrow theatre which life offers to a girl of twenty, who cannot conceive herself as anything else than a lady, or as in any position which would lack the tribute of respect. She had no permanent consciousness of other fetters, or of more spiritual restraints, having always disliked whatever was presented to her under the name of religion, in the same way that some people dislike arithmetic and accounts: it had raised no other emotion in her, no alarm, no longing; so that the question whether she believed it had not occurred to her, any more than it had occurred to her to inquire into the conditions of colonial property and banking, on which, as she had had many opportunities of knowing, the family fortune was dependent. All these facts about herself she would have been ready to admit, and even, more or less indirectly, to state. What she unwillingly recognized, and would have been glad for others to be unaware of, was that liability of hers to fits of spiritual dread, though this fountain of awe within her had not found its way into connection with the religion taught her or with any human relations. She was ashamed and frightened, as at what might happen again, in remembering her tremor on suddenly feeling herself alone, when, for example, she was walking without companionship and there came some rapid change in the light. Solitude in any wide scene impressed her with an undefined feeling of immeasurable existence aloof from her, in the midst of which she was helplessly incapable of asserting herself. The little astronomy taught her at school used sometimes to set her imagination at work in a way that made her tremble: but always when some one joined her she recovered her indifference to the vastness in which she seemed an exile; she found again her usual world in which her will was of some avail, and the religious nomenclature belonging to this world was no more identified for her with those uneasy impressions of awe than her uncle's surplices seen out of use at the Rectory. With human ears and eyes about her, she had always hitherto recovered her confidence, and felt the possibility of winning empire.

To her mamma and others her fits of timidity or terror were sufficiently accounted for by her "sensitiveness" or the "excitability of her nature"; but these explanatory phrases required conciliation with much that seemed to be blank indifference or rare self-mastery. Heat is a great agent and a useful word, but considered as a means of explaining the universe it requires an extensive knowledge of differences; and as a means of explaining character, "sensitiveness" is in much the same predicament. But who, loving a creature like Gwendolen, would not be inclined to regard every peculiarity in her as a mark of pre-eminence? That was what Rex did. After the Hermione scene he was more persuaded than ever that she must be instinct with all feeling, and not only readier to respond to a worshipful love, but able to love better than other girls. Rex felt the summer on his young wings and soared happily.

CHAPTER VII.

"*Perigot.* As the bonny lasse passed bye,
  Willie. Hey, ho, bonnilasse!
    P. She roode at me with glauncing eye,
    W. As clear as the crystall glasse.
    P. All as the sunny beame so bright,
    W. Hey, ho, the sunnebeame!
    P. Glaunceth from Phœbus' face forthright,
    W. So love into thy heart did streame."
                    —SPENSER: *Shepheard's Calendar.*

"The kindliest symptom, yet the most alarming crisis in the ticklish state of youth; the nourisher and destroyer of hopeful wits; . . . the servitude above freedom; the gentle mind's religion; the liberal superstition."—CHARLES LAMB.

THE first sign of the unimagined snow-storm was like the transparent white cloud that seems to set off the blue. Anna was in the secret of Rex's feeling; though for the first time in their lives he had said nothing to her about what he most thought of, and he only took it for granted that she knew it. For the first time, too, Anna could not say to Rex what was continually in her mind. Perhaps it might have been a pain which she would have had to conceal, that he should so soon care for some one else more than for herself, if such a feeling had not been thoroughly neutralized by doubt and anxiety on his behalf. Anna admired her cousin—would have said with simple sincerity, " Gwendolen is always very good to me," and held it in the order of things for herself to be entirely subject to this cousin; but she looked at her with mingled fear and distrust, with a puzzled contemplation as of some wondrous and beautiful animal whose nature was a mystery, and who, for anything Anna knew, might have an appetite for devouring all the small creatures that were her own particular pets. And now Anna's heart was sinking under the heavy conviction which she dared not utter, that Gwendolen would never care for Rex. What she herself held in tenderness and reverence had constantly seemed indifferent to Gwendolen, and it was easier to imagine her scorning Rex than returning any tenderness of his. Besides, she was always thinking of being something extraordinary. And poor Rex! Papa would be angry with him, if he knew. And of course he was too young to be in love in that way; and she, Anna, had thought that it would be years and years before anything of that sort came, and that she would be Rex's housekeeper ever so long. But what a heart must that be which did not return his love! Anna, in the prospect of his suffering, was beginning to dislike her too fascinating cousin.

It seemed to her, as it did to Rex, that the weeks had been filled with a tumultuous life evident to all observers: if he had been questioned on the subject he would have said that he had no wish to conceal what he hoped would be an engagement which he should immediately tell his father of; and yet for the first time in his life he was reserved not only about his feelings, but—which was more remarkable to Anna—about certain actions. She, on her side, was nervous each time her father or mother began to speak to her in private lest they should say anything about Rex and Gwendolen. But the elders were not in the least alive to this agitating drama, which went forward chiefly in a sort of pantomime extremely lucid in the minds thus expressing themselves, but easily missed by spectators who were running their eyes over the *Guardian* or the *Clerical Gazette*, and regarded the trivialities of the young ones with scarcely more interpretation than they gave to the actions of lively ants.

" Where are you going, Rex? " said Anna one gray morning when her father had set off in the carriage to the sessions, Mrs. Gascoigne with him, and she had observed that her brother had on his antigropelos, the utmost approach he possessed to a hunting equipment.

" Going to see the hounds throw off at the Three Barns."

" Are you going to take Gwendolen? " said Anna, timidly.

" She told you, did she? "

" No, but I thought—— Does papa know you are going? "

" Not that I am aware of. I don't suppose he would trouble himself about the matter."

" You are going to use his horse? "

" He knows I do that whenever I can."

" Don't let Gwendolen ride after the hounds, Rex," said Anna, whose fears gifted her with second-sight.

" Why not? " said Rey, smiling rather provokingly.

"Papa and mamma and aunt Davilow all wish her not to. They think it is not right for her."

"Why should you suppose she is going to do what is not right?"

"Gwendolen minds nobody sometimes," said Anna, getting bolder by dint of a little anger.

"Then she would not mind me," said Rex, perversely making a joke of poor Anna's anxiety.

"Oh, Rex, I cannot bear it. You will make yourself very unhappy." Here Anna burst into tears.

"Nannie, Nannie, what on earth is the matter with you?" said Rex, a little impatient at being kept in this way, hat on and whip in hand.

"She will not care for you one bit—I know she never will!" said the poor child in a sobbing whisper. She had lost all control of herself.

Rex reddened and hurried away from her out of the hall door, leaving her to the miserable consciousness of having made herself disagreeable in vain.

He did think of her words as he rode along; they had the unwelcomeness which all unfavorable fortune-telling has, even when laughed at; but he quickly explained them as springing from little Anna's tenderness, and began to be sorry that he was obliged to come away without soothing her. Every other feeling on the subject, however, was quickly merged in a resistant belief to the contrary of hers, accompanied with a new determination to prove that he was right. This sort of certainty had just enough kinship to doubt and uneasiness to hurry on a confession which an untouched security might have delayed.

Gwendolen was already mounted, and riding up and down the avenue when Rex appeared at the gate. She had provided herself against disappointment in case he did not appear in time by having the groom ready behind her, for she would not have waited beyond a reasonable time. But now the groom was dismissed, and the two rode away in delightful freedom. Gwendolen was in her highest spirits, and Rex thought that she had never looked so lovely before: her figure, her long white throat, and the curves of her cheek and chin were always set off to perfection by the compact simplicity of her riding dress. He could not conceive a more perfect girl; and to a youthful lover like Rex it seems that the fundamental identity of the good, the true, and the beautiful is already extant and manifest in the object of his love. Most observers would have held it more than equally accountable that a girl should have like impressions about Rex, for in his handsome face there was nothing corresponding to the undefinable stinging quality—as it were a trace of demon ancestry—which made some beholders hesitate in their admiration of Gwendolen.

It was an exquisite January morning in which there was no threat of rain, but a gray sky making the calmest background for the charms of a mild winter scene:—the grassy borders of the lanes, the hedgerows sprinkled with red berries and haunted with low twitterings, the purple bareness of the elms, the rich brown of the furrows. The horses' hoofs made a musical chime, accompanying their young voices. She was laughing at his equipment, for he was the reverse of a dandy, and he was enjoying her laughter: the freshness of the morning mingled with the freshness of their youth; and every sound that came from their clear throats, every glance they gave each other, was the bubbling outflow from a spring of joy. It was all morning to them, within and without. And thinking of them in these moments one is tempted to that futile sort of wishing—if only things could have been a little otherwise then, so as to have been greatly otherwise after—if only these two beautiful young creatures could have pledged themselves to each other then and there, and never through life have swerved from that pledge! For some of the goodness which Rex believed in was there. Goodness is a large, often a prospective word; like harvest, which at one stage when we talk of it lies all underground, with an indeterminate future: is the germ prospering in the darkness? at another, it has put forth delicate green blades, and by and by the trembling blossoms are ready to be dashed off by an hour of rough wind or rain. Each stage has its peculiar blight, and may have the healthy life choked out of it by a particular action of the foul land which rears or neighbors it, or by damage brought from foulness afar.

"Anna had got it into her head that you would want to ride after the hounds this morning," said Rex, whose secret associations with Anna's words made this speech seem quite perilously near the most momentous of subjects.

"Did she?" said Gwendolen, laughingly. "What a little clairvoyant she is!"

"Shall you?" said Rex, who had not believed in her intending to do it if the elders objected, but confided in her having good reasons.

"I don't know. I can't tell what I shall do till I get there. Clairvoyants are often wrong: they foresee what is likely. I am not fond of what is likely; it is always dull. I do what is unlikely."

"Ah, there you tell me a secret. When once I knew what people in general would be likely to do, I should know you would do the opposite. So you would have come round to a likelihood of your own sort. I shall be able to calculate on you. You couldn't surprise me."

"Yes, I could. I should turn round and do what was likely for people in general," said Gwendolen, with a musical laugh.

"You see you can't escape some sort of likelihood. And contradictoriness makes the strongest likelihood of all. You must give up a plan."

"No, I shall not. My plan is to do what pleases me." (Here should any young lady incline to imitate Gwendolen, let her consider the set of her head and neck: if the angle there had been different, the chin protrusive, and the cervical vertebræ a trifle more curved in their position, ten to one Gwendolen's words would have had a jar in them for the sweet-natured Rex. But everything odd in her speech was humor and pretty banter, which he was only anxious to turn toward one point.)

"Can you manage to feel only what pleases you?" said he.

"Of course not; that comes from what other people do. But if the world were pleasanter, one would only feel what was pleasant. Girls' lives are so stupid: they never do what they like."

"I thought that was more the case of the men. They are forced to do hard things, and are often dreadfully bored, and knocked to pieces too. And then, if we love a girl very dearly we want to do as she likes, so after all you have your own way."

"I don't believe it. I never saw a married woman who had her own way."

"What should you like to do?" said Rex, quite guilelessly, and in real anxiety.

"Oh, I don't know!—go to the North Pole, or ride steeple-chases, or go to be a queen in the East like Lady Hester Stanhope," said Gwendolen, flightily. Her words were born on her lips, but she would have been at a loss to give an answer of deeper origin.

"You don't mean you would never be married?"

"No; I didn't say that. Only when I married, I should not do as other women do."

"You might do just as you liked if you married a man who loved you more dearly than anything else in the world," said Rex, who, poor youth, was moving in themes outside the curriculum in which he had promised to win distinction. "I know one who does."

"Don't talk of Mr. Middleton, for heaven's sake," said Gwendolen, hastily, a quick blush spreading over her face and neck; "that is Anna's chant. I hear the hounds. Let us go on."

She put her chestnut to a canter, and Rex had no choice but to follow her. Still he felt encouraged. Gwendolen was perfectly aware that her cousin was in love with her; but she had no idea that the matter was of any consequence, having never had the slightest visitation of painful love herself. She wished the small romance of Rex's devotion to fill up the time of his stay at Pennicote, and to avoid explanations which would bring it to an untimely end. Besides, she objected, with a sort of physical repulsion, to being directly made love to. With all her imaginative delight in being adored, there was a certain fierceness of maidenhood in her.

But all other thoughts were soon lost for her in the excitement of the scene at the Three Barns. Several gentlemen of the hunt knew her, and she exchanged pleasant greetings. Rex could not get another word with her. The color, the stir

of the field had taken possession of Gwendolen with a strength
which was not due to habitual association, for she had never
yet ridden after the hounds—only said she should like to do
it, and so drawn forth a prohibition; her mamma dreading the
danger, and her uncle declaring that for his part he held that
kind of violent exercise unseemly in a woman, and that whatever might be done in other parts of the country, no lady of
good position followed the Wessex hunt: no one but Mrs.
Gadsby, the yeomanry captain's wife, who had been a kitchen-
maid and still spoke like one. This last argument had some
effect on Gwendolen, and had kept her halting between her
desire to assert her freedom and her horror of being classed
with Mrs. Gadsby.

Some of the most unexceptionable women in the neighborhood occasionally went to see the hounds throw off; but it
happened that none of them were present this morning to
abstain from following, while Mrs. Gadsby, with her doubtful
antecedents, grammatical and otherwise, was not visible to
make following seem unbecoming. Thus Gwendolen felt no
check on the animal stimulus that came from the stir and tongue
of the hounds, the pawing of the horses, the varying voices
of men, the movement hither and thither of vivid color on the
background of green and gray stillness:—that utmost excitement of the coming chase which consists in feeling something
like a combination of dog and horse, with the superadded thrill
of social vanities and consciousness of centaur-power which
belong to human kind.

Rex would have felt more of the same enjoyment if he could
have kept nearer to Gwendolen, and not seen her constantly
occupied with acquaintances, or looked at by would-be acquaintances, all on lively horses which veered about and swept
the surrounding space as effectually as a revolving lever.

"Glad to see you here this fine morning, Miss Harleth,"
said Lord Brackenshaw, a middle-aged peer of aristocratic
seediness in stained pink, with easy-going manners which
would have made the threatened deluge seem of no consequence. "We shall have a first-rate run. A pity you don't
go with us. Have your ever tried your little chestnut at a
ditch? you wouldn't be afraid, eh?"

"Not the least in the world," said Gwendolen. And this was true: she was never fearful in action and companionship. " I have often taken him at some rails and a ditch, too, near——"

"Ah, by Jove! " said his lordship, quietly, in notation that something was happening which must break off the dialogue: and as he reined off his horse, Rex was bringing his sober hackney up to Gwendolen's side when—the hounds gave tongue, and the whole field was in motion as if the whirl of the earth were carrying it; Gwendolen along with everything else; no word of notice to Rex, who without a second thought followed too. Could he let Gwendolen go alone? under other circumstances he would have enjoyed the run, but he was just now perturbed by the check which had been put on the impetus to utter his love, and get utterance in return—an impetus which could not at once resolve itself into a totally different sort of chase, at least with the consciousness of being on his father's gray nag, a good horse enough in his way, but of sober years and ecclesiastical habits. Gwendolen on her spirited little chestnut was up with the best, and felt as secure as an immortal goddess, having, if she had thought of risk, a core of confidence that no ill luck would happen to her. But she thought of no such thing, and certainly not of any risk there might be for her cousin. If she had thought of him, it would have struck her as a droll picture that he should be gradually falling behind, and looking round in search of gates: a fine lithe youth, whose heart must be panting with all the spirit of a beagle, stuck as if under a wizard's spell on a stiff clerical hackney, would have made her laugh with a sense of fun much too strong for her to reflect on his mortification. But Gwendolen was apt to think rather of those who saw her than of those whom she could not see; and Rex was soon so far behind that if she had looked she would not have seen him. For I grieve to say that in the search for a gate, along a lane lately mended, Primrose fell, broke his knees, and undesignedly threw Rex over his head.

Fortunately a blacksmith's son who also followed the hounds under disadvantages, namely, on foot (a loose way of hunting which had struck some even frivolous minds as immoral), was naturally also in the rear, and happened to be within sight of Rex's misfortune.   He ran to give help which was greatly needed, for Rex was a great deal stunned, and the complete recovery of sensation came in the form of pain.   Joel Dagge on this occasion showed himself that most useful of personages, whose knowledge is of a kind suited to the immediate occasion: he not only knew perfectly well what was the matter with the horse, how far they were both from the nearest public house and from Pennicote Rectory, and could certify to Rex that his shoulder was only a bit out of joint, but also offered experienced surgical aid.

"Lord, sir, let me shove it in again for you!   I's seen Nash, the bone-setter, do it, and done it myself for our little Sally twice over.   It's all one and the same, shoulders is.   If you'll trusten to me and tighten your mind up a bit, I'll do it for you in no time."

"Come, then, old fellow," said Rex, who could tighten his mind better than his seat in the saddle.   And Joel managed the operation, though not without considerable expense of pain to his patient, who turned so pitiably pale while tightening his mind, that Joel remarked: "Ah, sir, you aren't used to it, that's how it is.   I's see lots and lots o' joints out.   I see a man with his eye pushed out once—that was a rum go as ever I see.   You can't have a bit o' fun wi'out such a sort o' things. But it went in again.   I's swallowed three teeth mysen, as sure as I'm alive.   Now, sirrey" (this was addressed to Primrose), "come alonk—you mustn't make believe as you can't."

Joel being clearly a low character, it is, happily, not necessary to say more of him to the refined reader, than that he helped Rex to get home with as little delay as possible.   There was no alternative but to get home, though all the while he was in anxiety about Gwendolen, and more miserable in the thought that she, too, might have had an accident, than in the pain of his own bruises and the annoyance he was about to cause his father.   He comforted himself about her by reflecting that every one would be anxious to take care of her, and that some acquaintance would be sure to conduct her home.

Mr. Gascoigne was already at home, and was writing letters in his study, when he was interrupted by seeing poor Rex come in with a face which was not the less handsome and ingratiating for being pale and a little distressed. He was secretly the favorite son, and a young portrait of the father; who, however, never treated him with any partiality—rather, with an extra rigor. Mr. Gascoigne having inquired of Anna, knew that Rex had gone with Gwendolen to the meet at the Three Barns.

"What's the matter?" he said hastily, not laying down his pen.

"I'm very sorry, sir; Primrose has fallen down and broken his knees."

"Where have you been with him?" said Mr. Gascoigne, with a touch of severity. He rarely gave way to temper.

"To the Three Barns to see the hounds throw off."

"And you were fool enough to follow?"

"Yes, sir. I didn't go at any fences, but the horse got his leg into a hole."

"And you got hurt yourself, I hope, eh?"

"I got my shoulder put out, but a young blacksmith put it in again for me. I'm just a little battered, that's all."

"Well, sit down."

"I'm very sorry about the horse, sir; I knew it would be a vexation to you."

"And what has become of Gwendolen?" said Mr. Gascoigne, abruptly. Rex, who did not imagine that his father had made any inquiries about him, answered at first with a blush, which was the more remarkable for his previous paleness. Then he said, nervously:

"I am anxious to know—I should like to go or send at once to Offendene—but she rides so well, and I think she would keep up—there would most likely be many round her."

"I suppose it was she who led you on, eh?" said Mr. Gascoigne, laying down his pen, leaning back in his chair, and looking at Rex with more marked examination.

"It was natural for her to want to go; she didn't intend it beforehand—she was led away by the spirit of the thing. And, of course, I went when she went."

Mr. Gascoigne left a brief of silence, and then said, with quiet irony: "But now you observe, young gentleman, that you are not furnished with a horse which will enable you to play the squire to your cousin. You must give up that amusement. You have spoiled my nag for me, and that is enough mischief for one vacation. I shall beg you to get ready to start for Southampton to-morrow and join Stilfox, till you go up to Oxford with him. That will be good for your bruises as well as your studies."

Poor Rex felt his heart swelling and comporting itself as if it had been no better than a girl's.

"I hope you will not insist on my going immediately, sir."

"Do you feel too ill?"

"No, not that—but——" here Rex bit his lips and felt the tears starting, to his great vexation; then he rallied and tried to say more firmly: "I want to go to Offendene, but I can go this evening."

"I am going there myself. I can bring word about Gwendolen, if that is what you want."

Rex broke down. He thought he discerned an intention fatal to his happiness, nay, his life. He was accustomed to believe in his father's penetration, and to expect firmness. "Father, I can't go away without telling her that I love her, and knowing that she loves me."

Mr. Gascoigne was inwardly going through some self-rebuke for not being more wary, and was now really sorry for the lad; but every consideration was subordinate to that of using the wisest tactics in the case. He had quickly made up his mind, and could answer the more quietly:

"My dear boy, you are too young to be taking momentous, decisive steps of that sort. This is a fancy which you have got into your head during an idle week or two: you must set to work at something and dismiss it. There is every reason against it. An engagement at your age would be totally rash and unjustifiable; and, moreover, alliances between first cousins are undesirable. Make up your mind to a brief disappointment. Life is full of them. We have all got to be broken in; and this is a mild beginning for you."

"No, not mild. I can't bear it. I shall be good for nothing. I shouldn't mind anything, if it were settled between us. I could do anything then," said Rex, impetuously. "But it's of no use to pretend that I will obey you. I can't do it. If I said I would, I should be sure to break my word. I should see Gwendolen again."

"Well, wait till to-morrow morning, that we may talk of the matter again—you will promise me that," said Mr. Gascoigne, quietly; and Rex did not, could not, refuse.

The Rector did not even tell his wife that he had any other reason for going to Offendene that evening than his desire to ascertain that Gwendolen had got home safely. He found her more than safe—elated. Mr. Quallon, who had won the brush, had delivered the trophy to her, and she had brought it before her, fastened on the saddle; more than that, Lord Brackenshaw had conducted her home, and had shown himself delighted with her spirited riding. All this was told at once to her uncle, that he might see how well justified she had been in acting against his advice; and the prudential Rector did feel himself in a slight difficulty, for at that moment he was particularly sensible that it was his niece's serious interest to be well regarded by the Brackenshaws, and their opinion as to her following the hounds really touched the essence of his objection. However, he was not obliged to say anything immediately, for Mrs. Davilow followed up Gwendolen's brief triumphant phrases with:

"Still, I do hope you will not do it again, Gwendolen. I should never have a moment's quiet. Her father died by an accident, you know."

Here Mrs. Davilow had turned away from Gwendolen, and looked at Mr. Gascoigne.

"Mamma, dear," said Gwendolen, kissing her merrily, and passing over the question of the fears which Mrs. Davilow had meant to account for, "children don't take after their parents in broken legs."

Not one word had yet been said about Rex. In fact, there had been no anxiety about him at Offendene. Gwendolen had observed to her mamma, "Oh, he must have been left far behind, and gone home in despair," and it could not be denied that this was fortunate so far as it made way for Lord Brackenshaw's bringing her home. But now Mr. Gascoigne said, with some emphasis, looking at Gwendolen:

"Well, the exploit has ended better for you than for Rex."

"Yes, I dare say he had to make a terrible round. You have not taught Primrose to take the fences, uncle," said Gwendolen, without the faintest shade of alarm in her looks and tone.

"Rex has had a fall," said Mr. Gascoigne, curtly, throwing himself into an arm-chair, resting his elbows and fitting his palms and fingers together, while he closed his lips and looked at Gwendolen, who said:

"Oh, poor fellow! he is not hurt, I hope?" with a correct look of anxiety such as elated mortals try to superinduce when their pulses are all the while quick with triumph; and Mrs. Davilow, in the same moment, uttered a low "Good heavens! There!"

Mr. Gascoigne went on: "He put his shoulder out, and got some bruises, I believe." Here he made another little pause of observation; but Gwendolen, instead of any such symptoms as pallor and silence, had only deepened the compassionateness of her brow and eyes, and said again: "Oh, poor fellow! it is nothing serious, then?" and Mr. Gascoigne held his diagnosis complete. But he wished to make assurance doubly sure, and went on still with a purpose.

"He got his arm set again rather oddly. Some blacksmith —not a parishioner of mine—was on the field—a loose fish, I suppose, but handy, and set the arm for him immediately. So after all, I believe, I and Primrose come off worst. The horse's knees are cut to pieces. He came down in a hole, it seems, and pitched Rex over his head."

Gwendolen's face had allowably become contented again, since Rex's arm had been reset; and now, at the descriptive suggestions in the latter part of her uncle's speech, her elated spirits made her features less manageable than usual; the smiles broke forth, and finally a descending scale of laughter.

"You are a pretty young lady—to laugh at other people's calamities," said Mr. Gascoigne, with a milder sense of disapprobation than if he had not had counteracting reasons to be glad that Gwendolen showed no deep feeling on the occasion.

"Pray forgive me, uncle. Now Rex is safe, it is so droll

to fancy the figure he and Primrose would cut—in a lane all by themselves—only a blacksmith running up. It would make a capital caricature of ' Following the Hounds.' "

Gwendolen rather valued herself on her superior freedom in laughing where others might only see matter for seriousness. Indeed, the laughter became her person so well that her opinion of its gracefulness was often shared by others; and it even entered into her uncle's course of thought at this moment, that it was no wonder a boy should be fascinated by this young witch—who, however, was more mischievous than could be desired.

"How can you laugh at broken bones, child?" said Mrs. Davilow, still under her dominant anxiety. "I wish we had never allowed you to have the horse. You will see that we were wrong," she added, looking with a grave nod at Mr. Gascoigne—"at least I was, to encourage her in asking for it."

"Yes, seriously, Gwendolen," said Mr. Gascoigne, in a judicious tone of rational advice to a person understood to be altogether rational, "I strongly recommend you—I shall ask you to oblige me so far—not to repeat your adventure of to-day. Lord Brackenshaw is very kind, but I feel sure that he would concur with me in what I say. To be spoken of as 'the young lady who hunts ' by way of exception, would give a tone to the language about you which I am sure you would not like. Depend upon it, his lordship would not choose that Lady Beatrice or Lady Maria should hunt in this part of the country, if they were old enough to do so. When you are married, it will be different: you may do whatever your husband sanctions. But if you intend to hunt, you must· marry a man who can keep horses."

"I don't know why I should do anything so horrible as to marry without *that* prospect, at least," said Gwendolen, pettishly. Her uncle's speech had given her annoyance, which she could not show more directly; but she felt that she was committing herself, and after moving carelessly to another part of the room, went out.

"She always speaks in that way about marriage," said Mrs. Davilow; "but it will be different when she has seen the right person."

"Her heart has never been in the least touched, that you know of?" said Mr. Gascoigne.

Mrs. Davilow shook her head silently. "It was only last night she said to me: 'Mamma, I wonder how girls manage to fall in love. It is easy to make them do it in books. But men are too ridiculous.'"

Mr. Gascoigne laughed a little, and made no further remark on the subject. The next morning at breakfast he said:

"How are your bruises, Rex?"

"Oh, not very mellow yet, sir; only beginning to turn a little."

"You don't feel quite ready for a journey to Southampton?"

"Not quite," answered Rex, with his heart metaphorically in his mouth.

"Well, you can wait till to-morrow, and go to say good-by to them at Offendene."

Mrs. Gascoigne, who now knew the whole affair, looked steadily at her coffee lest she also should begin to cry, as Anna was doing already.

Mr. Gascoigne felt that he was applying a sharp remedy to poor Rex's acute attack, but he believed it to be in the end the kindest. To let him know the hopelessness of his love from Gwendolen's own lips might be curative in more ways than one.

"I can only be thankful that she doesn't care about him," said Mrs. Gascoigne, when she joined her husband in his study. "There are things in Gwendolen I cannot reconcile myself to. My Anna is worth two of her, with all her beauty and talent. It looks so very ill in her that she will not help in the schools with Anna—not even in the Sunday-school. What you or I advise is of no consequence to her: and poor Fannie is completely under her thumb. But I know you think better of her," Mrs. Gascoigne ended with a deferential hesitation.

"Oh, my dear, there is no harm in the girl. It is only that she has a high spirit, and it will not do to hold the reins too tight. The point is, to get her well married. She has a little too much fire in her for the present life with her mother and sisters. It is natural and right that she should be married soon—not to a poor man, but one who can give her a fitting position."

Presently Rex, with his arm in a sling, was on his two miles' walk to Offendene. He was rather puzzled by the unconditional permission to see Gwendolen, but his father's real ground of action could not enter into his conjectures. If it had, he would first have thought it horribly cold-blooded, and then have disbelieved in his father's conclusions.

When he got to the house, everybody was there but Gwendolen. The four girls, hearing him speak in the hall, rushed out of the library, which was their schoolroom, and hung round him with compassionate inquiries about his arm. Mrs. Davilow wanted to know exactly what had happened, and where the blacksmith lived, that she might make him a present; while Miss Merry, who took a subdued and melancholy part in all family affairs, doubted whether it would not be giving too much encouragement to that kind of character. Rex had never found the family troublesome before, but just now he wished them all away and Gwendolen there, and he was too uneasy for good-natured feigning. When at last he had said, " Where is Gwendolen? " and Mrs. Davilow had told Alice to go and see if her sister were come down, adding, " I sent up her breakfast this morning; she needed a long rest,"— Rex took the shortest way out of his endurance by saying, almost impatiently : " Aunt, I want to speak to Gwendolen— I want to see her alone."

"Very well, dear; go into the drawing-room. I will send her there," said Mrs. Davilow, who had observed that he was fond of being with Gwendolen, as was natural, but had not thought of this as having any bearing on the realities of life: it seemed merely part of the Christmas holidays which were spinning themselves out.

Rex for his part thought that the realities of life were all hanging on this interview. He had to walk up and down the drawing-room in expectation for nearly ten minutes—ample space for all imaginative fluctuations; yet, strange to say, he was unvaryingly occupied in thinking what and how much he could do, when Gwendolen had accepted him, to satisfy his father that the engagement was the most prudent thing in the world, since it inspired him with double energy for work. He was to be a lawyer, and what reason was there why he should not rise as high as Eldon did? He was forced to look at life in the light of his father's mind.

But when the door opened and she whose presence he was longing for entered, there came over him suddenly and mysteriously a state of tremor and distrust which he had never felt before. Miss Gwendolen, simple as she stood there, in her black silk, cut square about the round white pillar of her throat, a black band fastening her hair which streamed backward in smooth silky abundance, seemed more queenly than usual. Perhaps it was that there was none of the latent fun and tricksiness which had always pierced in her greeting of Rex. How much of this was due to her presentiment from what he had said yesterday that he was going to talk of love? How much from her desire to show regret about his accident? Something of both. But the wisdom of ages has hinted that there is a side of the bed which has a malign influence if you happen to get out on it; and this accident befalls some charming persons rather frequently. Perhaps it had befallen Gwendolen this morning. The hastening of her toilet, the way in which Bugle used the brush, the quality of the shilling serial mistakenly written for her amusement, the probabilities of the coming day, and, in short, social institutions generally, were all objectionable to her. It was not that she was out of temper, but that the world was not equal to the demands of her fine organism.

However it might be, Rex saw an awful majesty about her as she entered and put out her hand to him, without the least approach to a smile in eyes or mouth. The fun which had moved her in the evening had quite evaporated from the image of his accident, and the whole affair seemed stupid to her. But she said with perfect propriety: "I hope you are not much hurt, Rex; I deserve that you should reproach me for your accident."

"Not at all," said Rex, feeling the soul within him spreading itself like an attack of illness. "There is hardly anything the matter with me. I am so glad you had the pleasure: I would willingly pay for it by a tumble, only I was sorry to break the horse's knees."

Gwendolen walked to the hearth and stood looking at the

fire in the most inconvenient way for conversation, so that he could only get a side view of her face.

"My father wants me to go to Southampton for the rest of the vacation," said Rex, his baritone trembling a little.

"Southampton! That's a stupid place to go to, isn't it?" said Gwendolen, chilly.

"It would be to me, because you would not be there."

Silence.

"Should you mind about my going away, Gwendolen?"

"Of course. Every one is of consequence in this dreary country," said Gwendolen, curtly. The perception that poor Rex wanted to be tender made her curl up and harden like a sea-anemone at the touch of a finger.

"Are you angry with me, Gwendolen? Why do you treat me in this way all at once?" said Rex, flushing, and with more spirit in his voice, as if he, too, were capable of being angry.

Gwendolen looked round at him and smiled. "Treat you? Nonsense! I am only rather cross. Why did you come so very early? You must expect to find tempers in dishabille."

"Be as cross with me as you like—only don't treat me with indifference," said Rex, imploringly. "All the happiness of my life depends on your loving me—if only a little—better than any one else."

He tried to take her hand, but she hastily eluded his grasp and moved to the other end of the hearth, facing him.

"Pray don't make love to me! I hate it!" She looked at him fiercely.

Rex turned pale and was silent, but could not take his eyes off her, and the impetus was not yet exhausted that made hers dart death at him. Gwendolen herself could not have foreseen that she should feel in this way. It was all a sudden, new experience to her. The day before she had been quite aware that her cousin was in love with her—she did not mind how much, so that he said nothing about it; and if any one had asked her why she objected to love-making speeches, she would have said, laughingly, "Oh, I am tired of them all in the books." But now the life of passion had begun negatively in her. She felt passionately averse to this volunteered love.

To Rex at twenty the joy of life seemed at an end more absolutely than it can do to a man at forty. But before they
had ceased to look at each other, he did speak again.

"Is that the last word you have to say to me, Gwendolen?
Will it always be so?"

She could not help seeing his wretchedness and feeling a little regret for the old Rex who had not offended her. Decisively, but yet with some return of kindliness, she said:

"About making love? Yes. But I don't dislike you for
anything else."

There was just a perceptible pause before he said a low
"Good-by," and passed out of the room. Almost immediately
after, she heard the heavy hall door bang behind him.

Mrs. Davilow, too, had heard Rex's hasty departure, and
presently came into the drawing-room, where she found Gwendolen seated on the low couch, her face buried, and her hair
falling over her figure like a garment. She was sobbing bitterly. "My child, my child, what is it?" cried the mother,
who had never before seen her darling struck down in this
way, and felt something of the alarmed anguish that women
feel at the sight of overpowering sorrow in a strong man; for
this child had been her ruler. Sitting down by her with cir-
cling arms, she pressed her cheek against Gwendolen's head,
and then tried to draw it upward. Gwendolen gave way, and
letting her head rest against her mother, cried out sobbingly:
"Oh, mamma, what can become of my life? There is nothing
worth living for!"

"Why, dear?" said Mrs. Davilow. Usually she herself had
been rebuked by her daughter for involuntary signs of despair.

"I shall never love anybody. I can't love people. I hate
them."

"The time will come, dear, the time will come."

Gwendolen was more and more convulsed with sobbing; but
putting her arms round her mother's neck with an almost
painful clinging, she said brokenly: "I can't bear any one to
be very near me but you."

Then the mother began to sob, for this spoiled child had
never shown such dependence on her before: and so they
clung to each other.

CHAPTER VIII.

What name doth Joy most borrow
When life is fair?
" To-morrow."

What name doth best fit Sorrow
In young despair?
" To-morrow."

THERE was a much more lasting trouble at the Rectory.
Rex arrived there only to throw himself on his bed in a state
of apparent apathy, unbroken till the next day, when it began
to be interrupted by more positive signs of illness. Nothing
could be said about his going to Southampton: instead of that,
the chief thought of his mother and Anna was how to tend
this patient who did not want to be well, and from being the
brightest, most grateful spirit in the household, was metamorphosed into an irresponsive, dull-eyed creature who met all
affectionate attempts with a murmur of " Let me alone." His
father looked beyond the crisis, and believed it to be the shortest way out of an unlucky affair; but he was sorry for the
inevitable suffering, and went now and then to sit by him in
silence for a few minutes, parting with a gentle pressure of
his hand on Rex's blank brow, and a " God bless you, my
boy." Warham and the younger children used to peep round
the edge of the door to see this incredible thing of their lively
brother being laid low; but fingers were immediately shaken
at them to drive them back. The guardian who was always
there was Anna, and her little hand was allowed to rest within
her brother's, though he never gave it a welcoming pressure.
Her soul was divided between anguish for Rex and reproach
of Gwendolen.

"Perhaps it is wicked of me, but I think I never *can* love
her again," came as the recurrent burden of poor little Anna's
inward monody. And even Mrs. Gascoigne had an angry feeling toward her niece which she could not refrain from expressing (apologetically) to her husband.

"I know, of course, it is better, and we ought to be thankful that she is not in love with the poor boy; but really,

Henry, I think she is hard: she has the heart of a coquette.
I cannot help thinking that she must have made him believe
something, or the disappointment would not have taken hold
of him in that way. And some blame attaches to poor Fanny;
she is quite blind about that girl."

Mr. Gascoigne answered imperatively: "The less said on
that point the better, Nancy. I ought to have been more
awake myself. As to the boy, be thankful if nothing worse
ever happens to him. Let the thing die out as quickly as
possible; and especially with regard to Gwendolen—let it be
as if it had never been."

The Rector's dominant feeling was that there had been a
great escape. Gwendolen in love with Rex in return would
have made a much harder problem, the solution of which
might have been taken out of his hands. But he had to go
through some further difficulty.

One fine morning Rex asked for his bath, and made his toilet
as usual. Anna, full of excitement at this change, could do
nothing but listen for his coming down, and at last hearing
his step, ran to the foot of the stairs to meet him. For the
first time he gave her a faint smile, but it looked so melancholy on his pale face that she could hardly help crying.

"Nannie!" he said gently, taking her hand and leading her
slowly along with him to the drawing-room. His mother was
there, and when she came to kiss him, he said: "What a
plague I am!"

Then he sat still and looked out of the bow-window on the
lawn and shrubs covered with hoar-frost, across which the sun
was sending faint occasional gleams—something like that sad
smile on Rex's face, Anna thought. He felt as if he had had
a resurrection into a new world, and did not know what to do
with himself there, the old interests being left behind. Anna
sat near him, pretending to work, but really watching him
with yearning looks. Beyond the garden hedge there was a
road where wagons and carts sometimes went on field-work: a
railed opening was made in the hedge, because the upland with
its bordering wood and clump of ash-trees against the sky was
a pretty sight. Presently there came along a wagon laden
with timber; the horses were straining their grand muscles,

and the driver having cracked his whip, ran along anxiously
to guide the leader's head, fearing a swerve. Rex seemed to
be shaken into attention, rose, and looked till the last quivering trunk of the timber had disappeared, and then walked
once or twice along the room. Mrs. Gascoigne was no longer
there, and when he came to sit down again, Anna, seeing a
return of speech in her brother's eyes, could not resist the impulse to bring a little stool and seat herself against his knee,
looking up at him with an expression which seemed to say
"Do speak to me." And he spoke.

"I'll tell you what I'm thinking of, Nannie. I will go to
Canada, or somewhere of that sort." (Rex had not studied
the character of our colonial possessions.)

"Oh, Rex, not for always!"

"Yes, to get my bread there. I should like to build a hut,
and work hard at clearing, and have everything wild about
me, and a great wide quiet."

"And not take me with you?" said Anna, the big tears
coming fast.

"How could I?"

"I should like it better than anything; and settlers go with
their families. I would sooner go there than stay here in England. I could make the fires, and mend the clothes, and cook
the food; and I could learn how to make the bread before we
went. It would be nicer than anything—like playing at life
over again, as we used to do when we made our tent with the
drugget, and had our little plates and dishes."

"Father and mother would not let you go."

"Yes, I think they would, when I explained everything.
It would save money; and papa would have more to bring up
the boys with."

There was further talk of the same practical kind at intervals, and it ended in Rex's being obliged to consent that Anna
should go with him when he spoke to his father on the subject.

Of course it was when the Rector was alone in his study.
Their mother would become reconciled to whatever he decided
on; but mentioned to her first, the question would have distressed her.

"Well, my children!" said Mr. Gascoigne, cheerfully, as they entered. It was a comfort to see Rex about again.

"May we sit down with you a little, papa?" said Anna. "Rex has something to say."

"With all my heart."

It was a noticeable group that these three creatures made, each of them with a face of the same structural type—the straight brow, the nose suddenly straightened from an intention of being aquiline, the short upper lip, the short but strong and well-hung chin: there was even the same tone of complexion and set of the eye. The gray-haired father was at once massive and keen-looking; there was a perpendicular line in his brow which, when he spoke with any force of interest, deepened; and the habit of ruling gave him an air of reserved authoritativeness. Rex would have seemed a vision of the father's youth, if it had been possible to imagine Mr. Gascoigne without distinct plans and without command, smitten with a heart sorrow, and having no more notion of concealment than a sick animal; and Anna was a tiny copy of Rex, with hair drawn back and knotted, her face following his in its changes of expression, as if they had one soul between them.

"You know all about what has upset me, father," Rex began, and Mr. Gascoigne nodded.

"I am quite done up for life in this part of the world. I am sure it will be no use my going back to Oxford. I couldn't do any reading. I should fail, and cause you expense for nothing. I want to have your consent to take another course, sir."

Mr. Gascoigne nodded more slowly, the perpendicular line on his brow deepened, and Anna's trembling increased.

"If you would allow me a small outfit, I should like to go to the colonies and work on the land there." Rex thought the vagueness of the phrase prudential; "the colonies" necessarily embracing more advantages, and being less capable of being rebutted on a single ground than any particular settlement.

"Oh, and with me, papa," said Anna, not bearing to be left out from the proposal even temporarily. "Rex would want some one to take care of him, you know—some one to keep house. And we shall never, either of us, be married. And I should cost nothing, and I should be so happy. I know it would be hard to leave you and mamma; but there are all the others to bring up, and we two should be no trouble to you any more."

Anna had risen from her seat, and used the feminine argument of going closer to her papa as she spoke. He did not smile, but he drew her on his knee and held her there, as if to put her gently out of the question while he spoke to Rex.

"You will admit that my experience gives me some power of judging for you, and that I can probably guide you in practical matters better than you can guide yourself?"

Rex was obliged to say: "Yes, sir."

"And perhaps you will admit—though I don't wish to press that point—that you are bound in duty to consider my judgment and wishes?"

"I have never yet placed myself in opposition to you, sir." Rex in his secret soul could not feel that he was bound not to go to the colonies, but to go to Oxford again—which was the point in question.

"But you will do so if you persist in setting your mind toward a rash and foolish procedure, and deafening yourself to considerations which my experience of life assures me of. You think, I suppose, that you have had a shock which has changed all your inclinations, stupefied your brains, unfitted you for anything but manual labor, and given you a dislike to society? Is that what you believe?"

"Something like that. I shall never be up to the sort of work I must do to live in this part of the world. I have not the spirit for it. I shall never be the same again. And without any disrespect to you, father, I think a young fellow should be allowed to choose his way of life, if he does nobody any harm. There are plenty to stay at home, and those who like might be allowed to go where there are empty places."

"But suppose I am convinced on good evidence—as I am—that this state of mind of yours is transient, and that if you went off as you propose, you would by and by repent, and feel that you had let yourself slip back from the point you have been gaining by your education till now? Have you not strength of mind enough to see that you had better act on my assurance for a time, and test it? In my opinion, so far from agreeing with you that you should be free to turn yourself in-to a colonist and work in your shirt-sleeves with spade and hatchet—in my opinion you have no right whatever to expatriate yourself until you have honestly endeavored to turn to account the education you have received here. I say nothing of the grief to your mother and me."

"I'm very sorry; but what can I do? I can't study—that's certain," said Rex.

"Not just now, perhaps. You will have to miss a term. I have made arrangements for you—how you are to spend the next two months. But I confess I am disappointed in you, Rex. I thought you had more sense than to take up such ideas—to suppose that because you have fallen into a very common trouble, such as most men have to go through, you are loosened from all bonds of duty—just as if your brain had softened and you were no longer a responsible being."

What could Rex say? Inwardly he was in a state of rebellion, but he had no arguments to meet his father's; and while he was feeling, in spite of anything that might be said, that he should like to go off to "the colonies" to-morrow, it lay in a deep fold of his consciousness that he ought to feel—if he had been a better fellow he would have felt—more about his old ties. That is the sort of faith we live by in our soul-sicknesses.

Rex got up from his seat, as if he held the conference to be at an end.

"You assent to my arrangement, then?" said Mr. Gascoigne, with that distinct resolution of tone which seems to hold one in a vise.

There was a little pause before Rex answered: "I'll try what I can do, sir. I can't promise." His thought was, that trying would be of no use.

Her father kept Anna, holding her fast, though she wanted to follow Rex. "Oh, papa," she said, the tears coming with her words when the door had closed; "it is very hard for him. Doesn't he look ill?"

"Yes, but he will soon be better; it will all blow over.

And now, Anna, be as quiet as a mouse about it all. Never let it be mentioned when he is gone."

"No, papa. But I would not be like Gwendolen for anything—to have people fall in love with me so. It is very dreadful."

Anna dared not say that she was disappointed at not being allowed to go to the colonies with Rex; but that was her secret feeling, and she often afterward went inwardly over the whole affair, saying to herself: "I should have done with going out, and gloves, and crinoline, and having to talk when I am taken to dinner—and all that!"

I like to mark the time, and connect the course of individual lives with the historic stream, for all classes of thinkers. This was the period when the broadening of gauge in crinolines seemed to demand an agitation for the general enlargement of churches, ball-rooms, and vehicles. But Anna Gascoigne's figure would only allow the size of skirt manufactured for young ladies of fourteen.

CHAPTER IX.

I'll tell thee, Berthold, what men's hopes are like:
A silly child that, quivering with joy,
Would cast its little mimic fishing-line
Baited with loadstone for a bowl of toys
In the salt ocean.

EIGHT months after the arrival of the family at Offendene, that is to say, in the end of the following June, a rumor was spread in the neighborhood which to many persons was matter of exciting interest. It had no reference to the results of the American war, but it was one which touched all classes within a certain circuit round Wanchester: the corn-factors, the brewers, the horse-dealers, and saddlers, all held it a laudable thing, and one which was to be rejoiced in on abstract grounds, as showing the value of an aristocracy in a free country like England; the blacksmith in the hamlet of Diplow felt that a good time had come round; the wives of laboring men hoped their nimble boys of ten or twelve would be taken into employ by the gentlemen in livery; and the farmers about Diplow admitted, with a tincture of bitterness and reserve, that a man might now again perhaps have an easier market or exchange for a rick of old hay or a wagon-load of straw. If such were the hopes of low persons not in society, it may be easily inferred that their betters had better reasons for satisfaction, probably connected with the pleasures of life rather than its business. Marriage, however, must be considered as coming under both heads; and just as when a visit of majesty is announced, the dream of knighthood or a baronetcy is to be found under various municipal nightcaps, so the news in question raised a floating indeterminate vision of marriage in several well-bred imaginations.

The news was that Diplow Hall, Sir Hugo Mallinger's place, which had for a couple of years turned its white window-shutters in a painfully wall-eyed manner on its fine elms and beeches, its lilied pool and grassy acres specked with deer, was being prepared for a tenant, and was for the rest of the summer and through the hunting season to be inhabited in a fitting style both as to house and stable. But not by Sir Hugo himself: by his nephew, Mr. Mallinger Grandcourt, who was presumptive heir to the baronetcy, his uncle's marriage having produced nothing but girls. Nor was this the only contingency with which fortune flattered young Grandcourt, as he was pleasantly called; for while the chance of the baronetcy came through his father, his mother had given a baronial streak to his blood, so that if certain intervening persons slightly painted in the middle distance died, he would become a baron and peer of this realm.

It is the uneven allotment of nature that the male bird alone has the tuft, but we have not yet followed the advice of hasty philosophers who would have us copy nature entirely in these matters; and if Mr. Mallinger Grandcourt became a baronet or a peer, his wife would share the title—which in addition to his actual fortune was certainly a reason why that wife, being at present unchosen, should be thought of by more than one person with sympathetic interest as a woman sure to be well provided for.

Some readers of this history will doubtless regard it as incredible that people should construct matrimonial prospects on the mere report that a bachelor of good fortune and possibilities was coming within reach, and will reject the statement as a mere outflow of gall: they will aver that neither they nor their first cousins have minds so unbridled; and that in fact this is not human nature, which would know that such speculations might turn out to be fallacious, and would therefore not entertain them. But, let it be observed, nothing is here narrated of human nature generally: the history in its present stage concerns only a few people in a corner of Wessex—whose reputation, however, was unimpeached, and who, I am in the proud position of being able to state, were all on visiting terms with persons of rank.

There were the Arrowpoints, for example, in their beautiful place at Quetcham: no one could attribute sordid views in relation to their daughter's marriage to parents who could leave her at least half a million; but having affectionate anxieties about their Catherine's position (she having resolutely refused Lord Slogan, an unexceptionable Irish peer, whose estate wanted nothing but drainage and population), they wondered, perhaps from something more than a charitable impulse, whether Mr. Grandcourt was good-looking, of sound constitution, virtuous, or at least reformed, and if liberal-conservative, not too liberal-conservative; and without wishing anybody to die, thought his succession to the title an event to be desired.

If the Arrowpoints had such ruminations, it is the less surprising that they were stimulated in Mr. Gascoigne, who for being a clergyman was not the less subject to the anxieties of a parent and guardian; and we have seen how both he and Mrs. Gascoigne might by this time have come to feel that he was overcharged with the management of young creatures who were hardly to be held in with bit or bridle, or any sort of metaphor that would stand for judicious advice.

Naturally, people did not tell each other all they felt and thought about young Grandcourt's advent: on no subject is this openness found prudentially practicable—not even on the generation of acids, or the destination of the fixed stars; for either your contemporary with a mind turned toward the same subjects may find your ideas ingenious and forestall you in applying them, or he may have other views on acids and fixed stars, and think ill of you in consequence.   Mr. Gascoigne did not ask Mr. Arrowpoint if he had any trustworthy source of information about Grandcourt considered as a husband for a charming girl; nor did Mrs. Arrowpoint observe to Mrs. Davilow that if the possible peer sought a wife in the neighborhood of Diplow, the only reasonable expectation was that he would offer his hand to Catherine, who, however, would not accept him unless he were in all respects fitted to secure her happiness.   Indeed, even to his wife the Rector was silent as to the contemplation of any matrimonial result, from the probability that Mr. Grandcourt would see Gwendolen at the next Archery Meeting; though Mrs. Gascoigne's mind was very likely still more active in the same direction.   She had said interjectionally to her sister, "It would be a mercy, Fanny, if that girl were well married!" to which Mrs. Davilow, discerning some criticism of her darling in the fervor of that wish, had not chosen to make any audible reply, though she had said inwardly, "You will not get her to marry for your pleasure"; the mild mother becoming rather saucy when she identified herself with her daughter.

To her husband, Mrs. Gascoigne said: "I hear Mr. Grandcourt has two places of his own, but he comes to Diplow for the hunting.   It is to be hoped he will set a good example in the neighborhood.   Have you heard what sort of young man he is, Henry?"

"Mr. Gascoigne had not heard; at least, if his male acquaintances had gossiped in his hearing, he was not disposed to repeat their gossip, or give it any emphasis in his own mind.   He held it futile, even if it had been becoming, to show any curiosity as to the past of a young man whose birth, wealth, and consequent leisure made many habits venial which under other circumstances would have been inexcusable. Whatever Grandcourt had done, he had not ruined himself; and it is well known that in gambling, for example, whether of the business or holiday sort, a man who has the strength of mind to leave off when he has only ruined others, is a reformed character.   This is an illustration merely: Mr. Gascoigne had not heard that Grandcourt had been a gambler; and we can hardly pronounce him singular in feeling that a landed proprietor with a mixture of noble blood in his veins was not to be an object of suspicious inquiry like a reformed character who offers himself as your butler or footman. Reformation, where a man can afford to do without it, can hardly be other than genuine. Moreover, it was not certain on any other showing hitherto that Mr. Grandcourt had needed reformation more than other young men in the ripe youth of five-and-thirty; and, at any rate, the significance of what he had been must be determined by what he actually was.

Mrs. Davilow, too, although she would not respond to her sister's pregnant remark, could not be inwardly indifferent to an event that might promise a brilliant lot for Gwendolen. A little speculation on "what may be" comes naturally, without encouragement—comes inevitably in the form of images, when unknown persons are mentioned; and Mr. Grandcourt's name raised in Mrs. Davilow's mind first of all the picture of a handsome, accomplished excellent young man whom she would be satisfied with as a husband for her daughter; but then came the further speculation—would Gwendolen be satisfied with him? There was no knowing what would meet that girl's taste or touch her affections—it might be something else than excellence; and thus the image of the perfect suitor gave way before a fluctuating combination of qualities that might be imagined to win Gwendolen's heart. In the difficulty of arriving at the particular combination which would insure that result, the mother even said to herself: "It would not signify about her being in love, if she would only accept the right person." For whatever marriage had been for herself, how could she the less desire it for her daughter? The difference her own misfortunes made was, that she never dared to dwell much to Gwendolen on the desirableness of marriage, dreading an answer something like that of the future Madame Roland, when her gentle mother, urging the acceptance of a suitor, said, "Tu seras heureuse, ma chère." "Oui, maman, comme toi."

In relation to the problematic Mr. Grandcourt, least of all would Mrs. Davilow have willingly let fall a hint of the aerial castle-building which she had the good taste to be ashamed of;

for such a hint was likely enough to give an adverse poise to Gwendolen's own thought, and make her detest the desirable husband beforehand. Since that scene after poor Rex's fare-well visit, the mother had felt a new sense of peril in touching the mystery of her child's feeling, and in rashly determining what was her welfare: only she could think of welfare in no other shape than marriage.

The discussion of the dress that Gwendolen was to wear at the Archery Meeting was a relevant topic, however; and when it had been decided that as a touch of color on her white cash-mere, nothing, for her complexion, was comparable to pale green—a feather which she was trying in her hat before the looking-glass having settled the question—Mrs. Davilow felt her ears tingle when Gwendolen, suddenly throwing herself into the attitude of drawing her bow, said, with a look of comic enjoyment:

"How I pity all the other girls at the Archery Meeting—all thinking of Mr. Grandcourt! And they have not a shadow of a chance."

Mrs. Davilow had not presence of mind to answer immedi-ately, and Gwendolen turned round quickly toward her, say-ing wickedly:

"Now you know they have not, mamma. You and my uncle and aunt—you all intend him to fall in love with me."

Mrs. Davilow, piqued into a little stratagem, said: "Oh, my dear, that is not so certain. Miss Arrowpoint has charms which you have not."

"I know; but they demand thought. My arrow will pierce him before he has time for thought. He will declare himself my slave—I shall send him round the world to bring me back the wedding-ring of a happy woman—in the meantime all the men who are between him and the title will die of different diseases—he will come back Lord Grandcourt—but without the ring—and fall at my feet. I shall laugh at him—he will rise in re-sentment—I shall laugh more—he will call for his steed and ride to Quetcham, where he will find Miss Arrowpoint just married to a needy musician, Mrs. Arrowpoint tearing her cap off, and Mr. Arrowpoint standing by. Exit Lord Grandcourt, who returns to Diplow, and, like M. Jabot, *change de linge.*"

Was ever any young witch like this? You thought of hiding things from her—sat upon your secret and looked innocent, and all the while she knew by the corner of your eye that it was exactly five pounds ten you were sitting on! As well turn the key to keep out the damp! It was probable that by dint of divination she already knew more than any one else did of Mr. Grandcourt. That idea in Mrs. Davilow's mind prompted the sort of question which often comes without any other apparent reason than the faculty of speech and the not knowing what to do with it.

"Why, what kind of man do you imagine him to be, Gwendolen?"

"Let me see!" said the witch, putting her forefinger to her lips, with a little frown, and then stretching out the finger with decision. "Short—just above my shoulder—trying to make himself tall by turning up his moustache and keeping his beard long—a glass in his right eye to give him an air of distinction—a strong opinion about his waistcoat, but uncertain and trimming about the weather, on which he will try to draw me out. He will stare at me all the while, and the glass in his eye will cause him to make horrible faces, especially when he smiles in a flattering way. I shall cast down my eyes in consequence, and he will perceive that I am not indifferent to his attentions. I shall dream that night that I am looking at the extraordinary face of a magnified insect—and the next morning he will make me an offer of his hand; the sequel as before."

"That is a portrait of some one you have seen already, Gwen. Mr. Grandcourt may be a delightful young man for what you know."

"Oh, yes," said Gwendolen, with a high note of careless admission, taking off her best hat and turning it round on her hand contemplatively. "I wonder what sort of behavior a delightful young man would have?" Then, with a merry change of face: I know he would have hunters and racers, and a London house and two country-houses—one with battlements and another with a veranda. And I feel sure that with a little murdering he might get a title."

The irony of this speech was of the doubtful sort that has

some genuine belief mixed up with it. Poor Mrs. Davilow felt uncomfortable under it. Her own meanings being usually literal and in intention innocent; and she said, with a distressed brow:

"Don't talk in that way, child, for heaven's sake! you do read such books—they give you such ideas of everything. I declare when your aunt and I were your age we knew nothing about wickedness. I think it was better so."

"Why did you not bring me up in that way, mamma?" said Gwendolen. But immediately perceiving in the crushed look and rising sob that she had given a deep wound, she tossed down her hat and knelt at her mother's feet, crying:

"Mamma, mamma! I was only speaking in fun. I meant nothing."

"How could I, Gwendolen?" said poor Mrs. Davilow, unable to hear the retractation, and sobbing violently while she made the effort to speak. "Your will was always too strong for me—if everything else had been different."

This disjointed logic was intelligible enough to the daughter. "Dear mamma, I don't find fault with you—I love you," said Gwendolen, really compunctious. "How can you help what I am? Besides, I am very charming. Come, now." Here Gwendolen with her handkerchief gently rubbed away her mother's tears. "Really—I am contented with myself. I like myself better than I should have liked my aunt and you. How dreadfully dull you must have been!"

Such tender cajolery served to quiet the mother, as it had often done before after like collisions. Not that the collisions had often been repeated at the same point; for in the memory of both they left an association of dread with the particular topics which had occasioned them: Gwendolen dreaded the unpleasant sense of compunction toward her mother, which was the nearest approach to self-condemnation and self-distrust that she had known; and Mrs. Davilow's timid maternal conscience dreaded whatever had brought on the slightest hint of reproach. Hence, after this little scene, the two concurred in excluding Mr. Grandcourt from their conversation.

When Mr. Gascoigne once or twice referred to him, Mrs. Davilow feared least Gwendolen should betray some of her alarming keen-sightedness about what was probably in her uncle's mind; but the fear was not justified. Gwendolen knew certain differences in the characters with which she was concerned as birds know climate and weather; and, for the very reason that she was determined to evade her uncle's control, she was determined not to clash with him. The good understanding between them was much fostered by their enjoyment of archery together: Mr. Gascoigne, as one of the best bowmen in Wessex, was gratified to find the elements of like skill in his niece; and Gwendolen was the more careful not to lose the shelter of his fatherly indulgence, because since the trouble with Rex both Mrs. Gascoigne and Anna had been unable to hide what she felt to be a very unreasonable alienation from her. Toward Anna she took some pains to behave with a regretful affectionateness; but neither of them dared to mention Rex's name, and Anna, to whom the thought of him was part of the air she breathed, was ill at ease with the lively cousin who had ruined his happiness. She tried dutifully to repress any sign of her changed feeling; but who in pain can imitate the glance and hand-touch of pleasure?

This unfair resentment had rather a hardening effect on Gwendolen, and threw her into a more defiant temper. Her uncle, too, might be offended if she refused the next person who fell in love with her; and one day when that idea was in her mind, she said:

"Mamma, I see now why girls are glad to be married—to escape being expected to please everybody but themselves."

Happily, Mr. Middleton was gone without having made any avowal; and notwithstanding the admiration for the handsome Miss Harleth, extending perhaps over thirty square miles in a part of Wessex well studded with families whose members included several disengaged young men, each glad to seat himself by the lively girl with whom it was so easy to get on in conversation—notwithstanding these grounds for arguing that Gwendolen was likely to have other suitors more explicit than the cautious curate, the fact was not so.

Care has been taken not only that the trees should not sweep the stars down, but also that every man who admires a fair girl should not be enamored of her, and even that every man who is enamored should not necessarily declare himself. There are various refined shapes in which the price of corn, known to be a potent cause in this relation, might, if inquired into, show why a young lady, perfect in person, accomplishments, and costume, has not the trouble of rejecting many offers; and nature's order is certainly benignant in not obliging us one and all to be desperately in love with the most admirable mortal we have ever seen. Gwendolen, we know, was far from holding that supremacy in the minds of all observers. Besides, it was but a poor eight months since she had come to Offendene, and some inclinations become manifest slowly, like the sunward creeping of plants.

In face of this fact, that not one of the eligible young men already in the neighborhood had made Gwendolen an offer, why should Mr. Grandcourt be thought of as likely to do what they had left undone?

Perhaps because he was thought of as still more eligible; since a great deal of what passes for likelihood in the world is simply the reflex of a wish. Mr. and Mrs. Arrowpoint, for example, having no anxiety that Miss Harleth should make a brilliant marriage, had quite a different likelihood in their minds.

CHAPTER X.

1ST GENT. What woman should be? Sir, consult the taste
Of marriageable men. This planet's store
In iron, cotton, wool, or chemicals—
All matter rendered to our plastic skill,
Is wrought in shapes responsive to demand:
The market's pulse makes index high or low,
By rule sublime. Our daughters must be wives,
And to be wives must be what men will choose:
Men's taste is women's test. You mark the phrase?
'Tis good, I think?—the sense well winged and poised
With t's and s's.

GENT. Nay, but turn it round:
Give us the test of taste. A fine *menu*—
Is it to-day what Roman epicures
Insisted that a gentleman must eat
To earn the dignity of dining well?

BRACKENSHAW PARK, where the Archery Meeting was held, looked out from its gentle heights far over the neighboring valley to the outlying eastern downs and the broad, slow rise of cultivated country, hanging like a vast curtain toward the west. The castle, which stood on the highest platform of the clustered hills, was built of rough-hewn limestone, full of lights and shadows made by the dark dust of lichens and the washings of the rain. Masses of beech and fir sheltered it on the north, and spread down here and there along the green slopes like flocks seeking the water which gleamed below. The archery-ground was a carefully kept enclosure on a bit of table-land at the farthest end of the park, protected toward the southwest by tall elms and a thick screen of hollies, which kept the gravel walk and the bit of newly mown turf where the targets were placed in agreeable afternoon shade. The Archery Hall with an arcade in front showed like a white temple against the greenery on the northern side.

What could make a better background for the flower-groups of ladies, moving and bowing and turning their necks as it would become the leisurely lilies to do if they took to locomotion? The sounds, too, were very pleasant to hear, even when the military band from Wanchester ceased to play: musical laughs in all the registers and a harmony of happy, friendly speeches, now rising toward mild excitement, now sinking to an agreeable murmur.

No open-air amusement could be much freer from those noisy, crowding conditions which spoil most modern pleasures; no Archery Meeting could be mcre select, the number of friends accompanying the members being restricted by an award of tickets, so as to keep the maximum within the limits of convenience for the dinner and ball to be held in the castle. Within the enclosure no plebeian spectators were admitted except Lord Brackenshaw's tenants and their families, and of these it was chiefly the feminine members who used the privilege, bringing their little boys and girls or younger brothers and sisters. The males among them relieved the insipidity of the entertainment by imaginative betting, in which the stake was "anything you like," on their favorite archers; but the young maidens, having a different principle of discrimination, were considering which of those sweetly dressed ladies they would choose to be, if the choice were allowed them. Probably the form these rural souls would most have striven for as a tabernacle, was some other than Gwendolen's—one with more pink in her cheeks and hair of the most fashionable yellow; but among the male judges in the ranks immediately surrounding her there was unusual unanimity in pronouncing her the finest girl present.

No wonder she enjoyed her existence on that July day. Pre-eminence is sweet to those who love it, even under mediocre circumstances. Perhaps it is not quite mythical that a slave has been proud to be bought first; and probably a barn-door fowl on sale, though he may not have understood himself to be called the best of a bad lot, may have a self-informed consciousness of his relative importance, and strut consoled. But for complete enjoyment the outward and the inward must concur. And that concurrence was happening to Gwendolen.

Who can deny that bows and arrows are among the prettiest weapons in the world for feminine forms to play with? They prompt attitudes full of grace and power, where that fine concentration of energy seen in all marksmanship is freed from associations of bloodshed. The time-honored British resource of "killing something" is no longer carried on with bow and quiver; bands defending their passes against an invading nation fight under another sort of shade than a cloud of arrows; and poisoned darts are harmless survivals either in rhetoric or in regions comfortably remote. Archery has no ugly smell of brimstone; breaks nobody's shins, breeds no athletic monsters; its only danger is that of failing, which for generous blood is enough to mould skilful action. And among the Brackenshaw archers the prizes were all of the nobler symbolic kind: not properly to be carried off in a parcel, degrading honor into gain; but the gold arrow and the silver, the gold star and the silver, to be worn for a time in sign of achievement and then transferred to the next who did excellently. These signs of pre-eminence had the virtue of wreaths without their inconveniences, which might have produced a melancholy effect in the heat of the ball-room. Altogether the Brackenshaw Archery Club was an institution framed with good taste, so as not to have by necessity any ridiculous incidents.

And to-day all incalculable elements were in its favor.

There was mild warmth, and no wind to disturb either hair
or drapery or the course of the arrow; all skilful preparation
had fair play, and when there was a general march to extract
the arrows, the promenade of joyous young creatures in light
speech and laughter, the graceful movement in common toward
a common object, was a show worth looking at. Here Gwendolen seemed a Calypso among her nymphs. It was in her
attitudes and movements that every one was obliged to admit
her surpassing charm.

"That girl is like a high-mettled racer," said Lord Brackenshaw to young Clintock, one of the invited spectators.

"First chop! tremendously pretty too," said the elegant
Grecian, who had been paying her assiduous attention; "I
never saw her look better."

Perhaps she had never looked so well. Her face was beaming with young pleasure in which there were no malign rays of
discontent; for being satisfied with her own chances, she felt
kindly toward everybody and was satisfied with the universe.
Not to have the highest distinction in rank, not to be marked
out as an heiress, like Miss Arrowpoint, gave an added triumph
in eclipsing those advantages. For personal recommendation
she would not have cared to change the family group accompanying her for any other: her mamma's appearance would
have suited an amiable duchess; her uncle and aunt Gascoigne
with Anna made equally gratifying figures in their way; and
Gwendolen was too full of joyous belief in herself to feel in
the least jealous, though Miss Arrowpoint was one of the best
archeresses.

Even the reappearance of the formidable Herr Klesmer,
which caused some surprise in the rest of the company, seemed
only to fall in with Gwendolen's inclination to be amused.
Short of Apollo himself, what great musical *maestro* could
make a good figure at an archery meeting? There was a very
satirical light in Gwendolen's eyes as she looked toward the
Arrowpoint party on their first entrance, when the contrast
between Klesmer and the average group of English county
people seemed at its utmost intensity in the close neighborhood of his hosts—or patrons, as Mrs. Arrowpoint would have
liked to hear them called, that she might deny the possibility

of any longer patronizing genius, its royalty being universally acknowledged.   The contrast might have amused a graver personage than Gwendolen.   We English are a miscellaneous people, and any chance fifty of us will present many varieties of animal architecture or facial ornament; but it must be admitted that our prevailing expression is not that of a lively, impassioned race, preoccupied with the ideal and carrying the real as a mere makeweight.   The strong point of the English gentleman pure is the easy style of his figure and clothing; he objects to marked ins and outs in his costume, and he also objects to looking inspired.

Fancy an assemblage where the men had all that ordinary stamp of the well-bred Englishman, watching the entrance of Herr Klesmer—his mane of hair floating backward in massive inconsistency with the chimney-pot hat, which had the look of having been put on for a joke above his pronounced but well-modelled features and powerful clean-shaven mouth and chin; his tall, thin figure clad in a way which, not being strictly English, was all the worse for its apparent emphasis of intention.   Draped in a loose garment with a Florentine *berretta* on his head, he would have been fit to stand by the side of Leonardo da Vinci; but how when he presented himself in trousers which were not what English feeling demanded about the knees?—and when the fire that showed itself in his glances and the movements of his head, as he looked round him with curiosity, was turned into comedy by a hat which ruled that mankind should have well-cropped hair and a staid demeanor, such, for example, as Mr. Arrowpoint's, whose nullity of face and perfect tailoring might pass everywhere without ridicule?   One sees why it is often better for greatness to be dead, and to have got rid of the outward man.

Many present knew Klesmer, or knew of him; but they had only seen him on candle-light occasions when he appeared simply as a musician, and he had not yet that supreme, world-wide celebrity which makes an artist great to the most ordinary people by their knowledge of his great expensiveness. It was literally a new light for them to see him in—presented unexpectedly on this July afternoon in an exclusive society: some were inclined to laugh, others felt a little disgust at the want of judgment shown by the Arrowpoints in this use of an introductory card.

"What extreme guys those artistic fellows usually are!" said young Clintock to Gwendolen. "Do look at the figure he cuts, bowing with his hand on his heart to Lady Brackenshaw—and Mrs. Arrowpoint's feather pust reaching his shoulder."

"You are one of the profane," said Gwendolen. "You are blind to the majesty of genius. Herr Klesmer smites me with awe; I feel crushed in his presence; my courage all oozes from me."

"Ah, you understand all about his music."

"No, indeed," said Gwendolen, with a light laugh; "it is he who understands all about mine and thinks it pitiable." Klesmer's verdict on her singing had been an easier joke to her since he had been struck by her *plastik*.

"It is not addressed to the ears of the future, I suppose. I'm glad of that: it suits mine."

"Oh, you are very kind. But how remarkably well Miss Arrowpoint looks to-day! She would make quite a fine picture in that gold-colored dress."

"Too splendid, don't you think?"

"Well, perhaps a little too symbolical—too much like the figure of Wealth in an allegory."

This speech of Gwendolen's had rather a malicious sound, but it was not really more than a bubble of fun. She did not wish Miss Arrowpoint or any one else to be out of the way, believing in her own good fortune even more than in her skill. The belief in both naturally grew stronger as the shooting went on, for she promised to achieve one of the best scores—a success which astonished every one in a new member; and to Gwendolen's temperament one success determined another. She trod on air, and all things pleasant seemed possible. The hour was enough for her, and she was not obliged to think what she should do next to keep her life at the due pitch.

"How does the scoring stand, I wonder?" said Lady Brackenshaw, a gracious personage who, adorned with two little girls and a boy of stout make, sat as lady paramount.

Her lord had come up to her in one of the intervals of shooting. "It seems to me that Miss Harleth is likely to win the gold arrow."

"Gad, I think she will, if she carries it on! she is running Juliet Fenn hard. It is wonderful for one in her first year. Catherine is not up to her usual mark," continued his lordship, turning to the heiress's mother who sat near. "But she got the gold arrow last time. And there's a luck even in these games of skill. That's better. It gives the hinder ones a chance."

"Catherine will be very glad for others to win," said Mrs. Arrowpoint, "she is so magnanimous. It was entirely her considerateness that made us bring Herr Klesmer instead of Canon Stopley, who had expressed a wish to come. For her own pleasure, I am sure she would rather have brought the Canon; but she is always thinking of others. I told her it was not quite *en règle* to bring one so far out of our own set; but she said, 'Genius itself is not *en règle*; it comes into the world to make new rules.' And one must admit that."

"Ay, to be sure," said Lord Brackenshaw, in a tone of careless dismissal, adding quickly, "For my part, I am not magnanimous; I should like to win. But, confound it! I never have the chance now. I'm getting old and idle. The young ones beat me. As old Nestor says—the gods don't give us everything at one time: I was a young fellow once, and now I am getting an old and wise one. Old, at any rate; which is a gift that comes to everybody if they live long enough, so it raises no jealousy." The Earl smiled comfortably at his wife.

"Oh, my lord, people who have been neighbors twenty years must not talk to each other about age," said Mrs. Arrowpoint. "Years, as the Tuscans say, are made for the letting of houses. But where is our new neighbor? I thought Mr. Grandcourt was to be here to-day."

"Ay, by the way, so he was. The time's getting on too," said his lordship, looking at his watch. "But he only got to Diplow the other day. He came to us on Tuesday and said he had been a little bothered. He may have been pulled in another direction. Why, Gascoigne"—the rector was just then crossing at a little distance with Gwendolen on his arm, and turned in compliance with the call—"this is a little too bad; you not only beat us yourself, but you bring up your niece to beat all the archeresses."

"It *is* rather scandalous in her to get the better of elder members," said Mr. Gascoigne, with much inward satisfaction curling his short upper lip. "But it is not my doing, my lord. I only meant her to make a tolerable figure, without surpassing any one."

"It is not my fault, either," said Gwendolen, with pretty archness. "If I am to aim, I can't help hitting."

"Ay, ay, that may be a fatal business for some people," said Lord Brackenshaw, good-humoredly; then taking out his watch and looking at Mrs. Arrowpoint again: "The time's getting on, as you say. But Grandcourt is always late. I notice in town he's always late, and he's no bowman—understands nothing about it. But I told him he must come; he would see the flower of the neighborhood here. He asked about you—had seen Arrowpoint's card. I think you had not made his acquaintance in town. He has been a good deal abroad. People don't know him much."

"No; we are strangers," said Mrs. Arrowpoint. "But that is not what might have been expected. For his uncle Sir Hugo Mallinger and I are great friends when we meet."

"I don't know; uncles and nephews are not so likely to be seen together as uncles and nieces," said his lordship, smiling toward the Rector. "But just come with me one instant, Gascoigne, will you? I want to speak a word about the clout-shooting."

Gwendolen chose to go too, and be deposited in the same group with her mamma and aunt until she had to shoot again. That Mr. Grandcourt might after all not appear on the archery-ground, had begun to enter into Gwendolen's thought as a possible deduction from the completeness of her pleasure. Under all her saucy satire, provoked chiefly by her divination that her friends thought of him as a desirable match for her, she felt something very far from indifference as to the impression she would make on him. True, he was not to have the slightest power over her (for Gwendolen had not

considered that the desire to conquer is itself a sort of subjection); she had made up her mind that he was to be one of
those complimentary and assiduously admiring men of whom
even her narrow experience had shown her several with vari-
ous-colored beards and various styles of bearing; and the
sense that her friends would want her to think him delightful
gave her a resistant inclination to presuppose him ridiculous.
But that was no reason why she could spare his presence:
and even a passing prevision of trouble in case she despised
and refused him raised not the shadow of a wish that he
should save her that trouble by showing no disposition to
make her an offer.   Mr. Grandcourt taking hardly any notice
of her, and becoming shortly engaged to Miss Arrowpoint,
was not a picture which flattered her imagination.

Hence Gwendolen had been all ear to Lord Brackenshaw's
mode of accounting for Grandcourt's non-appearance; and
when he did arrive, no consciousness—not even Mrs. Arrowpoint's or Mr. Gascoigne's—was more awake to the fact than
hers, although she steadily avoided looking toward any point
where he was likely to be.   There should be no slightest
shifting of angles to betray that it was of any consequence
to her whether the much-talked-of Mr. Mallinger Grandcourt
presented himself or not.   She became again absorbed in the
shooting, and so resolutely abstained from looking round ob-
servantly that, even supposing him to have taken a conspicuous place among the spectators, it might be clear she was not
aware of him.   And all the while the certainty that he was
there made a distinct thread in her consciousness.   Perhaps
her shooting was the better for it: at any rate, it gained in
precision, and she at last raised a delightful storm of clapping
and applause by three hits running in the gold—a feat which
among the Brackenshaw archers had not the vulgar reward of
a shilling poll-tax, but that of a special gold star to be worn
on the breast.   That moment was not only a happy one to
herself—it was just what her mamma and her uncle would
have chosen for her.   There was a general falling into ranks
to give her space that she might advance conspicuously to
receive the gold star from the hands of Lady Brackenshaw;
and the perfect movement of her fine form was certainly a

pleasant thing to behold in the clear afternoon light when the shadows were long and still. She was the central object of that pretty picture, and every one present must gaze at her. That was enough: she herself was determined to see nobody in particular, or to turn her eyes any way except toward Lady Brackenshaw, but her thoughts undeniably turned in other ways. It entered a little into her pleasure that Herr Klesmer must be observing her at a moment when music was out of the question, and his superiority very far in the background; for vanity is as ill at ease under indifference as tenderness is under a love which it cannot return; and the unconquered Klesmer threw a trace of his malign power even across her pleasant consciousness that Mr. Grandcourt was seeing her to the utmost advantage, and was probably giving her an admiration unmixed with criticism. She did not expect to admire *him*, but that was not necessary to her peace of mind.

Gwendolen met Lady Brackenshaw's gracious smile without blushing (which only came to her when she was taken by surprise), but with a charming gladness of expression, and then bent with easy grace to have the star fixed near her shoulder. That little ceremony had been over long enough for her to have exchanged playful speeches and received congratulations as she moved among the groups who were now interesting themselves in the results of the scoring; but it happened that she stood outside examining the point of an arrow with rather an absent air when Lord Brackenshaw came up to her and said:

"Miss Harleth, here is a gentleman who is not willing to wait any longer for an introduction. He has been getting Mrs. Davilow to send me with him. Will you allow me to introduce Mr. Mallinger Grandcourt?"

BOOK II.—MEETING STREAMS.

CHAPTER XI.

The beginning of an acquaintance whether with persons or things is to get a definite outline for our ignorance.

MR. GRANDCOURT'S wish to be introduced had no suddenness for Gwendolen; but when Lord Brackenshaw moved aside a little for the prefigured stranger to come forward and she felt herself face to face with the real man, there was a little shock which flushed her cheeks and vexatiously deepened with her consciousness of it. The shock came from the reversal of her expectations: Grandcourt could hardly have been more unlike all her imaginary portraits of him. He was slightly taller than herself, and their eyes seemed to be on a level; there was not the faintest smile on his face as he looked at her, not a trace of self-consciousness or anxiety in his bearing; when he raised his hat he showed an extensive baldness surrounded with a mere fringe of reddish-blond hair, but he also showed a perfect hand; the line of feature from brow to chin undisguised by beard was decidedly handsome, with only moderate departures from the perpendicular, and the slight whisker too was perpendicular. It was not possible for a human aspect to be freer from grimace or solicitous wrigglings; also it was perhaps not possible for a breathing man wide awake to look less animated. The correct Englishman, drawing himself up from his bow into rigidity, assenting severely, and seeming to be in a state of internal drill, suggests a suppressed vivacity, and may be suspected of letting go with some violence when he is released from parade; but Grandcourt's bearing had no rigidity, it inclined rather to the flaccid. His complexion had a faded fairness resembling that of an actress when bare of the artificial white and red; his

long narrow gray eyes expressed nothing but indifference.
Attempts at description are stupid: who can all at once de-
scribe a human being? even when he is presented to us we
only begin that knowledge of his appearance which must be
completed by innumerable impressions under differing circumstances. We recognize the alphabet; we are not sure of the
language. I am only mentioning the points that Gwendolen
saw by the light of a prepared contrast in the first minutes of
her meeting with Grandcourt: they were summed up in the
words, "He is not ridiculous." But forthwith Lord Brackenshaw was gone, and what is called conversation had begun,
the first and constant element in it being that Grandcourt
looked at Gwendolen persistently with a slightly exploring
gaze, but without change of expression, while she only occasionally looked at him with a flash of observation a little softened by coquetry. Also, after her answers there was a longer
or shorter pause before he spoke again.

"I used to think archery was a great bore," Grandcourt
began. He spoke with a fine accent, but with a certain broken
drawl, as of a distinguished personage with a distinguished
cold on his chest.

"Are you converted to-day?" said Gwendolen.

(Pause, during which she imagined various degrees and
modes of opinion about herself that might be entertained by
Grandcourt.)

"Yes, since I saw you shooting. In things of this sort one
generally sees people missing and simpering."

"I suppose you are a first-rate shot with a rifle."

(Pause, during which Gwendolen, having taken a rapid observation of Grandcourt, made a brief graphic description of
him to an indefinite hearer.)

"I have left off shooting."

"Oh, then, you are a formidable person. People who have
done things once and left them off make one feel very contemptible, as if one were using cast-off fashions. I hope you
have not left off all follies, because I practice a great many."

(Pause, during which Gwendolen made several interpreta-
tions of her own speech.)

"What do you call follies?"

"Well, in general, I think whatever is agreeable is called a folly. But you have not left off hunting, I hear."

(Pause, wherein Gwendolen recalled what she had heard about Grandcourt's position, and decided that he was the most aristocratic-looking man she had ever seen.)

"One must do something."

"And do you care about the turf?—or is that among the things you have left off?"

(Pause, during which Gwendolen thought that a man of extremely calm, cold manners might be less disagreeable as a husband than other men, and not likely to interfere with his wife's preferences.)

"I run a horse now and then; but I don't go in for the thing as some men do. Are you fond of horses?"

"Yes, indeed: I never like my life so well as when I am on horseback, having a great gallop. I think of nothing. I only feel myself strong and happy."

(Pause, wherein Gwendolen wondered whether Grandcourt would like what she said, but assured herself that she was not going to disguise her tastes.)

"Do you like danger?"

"I don't know. When I am on horseback I never think of danger. It seems to me that if I broke my bones I should not feel it. I should go at anything that came in my way."

(Pause, during which Gwendolen had run through a whole hunting season with two chosen hunters to ride at will.)

"You would perhaps like tiger-hunting or pig-sticking. I saw some of that for a season or two in the East. Everything here is poor stuff after that."

"*You* are fond of danger, then?"

(Pause, wherein Gwendolen speculated on the probability that the men of coldest manners were the most adventurous, and felt the strength of her own insight, supposing the question had to be decided.)

"One must have something or other. But one gets used to it."

"I begin to think I am very fortunate, because everything is new to me: it is only that I can't get enough of it. I am not used to anything except being dull, which I should like to leave off as you have left off shooting."

(Pause, during which it occurred to Gwendolen that a man of cold and distinguished manners might possibly be a dull companion; but on the other hand, she thought that most persons were dull, that she had not observed husbands to be companions—and that after all she was not going to accept Grandcourt.)

"Why are you dull?"

"This is a dreadful neighborhood. There is nothing to be done in it. That is why I practised my archery."

(Pause, during which Gwendolen reflected that the life of an unmarried woman who could not go about and had no command of anything must necessarily be dull through all the degrees of comparison as time went on.)

"You have made yourself queen of it. I imagine you will carry the first prize."

"I don't know that. I have great rivals. Did you not observe how well Miss Arrowpoint shot?"

(Pause, wherein Gwendolen was thinking that men had been known to choose some one else than the woman they most admired, and recalled several experiences of that kind in novels.)

"Miss Arrowpoint? No—that is, yes."

"Shall we go now and hear what the scoring says? Every one is going to the other end now—shall we join them? I think my uncle is looking toward me. He perhaps wants me."

Gwendolen found a relief for herself by thus changing the situation: not that the *tête-à-tête* was quite disagreeable to her; but while it lasted she apparently could not get rid of the unwonted flush in her cheeks and the sense of surprise which made her feel less mistress of herself than usual. And this Mr. Grandcourt, who seemed to feel his own importance more than he did hers—a sort of unreasonableness few of us can tolerate—must not take for granted that he was of great moment to her, or that because others speculated on him as a desirable match she held herself altogether at his beck. How Grandcourt had filled up the pauses will be more evident hereafter.

"You have just missed the gold arrow, Gwendolen," said Mr. Gascoigne. "Miss Juliet Fenn scores eight above you."

"I am very glad to hear it. I should have felt that I was making myself too disagreeable—taking the best of everything," said Gwendolen, quite easily.

It was impossible to be jealous of Juliet Fenn, a girl as middling as mid-day market in everything but her archery and plainness, in which last she was noticeably like her father: underhung and with receding brow resembling that of the more intelligent fishes. (Surely, considering the importance which is given to such an accident in female offspring, marriageable men, or what the new English calls "intending bridegrooms," should look at themselves dispassionately in the glass, since their natural selection of a mate prettier than themselves is not certain to bar the effect of their own ugliness.)

There was now a lively movement in the mingling groups, which carried the talk along with it. Every one spoke to every one else by turns, and Gwendolen, who chose to see what was going on around her now, observed that Grandcourt was having Klesmer presented to him by some one unknown to her—a middle-aged man, with dark, full face and fat hands, who seemed to be on the easiest terms with both, and presently led the way in joining the Arrowpoints, whose acquaintance had already been made by both him and Grandcourt. Who this stranger was she did not care much to know; but she wished to observe what was Grandcourt's manner toward others than herself. Precisely the same: except that he did not look much at Miss Arrowpoint, but rather at Klesmer, who was speaking with animation—now stretching out his long fingers horizontally, now pointing downward with his forefinger, now folding his arms and tossing his mane, while he addressed himself first to one and then the other, including Grandcourt, who listened with an impassive face and narrow eyes, his left forefinger in his waistcoat-pocket, and his right slightly touching his thin whisker.

"I wonder which style Miss Arrowpoint admires most," was a thought that glanced through Gwendolen's mind, while her eyes and lips gathered rather a mocking expression. But she would not indulge her sense of amusement by watching, as if she were curious, and she gave all her animation to those immediately around her, determined not to care whether Mr. Grandcourt came near her again or not.

He did come, however, and at a moment when he could propose to conduct Mrs. Davilow to her carriage. "Shall we meet again in the ball-room?" she said, as he raised his hat at parting. The "yes" in reply had the usual slight drawl and perfect gravity.

"You were wrong for once, Gwendolen," said Mrs. Davilow, during their few minutes' drive to the castle.

"In what, mamma?"

"About Mr. Grandcourt's appearance and manners. You can't find anything ridiculous in him."

"I suppose I could if I tried, but I don't want to do it," said Gwendolen, rather pettishly; and her mamma was afraid to say more.

It was the rule on these occasions for the ladies and gentlemen to dine apart, so that the dinner might make a time of comparative ease and rest for both. Indeed, the gentlemen had a set of archery stories about the epicurism of the ladies, who had somehow been reported to show a revolting masculine judgment in venison, even asking for the fat—a proof of the frightful rate at which corruption might go on in women, but for severe social restraint. And every year the amiable Lord Brackenshaw, who was something of a *gourmet*, mentioned Byron's opinion that a woman should never be seen eating,—introducing it with a confidential, "The fact is"—as if he were for the first time admitting his concurrence in that sentiment of the refined poet.

In the ladies' dining-room it was evident that Gwendolen was not a general favorite with her own sex; there were no beginnings of intimacy between her and other girls, and in conversation they rather noticed what she said than spoke to her in free exchange. Perhaps it was that she was not much interested in them, and when left alone in their company had a sense of empty benches. Mrs. Vulcany once remarked that Miss Harleth was too fond of the gentlemen; but we know that she was not in the least fond of them—she was only fond of their homage—and women did not give her homage. The exception to this willing aloofness from her was Miss Arrow-point, who often managed unostentatiously to be by her side, and talked to her with quiet friendliness.

"She knows, as I do, that our friends are ready to quarrel over a husband for us," thought Gwendolen, "and she is de-termined not to enter into the quarrel."

"I think Miss Arrowpoint has the best manners I ever saw," said Mrs. Davilow, when she and Gwendolen were in a dress-ing-room with Mrs. Gascoigne and Anna, but at a distance where they could have their talk apart.

"I wish I were like her," said Gwendolen.

"Why? Are you getting discontented with yourself, Gwen?"

"No; but I am discontented with things. She seems con-tented."

"I am sure you ought to be satisfied to-day. You must have enjoyed the shooting. I saw you did."

"Oh, that is over now, and I don't know what will come next," said Gwendolen, stretching herself with a sort of moan and throwing up her arms. They were bare now: it was the fashion to dance in the archery dress, throwing off the jacket; and the simplicity of her white cashmere with its border of pale green set off her form to the utmost. A thin line of gold round her neck, and the gold star on her breast, were her only ornaments. Her smooth soft hair piled up into a grand crown made a clear line about her brow. Sir Joshua would have been glad to take her portrait; and he would have had an easier task than the historian at least in this, that he would not have had to represent the truth of change—only to give stability to one beautiful moment.

"The dancing will come next," said Mrs. Davilow. "You are sure to enjoy that."

"I shall only dance in the quadrille. I told Mr. Clintock so. I shall not waltz or polk with any one."

"Why in the world do you say that all on a sudden?"

"I can't bear having ugly people so near me."

"Whom do you mean by ugly people?"

"Oh, plenty."

"Mr. Clintock, for example, is not ugly." Mrs Davilow dared not mention Grandcourt.

"Well, I hate woollen cloth touching me."

"Fancy!" said Mrs. Davilow to her sister who now came up from the other end of the room. "Gwendolen says she will not waltz or polk."

"She is rather given to whims, I think," said Mrs. Gascoigne, gravely. "It would be more becoming in her to behave as other young ladies do on such an occasion as this; especially when she has had the advantage of first-rate dancing lessons."

"Why should I waltz if I don't like it, aunt? It is not in the catechism."

"My *dear!*" said Mrs. Gascoigne, in a tone of severe check, and Anna looked frightened at Gwendolen's daring. But they all passed on without saying more.

Apparently something had changed Gwendolen's mood since the hour of exulting enjoyment in the archery-ground. But she did not look the worse under the chandeliers in the ballroom, where the soft splendor of the scene and the pleasant odors from the conservatory could not but be soothing to the temper, when accompanied with the consciousness of being pre-eminently sought for. Hardly a dancing man but was anxious to have her for a partner, and each whom she accepted was in a state of melancholy remonstrance that she would not waltz or polk.

"Are you under a vow, Miss Harleth?"—"Why are you so cruel to us all?"—"You waltzed with me in February."— "And you who waltz so perfectly!" were exclamations not without piquancy for her. The ladies who waltzed naturally thought that Miss Harleth only wanted to make herself particular; but her uncle when he overheard her refusal supported her by saying:

"Gwendolen has usually good reasons." He thought she was certainly more distinguished in not waltzing, and he wished her to be distinguished. The archery ball was intended to be kept at the subdued pitch that suited all dignities, clerical and secular: it was not an escapement for youthful high spirits, and he himself was of opinion that the fashionable dances were too much of a romp.

Among the remonstrant dancing men, however, Mr. Grandcourt was not numbered. After standing up for a quadrille with Miss Arrowpoint, it seemed that he meant to ask for no other partner. Gwendolen observed him frequently with the Arrowpoints, but he never took an opportunity of approaching her. Mr. Gascoigne was sometimes speaking to him; but Mr. Gascoigne was everywhere. It was in her mind now that she would probably after all not have the least trouble about him; perhaps he had looked at her without any particular admiration, and was too much used to everything in the world to think of her as more than one of the girls who were invited in that part of the country. Of course! It was ridiculous of elders to entertain notions about what a man would do, without having seen him even through a telescope. Probably he meant to marry Miss Arrowpoint. Whatever might come, she, Gwendolen, was not going to be disappointed; the affair was a joke whichever way it turned, for she had never committed herself even by a silent confidence in anything Mr. Grandcourt would do. Still, she noticed that he did sometimes quietly and gradually change his position according to hers, so that he could see her whenever she was dancing, and if he did not admire her—so much the worse for him.

This movement for the sake of being in sight of her was more direct than usual rather late in the evening, when Gwendolen had accepted Klesmer as a partner; and that wide-glancing personage, who saw everything and nothing by turns, said to her when they were walking, "Mr. Grandcourt is a man of taste. He likes to see you dancing."

"Perhaps he likes to look at what is against his taste," said Gwendolen, with a light laugh; she was quite courageous with Klesmer now. "He may be so tired of admiring that he likes disgust for a variety."

"Those words are not suitable to your lips," said Klesmer, quickly, with one of his grand frowns, while he shook his hand as if to banish the discordant sounds.

"Are you as critical of words as of music?"

"Certainly I am. I should require your words to be what

your face and form are—always among the meanings of a noble music."

"That is a compliment as well as a correction. I am obliged for both. But do you know I am bold enough to wish to correct *you*, and require you to understand a joke?"

"One may understand jokes without liking them," said the terrible Klesmer. "I have had opera books sent me full of jokes; it was just because I understood them that I did not like them. The comic people are ready to challenge a man because he looks grave. 'You don't see the witticism, sir?' 'No, sir, but I see what you meant.' Then I am what we call ticketed as a fellow without *esprit*. But, in fact," said Klesmer, suddenly dropping from his quick narrative to a reflective tone, with an impressive frown, "I am very sensible to wit and humor."

"I am glad you tell me that," said Gwendolen, not without some wickedness of intention. But Klesmer's thoughts had flown off on the wings of his own statement, as their habit was, and she had the wickedness all to herself. "Pray, who is that standing near the card-room door?" she went on, seeing there the same stranger with whom Klesmer had been in animated talk on the archery-ground. "He is a friend of yours, I think."

"No, no; an amateur I have seen in town: Lush, a Mr. Lush—too fond of Meyerbeer and Scribe—too fond of the mechanical-dramatic."

"Thanks. I wanted to know whether you thought his face and form required that his words should be among the meanings of noble music?" Klesmer was conquered, and flashed at her a delightful smile which made them quite friendly until she begged to be deposited by the side of her mamma.

Three minutes afterward her preparations for Grandcourt's indifference were all cancelled. Turning her head after some remark to her mother, she found that he had made his way up to her.

"May I ask if you are tired of dancing, Miss Harleth?" he began, looking down with his former unperturbed expression.

"Not in the least."

"Will you do me the honor—the next—or another quadrille?"

"I should have been very happy," said Gwendolen, looking at her card, "but I am engaged for the next to Mr. Clintock—and indeed I perceive that I am doomed for every quadrille; I have not one to dispose of." She was not sorry to punish Mr. Grandcourt's tardiness, yet at the same time she would have liked to dance with him. She gave him a charming smile as she looked up to deliver her answer, and he stood still looking down at her with no smile at all.

"I am unfortunate in being too late," he said, after a moment's pause.

"It seemed to me that you did not care for dancing," said Gwendolen. "I thought it might be one of the things you had left off."

"Yes, but I have not begun to dance with you," said Grandcourt. Always there was the same pause before he took up his cue. "You make dancing a new thing, as you make archery."

"Is novelty always agreeable?"

"No, no—not always."

"Then I don't know whether to feel flattered or not. When you had once danced with me there would be no more novelty in it."

"On the contrary; there would probably be much more."

"That is deep. I don't understand."

"Is it difficult to make Miss Harleth understand her power?" Here Grandcourt had turned to Mrs. Davilow, who, smiling gently at her daughter, said:

"I think she does not generally strike people as slow to understand."

"Mamma," said Gwendolen, in a deprecating tone, "I am adorably stupid, and want everything explained to me—when the meaning is pleasant."

"If you are stupid, I admit that stupidity is adorable," returned Grandcourt, after the usual pause, and without change of tone. But clearly he knew what to say.

"I begin to think that my cavalier has forgotten me,"

Gwendolen observed after a little while. "I see the quadrille is being formed."

"He deserves to be renounced," said Grandcourt.

"I think he is very pardonable," said Gwendolen.

"There must have been some misunderstanding," said Mrs. Davilow. "Mr. Clintock was too anxious about the engagement to have forgotten it."

But now Lady Brackenshaw came up and said: "Miss Harleth, Mr. Clintock has charged me to express to you his deep regret that he was obliged to leave without having the pleasure of dancing with you again. An express came from his father, the archdeacon: something important: he was obliged to go. He was *au désespoir*."

"Oh, he was very good to remember the engagement under the circumstances," said Gwendolen. "I am sorry he was called away." It was easy to be politely sorrowful on so felicitous an occasion.

"Then I can profit by Mr. Clintock's misfortune?" said Grandcourt. "May I hope that you will let me take his place?"

"I shall be very happy to dance the next quadrille with you."

The appropriateness of the event seemed an augury, and as Gwendolen stood up for the quadrille with Grandcourt, there was a revival in her of the exultation—the sense of carrying everything before her, which she had felt earlier in the day. No man could have walked through the quadrille with more irreproachable ease than Grandcourt; and the absence of all eagerness in his attention to her suited his partner's taste. She was now convinced that he meant to distinguish her, to mark his admiration of her in a noticeable way; and it began to appear probable that she would have it in her power to reject him, whence there was a pleasure in reckoning up the advantages which would make her rejection splendid, and in giving Mr. Grandcourt his utmost value. It was also agreeable to divine that his exclusive selection of her to dance with, from among all the unmarried ladies present, would attract observation; though she studiously avoided seeing this, and at the end of the quadrille walked away on Grandcourt's arm as if she had been one of the shortest sighted instead of the longest and widest sighted of mortals. They encountered

Miss Arrowpoint, who was standing with Lady Brackenshaw and a group of gentlemen. The heiress looked at Gwendolen invitingly, and said: "I hope you will vote with us, Miss Harleth, and Mr. Grandcourt, too, though he is not an archer." Gwendolen and Grandcourt paused to join the group, and found that the voting turned on the project of a picnic archery meeting to be held in Cardell Chase, where the evening entertainment would be more poetic than a ball under chandeliers —a feast of sunset lights along the glades and through the branches and over the solemn tree-tops.

Gwendolen thought the scheme delightful—equal to playing Robin Hood and Maid Marian; and Mr. Grandcourt, when appealed to a second time, said it was a thing to be done; whereupon Mr. Lush, who stood behind Lady Brackenshaw's elbow, drew Gwendolen's notice by saying with a familiar look and tone to Grandcourt: "Diplow would be a good place for the meeting, and more convenient: there's a fine bit between the oaks toward the north gate."

Impossible to look more unconscious of being addressed than Grandcourt; but Gwendolen took a new survey of the speaker, deciding, first, that he must be on terms of intimacy with the tenant of Diplow, and, secondly, that she would never, if she could help it, let him come within a yard of her. She was subject to physical antipathies, and Mr. Lush's prominent eyes, fat though not clumsy figure, and strong black gray-besprinkled hair of frizzy thickness, which, with the rest of his prosperous person, was enviable to many, created one of the strongest of her antipathies. To be safe from his looking at her, she murmured to Grandcourt, "I should like to continue walking."

He obeyed immediately; but when they were thus away from any audience, he spoke no word for several minutes, and she, out of a half-amused, half-serious inclination for experiment, would not speak first. They turned into the large conservatory, beautifully lit up with Chinese lamps. The other couples there were at a distance which would not have interfered with any dialogue, but still they walked in silence until they had reached the farther end, where there was a flush of pink light, and the second wide opening into the ball-room.

Grandcourt, when they had half turned round, paused and said languidly:

"Do you like this kind of thing?"

If the situation had been described to Gwendolen half an hour before, she would have laughed heartily at it, and could only have imagined herself returning a playful, satirical answer. But for some mysterious reason—it was a mystery of which she had a faint wondering consciousness—she dared not be satirical: she had begun to feel a wand over her that made her afraid of offending Grandcourt.

"Yes," she said, quietly, without considering what "kind of thing" was meant—whether the flowers, the scents, the ball in general, or this episode of walking with Mr. Grandcourt in particular. And they returned along the conservatory without farther interpretation. She then proposed to go and sit down in her old place, and they walked among scattered couples preparing for the waltz to the spot where Mrs. Davilow had been seated all the evening. As they approached it her seat was vacant, but she was coming toward it again, and, to Gwendolen's shuddering annoyance, with Mr. Lush at her elbow. There was no avoiding the confrontation: her mamma came close to her before they had reached the seats, and, after a quiet greeting smile, said innocently, "Gwendolen, dear, let me present Mr. Lush to you." Having just made the acquaintance of this personage, as an intimate and constant companion of Mr. Grandcourt's, Mrs. Davilow imagined it altogether desirable that her daughter also should make the acquaintance.

It was hardly a bow that Gwendolen gave—rather, it was the slightest forward sweep of the head away from the physiognomy that inclined itself toward her, and she immediately moved toward her seat, saying, "I want to put on my burnous." No sooner had she reached it, than Mr. Lush was there, and had the burnous in his hand: to annoy this supercilious young lady, he would incur the offence of forestalling Grandcourt; and, holding up the garment close to Gwendolen, he said, "Pray, permit me?" But she, wheeling away from him as if he had been a muddy hound, glided on to the ottoman, saying, "No, thank you."

A man who forgave this would have much Christian feeling, supposing he had intended to be agreeable to the young lady; but before he seized the burnous Mr. Lush had ceased to have that intention. Grandcourt quietly took the drapery from him, and Mr. Lush, with a slight bow, moved away.

"You had perhaps better put it on," said Mr. Grandcourt, looking down on her without change of expression.

"Thanks; perhaps it would be wise," said Gwendolen, rising, and submitting very gracefully to take the burnous on her shoulders.

After that, Mr. Grandcourt exchanged a few polite speeches with Mrs. Davilow, and, in taking leave, asked permission to call at Offendene the next day. He was evidently not offended by th insult directed toward his friend. Certainly Gwendolen's refusal of the burnous from Mr. Lush was open to the interpretation that she wished to receive it from Mr. Grandcourt. But she, poor child, had had no design in this action, and was simply following her antipathy and inclination, confiding in them as she did in the more reflective judgments into which they entered as sap into leafage. Gwendolen had no sense that these men were dark enigmas to her, or that she needed any help in drawing conclusions about them—Mr. Grandcourt at least. The chief question was, how far his character and ways might answer her wishes; and unless she were satisfied about that, she had said to herself that she would not accept his offer.

Could there be a slenderer, more insignificant thread in human history than this consciousness of a girl, busy with her small inferences of the way in which she could make her life pleasant?—in a time, too, when ideas were with fresh vigor making armies of themselves, and the universal kinship was declaring itself fiercely: when women on the other side of the world would not mourn for the husbands and sons who died bravely in a common cause, and men stinted of bread on our side of the world heard of that willing loss and were patient: a time when the soul of man was waking to pulses which had for centuries been beating in him unfelt, until their full sum made a new life of terror or of joy.

What in the midst of that mighty drama are girls and their blind visions? They are the Yea or Nay of that good for which men are enduring and fighting. In these delicate vessels is borne onward through the ages the treasure of human affections.

CHAPTER XII.

"O gentlemen, the time of life is short;
To spend that shortness basely were too long,
If life did ride upon a dial's point,
Still ending at the arrival of an hour."
—SHAKESPEARE: *Henry IV.*

ON the second day after the Archery Meeting, Mr. Henleigh Mallinger Grandcourt was at his breakfast-table with Mr. Lush. Everything around them was agreeable: the summer air through the open windows, at which the dogs could walk in from the old green turf on the lawn; the soft, purplish coloring of the park beyond, stretching toward a mass of bordering wood; the still life in the room, which seemed the stiller for its sober antiquated elegance, as if it kept a conscious, well-bred silence, unlike the restlessness of vulgar furniture.

Whether the gentlemen were agreeable to each other was less evident. Mr. Grandcourt had drawn his chair aside so as to face the lawn, and with his left leg over another chair, and his right elbow on the table, was smoking a large cigar, while his companion was still eating. The dogs—half a dozen of various kinds were moving lazily in and out, taking attitudes of brief attention—gave a vacillating preference first to one gentleman, then to the other; being dogs in such good circumstances that they could play at hunger, and liked to be served with delicacies which they declined to put into their mouths; all except Fetch, the beautiful liver-colored water-spaniel, which sat with its forepaws firmly planted and its expressive brown face turned upward, watching Grandcourt with unshaken constancy. He held in his lap a tiny Maltese dog with a tiny silver collar and bell, and when he had a hand unused by cigar or coffee-cup, it rested on this small parcel of animal warmth. I fear that Fetch was jealous, and wounded that her

6—Vol. 9

master gave her no word or look; at last it seemed that she could bear this neglect no longer, and she gently put her large silky paw on her master's leg. Grandcourt looked at her with unchanged face for half a minute, and then took the trouble to lay down his cigar while he lifted the unimpassioned Fluff close to his chin and gave it caressing pats, all the while gravely watching Fetch, who, poor thing, whimpered interruptedly, as if trying to repress that sign of discontent, and at last rested her head beside the appealing paw, looking up with piteous beseeching. So, at least, a lover of dogs must have interpreted Fetch, and Grandcourt kept so many dogs that he was reputed to love them; at any rate, his impulse to act just in this way started from such an interpretation. But when the amusing anguish burst forth in a howling bark, Grandcourt pushed Fetch down without speaking, and, depositing Fluff carelessly on the table (where his black nose predominated over a salt-cellar), began to look to his cigar, and found, with some annoyance against Fetch as the cause, that the brute of a cigar required relighting. Fetch, having begun to wail, found, like others of her sex, that it was not easy to leave off; indeed, the second howl was a louder one, and the third was like unto it.

"Turn out that brute, will you?" said Grandcourt to Lush, without raising his voice or looking at him—as if he counted on attention to the smallest sign.

And Lush immediately rose, lifted Fetch, though she was rather heavy, and he was not fond of stooping, and carried her out, disposing of her in some way that took him a couple of minutes before he returned. He then lit a cigar, placed himself at an angle where he could see Grandcourt's face without turning, and presently said:

"Shall you ride or drive to Quetcham to-day?"

"I am not going to Quetcham."

"You did not go yesterday."

Grandcourt smoked in silence for half a minute, and then said:

"I suppose you sent my card and inquiries."

"I went myself at four, and said you were sure to be there shortly. They would suppose some accident prevented you from fulfilling the intention. Especially if you go to-day."

Silence for a couple of minutes. Then Grandcourt said:
"What men are invited here with their wives?"

Lush drew out a note-book. "The Captain and Mrs. Torrington come next week. Then there are Mr. Hollis and Lady
Flora, and the Cushats and the Gogoffs."

"Rather a ragged lot," remarked Grandcourt, after a while.
"Why did you ask the Gogoffs? When you write invitations
in my name, be good enough to give me a list, instead of bringing down a giantess on me without my knowledge. She spoils
the look of the room."

"You invited the Gogoffs yourself, when you met them in
Paris."

"What has my meeting them in Paris to do with it? I told
you to give me a list."

Grandcourt, like many others, had two remarkably different
voices. Hitherto we have heard him speaking in a superficial
interrupted drawl suggestive chiefly of languor and *ennui.*
But this last brief speech was uttered, in subdued inward, yet
distinct tones, which Lush had long been used to recognize as
the expression of a peremptory will.

"Are there any other couples you would like to invite?"

"Yes; think of some decent people, with a daughter or
two. And one of your damned musicians. But not a comic
fellow."

"I wonder if Klesmer would consent to come to us when he
leaves Quetcham. Nothing but first-rate music will go down
with Miss Arrowpoint."

Lush spoke carelessly, but he was really seizing an opportunity and fixing an observant look on Grandcourt, who now
for the first time turned his eyes toward his companion, but
slowly and without speaking until he had given two long luxurious puffs, when he said, perhaps in a lower tone than ever,
but with a perceptible edge of contempt:

"What in the name of nonsense have I to do with Miss
Arrowpoint and her music?"

"Well, something," said Lush, jocosely. "You need not
give yourself much trouble, perhaps. But some forms must
be gone through before a man can marry a million."

"Very likely. But I am not going to marry a million."

"That's a pity—to fling away an opportunity of this sort, and knock down your own plans."

" *Your* plans, I suppose you mean."

" You have some debts, you know, and things may turn out inconveniently after all. The heirship is not *absolutely* certain."

Grandcourt did not answer, and Lush went on.

"It really is a fine opportunity. The father and mother ask for nothing better, I can see, and the daughter's looks and manners require no allowances, any more than if she hadn't a sixpence. She is not beautiful; but equal to carrying any rank. And she is not likely to refuse such prospects as you can offer her."

"Perhaps not."

" The father and mother would let you do anything you liked with them."

" But I should not like to do anything with them."

Here it was Lush who made a little pause before speaking again, and then he said in a deep voice of remonstrance: "Good God, Grandcourt! after your experience, will you let a whim interfere with your comfortable settlement in life? "

"Spare your oratory. I know what I am going to do."

"What? " Lush put down his cigar and thrust his hands into his side pockets, as if he had to face something exasperating, but meant to keep his temper.

" I am going to marry the other girl."

" Have you fallen in love? " This question carried a strong sneer.

" I am going to marry her."

" You have made her an offer already, then? "

" No."

" She is a young lady with a will of her own, I fancy. Extremely well fitted to make a rumpus. She would know what she liked."

" She doesn't like you," said Grandcourt, with a ghost of a smile.

"Perfectly true," said Lush, adding again in a markedly sneering tone, "However, if you and she are devoted to each other, that will be enough."

Grandcourt took no notice of this speech, but sipped his coffee, rose, and strolled out on the lawn, all the dogs following him.

Lush glanced after him a moment, then resumed his cigar and lit it, but smoked slowly, consulting his beard with inspecting eyes and fingers, till he finally stroked it with an air of having arrived at some conclusion, and said in a subdued voice:

"Check, old boy!"

Lush, being a man of some ability, had not known Grandcourt for fifteen years without learning what sort of measures were useless with him, though what sort might be useful remained often dubious. In the beginning of his career he held a fellowship, and was near taking orders for the sake of a college living; but not being fond of that prospect, accepted instead the office of travelling companion to a marquess, and afterward to young Grandcourt, who had lost his father early, and who found Lush so convenient that he had allowed him to become prime minister in all his more personal affairs. The habit of fifteen years had made Grandcourt more and more in need of Lush's handiness, and Lush more and more in need of the lazy luxury to which his transactions on behalf of Grandcourt made no interruption worth reckoning. I cannot say that the same lengthened habit had intensified Grandcourt's want of respect for his companion, since that want had been absolute from the beginning, but it had confirmed his sense that he might kick Lush if he chose—only he never did choose to kick any animal, because the act of kicking is a compromising attitude, and a gentleman's dogs should be kicked for him. He only said things which might have exposed himself to be kicked if his confidant had been a man of independent spirit. But what son of a vicar who has stinted his wife and daughters of calico in order to send his male offspring to Oxford, can keep an independent spirit when he is bent on dining with high discrimination, riding good horses, living generally in the most luxuriant honey-blossomed clover—and all without working? Mr. Lush had passed for a scholar once, and had still a sense of scholarship when he was not trying to remember much of it; but the bachelors' and other arts which softened manners are a time-honored preparation for sinecures; and Lush's present comfortable provision was as good as a sinecure in not requiring more than the odor of departed learning. He was not unconscious of being held kickable, but he preferred counting that estimate among the peculiarities of Grandcourt's character, which made one of his incalculable moods of judgments as good as another. Since in his own opinion he had never done a bad action, it did not seem necessary to consider whether he should be likely to commit one if his love of ease required it. Lush's love of ease was well satisfied at present, and if his puddings were rolled toward him in the dust, he took the inside bits and found them relishing.

This morning, for example, though he had encountered more annoyance than usual, he went to his private sitting-room and played a good hour on the violoncello.

CHAPTER XIII.

"Philistia, be thou glad of me!"

GRANDCOURT having made up his mind to marry Miss Harleth showed a power of adapting means to ends. During the next fortnight there was hardly a day on which by some arrangement or other he did not see her, or prove by emphatic attentions that she occupied his thoughts. His cousin, Mrs. Torrington, was now doing the honors of his house, so that Mrs. Davilow and Gwendolen could be invited to a large party at Diplow in which there were many witnesses how the host distinguished the dowerless beauty, and showed no solicitude about the heiress. The world—I mean Mr. Gascoigne and all the families worth speaking of within visiting distance of Pennicote—felt an assurance on the subject which in the Rector's mind converted itself into a resolution to do his duty by his niece and see that the settlements were adequate. Indeed, the wonder to him and Mrs. Davilow was that the offer for which so many suitable occasions presented themselves had not been already made; and in this wonder Grandcourt himself was not without a share. When he had told his resolution to Lush, he had thought that the affair would be concluded more quickly, and to his own surprise he had repeatedly promised himself in a morning that he would to-day give Gwendolen the opportunity of accepting him, and had found in the evening that the necessary formality was still unaccomplished. This remarkable fact served to heighten his determination on another day. He had never admitted to himself that Gwendolen might refuse him, but—heaven help us all!—we are often unable to act on our certainties; our objection to a contrary issue (were it possible) is so strong that it rises like a spectral illusion between us and our certainty; we are rationally sure that the blind-worm cannot bite us mortally, but it would be so intolerable to be bitten, and the creature has a biting look—we decline to handle it.

He had asked leave to have a beautiful horse of his brought for Gwendolen to ride. Mrs. Davilow was to accompany her in the carriage, and they were to go to Diplow to lunch, Grandcourt conducting them. It was a fine mid-harvest time, not too warm for a noonday ride of five miles to be delightful: the poppies glowed on the borders of the fields, there was enough breeze to move gently like a social spirit among the ears of uncut corn, and to wing the shadow of a cloud across the soft gray downs; here the sheaves were standing, there the horses were straining their muscles under the last load from a wide space of stubble, but everywhere the green pastures made a broader setting for the corn-fields, and the cattle took their rest under wide branches. The road lay through a bit of country where the dairy-farms looked much as they did in the days of our forefathers—where peace and permanence seemed to find a home away from the busy change that sent the railway train flying in the distance.

But the spirit of peace and permanence did not penetrate poor Mrs. Davilow's mind so as to overcome her habit of uneasy foreboding. Gwendolen and Grandcourt cantering in front of her, and then slackening their pace to a conversational walk till the carriage came up with them again, made a gratifying sight; but it served chiefly to keep up the conflict of hopes and fears about her daughter's lot. Here was an irresistible opportunity for a lover to speak and put an end

to all uncertainties, and Mrs. Davilow could only hope with
trembling that Gwendolen's .cision would be favorable.   Certainly if Rex's love had ¹ s w repugnant to her, Mr. Grandcourt had the adva..t ge   being in complete contrast with
Rex; and that he had produced some quite novel impression
on her seemed evident ι. ιer marked abstinence from satirical
observations, nay, her total silen about his characteristics—a
silence which Mrs. Davilow did not dare to break.   "Is he a
man she would be h   y with?" was a question that inevitably
arose in the mother's mind.   "Well, perhaps as happy as she
would be with any one else—or as most other women are,"
was the answer with which she tried to quiet herself; for she
could not imagine Gwendolen under the influence of any feeling which would make her satisfied in what we traditionally
call "mean circumstances."

Grandcourt's own thought was looking in the same direction:
he wanted to have done with the uncertainty that belonged to
his not having spoken.   As to any further uncertainty—well,
it was something without any reasonable basis, some quality
in the air which acted as an irritant to his wishes.

Gwendolen enjoyed the riding, but her pleasure did not
break forth in girlish, unpremeditated chat and laughter as it
did on that morning with Rex.   She spoke a little, and even
laughed, but with a lightness as of a far-off echo: for her too
there was some peculiar quality in the air—not, she was sure,
any subjugation of her will by Mr. Grandcourt, and the splendid prospects he meant to offer her; for Gwendolen desired
every one, that dignified gentleman himself included, to understand that she was going to do just as she liked, and that
they had better not calculate on her pleasing them.   If she
chose to take this husband, she would have him know that she
was not going to renounce her freedom, or, according to her
favorite formula, "not going to do as other women did."

Grandcourt's speeches this morning were, as usual, all of
that brief sort which never fails to make a conversational figure when the speaker is held important in his circle.   Stop-
ping so soon, they give signs of a suppressed and formidable
ability to say more, and have also the meritorious quality of
allowing lengthiness to others.

"How do you like Criterion's paces?" he said, after they had entered the park and were slack ing from a canter to a walk.

"He is delightful to ride. I ld like to have a leap with him, if it would not frighten mam . There was a good wide channel we passed five minutes ag I should like to have a gallop back and take it."

"Pray do. We can take it together."

"No, thanks. Mamma is so timid—if she saw me it might make her ill."

"Let me go and explain. Criterion would take it without fail."

"No—indeed—you are very kind—but it would alarm her too much. I dare take any leap when she is not by; but I do it and don't tell her about it."

"We can let the carriage pass and then set off."

"No, no, pray don't think of it any more: I spoke quite randomly," said Gwendolen; she began to feel a new objection to carrying out her own proposition.

"But Mrs. Davilow knows I shall take care of you."

"Yes, but she would think of you as having to take care of my broken neck."

There was a considerable pause before Grandcourt said, looking toward her: "I should like to have the right always to take care of you."

Gwendolen did not turn her eyes on him; it seemed to her a long while that she was first blushing, and then turning pale, but to Grandcourt's rate of judgment she answered soon enough, with the lightest flute-tone and a careless movement of the head: "Oh, I am not sure that I want to be taken care of: if I chose to risk breaking my neck, I should like to be at liberty to do it."

She checked her horse as she spoke, and turned in her saddle, looking toward the advancing carriage. Her eyes swept across Grandcourt as she made this movement, but there was no language in them to correct the carelessness of her reply. At that very moment she was aware that she was risking something—not her neck, but the possibility of finally checking Grandcourt's advances, and she did not feel contented with the possibility.

"Damn her!" thought Grandcourt, as he too checked his horse. He was not a wordy thinker, and this explosive phrase stood for mixed impression which eloquent interpreters might have expanded into some sentences full of an irritated sense that he was being mystified, and a determination that this girl should not make a fool of him. Did she want him to throw himself at her feet and declare that he was dying for her? It was not by that gate that she would enter on the privileges he could give her. Or did she expect him to write his proposals? Equally a delusion. He would not make his offer in any way that could place him definitely in the position of being rejected. But as to her accepting him, she had done it already in accepting his marked attentions; and anything which happened to break them off would be understood to her disadvantage. She was merely coquetting, then?

However, the carriage came up, and no further *tête-à-tête* could well occur before their arrival at the house, where there was abundant company, to whom Gwendolen, clad in riding-dress, with her hat laid aside, clad also in the repute of being chosen by Mr. Grandcourt, was naturally a centre of observation; and since the objectionable Mr. Lush was not there to look at her, this stimulus of admiring attention heightened her spirits, and dispersed, for the time, the uneasy consciousness of divided impulses which threatened her with repentance of her own acts. Whether Grandcourt had been offended or not, there was no judging: his manners were unchanged, but Gwendolen's acuteness had not gone deeper than to discern that his manners were no clew for her, and because these were unchanged she was not the less afraid of him.

She had not been at Diplow before except to dine; and since certain points of view from the windows and the garden were worth showing, Lady Flora Hollis proposed after luncheon, when some of the guests had dispersed, and the sun was sloping toward four o'clock, that the remaining party should make a little exploration. Here came frequent opportunities when Grandcourt might have retained Gwendolen apart, and have spoken to her unheard. But, no! He indeed spoke to no one else, but what he said was nothing more eager or intimate than it had been in their first interview. He looked at her not less than usual; and some of her defiant spirit having come back, she looked full at him in return, not caring—rather preferring—that his eyes had no expression in them.

But at last it seemed as if he entertained some contrivance. After they had nearly made the tour of the grounds, the whole party paused by the pool to be amused with Fetch's accomplishment of bringing a water-lily to the bank like Cowper's spaniel Beau, and having been disappointed in his first attempt insisted on his trying again.

Here Grandcourt, who stood with Gwendolen outside the group, turned deliberately, and fixing his eyes on a knoll planted with American shrubs, and having a winding path up it, said languidly :

"This is a bore. Shall we go up there?"

"Oh, certainly—since we are exploring," said Gwendolen. She was rather pleased, and yet afraid.

The path was too narrow for him to offer his arm, and they walked up in silence. When they were on the bit of platform at the summit, Grandcourt said:

"There is nothing to be seen here; the thing was not worth climbing."

How was it that Gwendolen did not laugh? She was perfectly silent, holding up the folds of her robe like a statue, and giving a harder grasp to the handle of her whip, which she had snatched up automatically with her hat when they had first set off.

"What sort of place do you like?" said Grandcourt.

"Different places are agreeable in their way. On the whole, I think, I prefer places that are open and cheerful. I am not fond of anything sombre."

"Your place at Offendene is too sombre."

"It is, rather."

"You will not remain there long, I hope."

"Oh, yes, I think so. Mamma likes to be near her sister."

Silence for a short space.

"It is not to be supposed that *you* will always live there, though Mrs. Davilow may."

"I don't know. We women can't go in search of adventures—to find out the Northwest Passage or the source of the Nile, or to hunt tigers in the East. We must stay where we grow, or where the gardeners like to transplant us. We are brought up like the flowers, to look as pretty as we can, and be dull without complaining. That is my notion about the plants: they are often bored, and that is the reason why some of them have got poisonous. What do you think?" Gwendolen had run on rather nervously, lightly whipping the rhododendron bush in front of her.

"I quite agree. Most things are bores," said Grandcourt, his mind having been pushed into an easy current, away from its intended track. But after a moment's pause he continued in his broken, refined drawl:

"But a woman can be married."

"Some women can."

"You certainly, unless you are obstinately cruel."

"I am not sure that I am not both cruel and obstinate." Here Gwendolen suddenly turned her head and looked full at Grandcourt, whose eyes she had felt to be upon her throughout their conversation. She was wondering what the effect of looking at him would be on herself rather than on him.

He stood perfectly still, half a yard or more away from her; and it flashed through her thought that a sort of lotos-eater's stupor had begun in him and was taking possession of her. Then he said:

"Are you as uncertain about yourself as you make others about you?"

"I am quite uncertain about myself; I don't know how uncertain others may be."

"And you wish them to understand that you don't care?" said Grandcourt, with a touch of new hardness in his tone.

"I did not say that," Gwendolen replied, hesitatingly, and turning her eyes away, whipped the rhododendron bush again. She wished she were on horseback that she might set off on a canter. It was impossible to set off running down the knoll.

"You do care, then," said Grandcourt, not more quickly, but with a softened drawl.

"Ha! my whip!" said Gwendolen, in a little scream of distress. She had let it go—what could be more natural in a slight agitation?—and—but this seemed less natural in a gold-handled whip which had been left altogether to itself—it had gone with some force over the immediate shrubs, and had lodged itself in the branches of an azalea half-way down the knoll. She could run down now, laughing prettily, and Grandcourt was obliged to follow; but she was beforehand with him in rescuing the whip, and continued on her way to the level ground, when she paused and looked at Grandcourt with an exasperating brightness in her glance and a heightened color, as if she had carried a triumph, and these indications were still noticeable to Mrs. Davilow when Gwendolen and Grandcourt joined the rest of the party.

"It is all coquetting," thought Grandcourt; "the next time I beckon she will come down."

It seemed to him likely that this final beckoning might happen the very next day, when there was to be a picnic archery meeting in Cardell Chase, according to the plan projected on the evening of the ball.

Even in Gwendolen's mind that result was one of two likelihoods that presented themselves alternately, one of two decisions toward which she was being precipitated, as if they were two sides of a boundary-line, and she did not know on which she should fall. This subjection to a possible self, a self not to be absolutely predicted about, caused her some astonishment and terror: her favorite key of life—doing as she liked—seemed to fail her, and she could not foresee what at a given moment she might like to do. The prospect of marrying Grandcourt really seemed more attractive to her than she had believed beforehand that any marriage could be: the dignities, the luxuries, the power of doing a great deal of what she liked to do, which had now come close to her, and within her choice to secure or to lose, took hold of her nature as if it had been the strong odor of what she had only imagined and longed for before. And Grandcourt himself? He seemed as little of a flaw in his fortunes as a lover and husband could possibly be. Gwendolen wished to mount the chariot and drive the plunging horses herself, with a spouse by her side who would fold his arms and give her his countenance without looking ridiculous. Certainly, with all her perspicacity, and all the reading which seemed to her mamma dangerously instructive, her judgment was consciously a little at fault before Grandcourt. He was adorably quiet and free from absurdities—he would be a husband to suit with the best appearance a woman could make. But what else was he? He had been everywhere, and seen everything. *That* was desirable, and especially gratifying as a preamble to his supreme preference for Gwendolen Harleth. He did not appear to enjoy anything much. That was not necessary: and the less he had of particular tastes or desires, the more freedom his wife was likely to have in following hers. Gwendolen conceived that after marriage she would most probably be able to manage him thoroughly.

How was it that he caused her unusual constraint now?— that she was less daring and playful in her talk with him than with any other admirer she had known? That absence of demonstrativeness which she was glad of, acted as a charm in more senses than one, and was slightly benumbing. Grandcourt after all was formidable—a handsome lizard of a hitherto unknown species, not of the lively, darting kind. But Gwendolen knew hardly anything about lizards, and ignorance gives one a large range of probabilities. This splendid specimen was probably gentle, suitable as a boudoir pet: what may not a lizard be, if you know nothing to the contrary? Her acquaintance with Grandcourt was such that no accomplishment suddenly revealed in him would have surprised her. And he was so little suggestive of drama that it hardly occurred to her to think with any detail how his life of thirty-six years had been passed: in general, she imagined him always cold and dignified, not likely ever to have committed himself. He had hunted the tiger—had he ever been in love or made love? The one experience and the other seemed alike remote in Gwendolen's fancy from the Mr. Grandcourt who had come to Diplow in order apparently to make a chief epoch in her destiny—perhaps by introducing her to that state of marriage which she had resolved to make a state of greater freedom than her girlhood. And on the whole she wished to marry him; he suited her purpose; her prevailing, deliberate intention was, to accept him.

But was she going to fulfil her deliberate intention? She

began to be afraid of herself, and to find out a certain difficulty in doing as she liked. Already her assertion of independence in evading his advances had been carried further than was necessary, and she was thinking with some anxiety what she might do on the next occasion.

Seated according to her habit with her back to the horses on their drive homeward, she was completely under the observation of her mamma, who took the excitement and changefulness in the expression of her eyes, her unwonted absence of mind and total silence, as unmistakable signs that something unprecedented had occurred between her and Grandcourt. Mrs. Davilow's uneasiness determined her to risk some speech on the subject: the Gascoignes were to dine at Offendene, and in what had occurred this morning there might be some reason for consulting the Rector; not that she expected him any more than herself to influence Gwendolen, but that her anxious mind wanted to be disburdened.

"Something has happened, dear?" she began, in a tender tone of question.

Gwendolen looked round, and seeming to be roused to the consciousness of her physical self, took off her gloves and then her hat, that the soft breeze might blow on her head. They were in a retired bit of the road, where the long afternoon shadows from the bordering trees fell across it, and no observers were within sight. Her eyes continued to meet her mother's, but she did not speak.

"Mr. Grandcourt has been saying something? Tell me, dear." The last words were uttered beseechingly.

"What am I to tell you, mamma?" was the perverse answer.

"I am sure something has agitated you. You ought to confide in me, Gwen. You ought not to leave me in doubt and anxiety." Mrs. Davilow's eyes filled with tears.

"Mamma, dear, please don't be miserable," said Gwendolen, with pettish remonstrance. "It only makes me more so. I am in doubt myself."

"About Mr. Grandcourt's intentions?" said Mrs. Davilow, gathering determination from her alarms.

"No; not at all," said Gwendolen, with some curtness and a pretty little toss of the head as she put on her hat again.

"About whether you will accept him, then?"

"Precisely."

"Have you given him a doubtful answer?"

"I have given him no answer at all."

"He *has* spoken so that you could not misunderstand him?"

"As far as I would let him speak."

"You expect him to persevere?" Mrs. Davilow put this question rather anxiously, and receiving no answer, asked another: "You don't consider that you have discouraged him?"

"I dare say not."

"I thought you liked him, dear," said Mrs. Davilow, timidly.

"So I do, mamma, as liking goes. There is less to dislike about him than about most men. He is quiet and *distingué*." Gwendolen so far spoke with a pouting sort of gravity; but suddenly she recovered some of her mischievousness, and her face broke into a smile as she added: "Indeed, he has all the qualities that would make a husband tolerable—battlement, veranda, stables, etc., no grins and no glass in his eye."

"Do be serious with me for a moment, dear. Am I to understand that you mean to accept him?"

"Oh, pray, mamma, leave me to myself," said Gwendolen, with a pettish distress in her voice.

And Mrs. Davilow said no more.

When they got home, Gwendolen declared that she would not dine. She was tired, and would come down in the evening after she had taken some rest. The probability that her uncle would hear what had passed did not trouble her. She was convinced that whatever he might say would be on the side of her accepting Grandcourt, and she wished to accept him if she could. At this moment she would willingly have had weights hung on her own caprice.

Mr. Gascoigne did hear—not Gwendolen's answers repeated verbatim, but a softened generalized account of them. The mother conveyed as vaguely as the keen Rector's questions would let her the impression that Gwendolen was in some uncertainty about her own mind, but inclined on the whole to acceptance. The result was that the uncle felt himself called on to interfere; he did not conceive that he should do his duty in withholding direction from his niece in a momentous crisis of this kind.   Mrs. Davilow ventured a hesitating opinion that perhaps it would be safer to say nothing—Gwendolen was so sensitive (she did not like to say wilful).   But the Rector's was a firm mind, grasping its first judgments tenaciously and acting on them promptly, whence counter-judgments were no more for him than shadows fleeting across the solid ground to which he adjusted himself.

This match with Grandcourt presented itself to him as a sort of public affair; perhaps there were ways in which it might even strengthen the Establishment.   To the Rector, whose father (nobody would have suspected it, and nobody was told) had risen to be a provincial corn-dealer, aristocratic heirship resembled regal heirship in excepting its possessor from the ordinary standard of moral judgments, Grandcourt, the almost certain baronet, the probable peer, was to be ranged with public personages, and was a match to be accepted on broad general grounds, national and ecclesiastical.   Such public personages, it is true, are often in the nature of giants which an ancient community may have felt pride and safety in possessing, though, regarded privately, these born eminences must often have been inconvenient and even noisome. But of the future husband personally Mr. Gascoigne was disposed to think the best.   Gossip is a sort of smoke that comes from the dirty tobacco-pipes of those who diffuse it: it proves nothing but the bad taste of the smoker.   But if Grandcourt had really made any deeper or more unfortunate experiments in folly than were common in young men of high prospects, he was of an age to have finished them.   All accounts can be suitably wound up when a man has not ruined himself, and the expense may be taken as an insurance against future error. This was the view of practical wisdom; with reference to higher views, repentance had a supreme moral and religious value.   There was every reason to believe that a woman of well-regulated mind would be happy with Grandcourt.

It was no surprise to Gwendolen on coming down to tea to be told that her uncle wished to see her in the dining-room. He threw aside the paper as she entered and greeted her with his usual kindness.   As his wife had remarked, he always "made much" of Gwendolen, and her importance had risen of late. "My dear," he said, in a fatherly way, moving a chair for her as he held her hand, "I want to speak to you on a subject which is more momentous than any other with regard to your welfare. You will guess what I mean. But I shall speak to you with perfect directness: in such matters I consider myself bound to act as your father. You have no objection, I hope?"

"Oh, dear, no, uncle. You have always been very kind to me," said Gwendolen, frankly. This evening she was willing, if it were possible, to be a little fortified against her troublesome self, and her resistant temper was in abeyance. The Rector's mode of speech always conveyed a thrill of authority, as of a word of command: it seemed to take for granted that there could be no wavering in the audience, and that every one was going to be rationally obedient.

"It is naturally a satisfaction to me that the prospect of a marriage for you—advantageous in the highest degree—has presented itself so early. I do not know exactly what has passed between you and Mr. Grandcourt, but I presume there can be little doubt, from the way in which he has distinguished you, that he desires to make you his wife."

Gwendolen did not speak immediately, and her uncle said with more emphasis:

"Have you any doubt of that yourself, my dear?"

"I suppose that is what he has been thinking of. But he may have changed his mind to-morrow," said Gwendolen.

"Why to-morrow? Has he made advances which you have discouraged?"

"I think he meant—he began to make advances—but I did not encourage them. I turned the conversation."

"Will you confide in me so far as to tell me your reasons?"

"I am not sure that I had any reasons, uncle." Gwendolen laughed rather artificially.

"You are quite capable of reflecting, Gwendolen. You are aware that this is not a trivial occasion, and it concerns your establishment for life under circumstances which may not occur again. You have a duty here both to yourself and your family. I wish to understand whether you have any ground for hesitating as to your acceptance of Mr. Grandcourt."

"I suppose I hesitate without grounds." Gwendolen spoke rather poutingly, and her uncle grew suspicious.

"Is he disagreeable to you personally?"

"No."

"Have you heard anything of him which has affected you disagreeably?" The Rector thought it impossible that Gwendolen could have heard the gossip he had heard, but in any case he must endeavor to put all things in the right light for her.

"I have heard nothing about him except that he is a great match," said Gwendolen, with some sauciness; "and that affects me very agreeably."

"Then, my dear Gwendolen, I have nothing further to say than this: you hold your fortune in your own hands—a fortune such as rarely happens to a girl in your circumstances— a fortune, in fact, which almost takes the question out of the range of mere personal feeling, and makes your acceptance of it a duty. If Providence offers you power and position— especially when unclogged by any conditions that are repugnant to you—your course is one of responsibility, into which caprice must not enter. A man does not like to have his attachment trifled with: he may not be at once repelled—these things are matters of individual disposition. But the trifling may be carried too far. And I must point out to you that in case Mr. Grandcourt were repelled without your having refused him—without your having intended ultimately to refuse him, your situation would be a humiliating and painful one. I, for my part, should regard you with severe disapprobation, as the victim of nothing else than your own coquetry and folly."

Gwendolen became pallid as she listened to this admonitory speech. The ideas it raised had the force of sensations. Her resistant courage would not help her here, because her uncle was not urging her against her own resolve; he was pressing upon her the motives of dread which she already felt; he was making her more conscious of the risks that lay within herself. She was silent, and the Rector observed that he had produced some strong effect.

"I mean this in kindness, my dear." His tone had softened.

"I am aware of that, uncle," said Gwendolen, rising and shaking her head back, as if to rouse herself out of painful passivity. "I am not foolish. I know that I must be married some time—before it is too late. And I don't see how I could do better than marry Mr. Grandcourt. I mean to accept him, if possible." She felt as if she were re-enforcing herself by speaking with this decisiveness to her uncle.

But the Rector was a little startled by so bare a version of his own meaning from those young lips. He wished that in her mind his advice should be taken in an infusion of sentiments proper to a girl, and such as are presupposed in the advice of a clergyman, although he may not consider them always appropriate to be put forward. He wished his niece parks, carriages, a title—everything that would make this world a pleasant abode; but he wished her not to be cynical— to be, on the contrary, religiously dutiful, and have warm domestic affections.

"My dear Gwendolen," he said, rising also, and speaking with benignant gravity, "I trust that you will find in marriage a new fountain of duty and affection. Marriage is the only true and satisfactory sphere of a woman, and if your marriage with Mr. Grandcourt should be happily decided upon, you will have probably an increasing power, both of rank and wealth, which may be used for the benefit of others. These considerations are something higher than romance. You are fitted by natural gifts for a position which, considering your birth and early prospects, could hardly be looked forward to as in the ordinary course of things; and I trust that you will grace it not only by those personal gifts, but by a good and consistent life."

"I hope mamma will be the happier," said Gwendolen, in a more cheerful way, lifting her hands backward to her neck and moving toward the door. She wanted to waive those higher considerations.

Mr. Gascoigne felt that he had come to a satisfactory understanding with his niece, and had furthered her happy settlement in life by furthering her engagement to Grandcourt. Meanwhile there was another person to whom the contemplation of that issue had been a motive for some activity, and who believed that he too on this particular day had done something toward bringing about a favorable decision in *his* sense— which happened to be the reverse of the Rector's.

Mr. Lush's absence from Diplow during Gwendolen's visit had been due not to any fear on his part of meeting that supercilious young lady, or of being abashed by her frank dislike, but to an engagement from which he expected important consequences. He was gone in fact to the Wanchester Station to meet a lady accompanied by a maid and two children, whom he put into a fly, and afterward followed to the hotel of the Golden Keys in that town. An impressive woman, whom many would turn to look at again in passing; her figure was slim and sufficiently tall, her face rather emaciated, so that its sculpturesque beauty was the more pronounced, her crisp hair perfectly black, and her large, anxious eyes also what we call black. Her dress was soberly correct, her age perhaps physically more advanced than the number of years would imply, but hardly less than seven-and-thirty. An uneasy-looking woman: her glance seemed to presuppose that people and things were going to be unfavorable to her, while she was nevertheless ready to meet them with resolution. The children were lovely—a dark-haired girl of six or more, a fairer boy of five. When Lush incautiously expressed some surprise at her having brought the children, she said, with a sharp-edged intonation:

"Did you suppose I should come wandering about here by myself? Why should I not bring all four if I liked?"

"Oh, certainly," said Lush, with his usual fluent nonchalance.

He stayed an hour or so in conference with her, and rode back to Diplow in a state of mind that was at once hopeful and busily anxious as to the execution of the little plan on which his hopefulness was based. Grandcourt's marriage to Gwendolen Harleth would not, he believed, be much of a good to either of them, and it would plainly be fraught with disagreeables to himself. But now he felt confident enough to say inwardly: "I will take, nay, I will lay, odds that the marriage will never happen."

CHAPTER XIV.

I will not clothe myself in wreck—wear gems
Sawed from cramped finger-bones of women drowned;
Feel chilly vaporous hands of ireful ghosts
Clutching my necklace; trick my maiden breast
With orphans' heritage. Let your dead love
Marry its dead.

GWENDOLEN looked lovely and vigorous as a tall, newly
opened lily the next morning: there was a reaction of young
energy in her, and yesterday's self-distrust seemed no more
than the transient shiver on the surface of a full stream. The
roving archery match in Cardell Chase was a delightful prospect for the sport's sake: she felt herself beforehand moving
about like a wood-nymph under the beeches (in appreciative
company), and the imagined scene lent a charm to further advances on the part of Grandcourt—not an impassioned lyrical
Daphnis for the wood-nymph, certainly: but so much the
better. To-day Gwendolen foresaw him making slow conversational approaches to a declaration, and foresaw herself
awaiting and encouraging it according to the rational conclusion which she had expressed to her uncle.

When she came down to breakfast (after every one had left
the table except Mrs. Davilow) there were letters on her plate.
One of them she read with a gathering smile, and then handed
it to her mamma, who, on returning it, smiled also, finding
new cheerfulness in the good spirits her daughter had shown
ever since waking, and said:

"You don't feel inclined to go a thousand miles away?"

"Not exactly so far."

"It was a sad omission not to have written again before
this. Can't you write now—before we set out this morning?"

"It is not so pressing. To-morrow will do. You see they
leave town to-day. I must write to Dover. They will be
there till Monday."

"Shall I write for you, dear—if it teases you?"

Gwendolen did not speak immediately, but after sipping her
coffee answered brusquely: "Oh no, let it be; I will write
to-morrow." Then, feeling a touch of compunction, she

looked up and said with playful tenderness, "Dear, old, beautiful mamma!"

"Old, child, truly."

"Please don't, mamma! I meant old for darling. You are hardly twenty-five years older than I am. When you talk in that way, my life shrivels up before me."

"One can have a great deal of happiness in twenty-five years, my dear."

"I must lose no time in beginning," said Gwendolen, merrily. "The sooner I get my palaces and coaches the better."

"And a good husband who adores you, Gwen," said Mrs. Davilow, encouragingly.

Gwendolen put out her lips saucily and said nothing.

It was a slight drawback on her pleasure in starting that the Rector was detained by magistrate's business and would probably not be able to get to Cardell Chase at all that day. She cared little that Mrs. Gascoigne and Anna chose not to go without him, but her uncle's presence would have seemed to make it a matter of course that the decision taken would be acted on. For decision in itself began to be formidable. Having come close to accepting Grandcourt, Gwendolen felt this lot of unhoped-for fulness rounding itself too definitely: when we take to wishing a great deal for ourselves, whatever we get soon turns into mere limitation and exclusion. Still there was the reassuring thought that marriage would be the gate into a larger freedom.

The place of meeting was a grassy spot called Green Arbor, where a bit of hanging wood made a sheltering amphitheatre. It was here that the coachful of servants with provisions had to prepare the picnic meal; and the warden of the Chase was to guide the roving archers so as to keep them within the due distance from this centre, and hinder them from wandering beyond the limit which had been fixed on—a curve that might be drawn through certain well-known points, such as the Double Oak, the Whispering Stones, and the High Cross. The plan was, to take only a preliminary stroll before luncheon, keeping the main roving expedition for the more exquisite lights of the afternoon. The muster was rapid enough to save every one from dull moments of waiting, and when the groups began to scatter themselves through the light and shadow made here by closely neighboring beeches and there by rarer oaks, one may suppose that a painter would have been glad to look on. This roving archery was far prettier than the stationary game, but success in shooting at variable marks was less favored by practice, and the hits were distributed among the volunteer archers otherwise than they would have been in target-shooting. From this cause perhaps, as well as from the twofold distraction of being preoccupied and wishing not to betray her preoccupation, Gwendolen did not greatly distinguish herself in these first experiments, unless it were by the lively grace with which she took her comparative failure. She was in her white and green as on the day of the former archery meeting, when it made an epoch for her that she was introduced to Grandcourt; he was continually by her side now, yet it would have been hard to tell from mere looks and manners that their relation to each other had at all changed since their first conversation. Still there were other grounds that made most persons conclude them to be, if not engaged already, on the eve of being so. And she believed this herself. As they were all returning toward Green Arbor in divergent groups, not thinking at all of taking aim, but merely chattering, words passed which seemed really the beginning of that end—the beginning of her acceptance. Grandcourt said: "Do you know how long it is since I first saw you in this dress?"

"The archery meeting was on the 25th, and this is the 13th," said Gwendolen, laughingly. "I am not good at calculating, but I will venture to say that it must be nearly three weeks."

A little pause, and then he said: "That is a great loss of time."

"That your knowing me has caused you? Pray don't be uncomplimentary; I don't like it."

Pause again. "It is because of the gain that I feel the loss."

Here Gwendolen herself left a pause. She was thinking: "He is really very ingenious. He never speaks stupidly." Her silence was so unusual that it seemed the strongest of favorable answers, and he continued:

"The gain of knowing you makes me feel the time I lose in uncertainty. Do *you* like uncertainty?"

"I think I do, rather," said Gwendolen, suddenly beaming on him with a playful smile. "There is more in it."

Grandcourt met her laughing eyes with a slow, steady look right into them, which seemed like vision in the abstract, and said: "Do you mean more torment for me?"

There was something so strange to Gwendolen in this moment that she was quite shaken out of her usual self-consciousness. Blushing and turning away her eyes, she said: "No, that would make me sorry."

Grandcourt would have followed up this answer, which the change in her manner made apparently decisive of her favorable intention; but he was not in any way overcome so as to be unaware that they were now, within sight of everybody, descending the slope into Green Arbor, and descending it at an ill-chosen point where it began to be inconveniently steep. This was a reason for offering his hand in the literal sense to help her; she took it, and they came down in silence, much observed by those already on the level—among others by Mrs. Arrowpoint, who happened to be standing with Mrs. Davilow. That lady had now made up her mind that Grandcourt's merits were not such as would have induced Catherine to accept him, Catherine having so high a standard as to have refused Lord Slogan. Hence she looked at the tenant of Diplow with dispassionate eyes.

"Mr. Grandcourt is not equal as a man to his uncle, Sir Hugo Mallinger—too languid. To be sure, Mr. Grandcourt is a much younger man, but I shouldn't wonder if Sir Hugo were to outlive him, notwithstanding the difference of years. It is ill calculating on successions," concluded Mrs. Arrowpoint, rather too loudly.

"It is indeed," said Mrs. Davilow, able to assent with quiet cheerfulness, for she was so well satisfied with the actual situation of affairs that her habitual melancholy in their general unsatisfactoriness was altogether in abeyance.

I am not concerned to tell of the food that was eaten in that green refectory, or even to dwell on the glories of the forest scenery that spread themselves out beyond the level front of the hollow; being just now bound to tell a story of life at a stage when the blissful beauty of earth and sky entered only by narrow and oblique inlets into the consciousness, which was busy with a small social drama almost as little penetrated by a feeling of wider relations as if it had been a puppet-show. It will be understood that the food and champagne were of the best—the talk and laughter too, in the sense of belonging to the best society, where no one makes an invidious display of anything in particular, and the advantages of the world are taken with that high-bred depreciation which follows from being accustomed to them. Some of the gentlemen strolled a little and indulged in a cigar, there being a sufficient interval before four o'clock—the time for beginning to rove again. Among these, strange to say, was Grandcourt; but not Mr. Lush, who seemed to be taking his pleasure quite generously to-day by making himself particularly serviceable, ordering everything for everybody, and by this activity becoming more than ever a blot on the scene to Gwendolen, though he kept himself amiably aloof from her, and never even looked at her obviously. When there was a general move to prepare for starting, it appeared that the bows had all been put under the charge of Lord Brackenshaw's valet, and Mr. Lush was concerned to save the ladies the trouble of fetching theirs from the carriage where they were propped. He did not intend to bring Gwendolen's, but she, fearful lest he should do so, hurried to fetch it herself. The valet seeing her approach met her with it, and in giving it into her hand gave also a letter addressed to her. She asked no question about it, perceived at a glance that the address was in a lady's handwriting (of the delicate kind which used to be esteemed feminine before the present uncial period), and moving away with her bow in her hand, saw Mr. Lush coming to fetch other bows. To avoid meeting him she turned aside and walked with her back toward the stand of carriages, opening the letter. It contained these words:

"If Miss Harleth is in doubt whether she should accept Mr. Grandcourt, let her break from her party after they have passed the Whispering Stones and return to that spot. She will then hear something to decide her, but she can only hear it by keeping this letter a strict secret from every one. If she does not act according to this letter, she will repent, as the woman who writes it has repented. The secrecy Miss Harleth will feel herself bound in honor to guard. "

Gwendolen felt an inward shock, but her immediate thought was, "It is come in time." It lay in her youthfulness that she was absorbed by the idea of the revelation to be made, and had not even a momentary suspicion of contrivance that could justify her in showing the letter. Her mind gathered itself up at once into the resolution that she would manage to go unobserved to the Whispering Stones; and thrusting the letter into her pocket, she turned back to rejoin the company, with that sense of having something to conceal which to her nature had a bracing quality and helped her to be mistress of herself.

It was a surprise to every one that Grandcourt was not, like the other smokers, on the spot in time to set out roving with the rest. "We shall alight on him by and by," said Lord Brackenshaw; "he can't be gone far." At any rate, no man could be waited for. This apparent forgetfulness might be taken for the distraction of a lover so absorbed in thinking of the beloved object as to forget an appointment which would bring him into her actual presence. And the good-natured Earl gave Gwendolen a distant jocose hint to that effect, which she took with suitable quietude. But the thought in her own mind was, "Can he too be starting away from a decision? " It was not exactly a pleasant thought to her; but it was near the truth. "Starting away," however, was not the right expression for the languor of intention that came over Grandcourt, like a fit of diseased numbness, when an end seemed within easy reach: to desist then, when all expectation was to the contrary, became another gratification of mere will, sublimely independent of definite motive. At that moment he had begun a second large cigar in a vague, hazy obstinacy which, if Lush or any other mortal who might be insulted with impunity had interrupted by overtaking him with a request for his return, would have expressed itself by a slow removal of his cigar to say, in an undertone, "You'll be kind enough to go to the devil, will you? "

But he was not interrupted, and the rovers set off without

any visible depression of spirits, leaving behind only a few of the less vigorous ladies, including Mrs. Davilow, who preferred a quiet stroll free from obligation to keep up with others. The enjoyment of the day was soon at its highest pitch, the archery getting more spirited and the changing scenes of the forest from roofed grove to open glade growing lovelier with the lengthening shadows, and the deeply felt but undefinable gradations of the mellowing afternoon. It was agreed that they were playing an extemporized "As You Like It"; and when a pretty compliment had been turned to Gwendolen about her having the part of Rosalind, she felt the more compelled to be surpassing in liveliness. This was not very difficult to her, for the effect of what had happened to-day was an excitement which needed a vent, a sense of adventure rather than alarm, and a straining toward the management of her retreat so as not to be impeded.

The roving had been lasting nearly an hour before the arrival at the Whispering Stones, two tall conical blocks that leaned toward each other like gigantic gray-mantled figures. They were soon surveyed and passed by with the remark that they would be good ghosts on a starlit night. But a soft sunlight was on them now, and Gwendolen felt daring. The stones were near a fine grove of beeches where the archers found plenty of marks.

"How far are we from Green Arbor now?" said Gwendolen, having got in front by the side of the warden.

"Oh, not more than half a mile, taking along the avenue we're going to cross up there: but I shall take round a couple of miles, by the High Cross."

She was falling back among the rest, when suddenly they seemed all to be hurrying obliquely forward under the guidance of Mr. Lush, and lingering a little where she was, she perceived her opportunity of slipping away. Soon she was out of sight, and without running she seemed to herself to fly along the ground and count the moments nothing till she found herself back again at the Whispering Stones. They turned their blank gray sides to her: what was there on the other side? If there were nothing after all? That was her only dread now—to have to turn back again in mystification;

and walking round the right-hand stone without pause, she found herself in front of some one whose large dark eyes met hers at a foot's distance. In spite of expectation she was startled and shrank back, but in doing so she could take in the whole figure of this stranger and perceive that she was unmistakably a lady, and one who must have been exceedingly handsome. She perceived, also, that a few yards from her were two children seated on the grass.

"Miss Harleth?" said the lady.

"Yes." All Gwendolen's consciousness was wonder.

"Have you accepted Mr. Grandcourt?"

"No."

"I have promised to tell you something. And you will promise to keep my secret. However you may decide, you will not tell Mr. Grandcourt, or any one else, that you have seen me?"

"I promise."

"My name is Lydia Glasher. Mr. Grandcourt ought not to marry any one but me. I left my husband and child for him nine years ago. Those two children are his, and we have two others—girls—who are older. My husband is dead now, and Mr. Grandcourt ought to marry me. He ought to make that boy his heir."

She looked toward the boy as she spoke, and Gwendolen's eyes followed hers. The handsome little fellow was puffing out his cheeks in trying to blow a tiny trumpet which remained dumb. His hat hung backward by a string, and his brown curls caught the sun-rays. He was a cherub.

The two women's eyes met again, and Gwendolen said proudly: "I will not interfere with your wishes." She looked as if she were shivering, and her lips were pale.

"You are very attractive, Miss Harleth. But when he first knew me, I too was young. Since then my life has been broken up and embittered. It is not fair that he should be happy and I miserable, and my boy thrust out of sight for another."

These words were uttered with a biting accent, but with a determined abstinence from anything violent in tone or manner. Gwendolen, watching Mrs. Glasher's face while she spoke, felt a sort of terror: it was as if some ghastly vision had come to her in a dream and said: "I am a woman's life."

"Have you anything more to say to me?" she asked in a low tone, but still proudly and coldly. The revulsion within her was not tending to soften her. Every one seemed hateful.

"Nothing. You know what I wished you to know. You can inquire about me, if you like. My husband was Colonel Glasher."

"Then I will go," said Gwendolen, moving away with a ceremonious inclination, which was returned with equal grace.

In a few minutes Gwendolen was in the beech-grove again, but her party had gone out of sight and apparently had not sent in search of her, for all was solitude till she had reached the avenue pointed out by the warden. She determined to take this way back to Green Arbor, which she reached quickly; rapid movements seeming to her just now a means of suspending the thoughts which might prevent her from behaving with due calm. She had already made up her mind what step she would take.

Mrs. Davilow was of course astonished to see Gwendolen returning alone, and was not without some uneasiness which the presence of other ladies hindered her from showing. In answer to her words of surprise, Gwendolen said:

"Oh, I have been rather silly. I lingered behind to look at the Whispering Stones, and the rest hurried on after something, so I lost sight of them. I thought it best to come home by the short way—the avenue that the warden had told me of. I'm not sorry after all. I had had enough walking."

"Your party did not meet Mr. Grandcourt, I presume," said Mrs. Arrowpoint, not without intention.

"No," said Gwendolen, with a little flash of defiance, and a light laugh. "And we didn't see any carvings on the trees either. Where can he be? I should think he has fallen into the pool or had an apoplectic fit."

With all Gwendolen's resolve not to betray any agitation, she could not help it that her tone was unusually high and hard, and her mother felt sure that something unpropitious had happened.

Mrs. Arrowpoint thought that the self-confident young lady

was much piqued, and that Mr. Grandcourt was probably
seeing reason to change his mind.

"If you have no objection, mamma, I will order the carriage," said Gwendolen. "I am tired. And every one will
be going soon."

Mrs. Davilow assented; but by the time the carriage was
announced as ready—the horses having to be fetched from the
stables on the warden's premises—the roving party reappeared,
and with them Mr. Grandcourt.

"Ah, there you are!" said Lord Brackenshaw, going up to
Gwendolen, who was arranging her mamma's shawl for the
drive. "We thought at first you had alighted on Grandcourt
and he had taken you home. Lush said so. But after that
we met Grandcourt. However, we didn't suppose you could
be in any danger. The warden said he had told you a near
way back."

"You are going?" said Grandcourt, coming up with his
usual air, as if he did not conceive that there had been any
omission on his part. Lord Brackenshaw gave place to him
and moved away.

"Yes, we are going," said Gwendolen, looking busily at her
scarf, which she was arranging across her shoulders Scotch
fashion.

"May I call at Offendene to-morrow?"

"Oh, yes, if you like," said Gwendolen, sweeping him from
a distance with her eyelashes. Her voice was light and sharp
as the first touch of frost.

Mrs. Davilow accepted his arm to lead her to the carriage;
but while that was happening, Gwendolen with incredible
swiftness had got in advance of them, and had sprung into the
carriage.

"I got in, mamma, because I wished to be on this side,"
she said, apologetically. But she had avoided Grandcourt's
touch: he only lifted his hat and walked away—with the not
unsatisfactory impression that she meant to show herself
offended by his neglect.

The mother and daughter drove for five minutes in silence.
Then Gwendolen said: "I intend to join the Langens at
Dover, mamma. I shall pack up immediately on getting

home, and set off by the early train. I shall be at Dover almost as soon as they are; we can let them know by telegraph."

"Good heavens, child! what can be your reason for saying so?"

"My reason for saying it, mamma, is that I mean to do it."

"But why do you mean to do it?"

"I wish to go away."

"Is it because you are offended with Mr. Grandcourt's odd behavior in walking off to-day?"

"It is useless to enter into such questions. I am not going in any case to marry Mr. Grandcourt. Don't interest yourself further about him."

"What can I say to your uncle, Gwendolen? Consider the position you place me in. You led him to believe only last night that you had made up your mind in favor of Mr. Grandcourt."

"I am very sorry to cause you annoyance, mamma, dear, but I can't help it," said Gwendolen, with still harder resistance in her tone. "Whatever you or my uncle may think or do, I shall not alter my resolve, and I shall not tell my reason. I don't care what comes of it. I don't care if I never marry any one. There is nothing worth caring for. I believe all men are bad, and I hate them."

"But need you set off in this way, Gwendolen?" said Mrs. Davilow, miserable and helpless.

"Now, mamma, don't interfere with me. If you have ever had any trouble in your own life, remember it and don't interfere with me. If I am to be miserable, let it be by my own choice."

The mother was reduced to trembling silence. She began to see that the difficulty would be lessened if Gwendolen went away.

And she did go. The packing was all carefully done that evening, and not long after dawn the next day Mrs. Davilow accompanied her daughter to the railway station. The sweet dews of morning, the cows and horses looking over the hedges without any particular reason, the early travellers on foot with their bundles, seemed all very melancholy and purposeless to them both. The dingy torpor of the railway station, before the ticket could be taken, was still worse. Gwendolen had certainly hardened in the last twenty-four hours: her mother's trouble evidently counted for little in her present state of mind, which did not essentially differ from the mood that makes men take to worse conduct when their belief in persons or things is upset. Gwendolen's uncontrolled reading, though consisting chiefly in what are called pictures of life, had somehow not prepared her for this encounter with reality. Is that surprising? It is to be believed that attendance at the *opéra bouffe* in the present day would not leave men's minds entirely without shock, if the manners observed there with some applause were suddenly to start up in their own families. Perspective, as its inventor remarked, is a beautiful thing. What horrors of damp huts, where human beings languish, may not become picturesque through aerial distance! What hymning of cancerous vices may we not languish over as sublimest art in the safe remoteness of a strange language and artificial phrase! Yet we keep a repugnance to rheumatism and other painful effects when presented in our personal experience.

Mrs. Davilow felt Gwendolen's new phase of indifference keenly, and as she drove back alone, the brightening morning was sadder to her than before.

Mr. Grandcourt called that day at Offendene, but nobody was at home.

CHAPTER XV.

"*Festina lente*—celerity should be contempered with cunctation."—SIR THOMAS BROWNE.

GWENDOLEN, we have seen, passed her time abroad in the new excitement of gambling, and in imagining herself an empress of luck, having brought from her late experience a vague impression that in this confused world it signified nothing what any one did, so that they amused themselves. We have seen, too, that certain persons, mysteriously symbolized as Grapnell & Co., having also thought of reigning in the realm of luck, and being also bent on amusing themselves, no

matter how, had brought about a painful change in her family
circumstances; whence she had returned home—carrying with
her, against her inclination, a necklace which she had pawned
and some one else had redeemed.

While she was going back to England, Grandcourt was coming to find her; coming, that is, after his own manner—not in
haste by express straight from Diplow to Leubronn, where she
was understood to be; but so entirely without hurry that he
was induced by the presence of some Russian acquaintances to
linger at Baden-Baden and make various appointments with
them, which, however, his desire to be at Leubronn ultimately
caused him to break. Grandcourt's passions were of the
intermittent, flickering kind: never flaming out strongly.
But a great deal of life goes on without strong passion: myri-
ads of cravats are carefully tied, dinners attended, even
speeches made proposing the health of august personages,
without the zest arising from a strong desire. And a man
may make a good appearance in high social positions—may be
supposed to know the classics, to have his reserves on science,
a strong though repressed opinion on politics, and all the
sentiments of the English gentleman, at a small expense of
vital energy. Also, he may be obstinate or persistent at the
same low rate, and may even show sudden impulses which
have a false air of dæmonic strength because they seem inexplicable, though perhaps their secret lies merely in the want
of regulated channels for the soul to move in—good and sufficient ducts of habit without which our nature easily turns to
mere ooze and mud, and at any pressure yields nothing but a
spurt or a puddle.

Grandcourt had not been altogether displeased by Gwendolen's running away from the splendid chance he was holding
out to her. The act had some piquancy for him. He liked
to think that it was due to resentment of his careless behavior
in Cardell Chase, which, when he came to consider it, did
appear rather cool. To have brought her so near a tender
admission, and then to have walked headlong away from further opportunities of winning the consent which he had made
her understand him to be asking for, was enough to provoke
a girl of spirit; and to be worth his mastering, it was proper

that she should have some spirit. Doubtless she meant him
to follow her, and it was what he meant too. But for a whole
week he took no measures toward starting, and did not even
inquire where Miss Harleth was gone. Mr. Lush felt a triumph that was mingled with much distrust; for Grandcourt
had said no word to him about her, and looked as neutral as
an alligator: there was no telling what might turn up in the
slowly churning chances of his mind. Still, to have put off a
decision was to have made room for the waste of Grandcourt's
energy.

The guests at Diplow felt more curiosity than their host.
How was it that nothing more was heard of Miss Harleth?
Was it credible that she had refused Mr. Grandcourt? Lady
Flora Hollis, a lively, middle-aged woman, well endowed with
curiosity, felt a sudden interest in making a round of calls
with Mrs. Torrington, including the Rectory, Offendene, and
Quetcham, and thus not only got twice over, but also discussed
with the Arrowpoints the information that Miss Harleth was
gone to Leubronn, with some old friends, the Baron and Baroness von Langen; for the immediate agitation and disappointment of Mrs. Davilow and the Gascoignes had resolved itself
into a wish that Gwendolen's disappearance should not be
interpreted as anything eccentric or needful to be kept secret.
The Rector's mind, indeed, entertained the possibility that
the marriage was only a little deferred, for Mrs. Davilow had
not dared to tell him of the bitter determination with which
Gwendolen had spoken. And in spite of his practical ability,
some of his experience had petrified into maxims and quota-
tions. Amaryllis fleeing desired that her hiding-place should
be known; and that love will find out the way "over the
mountain and over the wave" may be said without hyperbole
in this age of steam. Gwendolen, he conceived, was an Amaryllis of excellent sense but coquettish daring; the question
was whether she had dared too much.

Lady Flora, coming back charged with news about Miss
Harleth, saw no good reason why she should not try whether
she could electrify Mr. Grandcourt by mentioning it to him at
table; and in doing so shot a few hints of a notion having got
abroad that he was a disappointed adorer. Grandcourt heard

with quietude, but with attention; and the next day he ordered
Lush to bring about a decent reason for breaking up the party
at Diplow by the end of another week, as he meant to go
yachting to the Baltic or somewhere—it being impossible to
stay at Diplow as if he were a prisoner on parole, with a set
of people whom he had never wanted. Lush needed no clearer
announcement that Grandcourt was going to Leubronn; but he
might go after the manner of a creeping billiard-ball and stick
on the way. What Mr. Lush intended was to make himself
indispensable so that he might go too, and he succeeded;
Gwendolen's repulsion for him being a fact that only amused
his patron, and made him none the less willing to have Lush
always at hand.

This was how it happened that Grandcourt arrived at the
Czarina on the fifth day after Gwendolen had left Leubronn,
and found there his uncle, Sir Hugo Mallinger, with his
family, including Deronda. It is not necessarily a pleasure
either to the reigning power or the heir presumptive when
their separate affairs—a touch of gout, say, in the one, and a
touch of wilfulness in the other—happen to bring them to the
same spot. Sir Hugo was an easy-tempered man, tolerant
both of differences and defects; but a point of view different
from his own concerning the settlement of the family estates
fretted him rather more than if it had concerned Church discipline or the ballot, and faults were the less venial for belonging to a person whose existence was inconvenient to him. In
no case could Grandcourt have been a nephew after his own
heart; but as the presumptive heir to the Mallinger estates he
was the sign and embodiment of a chief grievance in the baronet's life—the want of a son to inherit the lands, in no portion of which had he himself more than a life-interest. For
in the ill-advised settlement which his father, Sir Francis,
had chosen to make by will, even Diplow with its modicum of
land had been left under the same conditions as the ancient
and wide inheritance of the two Toppings—Diplow, where Sir
Hugo had lived and hunted through many a season in his
younger years, and where his wife and daughters ought to
have been able to retire after his death.

This grievance had naturally gathered emphasis as the years

advanced, and Lady Mallinger, after having had three daughters in quick succession, had remained for eight years till now that she was over forty without producing so much as another girl; while Sir Hugo, almost twenty years older, was at a time of life when, notwithstanding the fashionable retardation of most things from dinners to marriages, a man's hopefulness is apt to show signs of wear, until restored by second childhood.

In fact, he had begun to despair of a son, and this confirmation of Grandcourt's interest in the estates certainly tended to make his image and presence the more unwelcome; but, on the other hand, it carried circumstances which disposed Sir Hugo to take care that the relation between them should be kept as friendly as possible. It led him to dwell on a plan which had grown up side by side with his disappointment of an heir; namely, to try and secure Diplow as a future residence for Lady Mallinger and her daughters, and keep this pretty bit of the family inheritance for his own offspring in spite of that disappointment. Such knowledge as he had of his nephew's disposition and affairs encouraged the belief that Grandcourt might consent to a transaction by which he would get a good sum of ready money, as an equivalent for his prospective interest in the domain of Diplow and the moderate amount of land attached to it. If, after all, the unhoped-for son should be born, the money would have been thrown away, and Grandcourt would have been paid for giving up interests that had turned out good for nothing; but Sir Hugo set down this risk as *nil*, and of late years he had husbanded his fortune so well by the working of mines and the sale of leases that he was prepared for an outlay.

Here was an object that made him careful to avoid any quarrel with Grandcourt. Some years before, when he was making improvements at the Abbey, and needed Grandcourt's concurrence in his felling an obstructive mass of timber on the demesne, he had congratulated himself on finding that there was no active spite against him in his nephew's peculiar mind; and nothing had since occurred to make them hate each other more than was compatible with perfect politeness, or with any accommodation that could be strictly mutual.

Grandcourt, on his side, thought his uncle a superfluity and a bore, and felt that the list of things in general would be improved whenever Sir Hugo came to be expunged. But he had been made aware through Lush, always a useful medium, of the baronet's inclinations concerning Diplow, and he was gratified to have the alternative of the money in his mind: even if he had not thought it in the least likely that he would choose to accept it, his sense of power would have been flattered by his being able to refuse what Sir Hugo desired. The hinted transaction had told for something among the motives which had made him ask for a year's tenancy of Diplow, which it had rather annoyed Sir Hugo to grant, because the excellent hunting in the neighborhood might decide Grandcourt not to part with his chance of future possession;—a man who has two places, in one of which the hunting is less good, naturally desiring a third where it is better. Also, Lush had thrown out to Sir Hugo the probability that Grandcourt would woo and win Miss Arrowpoint, and in that case ready money might be less of a temptation to him. Hence, on this unexpected meeting at Leubronn, the baronet felt much curiosity to know how things had been going on at Diplow, was bent on being as civil as possible to his nephew, and looked forward to some private chat with Lush.

Between Deronda and Grandcourt there was a more faintly marked but peculiar relation, depending on circumstances which have yet to be made known. But on no side was there any sign of suppressed chagrin on the first meeting at the *table d' hôte*, an hour after Grandcourt's arrival; and when the quartet of gentlemen afterward met on the terrace, without Lady Mallinger, they moved off together to saunter through the rooms, Sir Hugo saying as they entered the large *saal:*

"Did you play much at Baden, Grandcourt?"

"No; I looked on and betted a little with some Russians there."

"Had you luck?"

"What did I win, Lush?"

"You brought away about two hundred," said Lush.

"You are not here for the sake of the play, then?" said Sir Hugo.

"No; I don't care about play now. It's a confounded

strain," said Grandcourt, whose diamond ring and demeanor, as he moved along playing slightly with his whisker, were being a good deal stared at by rouged foreigners interested in a new milord.

"The fact is, somebody should invent a mill to do amusements for you, my dear fellow," said Sir Hugo, "as the Tartars get their praying done. But I agree with you; I never cared for play. It's monotonous—knits the brain up into meshes. And it knocks me up to watch it now. I suppose one gets poisoned with the bad air. I never stay here more than ten minutes. But where's your gambling beauty, Deronda? Have you seen her lately?"

"She's gone," said Deronda, curtly.

"An uncommonly fine girl, a perfect Diana," said Sir Hugo, turning to Grandcourt again. "Really worth a little straining to look at her. I saw her winning, and she took it as coolly as if she had known it all beforehand. The same day, Deronda happened to see her losing like wildfire, and she bore it with immense pluck. I suppose she was cleaned out, or was wise enough to stop in time. How do you know she's gone?"

"Oh, by the Visitor-list," said Deronda, with a scarcely perceptible shrug. "Vandernoodt told me her name was Harleth, and she was with the Baron and Baroness von Langen. I saw by the list that Miss Harleth was no longer there."

This held no further information for Lush than that Gwendolen had been gambling. He had already looked at the list, and ascertained that Gwendolen had gone, but he had no intention of thrusting this knowledge on Grandcourt before he asked for it; and he had not asked, finding it enough to believe that the object of search would turn up somewhere or other.

But now Grandcourt had heard what was rather piquant, and not a word about Miss Harleth had been missed by him. After a moment's pause he said to Deronda:

"Do you know those people—the Langens?"

"I have talked with them a little since Miss Harleth went away. I knew nothing of them before."

"Where is she gone—do you know?"

"She is gone home," said Deronda, coldly, as if he wished to say no more. But then, from a fresh impulse, he turned to look markedly at Grandcourt, and added: "But it is possible you know her. Her home is not far from Diplow: Offendene, near Wanchester."

Deronda, turning to look straight at Grandcourt who was on his left hand, might have been a subject for those old painters who liked contrasts of temperament. There was a calm intensity of life and richness of tint in his face that on a sudden gaze from him was rather startling, and often made him seem to have spoken, so that servants and officials asked him automatically, "What did you say, sir?" when he had been quite silent. Grandcourt himself felt an irritation, which he did not show except by a slight movement of the eyelids, at Deronda's turning round on him when he was not asked to do more than speak. But he answered, with his usual drawl, "Yes, I know her," and paused with his shoulder toward Deronda, to look at the gambling.

"What of her, eh?" asked Sir Hugo of Lush, as the three moved on a little way. "She must be a new-comer at Offendene. Old Blenny lived there after the dowager died."

"A little too much of her," said Lush, in a low, significant tone; not sorry to let Sir Hugo know the state of affairs.

"Why? how?" said the baronet. They all moved out of the *salon* into a more airy promenade.

"He has been on the brink of marrying her," Lush went on. "But I hope it's off now. She's a niece of the clergyman—Gascoigne—at Pennicote. Her mother is a widow with a brood of daughters. This girl will have nothing, and is as dangerous as gunpowder. It would be a foolish marriage. But she has taken a freak against him, for she ran off here without notice, when he had agreed to call the next day. The fact is, he's here after her; but he was in no great hurry, and between his caprice and hers they are likely enough not to get together again. But of course he has lost his chance with the heiress."

Grandcourt joining them said: "What a beastly den this is! —a worse hole than Baden. I shall go back to the hotel."

When Sir Hugo and Deronda were alone, the baronet began:

"Rather a pretty story. That girl has something in her. She must be worth running after—has *de l'imprévu.* I think her appearance on the scene has bettered my chance of getting Diplow, whether the marriage comes off or not."

"I should hope a marriage like that would not come off," said Deronda, in a tone of disgust.

"What! are you a little touched with the sublime lash?" said Sir Hugo, putting up his glasses to help his short sight in looking at his companion. "Are you inclined to run after her?"

"On the contrary," said Deronda, "I should rather be inclined to run away from her."

"Why, you would easily cut out Grandcourt. A girl with her spirit would think you the finer match of the two," said Sir Hugo, who often tried Deronda's patience by finding a joke in impossible advice. (A difference of taste in jokes is a great strain on the affections.)

"I suppose pedigree and land belong to a fine match," said Deronda, coldly.

"The best horse will win in spite of pedigree, my boy. You remember Napoleon's *mot—Je suis un ancêtre,*" said Sir Hugo, who habitually undervalued birth, as men after dining will often agree that the good of life is distributed with wonderful equality.

"I am not sure that I want to be an ancestor," said Deronda. "It doesn't seem to me the rarest sort of origination."

"You won't run after the pretty gambler, then?" said Sir Hugo, putting down his glasses.

"Decidedly not."

This answer was perfectly truthful; nevertheless it had passed through Deronda's mind that under other circumstances he should have given way to the interest this girl had raised in him, and tried to know more of her. But his history had given him a stronger bias in another direction. He felt himself in no sense free.

CHAPTER XVI.

Men, like planets, have both a visible and an invisible history. The astronomer threads the darkness with strict deduction, accounting so for every visible arc in the wanderer's orbit; and the narrator of human actions, if he did his work with the same completeness, would have to thread the hidden pathways of feeling and thought which lead up to every moment of action, and to those moments of intense suffering which take the quality of action—like the cry of Prometheus, whose chained anguish seems a greater energy than the sea and sky he invokes and the deity he defies.

DERONDA's circumstances, indeed, had been exceptional. One moment had been burnt into his life as its chief epoch— a moment full of July sunshine and large pink roses shedding their last petals on a grassy court enclosed on three sides by a Gothic cloister.   Imagine him in such a scene: a boy of thirteen, stretched prone on the grass where it was in shadow, his curly head propped on his arms over a book, while his tutor, also reading, sat on a camp-stool under shelter.   Deronda's book was Sismondi's History of the Italian Republics:—the lad had a passion for history, eager to know how time had been filled up since the Flood, and how things were carried on in the dull periods.   Suddenly he let down his left arm and looked at his tutor, saying in purest boyish tones:

"Mr. Fraser, how was it that the popes and cardinals always had so many nephews?"

The tutor, an able young Scotchman who acted as Sir Hugo Mallinger's secretary, roused rather unwillingly from his political economy, answered with the clear-cut, emphatic chant which makes a truth doubly telling in Scotch utterance:

"Their own children were called nephews."

"Why?" said Deronda.

"It was just for the propriety of the thing; because, as you know very well, priests don't marry, and the children were illegitimate."

Mr. Fraser, thrusting out his lower lip and making his chant of the last word the more emphatic for a little impatience at being interrupted, had already turned his eyes on his book again, while Deronda, as if something had stung him, started up in a sitting attitude with his back to the tutor.

He had always called Sir Hugo Mallinger his uncle, and when it once occurred to him to ask about his father and mother, the baronet had answered, "You lost your father and mother when you were quite a little one; that is why I take care of you." Daniel then straining to discern something in that early twilight, had a dim sense of having been kissed very much, and surrounded by thin, cloudy, scented drapery till his fingers caught in something hard, which hurt him, and he began to cry. Every other memory he had was of the little world in which he still lived. And at that time he did not mind about learning more, for he was too fond of Sir Hugo to be sorry for the loss of unknown parents. Life was very delightful to the lad, with an uncle who was always indulgent and cheerful—a fine man in the bright noon of life, whom Daniel thought absolutely perfect, and whose place was one of the finest in England, at once historical, romantic, and home-like: a picturesque architectural outgrowth from an abbey, which had still remnants of the old monastic trunk. Diplow lay in another county, and was a comparatively landless place which had come into the family from a rich lawyer on the female side who wore the perruque of the Restoration; whereas the Mallingers had the grant of Monk's Topping under Henry the Eighth, and ages before had held the neighboring lands of King's Topping, tracing indeed their origin to a certain Hugues le Malingre, who came in with the Conqueror—and also apparently with a sickly complexion which had been happily corrected in his descendants. Two rows of these descendants, direct and collateral, females of the male line, and males of the female, looked down in the gallery over the cloisters on the nephew Daniel as he walked there: men in armor with pointed beards and arched eyebrows, pinched ladies in hoops and ruffs with no face to speak of; gravelooking men in black velvet and stuffed hips, and fair, frightened women holding little boys by the hand; smiling politicians in magnificent perruques, and ladies of the prize-animal kind, with rosebud mouths and full eyelids, according to Lely; then a generation whose faces were revised and embellished in the taste of Kneller; and so on through refined editions of the family types in the time of Reynolds and Romney, till the line ended with Sir Hugo and his younger brother Henleigh. This last had married Miss Grandcourt, and taken her name along with her estates, thus making a junction between two equally old families, impaling the three Saracens' heads proper and three bezants of the one with the tower and falcons *argent* of the other, and, as it happened, uniting their highest advantages in the prospects of that Henleigh Mallinger Grandcourt who is at present more of an acquaintance to us than either Sir Hugo or his nephew Daniel Deronda.

In Sir Hugo's youthful portrait with rolled collar and high cravat, Sir Thomas Lawrence had done justice to the agreeable alacrity of expression and sanguine temperament still to be seen in the original, but had done something more than justice in slightly lengthening the nose, which was in reality shorter than might have been expected in a Mallinger. Happily the appropriate nose of the family reappeared in his younger brother, and was to be seen in all its refined regularity in his nephew Mallinger Grandcourt. But in the nephew Daniel Deronda the family faces of various types, seen on the walls of the gallery, found no reflex. Still he was handsomer than any of them, and when he was thirteen might have served as model for any painter who wanted to image the most memorable of boys: you could hardly have seen his face thoroughly meeting yours without believing that human creatures had done nobly in times past, and might do more nobly in time to come. The finest childlike faces have this consecrating power, and make us shudder anew at all the grossness and basely wrought griefs of the world, lest they should enter here and defile.

But at this moment on the grass among the rose petals, Daniel Deronda was making a first acquaintance with those griefs. A new idea had entered his mind, and was beginning to change the aspect of his habitual feelings as happy careless voyagers are changed when the sky suddenly threatens and the thought of danger arises. He sat perfectly still with his back to the tutor, while his face expressed rapid inward transition. The deep blush, which had come when he first started up, gradually subsided; but his features kept that indescribable look of subdued activity which often accompanies a new

mental survey of familiar facts. He had not lived with other
boys, and his mind showed the same blending of child's ignorance with surprising knowledge which is oftener seen in
bright girls. Having read Shakespeare as well as a great
deal of history, he could have talked with the wisdom of a
bookish child about men who were born out of wedlock and
were held unfortunate in consequence, being under disadvantages which required them to be a sort of heroes if they were
to work themselves up to an equal standing with their legally
born brothers. But he had never brought such knowledge
into any association with his own lot, which had been too easy
for him ever to think about it—until this moment when there
had darted into his mind with the magic of quick comparison,
the possibility that here was the secret of his own birth, and
that the man whom he called uncle was really his father.
Some children, even younger than Daniel, have known the
first arrival of care, like an ominous irremovable guest in their
tender lives, on the discovery that their parents, whom they
had imagined able to buy everything, were poor and in hard
money troubles. Daniel felt the presence of a new guest who
seemed to come with an enigmatic veiled face, and to carry
dimly conjectured, dreaded revelations. The ardor which he
had given to the imaginary world in his books suddenly rushed
toward his own history and spent its pictorial energy there,
explaining what he knew, representing the unknown. The
uncle whom he loved very dearly took the aspect of a father
who held secrets about him—who had done him a wrong—
yes, a wrong; and what had become of his mother, from whom
he must have been taken away? Secrets about which he,
Daniel, could never inquire; for to speak or be spoken to
about these new thoughts seemed like falling flakes of fire to
his imagination. Those who have known an impassioned
childhood will understand this dread of utterance about any
shame connected with their parents. The impetuous advent
of new images took possession of him with the force of fact
for the first time told, and left him no immediate power for
the reflection that he might be trembling at a fiction of his
own. The terrible sense of collision between a strong rush of
feeling and the dread of its betrayal found relief at length in

big slow tears, which fell without restraint until the voice of Mr. Fraser was heard saying:

"Daniel, do you see that you are sitting on the bent pages of your book?"

Daniel immediately moved the book without turning round, and after holding it before him for an instant, rose with it and walked away into the open grounds, where he could dry his tears unobserved. The first shock of suggestion past, he could remember that he had no certainty how things really had been, and that he had been making conjectures about his own history, as he had often made stories about Pericles or Columbus, just to fill up the blanks before they became famous. Only there came back certain facts which had an obstinate reality—almost like the fragments of a bridge, telling you unmistakably how the arches lay. And again there came a mood in which his conjectures seemed like a doubt of religion, to be banished as an offence, and a mean prying after what he was not meant to know; for there was hardly a delicacy of feeling this lad was not capable of. But the summing up of all his fluctuating experience at this epoch was, that a secret impression had come to him which had given him something like a new sense in relation to all the elements of his life. And the idea that others probably knew things concerning him which they did not choose to mention, and which he would not have had them mention, set up in him a premature reserve which helped to intensify his inward experience. His ears were open now to words which before that July day would have passed by him unnoted; and round every trivial incident which imagination could connect with his suspicions, a newly roused set of feelings were ready to cluster themselves.

One such incident a month later wrought itself deeply into his life. Daniel had not only one of those thrilling boy voices which seem to bring an idyllic heaven and earth before our eyes, but a fine musical instinct, and had early made out accompaniments for himself on the piano, while he sang from memory. Since then he had had some teaching, and Sir Hugo, who delighted in the boy, used to ask for his music in the presence of guests. One morning after he had been singing "Sweet Echo" before a small party of gentlemen whom the rain had kept in the house, the baronet, passing from a smiling remark to his next neighbor, said:

"Come here, Dan!"

The boy came forward with unusual reluctance. He wore an embroidered holland blouse which set off the rich coloring of his head and throat, and the resistant gravity about his mouth and eyes, as he was being smiled upon, made their beauty the more impressive. Every one was admiring him.

"What do you say to being a great singer? Should you like to be adored by the world and take the house by storm, like Mario and Tamberlik?"

Daniel reddened instantaneously, but there was a just perceptible interval before he answered with angry decision:

"No; I should hate it!"

"Well, well, well!" said Sir Hugo, with surprised kindliness intended to be soothing. But Daniel turned away quickly, left the room, and going to his own chamber, threw himself on the broad window-sill, which was a favorite retreat of his when he had nothing particular to do. Here he could see the rain gradually subsiding with gleams through the parting clouds which lit up a great reach of the park, where the old oaks stood apart from each other, and the bordering wood was pierced with a green glade which met the eastern sky. This was a scene which had always been part of his home—part of the dignified ease which had been a matter of course in his life. And his ardent clinging nature had appropriated it all with affection. He knew a great deal of what it was to be a gentleman by inheritance, and without thinking much about himself—for he was a boy of active perceptions and easily forgot his own existence in that of Robert Bruce—he had never supposed that he could be shut out from such a lot, or have a very different part in the world from that of the uncle who petted him. It is possible (though not greatly believed in at present) to be fond of poverty and take it for a bride, to prefer scoured deal, red quarries, and whitewash for one's private surroundings, to delight in no splendor but what has open doors for the whole nation, and to glory in having no privilege except such as nature insists on; and noble men have been known to run away from elaborate ease and the option of idleness, that they might bind themselves for small pay to hard-handed labor. But Daniel's tastes were altogether in keeping with his nurture: his disposition was one in which every-day scenes and habits beget not *ennui* or rebellion, but delight, affection, aptitudes; and now the lad had been stung to the quick by the idea that his uncle—perhaps his father— thought of a career for him which was totally unlike his own, and which he knew very well was not thought of among possible destinations for the sons of English gentlemen. He had often stayed in London with Sir Hugo, who to indulge the boy's ear had carried him to the opera to hear the great tenors, so that the image of a singer taking the house by storm was very vivid to him; but now, spite of his musical gift, he set himself bitterly against the notion of being dressed up to sing before all those fine people, who would not care about him except as a wonderful toy. That Sir Hugo should have thought of him in that position for a moment, seemed to Daniel an unmistakable proof that there was something about his birth which threw him out from the class of gentlemen to which the baronet belonged. Would it ever be mentioned to him? Would the time come when his uncle would tell him everything? He shrank from the prospect; in his imagination he preferred ignorance. If his father had been wicked— Daniel inwardly used strong words, for he was feeling the injury done him as a maimed boy feels the crushed limb which for others is merely reckoned in an average of accidents—if his father had done any wrong, he wished it might never be spoken of to him; it was already a cutting thought that such knowledge might be in other minds. Was it in Mr. Fraser's? Probably not, else he would not have spoken in that way about the pope's nephews. Daniel fancied, as older people do, that every one else's consciousness was as active as his own on a matter which was vital to him. Did Turvey the valet know? —and old Mrs. French, the housekeeper?—and Banks, the bailiff, with whom he had ridden about the farms on his pony? And now there came back the recollection of a day some years before when he was drinking Mrs. Banks's whey, and Banks said to his wife with a wink and a cunning laugh, "He features the mother, eh?" At that time little Daniel had merely thought that Banks made a silly face, as the common farming men often did—laughing at what was not laughable; and he rather resented being winked at and talked of as if he did not understand everything. But now that small incident became information; it was to be reasoned on. How could he be like his mother and not like his father? His mother must have been a Mallinger, if Sir Hugo were his uncle. But no! His father might have been Sir Hugo's brother, and have changed his name, as Mr. Henleigh Mallinger did when he married Miss Grandcourt. But then, why had he never heard Sir Hugo speak of his brother Deronda, as he spoke of his brother Grandcourt? Daniel had never before cared about the family tree—only about that ancestor who had killed three Saracens in one encounter. But now his mind turned to a cabinet of estate-maps in the library, where he had once seen an illuminated parchment hanging out, that Sir Hugo said was the family tree. The phrase was new and odd to him—he was a little fellow then, hardly more than half his present age—and he gave it no precise meaning. He knew more now, and wished that he could examine that parchment. He imagined that the cabinet was always locked, and longed to try it. But here he checked himself. He might be seen; and he would never bring himself near even a silent admission of the sore that had opened in him.

It is in such experiences of boy or girlhood, while elders are debating whether most education lies in science or literature, that the main lines of character are often laid down. If Daniel had been of a less ardently affectionate nature, the reserve about himself and the supposition that others had something to his disadvantage in their minds might have turned into a hard, proud antagonism. But inborn lovingness was strong enough to keep itself level with resentment. There was hardly any creature in his habitual world that he was not fond of; teasing them occasionally, of course—all except his uncle, or "Nunc," as Sir Hugo had taught him to say; for the baronet was the reverse of a strait-laced man, and left his dignity to take care of itself. Him Daniel loved in that deeprooted filial way which makes children always the happier for being in the same room with father or mother, though their occupations may be quite apart. Sir Hugo's watch-chain and seals, his handwriting, his mode of smoking and of talking to his dogs and horses, had all a rightness and charm about them to the boy which went along with the happiness of morning and breakfast-time. That Sir Hugo had always been a Whig made Tories and Radicals equally opponents of the truest and best; and the books he had written were all seen under the same consecration of loving belief which differenced what was his from what was not his, in spite of general resemblance. Those writings were various, from volumes of travel in the brilliant style, to articles on things in general, and pamphlets on political crises; but to Daniel they were alike in having an unquestionable rightness by which other people's information could be tested.

Who cannot imagine the bitterness of a first suspicion that something in this object of complete love was *not* quite right? Children demand that their heroes should be fleckless, and easily believe them so; perhaps a first discovery to the contrary is hardly a less revolutionary shock to a passionate child than the threatened downfall of habitual beliefs which makes the world seem to totter for us in maturer life.

But some time after this renewal of Daniel's agitation it appeared that Sir Hugo must have been making a merely playful experiment in his question about the singing. He sent for Daniel into the library, and looking up from his writing as the boy entered, threw himself sideways in his armchair. "Ah, Dan!" he said kindly, drawing one of the old embroidered stools close to him. "Come and sit down here."

Daniel obeyed, and Sir Hugo put a gentle hand on his shoulder, looking at him affectionately.

"What is it, my boy? Have you heard anything that has put you out of spirits lately?"

Daniel was determined not to let the tears come, but he could not speak.

"All changes are painful when people have been happy, you know," said Sir Hugo, lifting his hand from the boy's shoulder to his dark curls and rubbing them gently. "You can't be educated exactly as I wish you to be without our parting. And I think you will find a great deal to like at school."

This was not what Daniel expected, and was so far a relief, which gave him spirit to answer:

"Am I to go to school?"

"Yes, I mean you to go to Eton. I wish you to have the education of an English gentleman; and for that it is necessary that you should go to a public school in preparation for the university: Cambridge I mean you to go to; it was my own university."

Daniel's color came and went.

"What do you say, sirrah?" said Sir Hugo, smiling.

"I should like to be a gentleman," said Daniel, with firm distinctness, "and go to school, if that is what a gentleman's son must do."

Sir Hugo watched him silently for a few moments, thinking he understood now why the lad had seemed angry at the notion of becoming a singer. Then he said tenderly:

"And so you won't mind about leaving your old Nunc?"

"Yes, I shall," said Daniel, clasping Sir Hugo's caressing arm with both his hands. "But sha'n't I come home and be with you in the holidays?"

"Oh, yes, generally," said Sir Hugo. "But now I mean you to go at once to a new tutor, to break the change for you before you go to Eton."

After this interview Daniel's spirit rose again. He was meant to be a gentleman, and in some unaccountable way it might be that his conjectures were all wrong. The very keenness of the lad taught him to find comfort in his ignorance. While he was busying his mind in the construction of possibilities, it became plain to him that there must be possibilities of which he knew nothing. He left off brooding, young joy and the spirit of adventure not being easily quenched within him, and in the interval before his going away he sang about the house, danced among the old servants, making them parting gifts, and insisted many times to the groom on the care that was to be taken of the black pony.

"Do you think I shall know much less than the other boys,

Mr. Fraser?" said Daniel. It was his bent to think that every stranger would be surprised at his ignorance.

"There are dunces to be found everywhere," said the judicious Fraser. "You'll not be the biggest; but you've not the makings of a Porson in you, or a Leibnitz either."

"I don't want to be a Porson or a Leibnitz," said Daniel. "I would rather be a greater leader, like Pericles or Washington."

"Ay, ay; you've a notion they did with little parsing, and less algebra," said Fraser. But in reality he thought his pupil a remarkable lad, to whom one thing was as easy as another if he had only a mind to it.

Things went very well with Daniel in his new world, except that a boy with whom he was at once inclined to strike up a close friendship talked to him a great deal about his home and parents, and seemed to expect a like expansiveness in return. Daniel immediately shrank into reserve, and this experience remained a check on his naturally strong bent toward the formation of intimate friendships. Every one, his tutor included, set him down as a reserved boy, though he was so good-humored and unassuming, as well as quick both at study and sport, that nobody called his reserve disagreeable. Certainly his face had a great deal to do with that favorable interpretation; but in this instance the beauty of the closed lips told no falsehood.

A surprise that came to him before his first vacation strengthened the silent consciousness of a grief within, which might be compared in some ways with Byron's susceptibility about his deformed foot. Sir Hugo wrote word that he was married to Miss Raymond, a sweet lady whom Daniel must remember having seen. The event would make no difference about his spending the vacation at the Abbey; he would find Lady Mallinger a new friend whom he would be sure to love —and much more to the usual effect when a man, having done something agreeable to himself, is disposed to congratulate others on his own good fortune, and the deducible satisfactoriness of events in general.

Let Sir Hugo be partly excused until the grounds of his action can be more fully known. The mistakes in his be-

havior to Deronda were due to that dulness toward what may
be going on in other minds, especially the minds of children,
which is among the commonest deficiencies even in good-
natured men like him, when life has been generally easy to
themselves, and their energies have been quietly spent in feeling gratified. No one was better aware than he that Daniel
was generally suspected to be his own son. But he was
pleased with that suspicion; and his imagination had never
once been troubled with the way in which the boy himself
might be affected, either then or in the future, by the enigmatic aspect of his circumstances. He was as fond of him as
could be, and meant the best by him. And considering the
lightness with which the preparation of young lives seems to
lie on respectable consciences, Sir Hugo Mallinger can hardly
be held open to exceptional reproach. He had been a bachelor till he was five-and-forty, had always been regarded as a
fascinating man of elegant tastes; what could be more natural, even according to the index of language, than that he
should have a beautiful boy like the little Deronda to take
care of? The mother might even perhaps be in the great
world—met with in Sir Hugo's residences abroad. The only
person to feel any objection was the boy himself, who could
not have been consulted. And the boy's objections had never
been dreamed of by anybody but himself.

By the time Deronda was ready to go to Cambridge, Lady
Mallinger had already three daughters—charming babies, all
three, but whose sex was announced as a melancholy alternative, the offspring desired being a son; if Sir Hugo had no
son the succession must go to his nephew Mallinger Grandcourt. Daniel no longer held a wavering opinion about his
own birth. His fuller knowledge had tended to convince him
that Sir Hugo was his father, and he conceived that the baronet, since he never approached a communication on the subject, wished him to have a tacit understanding of the fact,
and to accept in silence what would be generally considered
more than the due love and nurture. Sir Hugo's marriage
might certainly have been felt as a new ground of resentment
by some youths in Deronda's position, and the timid Lady
Mallinger with her fast-coming little ones might have been

images to scowl at, as likely to divert much that was disposable in the feelings and possessions of the baronet from one who felt his own claim to be prior. But hatred of innocent human obstacles was a form of moral stupidity not in Deronda's grain; even the indignation which had long mingled itself with his affection for Sir Hugo took the quality of pain rather than of temper; and as his mind ripened to the idea of tolerance toward error, he habitually linked the idea with his own silent grievances.

The sense of an entailed disadvantage—the deformed foot doubtfully hidden by the shoe—makes a restlessly active spiritual yeast, and easily turns a self-centred, unloving nature into an Ishmaelite. But in the rarer sort, who presently see their own frustrated claim as one among a myriad, the inexorable sorrow takes the form of fellowship and makes the imagination tender. Deronda's early wakened susceptibility, charged at first with ready indignation and resistant pride, had raised in him a premature reflection on certain questions of life; it had given a bias to his conscience, a sympathy with certain ills, and a tension of resolve in certain directions, which marked him off from other youths much more than any talents he possessed.

One day near the end of the Long Vacation, when he had been making a tour in the Rhineland with his Eton tutor, and was come for a farewell stay at the Abbey before going to Cambridge, he said to Sir Hugo:

"What do you intend me to be, sir?" They were in the library, and it was the fresh morning. Sir Hugo had called him in to read a letter from a Cambridge Don who was to be interested in him; and since the baronet wore an air at once business-like and leisurely, the moment seemed propitious for entering on a grave subject which had never yet been thoroughly discussed.

"Whatever your inclination leads you to, my boy. I thought it right to give you the option of the army, but you shut the door on that, and I was glad. I don't expect you to choose just yet—by and by, when you have looked about you a little more and tried your mettle among older men. The university has a good wide opening into the forum. There are prizes to be won, and a bit of good fortune often gives the turn to a man's taste. From what I see and hear, I should think you can take up anything you like. You are in deeper water with your classics than I ever got into, and if you are rather sick of that swimming, Cambridge is the place where you can go into mathematics with a will, and disport yourself on the dry sand as much as you like. I floundered along like a carp."

"I suppose money will make some difference, sir," said Daniel, blushing. "I shall have to keep myself by and by."

"Not exactly. I recommend you not to be extravagant— yes, yes, I know—you are not inclined to that;—but you need not take up anything against the grain. You will have a bachelor's income—enough for you to look about with. Perhaps I had better tell you that you may consider yourself secure of seven hundred a year. You might make yourself a barrister—be a writer—take up politics. I confess that is what would please me best. I should like to have you at my elbow and pulling with me."

Deronda looked embarrassed. He felt that he ought to make some sign of gratitude, but other feelings clogged his tongue. A moment was passing by in which a question about his birth was throbbing within him, and yet it seemed more impossible than ever that the question should find vent—more impossible than ever that he could hear certain things from Sir Hugo's lips. The liberal way in which he was dealt with was the more striking because the baronet had of late cared particularly for money, and for making the utmost of his life-interest in the estate by way of providing for his daughters; and as all this flashed through Daniel's mind it was momentarily within his imagination that the provision for him might come in some way from his mother. But such vaporous conjecture passed away as quickly as it came.

Sir Hugo appeared not to notice anything peculiar in Daniel's manner, and presently went on with his usual chatty liveliness.

"I am glad you have done some good reading outside your classics, and have got a grip of French and German. The truth is, unless a man can get the prestige and income of a

Don and write donnish books, it's hardly worth while for him
to make a Greek and Latin machine of himself, and be able to
spin you out pages of the Greek dramatists at any verse you'll
give him as a cue. That's all very fine, but in practical life
nobody does give you the cue for pages of Greek. In fact,
it's a nicety of conversation which I would have you attend to—
much quotation of any sort, even in English, is bad. It tends
to choke ordinary remark. One couldn't carry on life comfortably without a little blindness to the fact that everything
has been said better than we can put it ourselves. But talking
of Dons, I have seen Dons make a capital figure in society;
and occasionally he can shoot you down a cart-load of learning
in the right place, which will tell in politics. Such men are
wanted; and if you have any turn for being a Don, I say nothing against it."

"I think there's not much chance of that. Quicksett and
Puller are both stronger than I am. I hope you will not be
much disappointed if I don't come out with high honors."

"No, no. I should like you to do yourself credit, but for
God's sake don't come out as a superior expensive kind of
idiot, like young Brecon, who got a Double First, and has
been learning to knit braces ever since. What I wish you to
get is a passport in life. I don't go against our university
system; we want a little disinterested culture to make head
against cotton and capital, especially in the House. My
Greek has all evaporated; if I had to construe a verse on a
sudden, I should get an apoplectic fit. But it formed my
taste. I dare say my English is the better for it."

On this point Daniel kept a respectful silence. The enthusiastic belief in Sir Hugo's writings as a standard, and in the
Whigs as the chosen race among politicians, had gradually
vanished along with the seraphic boy's face. He had not
been the hardest of workers at Eton. Though some kinds of
study and reading came as easily as boating to him, he was
not of the material that usually makes the first-rate Eton
scholar. There had sprung up in him a meditative yearning
after wide knowledge which is likely always to abate ardor in
the fight for prize acquirement in narrow tracts. Happily he
was modest, and took any second-rateness in himself simply

as a fact, not as a marvel necessarily to be accounted for by a superiority. Still Mr. Fraser's high opinion of the lad had not been altogether belied by the youth; Daniel had the stamp of rarity in a subdued fervor of sympathy, an activity of imagination on behalf of others, which did not show itself effusively, but was continually seen in acts of considerateness that struck his companions as moral eccentricity. "Deronda would have been first-rate if he had had more ambition"—was a frequent remark about him. But how could a fellow push his way properly when he objected to swop for his own advantage, knocked under by choice when he was within an inch of victory, and, unlike the great Clive, would rather be the calf than the butcher? It was a mistake, however, to suppose that Deronda had not his share of ambition; we know he had suffered keenly from the belief that there was a tinge of dishonor in his lot; but there are some cases, and his was one of them, in which the sense of injury breeds—not the will to inflict injuries and climb over them as a ladder, but—a hatred of all injury. He had his flashes of fierceness, and could hit out upon occasion; but the occasions were not always what might have been expected. For in what related to himself his resentful impulses had been early checked by a mastering affectionateness. Love has a habit of saying "Never mind" to angry self, who, sitting down for the nonce in the lower place, by and by gets used to it. So it was that as Deronda approached manhood his feeling for Sir Hugo, while it was getting more and more mixed with criticism, was gaining in that sort of allowance which reconciles criticism with tenderness. The dear old beautiful home and everything within it, Lady Mallinger and her little ones included, were consecrated for the youth as they had been for the boy—only with a certain difference of light on the objects. The altar-piece was no longer miraculously perfect, painted under infallible guidance, but the human hand discerned in the work was appealing to a reverent tenderness safer from the gusts of discovery. Certainly Deronda's ambition, even in his springtime, lay exceptionally aloof from conspicuous, vulgar triumph, and from other ugly forms of boyish energy; perhaps because he was early impassioned by ideas, and burned his fire on those

heights. One may spend a good deal of energy in disliking
and resisting what others pursue, and a boy who is fond of
somebody else's pencil-case may not be more energetic than
another who is fond of giving his own pencil-case away. Still,
it was not Deronda's disposition to escape from ugly scenes;
he was more inclined to sit through them and take care of the
fellow least able to take care of himself. It had helped to
make him popular that he was sometimes a little compromised
by this apparent comradeship. For a meditative interest in
learning how human miseries are wrought—as precocious in
him as another sort of genius in the poet who writes a Queen
Mab at nineteen—was so infused with kindliness that it easily
passed for comradeship. Enough. In many of our neighbors'
lives there is much not only of error and lapse, but of a certain exquisite goodness which can never be written or even
spoken—only divined by each of us, according to the inward
instruction of our own privacy.

The impression he made at Cambridge corresponded to his
position at Eton. Every one interested in him agreed that he
might have taken a high place if his motives had been of a
more pushing sort, and if he had not, instead of regarding
studies as instruments of success, hampered himself with the
notion that they were to feed motive and opinion—a notion
which set him criticising methods and arguing against his
freight and harness when he should have been using all his
might to pull. In the beginning his work at the university
had a new zest for him; indifferent to the continuation of the
Eton classical drill, he applied himself vigorously to mathematics, for which he had shown an early aptitude under Mr.
Fraser, and he had the delight of feeling his strength in a
comparatively fresh exercise of thought. That delight, and
the favorable opinion of his tutor, determined him to try for
a mathematical scholarship in the Easter of his second year;
he wished to gratify Sir Hugo by some achievement, and the
study of the higher mathematics, having the growing fascination inherent in all thinking which demands intensity, was
making him a more exclusive worker than he had been before.

But here came the old check which had been growing with
his growth. He found the inward bent toward comprehen-

sion and thoroughness diverging more and more from the track marked out by the standards of examination; he felt a heightening discontent with the wearing futility and enfeebling strain of a demand for excessive retention and dexterity without any insight into the principles which form the vital connections of knowledge. (Deronda's undergraduateship occurred fifteen years ago, when the perfection of our university methods was not yet indisputable.) In hours when his dissatisfaction was strong upon him he reproached himself for having been attracted by the conventional advantage of belonging to an English university, and was tempted toward the project of asking Sir Hugo to let him quit Cambridge and pursue a more independent line of study abroad. The germs of this inclination had been already stirring in his boyish love of universal history, which made him want to be at home in foreign countries, and follow in imagination the travelling students of the middle ages. He longed now to have the sort of apprenticeship to life which would not shape him too definitely, and rob him of the choice that might come from a free growth. One sees that Deronda's demerits were likely to be on the side of reflective hesitation, and this tendency was encouraged by his position; there was no need for him to get an immediate income, or to fit himself in haste for a profession; and his sensibility to the half-known facts of his parentage made him an excuse for lingering longer than others in a state of social neutrality. Other men, he inwardly said, had a more definite place and duties. But the project which flattered his inclination might not have gone beyond the stage of ineffective brooding, if certain circumstances had not quickened it into action.

The circumstances arose out of an enthusiastic friendship which extended into his after-life. Of the same year with himself, and occupying small rooms close to his, was a youth who had come as an exhibitioner from Christ's Hospital, and had eccentricities enough for a Charles Lamb. Only to look at his pinched features and blond hair hanging over his collar reminded one of pale quaint heads by early German painters; and when this faint coloring was lit up by a joke, there came sudden creases about the mouth and eyes which might have been moulded by the soul of an aged humorist. His father, an engraver of some distinction, had been dead eleven years, and his mother had three girls to educate and maintain on a meagre annuity. Hans Meyrick—he had been daringly christened after Holbein—felt himself the pillar, or rather the knotted and twisted trunk, round which these feeble climbing plants must cling. There was no want of ability or of honest, well-meaning affection to make the prop trustworthy; the ease and quickness with which he studied might serve him to win prizes at Cambridge, as he had done among the Blue Coats, in spite of irregularities. The only danger was, that the incalculable tendencies in him might be fatally timed, and that his good intentions might be frustrated by some act which was not due to habit but to capricious, scattered impulses. He could not be said to have any one bad habit; yet at longer or shorter intervals he had fits of impish recklessness, and did things that would have made the worst habits.

Hans in his right mind, however, was a lovable creature, and in Deronda he had happened to find a friend who was likely to stand by him with the more constancy from compassion for these brief aberrations that might bring a long repentance. Hans, indeed, shared Deronda's rooms nearly as much as he used his own; to Deronda he poured himself out on his studies, his affairs, his hopes; the poverty of his home, and his love for the creatures there; the itching of his fingers to draw, and his determination to fight it away for the sake of getting some sort of plum that he might divide with his mother and the girls. He wanted no confidence in return, but seemed to take Deronda as an Olympian who needed nothing—an egotism in friendship which is common enough with mercurial, expansive natures. Deronda was content, and gave Meyrick all the interest he claimed, getting at last a brotherly anxiety about him, looking after him in his erratic moments, and contriving by adroitly delicate devices not only to make up for his friend's lack of pence, but to save him from threatening chances. Such friendship easily becomes tender; the one spreads strong sheltering wings that delight in spreading, the other gets the warm protection which is also a delight. Meyrick was going in for a classical scholarship, and his success, in various ways momentous, was the more probable from the steadying influence of Deronda's friendship.

But an imprudence of Meyrick's, committed at the beginning of the autumn term, threatened to disappoint his hopes. With his usual alternation between unnecessary expense and self-privation, he had given too much money for an old engraving which fascinated him, and, to make up for it, had come from London in a third-class carriage with his eyes exposed to a bitter wind and any irritating particles the wind might drive before it. The consequence was a severe inflammation of the eyes, which for some time hung over him the threat of a lasting injury. This crushing trouble called out all Deronda's readiness to devote himself, and he made every other occupation secondary to that of being companion and eyes to Hans, working with him and for him at his classics, that if possible his chance of the classical scholarship might be saved. Hans, to keep the knowledge of his suffering from his mother and sisters, alleged his work as a reason for passing the Christmas at Cambridge, and his friend stayed up with him.

Meanwhile Deronda relaxed his hold on his mathematics, and Hans, reflecting on this, at length said: "Old fellow, while you are hoisting me you are risking yourself. With your mathematical cram one may be like Moses or Mahomet or somebody of that sort who had to cram, and forgot in one day what it had taken him forty to learn."

Deronda would not admit that he cared about the risk, and he had really been beguiled into a little indifference by double sympathy: he was very anxious that Hans should not miss the much-needed scholarship, and he felt a revival of interest in the old studies. Still, when Hans, rather late in the day, got able to use his own eyes, Deronda had tenacity enough to try hard and recover his lost ground. He failed, however; but he had the satisfaction of seeing Meyrick win.

Success, as a sort of beginning that urged completion, might have reconciled Deronda to his university course; but the emptiness of all things, from politics to pastimes, is never so striking to us as when we fail in them. The loss of the personal triumph had no severity for him, but the sense of having spent his time ineffectively in a mode of working which had been against the grain gave him a distaste for any renewal of the process, which turned his imagined project of quitting Cambridge into a serious intention. In speaking of his intention to Meyrick he made it appear that he was glad of the turn events had taken—glad to have the balance dip decidedly, and feel freed from his hesitations; but he observed that he must of course submit to any strong objection on the part of Sir Hugo.

Meyrick's joy and gratitude were disturbed by much uneasiness. He believed in Deronda's alleged preference, but he felt keenly that in serving him Daniel had placed himself at a disadvantage in Sir Hugo's opinion, and he said mournfully: "If you had got the scholarship, Sir Hugo would have thought that you asked to leave us with a better grace. You have spoilt your luck for my sake, and I can do nothing to mend it."

"Yes, you can; you are to be a first-rate fellow. I call that a first-rate investment of my luck."

"Oh, confound it! You save an ugly mongrel from drowning, and expect him to cut a fine figure. The poets have made tragedies enough about signing one's self over to wickedness for the sake of getting something plummy; I shall write a tragedy of a fellow who signed himself over to be good, and was uncomfortable ever after."

But Hans lost no time in secretly writing the history of the affair to Sir Hugo, making it plain that but for Deronda's generous devotion he could hardly have failed to win the prize he had been working for.

The two friends went up to town together: Meyrick to rejoice with his mother and the girls in their little home at Chelsea; Deronda to carry out the less easy task of opening his mind to Sir Hugo. He relied a little on the baronet's general tolerance of eccentricities, but he expected more opposition than he met with. He was received with even warmer kindness than usual, the failure was passed over lightly, and when he detailed his reasons for wishing to quit the university and go to study abroad, Sir Hugo sat for some time in a silence which was rather meditative than surprised. At last he said, looking at Daniel with examination: "So you don't want to be an Englishman to the backbone after all?"

"I want to be an Englishman, but I want to understand other points of view. And I want to get rid of a merely English attitude in studies."

"I see; you don't want to be turned out in the same mould as every other youngster. And I have nothing to say against your doffing some of our national prejudices. I feel the better myself for having spent a good deal of my time abroad., But, for God's sake, keep an English cut, and don't become indifferent to bad tobacco. And, my dear boy, it is good to be unselfish and generous; but don't carry that too far. It will not do to give yourself to be melted down for the benefit of the tallow-trade; you must know where to find yourself. However, I shall put no veto on your going. Wait until I can get off Committee, and I'll run over with you."

So Deronda went according to his will. But not before he had spent some hours with Hans Meyrick, and been introduced to the mother and sisters in the Chelsea home. The shy girls watched and registered every look of their brother's friend, declared by Hans to have been the salvation of him, a fellow like nobody else, and, in fine, a brick. They so thoroughly accepted Deronda as an ideal, that when he was gone the youngest set to work, under the criticism of the two elder girls, to paint him as Prince Camaralzaman.

CHAPTER XVII.

" This is truth the poet sings,
That a sorrow's crown of sorrow is remembering happier things."
—TENNYSON: *Locksley Hall.*

On a fine evening near the end of July, Deronda was rowing himself on the Thames. It was already a year or more since he had come back to England, with the understanding that his education was finished, and that he was somehow to take his place in English society; but though, in deference to Sir Hugo's wish, and to fence off idleness, he had begun to read law, this apparent decision had been without other result than to deepen the roots of indecision. His old love of boating had revived with the more force now that he was in town with the Mallingers, because he could nowhere else get the same still seclusion which the river gave him. He had a boat of his own at Putney, and whenever Sir Hugo did not want him, it was his chief holiday to row till past sunset and come in again with the stars. Not that he was in a sentimental stage; but he was in another sort of contemplative mood perhaps more common in the young men of our day—that of questioning whether it were worth while to take part in the battle of the world: I mean, of course, the young men in whom the unproductive labor of questioning is sustained by three or five per cent. on capital which somebody else has battled for. It puzzled Sir Hugo that one who made a splendid contrast with all that was sickly and puling should be hampered with ideas which, since they left an accomplished Whig like himself unobstructed, could be no better than spectral illusions; especially as Deronda set himself against authorship—a vocation which is understood to turn foolish thinking into funds.

Rowing in his dark-blue shirt and skull-cap, his curls closely clipped, his mouth beset with abundant soft waves of beard, he bore only disguised traces of the seraphic boy "trailing clouds of glory." Still, even one who had never seen him since his boyhood might have looked at him with slow recognition, due perhaps to the peculiarity of the gaze which Gwendolen chose to call "dreadful," though it had really a very mild sort of scrutiny. The voice, sometimes audible in subdued snatches of song, had turned out merely a high barytone; indeed, only to look at his lithe, powerful frame and the firm gravity of his face would have been enough for an experienced guess that he had no rare and ravishing tenor such as nature reluctantly makes at some sacrifice. Look at his hands: they are not small and dimpled, with tapering fingers that seem to have only a deprecating touch; they are long, flexible, firmly grasping hands, such as Titian has painted in a picture where he wanted to show the combination of refinement with force. And there is something of a likeness, too, between the faces belonging to the hands—in both the uniform pale-brown skin, the perpendicular brow, the calmly penetrating eyes. Not seraphic any longer: thoroughly terrestrial and manly; but still of a kind to raise belief in a human dignity which can afford to acknowledge poor relations.

Such types meet us here and there among average conditions; in a workman, for example, whistling over a bit of measurement and lifting his eyes to answer our question about the road. And often the grand meanings of faces as well as of written words may lie chiefly in the impressions of those who look on them. But it is precisely such impressions that happen just now to be of importance in relation to Deronda, rowing on the Thames in a very ordinary equipment for a young Englishman at leisure, and passing under Kew Bridge with no thought of an adventure in which his appearance was likely to play any part. In fact, he objected very strongly to the notion, which others had not allowed him to escape, that his appearance was of a kind to draw attention; and hints of this, intended to be complimentary, found an angry resonance in him, coming from mingled experiences, to which a clew has already been given. His own face in the glass had during many years been associated for him with thoughts of some one whom he must be like—one about whose character and lot he continually wondered, and never dared to ask.

In the neighborhood of Kew Bridge, between six and seven o'clock, the river was no solitude. Several persons were sauntering on the towing-path, and here and there a boat was plying. Deronda had been rowing fast to get over this spot, when, becoming aware of a great barge advancing toward him, he guided his boat aside, and rested on his oar within a couple of yards of the river-brink. He was all the while unconsciously continuing the low-toned chant which had haunted his throat all the way up the river—the gondolier's song in the "Otello," where Rossini has worthily set to music the immortal words of Dante:

> "Nessun maggior dolore
> Che ricordarsi del tempo felice
> Nella miseria"; [1]

and, as he rested on his oar, the pianissimo fall of the melodic wail "nella miseria" was distinctly audible on the brink of

---

[1] Dante's words are best rendered by our own poet in the lines at the head of the chapter.

the water. Three or four persons had paused at various spots
to watch the barge passing the bridge, and doubtless included
in their notice the young gentleman in the boat; but probably
it was only to one ear that the low vocal sounds came with
more significance than if they had been an insect murmur
amidst the sum of current noises. Deronda, awaiting the
barge, now turned his head to the riverside, and saw at a
few yards' distance from him a figure which might have been
an impersonation of the misery he was unconsciously giving
voice to: a girl hardly more than eighteen, of low slim figure,
with most delicate little face, her dark curls pushed behind
her ears under a large black hat, a long woollen cloak over her
shoulders. Her hands were hanging down clasped before her,
and her eyes were fixed on the river with a look of immovable, statue-like despair. This strong arrest of his attention
made him cease singing; apparently his voice had entered her
inner world without her having taken any note of whence it
came, for when it suddenly ceased she changed her attitude
slightly, and, looking round with a frightened glance, met
Deronda's face. It was but a couple of moments, but that
seems a long while for two people to look straight at each
other. Her look was something like that of a fawn or other
gentle animal before it turns to run away: no blush, no special
alarm, but only some timidity which yet could not hinder her
from a long look before she turned. In fact, it seemed to
Deronda that she was only half conscious of her surroundings;
was she hungry, or was there some other cause of bewilder-
ment? He felt an outleap of interest and compassion toward
her; but the next instant she had turned and walked away to
a neighboring bench under a tree. He had no right to linger
and watch her; poorly dressed, melancholy women are common sights; it was only the delicate beauty, the picturesque
lines and color of the image that were exceptional, and these
conditions made it the more markedly impossible that he
should obtrude his interest upon her. He began to row away,
and was soon far up the river; but no other thoughts were
busy enough quite to expel that pale image of unhappy girlhood. He fell again and again to speculating on the probable romance that lay behind that loneliness and look of deso-

lation; then to smile at his own share in the prejudice that
interesting faces must have interesting adventures; then to
justify himself for feeling that sorrow was the more tragic
when it befell delicate, childlike beauty.

"I should not have forgotten the look of misery if she had
been ugly and vulgar," he said to himself. But there was no
denying that the attractiveness of the image made it likelier
to last. It was clear to him as an onyx cameo: the brown-
black drapery, the white face with small, small features and
dark, long-lashed eyes. His mind glanced over the girl-
tragedies that are going on in the world, hidden, unheeded,
as if they were but tragedies of the copse or hedgerow, where
the helpless drag wounded wings forsakenly, and streak the
shadowed moss with the red moment-hand of their own death.
Deronda of late, in his solitary excursions, had been occupied
chiefly with uncertainties about his own course; but those
uncertainties, being much at their leisure, were wont to have
such wide-sweeping connections with all life and history that
the new image of helpless sorrow easily blent itself with what
seemed to him the strong array of reasons why he should
shrink from getting into that routine of the world which
makes men apologize for all its wrong-doing, and takes opinions as mere professional equipment—why he should not draw
strongly at any thread in the hopelessly entangled scheme of
things.

He used his oars little, satisfied to go with the tide and be
taken back by it. It was his habit to indulge himself in that
solemn passivity which easily comes with the lengthening
shadows and mellowing light, when thinking and desiring
melt together imperceptibly, and what in other hours may
have seemed argument takes the quality of passionate vision.
By the time he had come back again with the tide past Rich-
mond Bridge the sun was near setting; and the approach of
his favorite hour—with its deepening stillness, and darkening
masses of tree and building between the double glow of the
sky and the river—disposed him to linger as if they had been
an unfinished strain of music. He looked out for a perfectly
solitary spot where he could lodge his boat against the bank,
and, throwing himself on his back with his head propped on

the cushions, could watch out the light of sunset and the opening of that bead-roll which some Oriental poet describes as God's call to the little stars, who each answer, "Here I am." He chose a spot in the bend of the river just opposite Kew Gardens, where he had a great breadth of water before him reflecting the glory of the sky, while he himself was in shadow. He lay with his hands behind his head propped on a level with the boat's edge, so that he could see all around him, but could not be seen by any one at a few yards' distance; and for a long while he never turned his eyes from the view right in front of him. He was forgetting everything else in a half-speculative, half-involuntary identification of himself with the objects he was looking at, thinking how far it might be possible habitually to shift his centre till his own personality would be no less outside him than the landscape—when the sense of something moving on the bank opposite him where it was bordered by a line of willow-bushes made him turn his glance thitherward. In the first moment he had a darting presentiment about the moving figure; and now he could see the small face with the strange dying sunlight upon it. He feared to frighten her by a sudden movement, and watched her with motionless attention. She looked round, but seemed only to gather security from the apparent solitude, hid her hat among the willows, and immediately took off her woollen cloak. Presently she seated herself and deliberately dipped the cloak in the water, holding it there a little while, then taking it out with effort, rising from her seat as she did so. By this time Deronda felt sure that she meant to wrap the wet cloak round her as a drowning-shroud; there was no longer time to hesitate about frightening her. He rose and seized his oar to ply across; happily her position lay a little below him. The poor thing, overcome with terror at this sign of discovery from the opposite bank, sank down on the brink again, holding her cloak but half out of the water. She crouched and covered her face as if she kept a faint hope that she had not been seen, and that the boatman was accidentally coming toward her. But soon he was within brief space of her, steadying his boat against the bank, and speaking, but very gently:

"Don't be afraid. . . . You are unhappy. . . . Pray, trust me. . . . Tell me what I can do to help you."

She raised her head and looked up at him. His face now was toward the light, and she knew it again. But she did not speak for a few moments, which were a renewal of their former gaze at each other. At last she said in a low sweet voice, with an accent so distinct that it suggested foreignness and yet was not foreign, "I saw you before"; . . . and then added dreamily, after a like pause, "nella miseria."

Deronda, not understanding the connection of her thought, supposed that her mind was weakened by distress and hunger.

"It was you, singing?" she went on, hesitatingly—"Nessun maggior dolore." . . . The mere words themselves uttered in her sweet undertones seemed to give the melody to Deronda's ear.

"Ah, yes," he said, understanding now, "I am often singing them. But I fear you will injure yourself staying here. Pray, let me carry you in my boat to some place of safety. And that wet cloak—let me take it."

He would not attempt to take it without her leave, dreading lest he should scare her. Even at his words he fancied that she shrank and clutched the cloak more tenaciously. But her eyes were fixed on him with a question in them as she said: "You look good. Perhaps it is God's command."

"Do trust me. Let me help you. I will die before I will let any harm come to you."

She rose from her sitting posture, first dragging the saturated cloak and then letting it fall on the ground—it was too heavy for her tired arms. Her little woman's figure as she laid her delicate chilled hands together one over the other against her waist, and went a step backward while she leaned her head forward as if not to lose her sight of his face, was unspeakably touching.

"Great God!"—the words escaped Deronda in a tone so low and solemn that they seemed like a prayer become unconsciously vocal. The agitating impression this forsaken girl was making on him stirred a fibre that lay close to his deepest interest in the fates of women—"perhaps my mother was like this one." The old thought had come now with a new im-

petus of mingled feeling, and urged that exclamation in which
both East and West have for ages concentrated their awe in
the presence of inexorable calamity.

The low-toned words seemed to have some reassurance in
them for the hearer; she stepped forward close to the boat's
side, and Deronda put out his hand, hoping now that she
would let him help her in. She had already put her tiny hand
into his which closed round it, when some new thought struck
her, and drawing back, she said:

"I have nowhere to go—nobody belonging to me in all this
land."

"I will take you to a lady who has daughters," said
Deronda, immediately. He felt a sort of relief in gathering
that the wretched home and cruel friends he imagined her to
be fleeing from were not in the near background. Still she
hesitated, and said more timidly than ever:

"Do you belong to the theatre?"

"No; I have nothing to do with the theatre," said Deronda,
in a decided tone. Then beseechingly: "I will put you in
perfect safety at once; with a lady, a good woman; I am sure
she will be kind. Let us lose no time; you will make yourself ill. Life may still become sweet to you. There are good
people—there are good women who will take care of you."

She drew backward no more, but stepped in easily, as if
she were used to such action, and sat down on the cushions.

"You had a covering for your head," said Deronda.

"My hat?" (She lifted up her hands to her head.) "It
is quite hidden in the bush."

"I will find it," said Deronda, putting out his hand deprecatingly as she attempted to rise. "The boat is fixed."

He jumped out, found the hat, and lifted up the saturated
cloak, wringing it and throwing it into the bottom of the boat.

"We must carry the cloak away, to prevent any one who
may have noticed you from thinking you have been drowned,"
he said cheerfully, as he got in again and presented the old
hat to her. "I wish I had any other garment than my coat
to offer you. But shall you mind throwing it over your shoulders while we are on the water? It is quite an ordinary thing
to do, when people return late and are not enough provided

with wraps." He held out the coat toward her with a smile, and there came a faint melancholy smile in answer, as she took it and put it on very cleverly.

"I have some biscuits—should you like them?" said Deronda.

"No; I cannot eat. I had still some money left to buy bread."

He began to ply his oar without further remark, and they went along swiftly for many minutes without speaking. She did not look at him, but was watching the oar, leaning forward in an attitude of repose, as if she were beginning to feel the comfort of returning warmth and the prospect of life instead of death. The twilight was deepening; the red flush was all gone and the little stars were giving their answer one after another. The moon was rising, but was still entangled among trees and buildings. The light was not such that he could distinctly discern the expression of her features or her glance, but they were distinctly before him nevertheless—features and a glance which seemed to have given a fuller meaning for him to the human face. Among his anxieties, one was dominant: his first impression about her, that her mind might be disordered, had not been quite dissipated; the project of suicide was unmistakable, and gave a deeper color to every other suspicious sign. He longed to begin a conversation, but abstained, wishing to encourage the confidence that might induce her to speak first. At last she did speak.

"I like to listen to the oar."

"So do I."

"If you had not come, I should have been dead now."

"I cannot bear you to speak of that. I hope you will never be sorry that I came."

"I cannot see how I shall be glad to live. The *maggior dolore* and the *miseria* have lasted longer than the *tempo felice*." She paused, and then went on dreamily: "*Dolore-miseria*— I think those words are alive."

Deronda was mute; to question her seemed an unwarrantable freedom; he shrank from appearing to claim the authority of a benefactor, or to treat her with the less reverence because she was in distress. She went on, musingly:

"I thought it was not wicked. Death and life are one before the Eternal. I know our fathers slew their children and then slew themselves, to keep their souls pure. I meant it so. But now I am commanded to live. I cannot see how I shall live."

"You will find friends. I will find them for you."

She shook her head and said mournfully: "Not my mother and brother. I cannot find them."

"You are English? You must be—speaking English so perfectly."

She did not answer immediately, but looked at Deronda again, straining to see him in the doubtful light. Until now she had been watching the oar. It seemed as if she were half roused, and wondered which part of her impressions was dreaming and which waking. Sorrowful isolation had benumbed her sense of reality, and the power of distinguishing outward and inward was continually slipping away from her. Her look was full of wondering timidity, such as the forsaken one in the desert might have lifted to the angelic vision before she knew whether his message were in anger or in pity.

"You want to know if I am English?" she said at last, while Deronda was reddening nervously under a gaze which he felt more fully than he saw.

"I want to know nothing except what you like to tell me," he said, still uneasy in the fear that her mind was wandering. "Perhaps it is not good for you to talk."

"Yes, I will tell you. I am English-born. But I am a Jewess."

Deronda was silent, inwardly wondering that he had not said this to himself before, though any one who had seen delicate-faced Spanish girls might simply have guessed her to be Spanish.

"Do you despise me for it?" she said presently in low tones, which had a sadness that pierced like a cry from a small dumb creature in fear.

"Why should I?" said Deronda. "I am not so foolish."

"I know many Jews are bad."

"So are many Christians. But I should not think it fair for you to despise me because of that."

"My mother and brother were good. But I shall never find them. I am come a long way—from abroad. I ran away; but I cannot tell you—I cannot speak of it. I thought I might find my mother again—God would guide me. But then I despaired. This morning when the light came, I felt as if one word kept sounding within me—Never! never! But now —I begin—to think——" her words were broken by rising sobs—"I am commanded to live—perhaps we are going to her."

With an outburst of weeping she buried her head on her knees. He hoped that this passionate weeping might relieve her excitement. Meanwhile he was inwardly picturing in much embarrassment how he should present himself with her in Park Lane—the course which he had at first unreflectingly determined on. No one kinder and more gentle than Lady Mallinger; but it was hardly probable that she would be at home; and he had a shuddering sense of a lackey staring at this delicate, sorrowful image of womanhood—of glaring lights and fine staircases, and perhaps chilling suspicious manners from lady's maid and housekeeper, that might scare the mind already in a state of dangerous susceptibility. But to take her to any other shelter than a home already known to him was not to be contemplated: he was full of fears about the issue of the adventure which had brought on him a responsibility all the heavier for the strong and agitating impression this childlike creature had made on him. But another resource came to mind: he could venture to take her to Mrs. Meyrick's —to the small home at Chelsea, where he had been often enough since his return from abroad to feel sure that he could appeal there to generous hearts, which had a romantic readiness to believe in innocent need and to help it. Hans Meyrick was safe away in Italy, and Deronda felt the comfort of presenting himself with his charge at a house where he would be met by a motherly figure of quakerish neatness, and three girls who hardly knew of any evil closer to them than what lay in history books and dramas, and would at once associate a lovely Jewess with Rebecca in "Ivanhoe," besides thinking that everything they did at Deronda's request would be done for their idol, Hans. The vision of the Chelsea home once raised, Deronda no longer hesitated.

The rumbling thither in the cab after the stillness of the water seemed long. Happily his charge had been quiet since her fit of weeping, and submitted like a tired child. When they were in the cab, she laid down her hat and tried to rest her head, but the jolting movement would not let it rest; still she dozed, and her sweet head hung helpless first on one side, then on the other.

"They are too good to have any fear about taking her in," thought Deronda. Her person, her voice, her exquisite utterance, were one strong appeal to belief and tenderness. Yet what had been the history which had brought her to this desolation? He was going on a strange errand—to ask shelter for this waif. Then there occurred to him the beautiful story Plutarch somewhere tells of the Delphic women; how when the Mænads, outworn with their torch-lit wanderings, lay down to sleep in the market-place, the matrons came and stood silently round them to keep guard over their slumbers; then, when they waked, ministered to them tenderly and saw them safely to their own borders. He could trust the women he was going to for having hearts as good.

Deronda felt himself growing older this evening and entering on a new phase in finding a life to which his own had come—perhaps as a rescue; but how to make sure that snatching from death was rescue? The moment of finding a fellow-creature is often as full of mingled doubt and exultation as the moment of finding an idea.

CHAPTER· XVIII.

Life is a various mother: now she dons
Her plumes and brilliants, climbs the marble stairs
With head aloft, nor ever turns her eyes
On lackeys who attend her; now she dwells
Grim-clad up darksome alleys, breathes hot gin,
And screams in pauper riot.

But to these
She came a frugal matron, neat and deft,
With cheerful morning thoughts and quick device
To find the much in little.

MRS. MEYRICK's house was not noisy; the front parlor looked on the river, and the back on gardens, so that though she was reading aloud to her daughters, the window could be left open to freshen the air of the small double room where a lamp and two candles were burning. The candles were on a table apart for Kate, who was drawing illustrations for a publisher; the lamp was not only for the reader, but for Amy and Mab, who were embroidering satin cushions for "the great world."

Outside, the house looked very narrow and shabby, the bright light through the holland blind showing the heavy old-fashioned window-frame; but it is pleasant to know that many such grim-walled slices of space in our foggy London have been, and still are, the homes of a culture the more spotlessly free from vulgarity, because poverty has rendered everything like display an impersonal question, and all the grand shows of the world simply a spectacle which rouses no petty rivalry or vain effort after possession.

The Meyricks' was a home of that kind; and they all clung to this particular house in a row because its interior was filled with objects always in the same places, which for the mother held memories of her marriage-time, and for the young ones seemed as necessary and uncriticised a part of their world as the stars of the Great Bear seen from the back windows. Mrs. Meyrick had borne much stint of other matters that she might be able to keep some engravings specially cherished by her husband; and the narrow spaces of wall held a world-history in scenes and heads which the children had early learned by heart. The chairs and tables were also old friends preferred to new. But in these two little parlors with no furniture that a broker would have cared to cheapen except the prints and piano, there was space and apparatus for a wide-glancing, nicely select life, open to the highest things in music, painting, and poetry. I am not sure that in the times of greatest scarcity, before Kate could get paid work, these ladies had always had a servant to light their fires and sweep their rooms; yet they were fastidious in some points, and could not believe that the manners of ladies in the fashionable world were so full of coarse selfishness, petty quarrelling, and slang as they are represented to be in what are called literary photographs. The Meyricks had their little oddities, streaks of eccentricity from the mother's blood as well as their father's, their minds being like mediæval houses with unexpected recesses and openings from this into that, flights of steps and sudden outlooks.

But mother and daughters were all united by a triple bond —family love; admiration for the finest work, the best action; and habitual industry. Hans's desire to spend some of his money in making their lives more luxurious had been resisted by all of them, and both they and he had been thus saved from regrets at the threatened triumph of his yearning for art over the attractions of secured income—a triumph that would by and by oblige him to give up his fellowship. They could all afford to laugh at his Gavarni-caricatures and to hold him blameless in following a natural bent which their unselfishness and independence had left without obstacle. It was enough for them to go on in their old way, only having a grand treat of opera-going (to the gallery) when Hans came home on a visit.

Seeing the group they made this evening, one could hardly wish them to change their way of life. They were all alike small, and so in due proportion with their miniature rooms. Mrs. Meyrick was reading aloud from a French book; she was a lively little woman, half French, half Scotch, with a pretty articulateness of speech that seemed to make daylight in her hearer's understanding. Though she was not yet fifty, her rippling hair, covered by a quakerish net cap, was chiefly gray, but her eyebrows were brown as the bright eyes below them; her black dress, almost like a priest's cassock with its row of buttons, suited a neat figure hardly five feet high. The daughters were to match the mother, except that Mab had Hans's light hair and complexion, with a bossy irregular brow and other quaintnesses that reminded one of him. Everything about them was compact, from the firm coils of their hair, fastened back *à la Chinoise*, to their gray skirts in puritan nonconformity with the fashion, which at that time would have demanded that four feminine circumferences should fill all the free space in the front parlor. All four, if they had been wax-work, might have been packed easily in a fashionable lady's travelling trunk. Their faces seemed full of speech, as if their minds had been shelled, after the manner of horse-chestnuts, and become brightly visible. The only large thing of its kind in the room was Hafiz, the Persian cat, comfortably poised on the brown leather back of a chair, and opening his large eyes now and then to see that the lower animals were not in any mischief.

The book Mrs. Meyrick had before her was Erckmann-Chatrian's *Histoire d'un Conscrit*. She had just finished reading it aloud, and Mab, who had let her work fall on the ground while she stretched her head forward and fixed her eyes on the reader, exclaimed:

"I think that is the finest story in the world."

"Of course, Mab!" said Amy, "it is the last you have heard. Everything that pleases you is the best in its turn."

"It is hardly to be called a story," said Kate. "It is a bit of history brought near us with a strong telescope. We can see the soldiers' faces; no, it is more than that—we can hear everything—we can almost hear their hearts beat."

"I don't care what you call it," said Mab, flirting away her thimble. "Call it a chapter in Revelations. It makes me want to do something good, something grand. It makes me so sorry for everybody. It makes me like Schiller—I want to take the world in my arms and kiss it. I must kiss you instead, little mother!" She threw her arms round her mother's neck.

"Whenever you are in that mood, Mab, down goes your work," said Amy. "It would be doing something good to finish your cushion without soiling it."

"Oh—oh—oh!" groaned Mab, as she stooped to pick up her work and thimble. "I wish I had three wounded conscripts to take care of."

"You would spill their beef-tea while you were talking," said Amy.

"Poor Mab! don't be hard on her," said the mother. "Give me the embroidery now, child. You go on with your enthusiasm, and I will go on with the pink and white poppy."

"Well, ma, I think you are more caustic than Amy," said Kate, while she drew her head back to look at her drawing.

"Oh—oh—oh!" cried Mab again, rising and stretching her arms. "I wish something wonderful would happen. I feel like the deluge. The waters of the great deep are broken up, and the windows of heaven are opened. I must sit down and play the scales."

Mab was opening the piano while the others were laughing at this climax, when a cab stopped before the house, and there forthwith came a quick rap of the knocker.

"Dear me!" said Mrs. Meyrick, starting up, "it is after ten, and Phœbe is gone to bed." She hastened out, leaving the parlor door open.

"Mr. Deronda!" The girls could hear this exclamation from their mamma. Mab clasped her hands, saying in a loud whisper, "There now! something *is* going to happen"; Kate and Amy gave up their work in amazement. But Deronda's tone in reply was so low that they could not hear his words, and Mrs. Meyrick immediately closed the parlor door.

"I know I am trusting to your goodness in a most extraordinary way," Deronda went on, after giving his brief narrative, "but you can imagine how helpless I feel with a young creature like this on my hands. I could not go with her among strangers, and in her nervous state I should dread taking her into a house full of servants. I have trusted to your mercy. I hope you will not think my act unwarrantable."

"On the contrary. You have honored me by trusting me.

I see your difficulty. Pray bring her in. I will go and prepare the girls."

While Deronda went back to the cab, Mrs. Meyrick turned into the parlor again and said: "Here is somebody to take care of instead of your wounded conscripts, Mab: a poor girl who was going to drown herself in despair. Mr. Deronda found her only just in time to save her. He brought her along in his boat, and did not know what else it would be safe to do with her, so he has trusted us and brought her here. It seems she is a Jewess, but quite refined, he says—knowing Italian and music."

The three girls, wondering and expectant, came forward and stood near each other in mute confidence that they were all feeling alike under this appeal to their compassion. Mab looked rather awe-stricken, as if this answer to her wish were something preternatural.

Meanwhile Deronda, going to the door of the cab where the pale face was now gazing out with roused observation, said: "I have brought you to some of the kindest people in the world; there are daughters like you. It is a happy home. Will you let me take you to them?"

She stepped out obediently, putting her hand in his and forgetting her hat; and when Deronda led her into the full light of the parlor where the four little women stood awaiting her, she made a picture that would have stirred much duller sensibilities than theirs. At first she was a little dazed by the sudden light, and before she had concentrated her glance he had put her hand into the mother's. He was inwardly rejoicing that the Meyricks were so small: the dark-curled head was the highest among them. The poor wanderer could not be afraid of these gentle faces so near hers; and now she was looking at each of them in turn while the mother said: "You must be weary, poor child."

"We will take care of you—we will comfort you—we will love you," cried Mab, no longer able to restrain herself, and taking the small right hand caressingly between both her own. This gentle welcoming warmth was penetrating the bewildered one; she hung back just enough to see better the four faces in front of her, whose good-will was being reflected in

hers, not in any smile, but in that undefinable change which
tells us that anxiety is passing into contentment. For an
instant she looked up at Deronda, as if she were referring all
this mercy to him, and then again turning to Mrs. Meyrick,
said with more collectedness in her sweet tones than he had
heard before:

"I am a stranger. I am a Jewess. You might have
thought I was wicked."

"No, we are sure you are good," burst out Mab.

"We think no evil of you, poor child. You shall be safe
with us," said Mrs. Meyrick. "Come now and sit down.
You must have some food, and then go to rest."

The stranger looked up again at Deronda, who said:

"You will have no more fears with these friends? You will
rest to-night?"

"Oh, I should not fear. I should rest. I think these are
the ministering angels."

Mrs. Meyrick wanted to lead her to a seat, but again hanging back gently, the poor weary thing spoke as if with a scruple at being received without a further account of herself:

"My name is Mirah Lapidoth. I am come a long way, all
the way from Prague by myself. I made my escape. I ran
away from dreadful things. I came to find my mother and
brother in London. I had been taken from my mother when
I was little, but I thought I could find her again. I had trouble—the houses were all gone—I could not find her. It has
been a long while, and I had not much money. That is why
I am in distress."

"Our mother will be good to you," cried Mab. "See what
a nice little mother she is!"

"Do sit down now," said Kate, moving a chair forward,
while Amy ran to get some tea.

Mirah resisted no longer, but seated herself with perfect
grace, crossing her little feet, laying her hands one over the
other on her lap, and looking at her friends with placid
reverence; whereupon Hafiz, who had beeen watching the
scene restlessly, came forward with tail erect and rubbed
himself against her ankles. Deronda felt it time to take his
leave.

"Will you allow me to come again and inquire—perhaps at five to-morrow?" he said to Mrs. Meyrick.

"Yes, pray; we shall have had time to make acquaintance then."

"Good-by," said Deronda, looking down at Mirah, and putting out his hand. She rose as she took it, and the moment brought back to them both strongly the other moment when she had first taken that outstretched hand. She lifted her eyes to his, and said with reverential fervor: "The God of our fathers bless you and deliver you from all evil as you have delivered me. I did not believe there was any man so good. None before have thought me worthy of the best. You found me poor and miserable, yet you have given me the best."

Deronda could not speak, but, with silent adieus to the Meyricks, hurried away.

BOOK III.—MAIDENS CHOOSING.

CHAPTER XIX.

"I pity the man who can travel from Dan to Beersheba, and say, ''Tis all barren', and so it is: and so is all the world to him who will not cultivate the fruits it offers."
—STERNE: *Sentimental Journey.*

To say that Deronda was romantic would be to misrepresent him; but under his calm and somewhat self-repressed exterior there was a fervor which made him easily find poetry and romance among the events of every-day life. And perhaps poetry and romance are as plentiful as ever in the world except for those phlegmatic natures who I suspect would in any age have regarded them as a dull form of erroneous thinking. They exist very easily in the same room with the microscope, and even in railway carriages: what banishes them is the vacuum in gentlemen and lady passengers. How should all the apparatus of heaven and earth, from the farthest firmament to the tender bosom of the mother who nourished us, make poetry for a mind that has no movements of awe and tenderness, no sense of fellowship which thrills from the near to the distant, and back again from the distant to the near?

To Deronda this event of finding Mirah was as heart-stirring as anything that befell Orestes or Rinaldo. He sat up half the night, living again through the moments since he had first discerned Mirah on the river-brink, with the fresh and fresh vividness which belongs to emotive memory. When he took up a book to try and dull this urgency of inward vision, the printed words were no more than a network through which he saw and heard everything as clearly as before—saw not only the actual events of two hours, but possibilities of what had been and what might be which those events were enough to feed with the warm blood of passionate hope and fear.

Something in his own experience caused Mirah's search after her mother to lay hold with peculiar force on his imagination. The first prompting of sympathy was to aid her in the search: if given persons were extant in London there were ways of finding them, as subtle as scientific experiment, the right machinery being set at work. But here the mixed feelings which belonged to Deronda's kindred experience naturally transfused themselves into his anxiety on behalf of Mirah.

The desire to know his own mother, or to know about her, was constantly haunted with dread; and in imagining what might befall Mirah it quickly occurred to him that finding the mother and brother from whom she had been parted when she was a little one might turn out to be a calamity. When she was in the boat she said that her mother and brother were good; but the goodness might have been chiefly in her own ignorant innocence and yearning memory, and the ten or twelve years since the parting had been time enough for much worsening. Spite of his strong tendency to side with the objects of prejudice, and in general with those who got the worst of it, his interest had never been practically drawn toward existing Jews, and the facts he knew about them, whether they walked conspicuous in fine apparel or lurked in by-streets, were chiefly of the sort most repugnant to him. Of learned and accomplished Jews he took it for granted that they had dropped their religion, and wished to be merged in the people of their native lands. Scorn flung at a Jew as such would have roused all his sympathy in griefs of inheritance; but the indiscriminate scorn of a race will often strike a specimen who has well earned it on his own account, and might fairly be gibbeted as a rascally son of Adam. It appears that the Caribs, who know little of theology, regard thieving as a practice peculiarly connected with Christian tenets, and probably they could allege experimental grounds for this opinion. Deronda could not escape (who can?) knowing ugly stories of Jewish characteristics and occupations; and though one of his favorite protests was against the severance of past and present history, he was like others who shared his protest, in never having cared to reach any more special conclusions about actual Jews than that they retained the virtues and vices of a long-oppressed race. But now that Mirah's longing roused his mind to a closer survey of details, very disagreeable images urged themselves of what it might be to find out this middle-aged Jewess and her son. To be sure, there was the exquisite refinement and charm of the creature herself to make a presumption in favor of her immediate kindred, but—he must wait to know more: perhaps through Mrs. Meyrick he might gather some guiding hints from Mirah's own lips. Her voice, her accent, her looks—all the sweet purity that clothed her as with a consecrating garment, made him shrink the more from giving her, either ideally or practically, an association with what was hateful or contaminating. But these fine words with which we fumigate and becloud unpleasant facts are not the language in which we think. Deronda's thinking went on in rapid images of what might be: he saw himself guided by some official scout into a dingy street; he entered through a dim doorway, and saw a hawk-eyed woman, rough-headed, and unwashed, cheapening a hungry girl's last bit of finery; or in some quarter only the more hideous for being smarter, he found himself under the breath of a young Jew talkative and familiar, willing to show his acquaintance with gentlemen's tastes, and not fastidious in any transactions with which they would favor him—and so on through the brief chapter of his experience in this kind. Excuse him: his mind was not apt to run spontaneously into insulting ideas, or to practise a form of wit which identifies Moses with the advertisement sheet; but he was just now governed by dread, and if Mirah's parents had been Christian, the chief difference would have been that his forebodings would have been fed with wider knowledge. It was the habit of his mind to connect dread with unknown parentage, and in this case as well as his own there was enough to make the connection reasonable.

But what was to be done with Mirah? She needed shelter and protection in the fullest sense, and all his chivalrous sentiment roused itself to insist that the sooner and the more fully he could engage for her the interest of others besides himself, the better he should fulfil her claims on him. He had no right to provide for her entirely, though he might be able to do so; the very depth of the impression she had produced made him desire that she should understand herself to be entirely independent of him; and vague visions of the future which he tried to dispel as fantastic left their influence in an anxiety stronger than any motive he could give for it, that those who saw his actions closely should be acquainted from the first with the history of his relation to Mirah. He had learned to hate secrecy about the grand ties and obligations of his life—to hate it the more because a strong spell of interwoven sensibilities hindered him from breaking such secrecy. Deronda had made a vow to himself that—since the truths which disgrace mortals are not all of their own making—the truth should never be made a disgrace to another by his act. He was not without terror lest he should break this vow, and fall into the apologetic philosophy which explains the world into containing nothing better than one's own conduct.

At one moment he resolved to tell the whole of his adventure to Sir Hugo and Lady Mallinger the next morning at breakfast, but the possibility that something quite new might reveal itself on his next visit to Mrs. Meyrick's checked this impulse, and he finally went to sleep on the conclusion that he would wait until that visit had been made.

CHAPTER XX.

"It will hardly be denied that even in this frail and corrupted world, we sometimes meet persons who, in their very mien and aspect, as well as in the whole habit of life, manifest such a signature and stamp of virtue, as to make our judgment of them a matter of intuition rather than the result of continued examination."—ALEXANDER KNOX: quoted in Southey's Life of Wesley.

MIRAH said that she had slept well that night; and when she came down in Mab's black dress, her dark hair curling in fresh fibrils as it gradually dried from its plenteous bath, she looked like one who was beginning to take comfort after the long sorrow and watching which had paled her cheek and made deep blue semicircles under her eyes. It was Mab who carried her breakfast and ushered her down—with some pride in the effect produced by a pair of tiny felt slippers which she had rushed out to buy because there were no shoes in the house small enough for Mirah, whose borrowed dress ceased about her ankles, and displayed the cheap clothing that, moulding itself on her feet, seemed an adornment as choice as the sheaths of buds. The farthing buckles were bijoux.

"Oh, if you please, mamma!" cried Mab, clasping her hands and stooping toward Mirah's feet, as she entered the parlor; "look at the slippers, how beautifully they fit! I declare she is like the queen Budoor—'two delicate feet, the work of the protecting and all-recompensing Creator, support her; and I wonder how they can sustain what is above them.'"

Mirah looked down at her own feet in a childlike way, and then smiled at Mrs. Meyrick, who was saying inwardly: "One could hardly imagine this creature having an evil thought. But wise people would tell me to be cautious." She returned Mirah's smile, and said: "I fear the feet have had to sustain their burden a little too often lately. But to-day she will rest and be my companion."

"And she will tell you so many things and I shall not hear them," grumbled Mab, who felt herself in the first volume of a delightful romance, and obliged to miss some chapters because she had to go to pupils.

Kate was already gone to make sketches along the river, and Amy was away on business errands. It was what the mother wished, to be alone with this stranger, whose story must be a sorrowful one, yet was needful to be told.

The small front parlor was as good as a temple that morning. The sunlight was on the river, and soft air came in through the open window; the walls showed a glorious silent cloud of witnesses—the Virgin soaring amid her cherubic escort; grand Melancholia with her solemn universe; the Prophets and Sibyls; the School of Athens; the Last Supper; mystic groups where far-off ages made one moment; grave Holbein and Rembrandt heads; the Tragic Muse; last-century children at their musings or their play; Italian poets— all were there through the medium of a little black and white. The neat mother who had weathered her troubles, and come out of them with a face still cheerful, was sorting colored wools for her embroidery. Hafiz purred on the window-ledge, the clock on the mantelpiece ticked without hurry, and the occasional sound of wheels seemed to lie outside the more massive central quiet. Mrs. Meyrick thought that this quiet might be the best invitation to speech on the part of her companion, and chose not to disturb it by remark. Mirah sat opposite in her former attitude, her hands clasped on her lap, her ankles crossed, her eyes at first travelling slowly over the objects around her, but finally resting with a sort of placid reverence on Mrs. Meyrick. At length she began to speak softly.

"I remember my mother's face better than anything; yet I was not seven when I was taken away, and I am nineteen now."

"I can understand that," said Mrs. Meyrick. "There are some earliest things that last the longest."

"Oh, yes, it was the earliest. I think my life began with waking up and loving my mother's face: it was so near to me, and her arms were round me, and she sang to me. One hymn she sang so often, so often: and then she taught me to sing it with her: it was the first I ever sang. They were always Hebrew hymns she sang; and because I never knew the meaning of the words, they seemed full of nothing but our love and happiness. When I lay in my little bed and it was all white above me, she used to bend over me between me and the white, and sing in a sweet low voice. I can dream myself back into that time when I am awake, and often it comes back to me in my sleep—my hand is very little, I put it up to her face and she kisses it. Sometimes in my dream I begin to tremble and think that we are both dead; but then I wake up and my hand lies like this, and for a moment I hardly know myself. But if I could see my mother again, I should know her."

"You must expect some change after twelve years," said Mrs. Meyrick, gently. "See my gray hair: ten years ago it was bright brown. The days and the months pace over us like restless little birds, and leave the marks of their feet backward and forward; especially when they are like birds with heavy hearts—then they tread heavily."

"Ah, I am sure her heart has been heavy for want of me. But to feel her joy if we could meet again, and I could make her know how I love her and give her deep comfort after all her mourning! If that could be, I should mind nothing; I should be glad that I have lived through my trouble. I did despair. The world seemed miserable and wicked; none helped me so that I could bear their looks and words; I felt that my mother was dead, and death was the only way to her. But then in the last moment—yesterday, when I longed for the water to close over me—and I thought that death was the best image of mercy—then goodness came to me living, and I felt trust in the living. And—it is strange—but I began to hope that she was living too. And now I am with you—here —this morning, peace and hope have come into me like a flood. I want nothing; I can wait; because I hope and believe and am grateful—oh, so grateful! You have not thought evil of me—you have not despised me."

Mirah spoke with low-toned fervor, and sat as still as a picture all the while.

"Many others would have felt as we do, my dear," said Mrs. Meyrick, feeling a mist come over her eyes as she looked at her work.

"But I did not meet them—they did not come to me."

"How was it that you were taken from your mother?"

"Ah, I am a long while coming to that. It is dreadful to speak of, yet I must tell you—I must tell you everything. My father—it was he who took me away. I thought we were only going on a little journey; and I was pleased. There was a box with all my little things in. But we went on board a ship, and got farther and farther away from the land. Then I was ill; and I thought it would never end—it was the first misery, and it seemed endless. But at last we landed. I knew nothing then, and believed what my father said. He comforted me, and told me I should go back to my mother. But it was America we had reached, and it was long years before we came back to Europe. At first I often asked my father when we were going back; and I tried to learn writing fast, because I wanted to write to my mother; but one day when he found me trying to write a letter, he took me on his knee and told me that my mother and brother were dead; that was why we did not go back. I remember my brother a lit-

tle; he carried me once; but he was not always at home. I
believed my father when he said that they were dead. I saw
them under the earth when he said they were there, with
their eyes forever closed. I never thought of its not being
true; and I used to cry every night in my bed for a long while.
Then when she came so often to me, in my sleep, I thought
she must be living about me, though I could not always see
her, and that comforted me. I was never afraid in the dark,
because of that; and very often in the day I used to shut my
eyes and bury my face, and try to see her and to hear her singing. I came to do that at last without shutting my eyes."

Mirah paused with a sweet content in her face, as if she
were having her happy vision, while she looked out toward
the river.

"Still your father was not unkind to you, I hope," said
Mrs. Meyrick, after a minute, anxious to recall her.

"No; he petted me, and took pains to teach me. He was
an actor; and I found out, after, that the 'Coburg' I used to
hear of his going to at home was a theatre. But he had more
to do with the theatre than acting. He had not always been
an actor; he had been a teacher, and knew many languages.
His acting was not very good, I think; but he managed the
stage, and wrote and translated plays. An Italian lady, a
singer, lived with us a long time. They both taught me; and
I had a master besides, who made me learn by heart and recite.
I worked quite hard, though I was so little; and I was not
nine when I first went on the stage. I could easily learn
things, and I was not afraid. But then and ever since I hated
our way of life. My father had money, and we had finery
about us in a disorderly way; always there were men and
women coming and going, there was loud laughing and dis-
puting, strutting, snapping of fingers, jeering, faces I did not
like to look at—though many petted and caressed me. But
then I remembered my mother. Even at first when I understood nothing, I shrank away from all those things outside me
into companionship with thoughts that were not like them;
and I gathered thoughts very fast because I read many things
—plays and poetry, Shakespeare and Schiller, and learned evil
and good. My father began to believe that I might be a great

singer: my voice was considered wonderful for a child; and he had the best teaching for me. But it was painful that he boasted of me, and set me to sing for show at any minute, as if I had been a musical box. Once when I was nine years old, I played the part of a little girl who had been forsaken and did not know it, and sat singing to herself while she played with flowers. I did it without any trouble; but the clapping and all the sounds of the theatre were hateful to me; and I never liked the praise I had, because it seemed all very hard and unloving: I missed the love and the trust I had been born into. I made a life in my own thoughts quite different from everything about me: I chose what seemed to me beautiful out of the plays and everything, and made my world out of it; and it was like a sharp knife always grazing me that we had two sorts of life which jarred so with each other—women looking good and gentle on the stage, and saying good things as if they felt them, and directly after I saw them with coarse, ugly manners. My father sometimes noticed my shrinking ways; and Signora said one day when I had been rehearsing: "She will never be an artist: she has no notion of being anybody but herself. That does very well now, but by and by you will see—she will have no more face and action than a singing-bird." My father was angry, and they quarrelled. I sat alone and cried, because what she had said was like a long unhappy future unrolled before me. I did not want to be an artist; but this was what my father expected of me. After a while Signora left us, and a governess used to come and give me lessons in different things, because my father began to be afraid of my singing too much; but I still acted from time to time. Rebellious feelings grew stronger in me, and I wished to get away from this life; but I could not tell where to go, and I dreaded the world. Besides, I felt it would be wrong to leave my father: I dreaded doing wrong, for I thought I might get wicked and hateful to myself, in the same way that many others seemed hateful to me. For so long, so long I had never felt my outside world happy; and if I got wicked I should lose my world of happy thoughts where my mother lived with me. That was my childish notion all through those years. Oh, how long they were!"

Mirah fell to musing again.

"Had you no teaching about what was your duty?" said Mrs. Meyrick. She did not like to say "religion"—finding herself on inspection rather dim as to what the Hebrew religion might have turned into at this date.

"No—only that I ought to do what my father wished. He did not follow our religion at New York, and I think he wanted me not to know much about it. But because my mother used to take me to the synagogue, and I remembered sitting on her knee and looking through the railing and hearing the chanting and singing, I longed to go. One day when I was quite small I slipped out and tried to find the synagogue, but I lost myself a long while till a pedler questioned me and took me home. My father, missing me, had been in much fear, and was very angry. I too had been so frightened at losing myself that it was long before I thought of venturing out again. But after Signora left us we went to rooms where our landlady was a Jewess and observed her religion. I asked her to take me with her to the synagogue; and I read in her prayer-books and Bible, and when I had money enough I asked her to buy me books of my own, for these books seemed a closer companionship with my mother: I knew that she must have looked at the very words and said them. In that way I have come to know a little of our religion, and the history of our people, besides piecing together what I read in plays and other books about Jews and Jewesses; because I was sure that my mother obeyed her religion. I had left off asking my father about her. It is very dreadful to say it, but I began to disbelieve him. I had found that he did not always tell the truth, and made promises without meaning to keep them; and that raised my suspicion that my mother and brother were still alive, though he had told me that they were dead. For in going over the past again and again as I got older and knew more, I felt sure that my mother had been deceived, and had expected to see us back again after a very little while; and my father taking me on his knee and telling me that my mother and brother were both dead seemed to me now nothing but a bit of acting, to set my mind at rest. The cruelty of that falsehood sank into me, and hated all untruth because of it.

I wrote to my mother secretly: I knew the street, Colman Street, where we lived, and that it was near Blackfriars Bridge and the Coburg, and that our name was Cohen then, though my father called us Lapidoth, because, he said, it was a name of his forefathers in Poland. I sent my letter secretly; but no answer came, and I thought there was no hope for me. Our life in America did not last much longer. My father suddenly told me we were to pack up and go to Hamburg, and I was rather glad. I hoped we might get among a different sort of people, and I knew German quite well—some German plays almost all by heart. My father spoke it better than he spoke English. I was thirteen then, and I seemed to myself quite old—I knew so much, and yet so little. I think other children cannot feel as I did. I had often wished that I had been drowned when I was going away from my mother. But I set myself to obey and suffer; what else could I do? One day when we were on our voyage, a new thought came into my mind. I was not very ill that time, and I kept on deck a good deal. My father acted and sang and joked to amuse people on board, and I used often to overhear remarks about him. One day, when I was looking at the sea and nobody took notice of me, I overheard a gentleman say: ' Oh, he is one of those clever Jews—a rascal, I shouldn't wonder. There's no race like them for cunning in the men and beauty in the women. I wonder what market he means that daughter for.' When I heard this it darted into my mind that the unhappiness in my life came from my being a Jewess, and that always to the end the world would think slightly of me, and that I must bear it, for I should be judged by that name; and it comforted me to believe that my suffering was part of the affliction of my people, my part in the long song of mourning that has been going on through ages and ages. For if many of our race were wicked and made merry in their wickedness—what was that but part of the affliction borne by the just among them, who were despised for the sins of their brethren? —But you have not rejected me."

Mirah had changed her tone in this last sentence, having suddenly reflected that at this moment she had reason not for complaint, but for gratitude.

"And we will try to save you from being judged unjustly by others, my poor child," said Mrs. Meyrick, who had now given up all attempt at going on with her work, and sat listening with folded hands and a face hardly less eager than Mab's would have been. "Go on, go on: tell me all."

"After that we lived in different towns—Hamburg and Vienna the longest. I began to study singing again, and my father always got money about the theatres. I think he brought a good deal of money from America: I never knew why we left. For some time he was in great spirits about my singing, and he made me rehearse parts and act continually. He looked forward to my coming out in the opera. But by and by it seemed that my voice would never be strong enough —it did not fulfil its promise. My master at Vienna said: 'Don't strain it further: it will never do for the public:—it is gold, but a thread of gold dust.' My father was bitterly disappointed; we were not so well off at that time. I think I have not quite told you what I felt about my father. I knew he was fond of me and meant to indulge me, and that made me afraid of hurting him; but he always mistook what would please me and give me happiness. It was his nature to take everything lightly; and I soon left off asking him any question about things that I cared for much, because he always turned them off with a joke. He would even ridicule our own people; and once when he had been imitating their movements and their tones in praying, only to make others laugh, I could not restrain myself—for I always had an anger in my heart about my mother—and when we were alone I said: 'Father, you ought not to mimic our own people before Christians who mock them: would it not be bad if I mimicked you, that they might mock you?' But he only shrugged his shoulders and laughed, and pinched my chin, and said, 'You couldn't do it, my dear.' It was this way of turning off everything that made a great wall between me and my father, and whatever I felt most I took the most care to hide from him. For there were some things—when they were laughed at I could not bear it: the world seemed like a hell to me. Is this world and all the life upon it only like a farce or a vaudeville, where you find no great meanings? Why, then, are there tragedies and grand operas, where men do difficult things and choose to suffer? I think it is silly to speak of all things as a joke. And I saw that his wishing me to sing the greatest music and parts in grand operas was only wishing for what would fetch the greatest price. That hemmed in my gratitude for his affectionateness, and the tenderest feeling I had toward him was pity. Yes, I did sometimes pity him. He had aged and changed. Now he was no longer so lively. I thought he seemed worse—less good to others and to me. Every now and then in the latter years his gayety went away suddenly, and he would sit at home silent and gloomy; or he would come in and fling himself down and sob, just as I have done myself when I have been in trouble. If I put my hand on his knee and said, 'What is the matter, father?' he would make no answer, but would draw my arm round his neck and put his arm round me and go on crying. There never came any confidence between us; but, oh, I was sorry for him. At those moments I knew he must feel his life bitter, and I pressed my cheek against his head and prayed. Those moments were what most bound me to him; and I used to think how much my mother once loved him, else she would not have married him.

"But soon there came the dreadful time. We had been at Pesth and we came back to Vienna. In spite of what my master Leo had said, my father got me an engagement, not at the opera, but to take singing parts at a suburb theatre in Vienna. He had nothing to do with the theatre then; I did not understand what he did, but I think he was continually at a gambling-house, though he was careful always about taking me to the theatre. I was very miserable. The plays I acted in were detestable to me. Men came about us and wanted to talk to me: women and men seemed to look at me with a sneering smile: it was no better than a fiery furnace. Perhaps I make it worse than it was—you don't know that life; but the glare and the faces and my having to go on and act and sing what I hated, and then see people who came to stare at me behind the scenes—it was all so much worse than when I was a little girl. I went through with it; I did it; I had set my mind to obey my father and work, for I saw nothing better that I could do. But I felt that my voice wa getting weaker, and I knew that my acting was not good except when it was not really acting, but the part was one that I could be myself in, and some feeling within me carried me along. That was seldom.

"Then in the midst of all this, the news came to me one morning that my father had been taken to prison, and he had sent for me. He did not tell me the reason why he was there, but he ordered me to go to an address he gave me, to see a Count who would be able to get him released. The address was to some public rooms where I was to ask for the Count, and beg him to come to my father. I found him, and recognized him as a gentleman whom I had seen the other night for the first time behind the scenes. That agitated me, for I remembered his way of looking at me and kissing my hand—I thought it was in mockery. But I delivered my errand and he promised to go immediately to my father, who came home again that very evening, bringing the Count with him. I now began to feel a horrible dread of this man, for he worried me with his attentions, his eyes were always on me: I felt sure that whatever else there might be in his mind toward me, below it all there was scorn for the Jewess and the actress. And when he came to me the next day in the theatre and would put my shawl round me, a terror took hold of me; I saw that my father wanted me to look pleased. The Count was neither very young nor very old: his hair and eyes were pale; he was tall and walked heavily, and his face was heavy and grave except when he looked at me. He smiled at me, and his smile went through me with horror: I could not tell why he was so much worse to me than other men. Some feelings are like our hearing: they come as sounds do, before we know their reason. My father talked to me about him when we were alone, and praised him—said what a good friend he had been. I said nothing, because I supposed he had got my father out of prison. When the Count came again, my father left the room. He asked me if I liked being on the stage. I said No, I only acted in obedience to my father. He always spoke French, and called me ' *petit ange* ' and such things, which I felt insulting. I knew he meant to make love to me,

and I had it firmly in my mind that a nobleman and one who
was not a Jew could have no love for me that was not half
contempt. But then he told me that I need not act any longer; he wished me to visit him at his beautiful place, where I
might be queen of everything. It was difficult to me to speak,
I felt so shaken with anger: I could only say, ' I would rather
stay on the stage forever,' and I left him there. Hurrying
out of the room, I saw my father sauntering in the passage.
My heart was crushed. I went past him and locked myself
up. It had sunk into me that my father was in a conspiracy
with that man against me. But the next day he persuaded
me to come out: he said that I had mistaken everything, and
he would explain: if I did not come out and act and fulfil my
engagement, we should be ruined and he must starve. So I
went on acting, and for a week or more the Count never came
near me. My father changed our lodgings, and kept at home
except when he went to the theatre with me. He began one
day to speak discouragingly of my acting, and say, I could
never go on singing in public—I should lose my voice—I ought
to think of my future, and not put my nonsensical feelings
between me and my fortune. He said: ' What will you do?
You will be brought down to sing and beg at people's doors.
You have had a splendid offer and ought to accept it.' I
could not speak: a horror took possession of me when I
thought of my mother and of him. I felt for the first time
that I should not do wrong to leave him. But the next day
he told me that he had put an end to my engagement at the
theatre, and that we were to go to Prague. I was getting
suspicious of everything, and my will was hardening to act
against him. It took us two days to pack and get ready; and
I had it in my mind that I might be obliged to run away from
my father, and then I would come to London and try if it were
possible to find my mother. I had a little money, and I sold
some things to get more. I packed a few clothes in a little
bag that I could carry with me, and I kept my mind on the
watch. My father's silence—his letting drop that subject of
the Count's offer—made me feel sure that there was a plan
against me. I felt as if it had been a plan to take me to a
madhouse. I once saw a picture of a madhouse, that I could

never forget; it seemed to me very much like some of the life I had seen—the people strutting, quarrelling, leering—the faces with cunning and malice in them. It was my will to keep myself from wickedness; and I prayed for help. I had seen what despised women were: and my heart turned against my father, for I saw always behind him that man who made me shudder. You will think I had not enough reason for my suspicions, and perhaps I had not, outside my own feeling; but it seemed to me that my mind had been lit up, and all that might be stood out clear and sharp. If I slept, it was only to see the same sort of things, and I could hardly sleep at all. Through our journey I was everywhere on the watch. I don't know why, but it came before me like a real event, that my father would suddenly leave me and I should find myself with the Count where I could not get away from him. I thought God was warning me: my mother's voice was in my soul. It was dark when we reached Prague, and though the strange bunches of lamps were lit, it was difficult to distinguish faces as we drove along the street. My father chose to sit outside—he was always smoking now—and I watched everything in spite of the darkness. I do believe I could see better then than ever I did before: the strange clearness within seemed to have got outside me. It was not my habit to notice faces and figures much in the street; but this night I saw every one; and when we passed before a great hotel I caught sight only of a back that was passing in—the light of the great bunch of lamps a good way off fell on it. I knew it—before the face was turned, as it fell into shadow, I knew who it was. Help came to me. I feel sure help came to me. I did not sleep that night. I put on my plainest things—the cloak and hat I have worn ever since; and I sat watching for the light and the sound of the doors being unbarred. Some one rose early—at four o'clock, to go to the railway. That gave me courage. I slipped out with my little bag under my cloak, and none noticed me. I had been a long while attending to the railway guide that I might learn the way to England; and before the sun had risen I was in the train for Dresden. Then I cried for joy. I did not know whether my money would last out, but I trusted. I could sell the things in my bag and the little rings in my ears, and I could live on bread only. My only terror was lest my father should follow me. But I never paused. I came on, and on, and on, only eating bread now and then. When I got to Brussels, I saw that I should not have enough money, and I sold all that I could sell; but here a strange thing happened. Putting my hand into the pocket of my cloak, I found a half-napoleon. Wondering and wondering how it came there, I remembered that on the way from Cologne there was a young workman sitting against me. I was frightened at every one, and did not like to be spoken to. At first he tried to talk, but when he saw that I did not like it, he left off. It was a long journey; I ate nothing but a bit of bread, and he once offered me some of the food he brought in, but I refused it. I do believe it was he who put that bit of gold in my pocket. Without it I could hardly have got to Dover, and I did walk a good deal of the way from Dover to London. I knew I should look like a miserable beggar-girl. I wanted not to look very miserable, because if I found my mother it would grieve her to see me so. But, oh, how vain my hope was that she would be there to see me come! As soon as I set foot in London, I began to ask for Lambeth and Blackfriars Bridge, but they were a long way off, and I went wrong. At last I got to Blackfriars Bridge and asked for Colman Street. People shook their heads. None knew it. I saw it in my mind—our doorsteps, and the white tiles hung in the windows, and the large brick building opposite with wide doors. But there was nothing like it. At last when I asked a tradesman where the Coburg Theatre and Colman Street were, he said: 'Oh, my little woman, that's all done away with. The old streets have been pulled down; everything is new.' I turned away, and felt as if death had laid a hand on me. He said: 'Stop, stop! young woman; what is it you're wanting with Colman Street, eh?' meaning well, perhaps. But his tone was what I could not bear; and how could I tell him what I wanted? I felt blinded and bewildered with a sudden shock. I suddenly felt that I was very weak and weary, and yet where could I go? for I looked so poor and dusty, and had nothing with me—I looked like a street-beggar. And I was afraid of all places where I could enter. I lost my trust. I thought I was forsaken. It seemed that I had been in a fever of hope—delirious—all the way from Prague: I thought that I was helped, and I did nothing but strain my mind forward and think of finding my mother; and now— there I stood in a strange world. All who saw me would think ill of me, and I must herd with beggars. I stood on the bridge and looked along the river. People were going on to a steamboat. Many of them seemed poor, and I felt as if it would be a refuge to get away from the streets: perhaps the boat would take me where I could soon get into a solitude. I had still some pence left, and I bought a loaf when I went on the boat. I wanted to have a little time and strength to think of life and death. How could I live? And now again it seemed that if ever I were to find my mother again, death was the way to her. I ate, that I might have strength to think. The boat set me down at a place along the river—I don't know where—and it was late in the evening. I found some large trees apart from the road, and I sat down under them that I might rest through the night. Sleep must have soon come to me, and when I awoke it was morning. The birds were singing, the dew was white about me, I felt chill and oh so lonely! I got up and walked and followed the river a long way, and then turned back again. There was no reason why I should go anywhere. The world about me seemed like a vision that was hurrying by while I stood still with my pain. My thoughts were stronger than I was: they rushed in and forced me to see all my life from the beginning; ever since I was carried away from my mother I had felt myself a lost child taken up and used by strangers, who did not care what my life was to me, but only what I could do for them. It seemed all a weary wandering and heart-loneliness—as if I had been forced to go to merry-makings without the expectation of joy. And now it was worse. I was lost again, and I dreaded lest any stranger should notice me and speak to me. I had a terror of the world. None knew me; all would mistake me. I had seen so many in my life who made themselves glad with scorning, and laughed at another's shame. What could I do? This life seemed to be closing in upon me with a wall of fire— everywhere there was scorching that made me shrink. The

high sunlight made me shrink. And I began to think that
my despair was the voice of God telling me to die. But it
would take me long to die of hunger. Then I thought of my
People, how they had been driven from land to land and been
afflicted, and multitudes had died of misery in their wandering
—was I the first? And in the wars and troubles when Christians were cruelest, our fathers had sometimes slain their children and afterward themselves; it was to save them from being
false apostates. That seemed to make it right for me to put
an end to my life; for calamity had closed me in, too, and I
saw no pathway but to evil. But my mind got into war with
itself, for there were contrary things in it. I knew that some
had held it wrong to hasten their own death, though they were
in the midst of flames: and while I had some strength left it
was a longing to bear if I ought to bear—else where was the
good of all my life? It had not been happy since the first
years: when the light came every morning I used to think, ' I
will bear it.' But always before I had some hope; now it
was gone. With these thoughts I wandered and wandered,
inwardly crying to the Most High, from whom I should not flee
in death more than in life—though I had no strong faith that
He cared for me. The strength seemed departing from my
soul: deep below all my cries was the feeling that I was alone
and forsaken. The more I thought the wearier I got, till it
seemed I was not thinking at all, but only the sky and the
river and the Eternal God were in my soul. And what was it
whether I died or lived? If I lay down to die in the river,
was it more than lying down to sleep?—for there, too, I committed my soul—I gave myself up. I could not hear memories any more: I could only feel what was present in me—
it was all one longing to cease from my weary life, which
seemed only a pain outside the great peace that I might
enter into. That was how it was. When the evening
came and the sun was gone, it seemed as if that was all I
had to wait for. And a new strength came into me to will
what I would do. You know what I did. I was going to
die. You know what happened—did he not tell you? Faith
came to me again: I was not forsaken. He told you how
he found me? "

Mrs. Meyrick gave no audible answer, but pressed her lips against Mirah's forehead.

"She's just a pearl: the mud has only washed her," was the fervid little woman's closing commentary when, *tête-à-tête* with Deronda in the back parlor that evening, she had conveyed Mirah's story to him with much vividness.

"What is your feeling about a search for this mother?" said Deronda. "Have you no fears? I have, I confess."

"Oh, I believe the mother's good," said Mrs. Meyrick, with rapid decisiveness; "or *was* good. She may be dead—that's my fear. A good woman, you may depend: you may know it by the scoundrel the father is. Where did the child get her goodness from? Wheaten flour has to be accounted for."

Deronda was rather disappointed at this answer: he had wanted a confirmation of his own judgment, and he began to put in demurrers. The argument about the mother would not apply to the brother; and Mrs. Meyrick admitted that the brother might be an ugly likeness of the father. Then, as to advertising, if the name was Cohen, you might as well advertise for two undescribed terriers: and here Mrs. Meyrick helped him, for the idea of an advertisement, already mentioned to Mirah, had roused the poor child's terror: she was convinced that her father would see it—he saw everything in the papers. Certainly there were safer means than advertising: men might be set to work whose business it was to find missing persons; but Deronda wished Mrs. Meyrick to feel with him that it would be wiser to wait, before seeking a dubious, perhaps a deplorable, result; especially as he was engaged to go abroad the next week for a couple of months. If a search were made, he would like to be at hand, so that Mrs. Meyrick might not be unaided in meeting any consequences—supposing that she would generously continue to watch over Mirah.

"We should be very jealous of any one who took the task from us," said Mrs. Meyrick. "She will stay under my roof: there is Hans's old room for her."

"Will she be content to wait?" said Deronda, anxiously.

"No trouble there. It is not her nature to run into plan-
ning and devising: only to submit. See how she submitted
to that father! It was a wonder to herself how she found the
will and contrivance to run away from him. About finding
her mother, her only notion now is to trust: since you were
sent to save her and we are good to her, she trusts that her
mother will be found in the same unsought way. And when
she is talking I catch her feeling like a child."

Mrs. Meyrick hoped that the sum Deronda put into her
hands as a provision for Mirah's wants was more than would
be needed: after a little while Mirah would perhaps like to
occupy herself as the other girls did, and make herself independent. Deronda pleaded that she must need a long rest.

"Oh, yes; we will hurry nothing," said Mrs. Meyrick.
"Rely upon it, she shall be taken tender care of. If you like
to give me your address abroad, I will write to let you know
how we get on. It is not fair that we should have all the
pleasure of her salvation to ourselves. And, besides, I want
to make believe that I am doing something for you as well as
for Mirah."

"That is no make-believe. What should I have done without you last night? Everything would have gone wrong. I
shall tell Hans that the best of having him for a friend is,
knowing his mother."

After that they joined the girls in the other room, where
Mirah was seated placidly, while the others were telling her
what they knew about Mr. Deronda—his goodness to Hans,
and all the virtues that Hans had reported of him.

"Kate burns a pastille before his portrait every day," said
Mab. "And I carry his signature in a little black silk bag
round my neck to keep off the cramp. And Amy says the
multiplication-table in his name. We must all do something
extra in honor of him, now he has brought you to us."

"I suppose he is too great a person to want anything," said
Mirah, smiling at Mab, and appealing to the graver Amy.
"He is perhaps very high in the world?"

"He is very much above us in rank," said Amy. "He is
related to grand people. I dare say he leans on some of the
satin cushions we prick our fingers over."

"I am glad he is of high rank," said Mirah, with her usual quietness.

"Now, why are you glad of that?" said Amy, rather suspicious of this sentiment, and on the watch for Jewish peculiarities which had not appeared.

"Because I have always disliked men of high rank before."

"Oh, Mr. Deronda is not so very high," said Kate. "He need not hinder us from thinking ill of the whole peerage and baronetage if we like."

When he entered, Mirah arose with the same look of grateful reverence that she had lifted to him the evening before: impossible to see a creature freer at once from embarrassment and boldness. Her theatrical training had left no recognizable trace; probably her manners had not much changed since she played the forsaken child at nine years of age; and she had grown up in her simplicity and truthfulness like a little flower-seed that absorbs the chance confusion of its surroundings into its own definite mould of beauty. Deronda felt that he was making acquaintance with something quite new to him in the form of womanhood. For Mirah was not childlike from ignorance: her experience of evil and trouble was deeper and stranger than his own. He felt inclined to watch her and listen to her as if she had come from a far-off shore inhabited by a race different from our own.

But for that very reason he made his visit brief: with his usual activity of imagination as to how his conduct might affect others, he shrank from what might seem like curiosity, or the assumption of a right to know as much as he pleased of one to whom he had done a service. For example, he would have liked to hear her sing, but he would have felt the expression of such a wish to be a rudeness in him—since she could not refuse, and he would all the while have a sense that she was being treated like one whose accomplishments were to be ready on demand. And whatever reverence could be shown to woman, he was bent on showing to this girl. Why? He gave himself several good reasons; but whatever one does with a strong unhesitating outflow of will has a store of motive that it would be hard to put into words. Some deeds seem

little more than interjections which give vent to the long passion of a life.

So Deronda soon took his farewell for the two months during which he expected to be absent from London, and in a few
days he was on his way with Sir Hugo and Lady Mallinger to
Leubronn.

He had fulfilled his intention of telling them about Mirah.
The baronet was decidedly of opinion that the search for the
mother and brother had better be let alone. Lady Mallinger
was much interested in the poor girl, observing that there was
a Society for the Conversion of the Jews, and that it was to
be hoped Mirah would embrace Christianity; but perceiving
that Sir Hugo looked at her with amusement, she concluded
that she had said something foolish. Lady Mallinger felt
apologetically about herself as a woman who had produced
nothing but daughters in a case where sons were required, and
hence regarded the apparent contradictions of the world as
probably due to the weakness of her own understanding. But
when she was much puzzled, it was her habit to say to herself, "I will ask Daniel." Deronda was altogether a convenience in the family; and Sir Hugo, too, after intending to do
the best for him, had begun to feel that the pleasantest result
would be to have this substitute for a son always ready at his
elbow.

This was the history of Deronda, so far as he knew it, up
to the time of that visit to Leubronn in which he saw Gwendolen Harleth at the gaming-table.

CHAPTER XXI.

It is a common sentence that Knowledge is power; but who hath duly considered or set forth the power of Ignorance? Knowledge slowly builds up what Ignorance in an hour pulls down. Knowledge, through patient and frugal centuries, enlarges discovery and makes record of it; Ignorance, wanting its day's dinner, lights a fire with the record, and gives a flavor to its one roast with the burnt souls of many generations. Knowledge, instructing the sense, refining and multiplying needs, transforms itself into skill and makes life various with a new six days' work; comes Ignorance drunk on the seventh, with a firkin of oil and a match and an easy "Let there not be" — and the many-colored creation is shrivelled up in blackness. Of a truth, Knowledge is power, but it is a power reined by scruple, having a conscience of what must be and what may be; whereas Ignorance is a blind giant who, let him but wax unbound, would make it a sport to seize the pillars that hold up the long-wrought fabric of human good, and turn all the places of joy dark as a buried Babylon. And looking at life parcel-wise, in the growth of a single lot, who having a practised vision may not see that ignorance of the true bond between events, and false conceit of means whereby sequences may be compelled — like that falsity of eyesight which overlooks the gradations of distance, seeing that which is afar off as if it were within a step or a grasp — precipitates the mistaken soul on destruction?

It was half-past ten in the morning when Gwendolen Harleth, after her gloomy journey from Leubronn, arrived at the station from which she must drive to Offendene. No carriage or friend was awaiting her, for in the telegram she had sent from Dover she had mentioned a later train, and in her impatience of lingering at a London station she had set off without picturing what it would be to arrive unannounced at half an hour's drive from home—at one of those stations which have been fixed on not as near anywhere, but as equidistant from everywhere. Deposited as a *feme sole* with her large trunks, and having to wait while a vehicle was being got from the large-sized lantern called the Railway Inn, Gwendolen felt that the dirty paint in the waiting-room, the dusty decanter of flat water, and the texts in large letters calling on her to repent and be converted, were part of the dreary prospect opened by her family troubles; and she hurried away to the outer door looking toward the lane and fields. But here the very gleams of sunshine seemed melancholy, for the autumnal leaves and grass were shivering, and the wind was turning up the feathers of a cock and two croaking hens which had doubtless parted with their grown-up offspring and did not know what to do with themselves. The railway official also seemed without resources, and his innocent demeanor in observing

Gwendolen and her trunks was rendered intolerable by the
cast in his eye; especially since, being a new man, he did not
know her, and must conclude that she was not very high in
the world. The vehicle—a dirty old barouche—was within
sight, and was being slowly prepared by an elderly laborer.
Contemptible details these, to make part of a history; yet the
turn of most lives is hardly to be accounted for without them.
They are continually entering with cumulative force into a
mood until it gets the mass and momentum of a theory or a
motive. Even philosophy is not quite free from such determining influences; and to be dropt solitary at an ugly irrele-
vant-looking spot, with a sense of no income on the mind,
might well prompt a man to discouraging speculation on the
origin of things and the reason of a world where a subtle
thinker found himself so badly off. How much more might
such trifles tell on a young lady equipped for society with a
fastidious taste, an Indian shawl over her arm, some twenty
cubic feet of trunks by her side, and a mortal dislike to the
new consciousness of poverty which was stimulating her imagination of disagreeables? At any rate they told heavily on
poor Gwendolen, and helped to quell her resistant spirit.
What was the good of living in the midst of hardships, ugliness, and humiliation? This was the beginning of being at
home again, and it was a sample of what she had to expect.

Here was the theme on which her discontent rung its sad
changes during her slow drive in the uneasy barouche, with
one great trunk squeezing the meek driver, and the other fastened with a rope on the seat in front of her. Her ruling
vision all the way from Leubronn had been that the family
would go abroad again; for of course there must be some little
income left—her mamma did not mean that they would have
literally nothing. To go to a dull place abroad and live
poorly, was the dismal future that threatened her: she had
seen plenty of poor English people abroad, and imagined herself plunged in the despised dulness of their ill-plenished lives,
with Alice, Bertha, Fanny, and Isabel all growing up in tedi-
ousness around her, while she advanced toward thirty, and her
mamma got more and more melancholy. But she did not
mean to submit, and let misfortune do what it would with her:

she had not yet quite believed in the misfortune; but weariness, and disgust with this wretched arrival, had begun to affect her like an uncomfortable waking, worse than the uneasy dreams which had gone before. The self-delight with which she had kissed her image in the glass had faded before the sense of futility in being anything whatever—charming, clever, resolute—what was the good of it all? Events might turn out anyhow, and men were hateful. Yes, men were hateful. Those few words were filled out with very vivid memories. But in these last hours, a certain change had come over their meaning. It is one thing to hate stolen goods, and another thing to hate them the more because their being stolen hinders us from making use of them. Gwendolen had begun to be angry with Grandcourt for being what had hindered her from marrying him, angry with him as the cause of her present dreary lot.

But the slow drive was nearly at an end, and the lumbering vehicle coming up the avenue was within sight of the windows. A figure appearing under the portico brought a rush of new and less selfish feeling in Gwendolen, and when springing from the carriage she saw the dear beautiful face with fresh lines of sadness in it, she threw her arms round her mother's neck, and for the moment felt all sorrows only in relation to her mother's feeling about them.

Behind, of course, were the sad faces of the four superfluous girls, each, poor thing—like those other many thousand sisters of us all—having her peculiar world which was of no importance to any one else, but all of them feeling Gwendolen's presence to be somehow a relenting of misfortune: where Gwendolen was, something interesting would happen; even her hurried submission to their kisses, and "Now go away, girls," carried the sort of comfort which all weakness finds in decision and authoritativeness. Good Miss Merry, whose air of meek depression, hitherto held unaccountable in a governess affectionately attached to the family, was now at the general level of circumstances, did not expect any greeting, but busied herself with the trunks and the coachman's pay; while Mrs. Davilow and Gwendolen hastened upstairs and shut themselves in the black and yellow bedroom.

"Never mind, mamma dear," said Gwendolen, tenderly
pressing her handkerchief against the tears that were rolling
down Mrs. Davilow's cheeks. "Never mind. I don't mind.
I will do something. I will be something. Things will come
right. It seemed worse because I was away. Come, now!
you must be glad because I am here."

Gwendolen felt every word of that speech. A rush of compassionate tenderness stirred all her capability of generous
resolution; and the self-confident projects which had vaguely
glanced before her during her journey sprang instantaneously
into new definiteness. Suddenly she seemed to perceive how
she could be "something." It was one of her best moments,
and the fond mother, forgetting everything below that tide-
mark, looked at her with a sort of adoration. She said:

"Bless you, my good, good darling! I can be happy, if
you can!"

But later in the day there was an ebb; the old slippery
rocks, the old weedy places reappeared. Naturally, there was
a shrinking of courage as misfortune ceased to be a mere announcement, and began to disclose itself as a grievous tyran-
nical inmate. At first—that ugly drive at an end—it was still
Offendene that Gwendolen had come home to, and all surroundings of immediate consequence to her were still there to
sceure her personal ease; the roomy stillness of the large solid
house while she rested; all the luxuries of her toilet cared for
without trouble to her; and a little tray with her favorite food
brought to her in private. For she had said: "Keep them
all away from us to-day, mamma. Let you and me be alone
together."

When Gwendolen came down into the drawing-room, fresh
as a newly dipped swan, and sat leaning against the cushions
of the settee beside her mamma, their misfortune had not yet
turned its face and breath upon her. She felt prepared to
hear everything, and began in a tone of deliberate intention:

"What have you thought of doing exactly, mamma?"

"Oh, my dear, the next thing to be done is to move away
from this house. Mr. Haynes most fortunately is as glad to
have it now as he would have been when wo took it. Lord
Brackenshaw's agent is to arrange everything with him to the

best advantage for us: Bazley, you know; not at all an ill-natured man."

"I cannot help thinking that Lord Brackenshaw would let you stay here rent-free, mamma," said Gwendolen, whose talents had not been applied to business so much as to discernment of the admiration excited by her charms.

"My dear child, Lord Brackenshaw is in Scotland, and knows nothing about us. Neither your uncle nor I would choose to apply to him. Besides, what could we do in this house without servants, and without money to warm it? The sooner we are out the better. We have nothing to carry but our clothes, you know."

"I suppose you mean to go abroad, then?" said Gwendolen. After all, this is what she had familiarized her mind with.

"Oh, no, dear—no. How could we travel? You never did learn anything about income and expenses," said Mrs. Davilow, trying to smile, and putting her hand on Gwendolen's as she added, mournfully, "That makes it so much harder for you, my pet."

"But where are we to go?" asid Gwendolen, with a trace of sharpness in her tone. She felt a new current of fear passing through her.

"It is all decided. A little furniture is to be got in from the Rectory—all that can be spared." Mrs. Davilow hesitated. She dreaded the reality for herself less than the shock she must give Gwendolen, who looked at her with tense expectancy, but was silent.

"It is Sawyer's Cottage we are to go to."

At first Gwendolen remained silent, paling with anger—jus tifiable anger, in her opinion. Then she said with haughtiness:

"That is impossible. Something else than that ought to have been thought of. My uncle ought not to allow that. I will not submit to it."

"My sweet child, what else could have been thought of? Your uncle, I am sure, is as kind as he can be; but he is suffering himself: he has his family to bring up. And do you quite understand? You must remember—we have nothing. We shall have absolutely nothing except what he and my sister g··e us. They have been as wise and active as possible, and we must try to earn something. I and the girls are going to work a table-cloth border for the Ladies' Charity at Wanchester, and a communion-cloth that the parishioners are to present to Pennicote Church."

Mrs. Davilow went into these details timidly; but how else was she to bring the fact of their position home to this poor child?—who, alas! must submit at present, whatever might be in the background for her. And she herself had a superstition that there must be something better in the background.

"But surely somewhere else than Sawyer's Cottage might have been found," Gwendolen persisted—taken hold of (as if in a nightmare) by the image of this house where an exciseman had lived.

"No, indeed, dear. You know houses are scarce, and we may be thankful to get anything so private. It is not so very bad. There are two little parlors and four bedrooms. You shall sit alone whenever you like."

The ebb of sympathetic care for her mamma had gone so low just now that Gwendolen took no notice of these deprecatory words.

"I cannot conceive that all your property is gone at once, mamma. How can you be sure in so short a time? It is not a week since you wrote to me."

"The first news came much earlier, dear. But I would not spoil your pleasure till it was quite necessary."

"Oh, how vexatious!" said Gwendolen, coloring with fresh anger. "If I had known, I could have brought home the money I had won; and for want of knowing, I stayed and lost it. I had nearly two hundred pounds, and it would have done for us to live on a little while, till I could carry out some plan." She paused an instant, and then added more impetuously: "Everything has gone against me. People have come near me only to blight me."

Among the "people" she was including Deronda. If he had not interfered in her life, she would have gone to the gaming-table again with a few napoleons, and might have won back her losses.

"We must resign ourselves to the will of Providence, my

child," said poor Mrs. Davilow, startled by this revelation of the gambling, but not daring to say more. She felt sure that "people" meant Grandcourt, about whom her lips were sealed. And Gwendolen answered immediately:

"But I don't resign myself. I shall do what I can against it. What is the good of calling people's wickedness Providence? You said in your letter it was Mr. Lassmann's fault we had lost our money. Has he run away with it all?"

"No, dear, you don't understand. There were great speculations: he meant to gain. It was all about mines and things of that sort. He risked too much."

"I don't call that Providence: it was his improvidence with our money, and he ought to be punished. Can't we go to law and recover our fortune? My uncle ought to take measures, and not sit down by such wrongs. We ought to go to law."

"My dear child, law can never bring back money lost in that way. Your uncle says it is milk spilt upon the ground. Besides, one must have a fortune to get any law: there is no law for people who are ruined. And our money has only gone along with other people's. We are not the only sufferers: others have to resign themselves besides us."

"But I don't resign myself to live at Sawyer's Cottage and see you working for sixpences and shillings because of that. I shall not do it. I shall do what is more befitting our rank and education."

"I am sure your uncle and all of us will approve of that, dear, and admire you the more for it," said Mrs. Davilow, glad of an unexpected opening for speaking on a difficult subject. "I didn't mean that you should resign yourself to worse when anything better offered itself. Both your uncle and aunt have felt that your abilities and education were a fortune for you, and they have already heard of something within your reach."

"What is that, mamma?" Some of Gwendolen's anger gave way to interest, and she was not without romantic conjectures.

"There are two situations that offer themselves. One is in a bishop's family, where there are three daughters, and the other is in quite a high class of school; and in both, your

French and music and dancing—and then your manners and
habits as a lady, are exactly what is wanted.   Each is a hundred a year—and—just for the present"—Mrs. Davilow had
become frightened and hesitating—"to save you from the
petty, common way of living that we must go to—you would
perhaps accept one of the two."

"What! be like Miss Graves at Madame Meunier's?   No."

"I think, myself, that Dr. Mompert's would be more suitable.   There could be no hardship in a bishop's family."

"Excuse me, mamma.   There are hardships everywhere for
a governess.   And I don't see that it would be pleasanter to
be looked down on in a bishop's family than in any other.
Besides, you know very well I hate teaching.   Fancy me shut
up with three awkward girls something like Alice!   I would
rather emigrate than be a governess."

What it precisely was to emigrate, Gwendolen was not
called on to explain.   Mrs. Davilow was mute, seeing no outlet, and thinking with dread of the collision that might happen
when Gwendolen had to meet her uncle and aunt.   There was
an air of reticence in Gwendolen's haughty resistant speeches,
which implied that she had a definite plan in reserve; and her
practical ignorance, continually exhibited, could not nullify
the mother's belief in the effectiveness of that forcible will
and daring which had held the mastery over herself.

"I have some ornaments, mamma, and I could sell them,"
said Gwendolen.   "They would make a sum: I want a little
sum—just to go on with.   I dare say Marshall at Wanchester
would take them: I know he showed me some bracelets once
that he said he had bought from a lady.   Jocosa might go and
ask him.   Jocosa is going to leave us, of course.   But she
might do that first."

"She would do anything she could, poor dear soul.   I have
not told you yet—she wanted me to take all her savings—her
three hundred pounds.   I tell her to set up a little school.
It will be hard for her to go into a new family now, she has
been so long with us."

"Oh, recommend her for the bishop's daughters," said
Gwendolen, with a sudden gleam of laughter in her face.   "I
am sure she will do better than I should."

"Do take care not to say such things to your uncle," said Mrs. Davilow. "He will be hurt at your despising what he has exerted himself about. But I dare say you have something else in your mind that he might not disapprove, if you consulted him."

"There is some one else I want to consult first. Are the Arrowpoints at Quetcham still, and is Herr Klesmer there? But I dare say you know nothing about it, poor dear mamma. Can Jeffries go on horseback with a note?"

"Oh, my dear, Jeffries is not here, and the dealer has taken the horses. But some one could go for us from Leek's farm. The Arrowpoints are at Quetcham, I know. Miss Arrowpoint left her card the other day: I could not see her. But I don't know about Herr Klesmer. Do you want to send before to-morrow?"

"Yes, as soon as possible. I will write a note," said Gwendolen, rising.

"What can you be thinking of, Gwen?" said Mrs. Davilow, relieved in the midst of her wonderment by signs of alacrity and better humor.

"Don't mind what, there's a dear good mamma," said Gwendolen, reseating herself a moment to give atoning caresses. "I mean to do something. Never mind what, until it is all settled. And then you shall be comforted. The dear face!—it is ten years older in these three weeks. Now, now, now!—don't cry"—Gwendolen, holding her mamma's head with both hands, kissed the trembling eyelids. "But mind you don't contradict me or put hindrances in my way. I must decide for myself. I cannot be dictated to by my uncle or any one else. My life is my own affair. And I think"— here her tone took an edge of scorn—"I think I can do better for you than let you live in Sawyer's Cottage."

In uttering this last sentence, Gwendolen again rose, and went to a desk, where she wrote the following note to Klesmer:

"Miss Harleth presents her compliments to Herr Klesmer, and ventures to request of him the very great favor that he will call upon her, if possible to-morrow. Her reason for presuming so far on his kindness is of a very serious nature. Unfortunate family circumstances have obliged her to take a course in which she can only turn for advice to the great knowledge and judgment of Herr Klesmer."

"Pray get this sent to Quetcham at once, mamma," said Gwendolen, as she addressed the letter. "The man must be told to wait for an answer. Let no time be lost."

For the moment, the absorbing purpose was to get the letter despatched; but when she had been assured on this point, another anxiety arose and kept her in a state of uneasy excitement. If Klesmer happened not to be at Quetcham, what could she do next? Gwendolen's belief in her star, so to speak, had had some bruises. Things had gone against her. A splendid marriage which presented itself within reach had shown a hideous flaw. The chances of roulette had not adjusted themselves to her claims; and a man of whom she knew nothing had thrust himself between her and her intentions. The conduct of those uninteresting people who managed the business of the world had been culpable just in the points most injurious to her in particular. Gwendolen Harleth, with all her beauty and conscious force, felt the close threats of humiliation: for the first time the conditions of this world seemed to her like a hurrying, roaring crowd in which she had got astray, no more cared for and protected than a myriad of other girls, in spite of its being a peculiar hardship to her. If Klesmer were not at Quetcham—that would be all of a piece with the rest: the unwelcome negative urged itself as a probability, and set her brain working at desperate alternatives which might deliver her from Sawyer's Cottage or the ultimate necessity of "taking a situation," a phrase that summed up for her the disagreeables most wounding to her pride, most irksome to her tastes—at least so far as her experience enabled her to imagine disagreeables.

Still Klesmer might be there, and Gwendolen thought of the result in that case with a hopefulness which even cast a satisfactory light over her peculiar troubles, as what might well enter into the biography of celebrities and remarkable persons. And if she had heard her immediate acquaintances cross-examined as to whether they thought her remarkable, the first who said "No" would have surprised her.

CHAPTER XXII.

We please our fancy with ideal webs
Of innovation, but our life meanwhile
Is in the loom, where busy passion plies
The shuttle to and fro, and gives our deeds
The accustomed pattern.

GWENDOLEN's note, coming "pat betwixt too early and too late," was put into Klesmer's hands just when he was leaving Quetcham, and in order to meet her appeal to his kindness he with some inconvenience to himself spent the night at Wanchester. There were reasons why he would not remain at Quetcham.

That magnificent mansion, fitted with regard to the greatest expense, had in fact become too hot for him, its owners having, like some great politicians, been astonished at an insurrection against the established order of things, which we plain people after the event can perceive to have been prepared under their very noses.

There were as usual many guests in the house, and among them one in whom Miss Arrowpoint foresaw a new pretender to her hand: a political man of good family who confidently expected a peerage, and felt on public grounds that he required a larger fortune to support the title properly. Heiresses vary, and persons interested in one of them beforehand are prepared to find that she is too yellow or too red, tall and toppling or short and square, violent and capricious or moody and insipid; but in every case it is taken for granted that she will consider herself an appendage to her fortune, and marry where others think her fortune ought to go. Nature, however, not only accommodates herself ill to our favorite practices by making "only children" daughters, but also now and then endows the misplaced daughter with a clear head and a strong will. The Arrowpoints had already felt some anxiety owing to these endowments of their Catherine. She would not accept the view of her social duty which required her to marry a needy nobleman or a commoner on the ladder toward nobility; and they were not without uneasiness concerning her persistence in declining suitable offers. As to the possibility of her being in love with Klesmer, they were not at all uneasy—a very common sort of blindness. For in general mortals have a great power of being astonished at the presence of an effect toward which they have done everything, and at the absence of an effect toward which they have done nothing but desire it. Parents are astonished at the ignorance of their sons, though they have used the most time-honored and expensive means of securing it; husbands and wives are mutually astonished at the loss of affection which they have taken no pains to keep; and all of us in our turn are apt to be astonished that our neighbors do not admire us. In this way it happens that the truth seems highly improbable. The truth is something different from the habitual lazy combinations begotten by our wishes. The Arrowpoints' hour of astonishment was come.

When there is a passion between an heiress and a proud, independent-spirited man, it is difficult for them to come to an understanding; but the difficulties are likely to be overcome unless the proud man secures himself by a constant *alibi.* Brief meetings after studied absence are potent in disclosure: but more potent still is frequent companionship, with full sympathy in taste, and admirable qualities on both sides; especially where the one is in the position of teacher, and the other is delightedly conscious of receptive ability which also gives the teacher delight. The situation is famous in history, and has no less charm now than it had in the days of Abelard.

But this kind of comparison had not occurred to the Arrowpoints when they first engaged Klesmer to come down to Quetcham. To have a first-rate musician in your house is a privilege of wealth; Catherine's musical talent demanded every advantage; and she particularly desired to use her quieter time in the country for more thorough study. Klesmer was not yet a Liszt, understood to be adored by ladies of all European countries with the exception of Lapland: and even with that understanding it did not follow that he would make proposals to an heiress. No musician of honor would do so. Still less was it conceivable that Catherine would give him the slightest pretext for such daring. The large check that Mr. Arrowpoint was to draw in Klesmer's name seemed to make him as safe an inmate as a footman. Where marriage is inconceivable, a girl's sentiments are safe.

Klesmer was eminently a man of honor, but marriages rarely begin with formal proposals, and moreover, Catherine's limit of the conceivable did not exactly correspond with her mother's.

Outsiders might have been more apt to think that Klesmer's position was dangerous for himself if Miss Arrowpoint had been an acknowledged beauty; not taking into account that the most powerful of all beauty is that which reveals itself after sympathy, and not before it. There is a charm of eye and lip which comes with every little phrase that certifies delicate perception or fine judgment, with every unostentatious word or smile that shows a heart awake to others; and no sweep of garment or turn of figure is more satisfying than that which enters as a restoration of confidence that one person is present on whom no intention will be lost. What dignity of meaning goes on gathering in frowns and laughs which are never observed in the wrong place; what suffused adorableness in a human frame where there is a mind that can flash out comprehension and hands that can execute finely! The more obvious beauty, also adorable sometimes—one may say it without blasphemy—begins by being an apology for folly, and ends like other apologies in becoming tiresome by iteration; and that Klesmer, though very susceptible to it, should have a passionate attachment to Miss Arrowpoint, was no more a paradox than any other triumph of a manifold sympathy over a monotonous attraction. We object less to be taxed with the enslaving excess of our passions than with our deficiency in wider passion; but if the truth were known, our reputed intensity is often the dulness of not knowing what else to do with ourselves. Tannhäuser, one suspects, was a knight of ill-furnished imagination, hardly of larger discourse than a heavy guardsman; Merlin had certainly seen his best days, and was merely repeating himself, when he fell into that hopeless captivity; and we know that Ulysses felt so manifest an *ennui* under similar circumstances that Calypso herself furthered his departure. There is indeed a report that he afterward left Penelope; but since she was habitually absorbed in worsted work, and it was probably from her that Telemachus got his mean, pettifogging disposition, always anxious about the property and the daily consumption of meat, no inference can be drawn from this already dubious scandal as to the relation between companionship and constancy.

Klesmer was as versatile and fascinating as a young Ulysses on a sufficient acquaintance—one whom nature seemed to have first made generously, and then to have added music as a dominant power using all the abundant rest, and, as in Mendelssohn, finding expression for itself not only in the highest finish of execution, but in the fervor of creative work and theoretic belief which pierces the whole future of a life with the light of congruous, devoted purpose. His foibles of arrogance and vanity did not exceed such as may be found in the best English families; and Catherine Arrowpoint had no corresponding restlessness to clash with his: notwithstanding her native kindliness she was perhaps too coolly firm and self-sustained. But she was one of those satisfactory creatures whose intercourse has the charm of discovery; whose integrity of faculty and expression begets a wish to know what they will say on all subjects or how they will perform whatever they undertake; so that they end by raising not only a continual expectation, but a continual sense of fulfilment—the systole and diastole of blissful companionship. In such cases the outward presentment easily becomes what the image is to the worshipper. It was not long before the two became aware that each was interesting to the other; but the "how far" remained a matter of doubt. Klesmer did not conceive that Miss Arrowpoint was likely to think of him as a possible lover, and she was not accustomed to think of herself as likely to stir more than a friendly regard, or to fear the expression of more from any man who was not enamoured of her fortune. Each was content to suffer some unshared sense of denial for the sake of loving the other's society a little too well; and under these conditions no need had been felt to restrict Klesmer's visits for the last year either in country or in town. He knew very well that if Miss Arrowpoint had been poor he would have made ardent love to her instead of sending a storm through the piano, or folding his arms and pouring out a hyperbolical tirade about something as impersonal as the North Pole; and she was not less aware that if it had been possible for Klesmer to wish for her hand she would have found overmastering reasons for giving it to him. Here was the safety of full cups, which are as secure from overflow as the half-empty, always supposing no disturbance. Naturally, silent feeling had not remained at the same point any more than the stealthy dial-hand, and in the present visit to Quetcham, Klesmer had begun to think that he would not come again; while Catherine was more sensitive to his frequent *brusquerie*, which she rather resented as a needless effort to assert his footing of superior in every sense except the conventional.

Meanwhile enters the expectant peer, Mr. Bult, an esteemed party man, who, rather neutral in private life, had strong opinions concerning the districts of the Niger, was much at home also in the Brazils, spoke with decision of affairs in the South Seas, was studious of his Parliamentary and itinerant speeches, and had the general solidity and suffusive pinkness of a healthy Briton on the central table-land of life. Catherine, aware of a tacit understanding that he was an undeniable husband for an heiress, had nothing to say against him but that he was thoroughly tiresome to her. Mr. Bult was amiably confident, and had no idea that his insensibility to counterpoint could ever be reckoned against him. Klesmer he hardly regarded in the light of a serious human being who ought to have a vote, and he did not mind Miss Arrowpoint's addiction to music any more than her probable expenses in antique lace. He was consequently a little amazed at an after-dinner outburst of Klesmer's on the lack of idealism in English politics, which left all mutuality between distant races to be determined simply by the need of a market: the crusades, to his mind, had at least this excuse, that they had a banner of sentiment round which generous feelings could rally: of course, the scoundrels rallied too; but what then? they rally in equal force round your advertisement van of "Buy cheap, sell dear." On this theme Klesmer's eloquence, gesticulatory and other, went on for a little while like stray fireworks accidentally

ignited, and then sank into immovable silence. Mr. Bult was
not surprised that Klesmer's opinions should be flighty, but
was astonished at his command of English idiom and his ability to put a point in a way that would have told at a constituents' dinner—to be accounted for probably by his being a
Pole, or a Czech, or something of that fermenting sort, in a
state of political refugeeism which had obliged him to make a
profession of his music; and that evening in the drawing-room
he for the first time went up to Klesmer at the piano, Miss
Arrowpoint being near, and said:

"I had no idea before that you were a political man."

Klesmer's only answer was to fold his arms, put out his
nether lip, and stare at Mr. Bult.

"You must have been used to public speaking. You speak
uncommonly well, though I don't agree with you. From
what you said about sentiment, I fancy you are a Pan-
slavist."

"No; my name is Elijah. I am the Wandering Jew," said
Klesmer, flashing a smile at Miss Arrowpoint, and suddenly
making a mysterious wind-like rush backward and forward
on the piano. Mr. Bult felt this buffoonery rather offensive
and Polish, but—Miss Arrowpoint being there—did not like
to move away.

"Herr Klesmer has cosmopolitan ideas," said Miss Arrowpoint, trying to make the best of the situation. "He looks
forward to a fusion of races."

"With all my heart," said Mr. Bult, willing to be gracious.
"I was sure he had too much talent to be a mere musician."

"Ah, sir; you are under some mistake there," said Klesmer, firing up. "No man has too much talent to be a musician. Most men have too little. A creative artist is no more a
mere musician than a great statesman is a mere politician. We
are not ingenious puppets, sir, who live in a box and look out
on the world only when it is gaping for amusement. We help
to rule the nations and make the age as much as any other
public men. We count ourselves on level benches with legis-
lators. And a man who speaks effectively through music is
compelled to something more difficult than parliamentary eloquence."

With the last word Klesmer wheeled from the piano and walked away.

Miss Arrowpoint colored, and Mr. Bult observed with his usual phlegmatic stolidity, "Your pianist does not think small beer of himself."

"Herr Klesmer is something more than a pianist," said Miss Arrowpoint, apologetically. "He is a great musician in the fullest sense of the word. He will rank with Schubert and Mendelssohn."

"Ah, you ladies understand these things," said Mr. Bult, none the less convinced that these things were frivolous because Klesmer had shown himself a coxcomb.

Catherine, always sorry when Klesmer gave himself airs, found an opportunity the next day in the music-room to say: "Why were you so heated last night with Mr. Bult? He meant no harm."

"You wish me to be complaisant to him?" said Klesmer, rather fiercely.

"I think it is hardly worth your while to be other than civil."

"You find no difficulty in tolerating him, then?—you have a respect for a political platitudinarian as insensible as an ox to everything he can't turn into political capital. You think his monumental obtuseness suited to the dignity of the English gentleman."

"I did not say that."

"You mean that I acted without dignity and you are offended with me."

"Now you are slightly nearer the truth," said Catherine, smiling.

"Then I had better put my burial-clothes in my portmanteau and set off at once."

"I don't see that. If I have to bear your criticism of my operetta, you should not mind my criticism of your impatience."

"But I do mind it. You would have wished me to take his ignorant impertinence about a ' mere musician ' without letting him know his place. I am to hear my gods blasphemed as well as myself insulted. But I beg pardon. It is impos-

sible you should see the matter as I do. Even you can't understand the wrath of the artist: he is of another caste for
you."

"That is true," said Catherine, with some betrayal of feeling. "He is of a caste to which I look up—a caste above
mine."

Klesmer, who had been seated at a table looking over
scores, started up and walked to a little distance, from which
he said:

"That is finely felt—I am grateful. But I had better go,
all the same. I have made up my mind to go, for good and
all. You can get on exceedingly well without me: your operetta is on wheels—it will go of itself. And your Mr. Bult's
company fits me 'wie die Faust ins Auge.' I am neglecting
my engagements. I must go off to St. Petersburg."

There was no answer.

"You agree with me that I had better go?" said Klesmer,
with some irritation.

"Certainly; if that is what your business and feeling
prompt. I have only to wonder that you have consented to
give us so much of your time in the last year. There must
be treble the interest to you anywhere else. I have never
thought of your consenting to come here an anything else than
a sacrifice."

"Why should I make the sacrifice?" said Klesmer, going
to seat himself at the piano, and touching the keys so as to
give with the delicacy of an echo in the far distance a melody
which he had set to Heine's "Ich hab' dich geliebet und liebe
dich noch."

"That is the mystery," said Catherine, not wanting to affect
anything, but from mere agitation. From the same cause she
was tearing a piece of paper into minute morsels, as if at a
task of utmost multiplication imposed by a cruel fairy.

"You can conceive no motive?" said Klesmer, folding his
arms.

"None that seems in the least probable."

"Then I shall tell you. It is because you are to me the
chief woman in the world—the throned lady whose colors I
carry between my heart and my armor."

Catherine's hands trembled so much that she could no longer tear the paper: still less could her lips utter a word. Klesmer went on:

"This would be the last impertinence in me, if I meant to found anything upon it. That is out of the question. I mean no such thing. But you once said it was your doom to suspect every man who courted you of being an adventurer, and what made you angriest was men's imputing to you the folly of believing that they courted you for your own sake. Did you not say so?"

"Very likely," was the answer, in a low murmur.

"It was a bitter word. Well, at least one man who has seen women as plenty as flowers in May has lingered about you for your own sake. And since he is one whom you can never marry, you will believe him. That is an argument in favor of some other man. But don't give yourself for a meal to a minotaur like Bult. I shall go now and pack. I shall make my excuses to Mrs. Arrowpoint." Klesmer rose as he ended, and walked quickly toward the door.

"You must take this heap of manuscript, then," said Catherine, suddenly making a desperate effort. She had risen to fetch the heap from another table. Klesmer came back, and they had the length of the folio sheets between them.

"Why should I not marry the man who loves me, if I love him?" said Catherine. To her the effort was something like the leap of a woman from the deck into the life-boat.

"It would be too hard—impossible—you could not carry it through. I am not worth what you would have to encounter. I will not accept the sacrifice. It would be thought a *mésalliance* for you, and I should be liable to the worst accusations."

"Is it the accusations you are afraid of? I am afraid of nothing but that we should miss the passing of our lives together."

The decisive word had been spoken: there was no doubt concerning the end willed by each: there only remained the way of arriving at it, and Catherine determined to take the straightest possible. She went to her father and mother in the library, and told them that she had promised to marry Klesmer.

Mrs. Arrowpoint's state of mind was pitiable. Imagine Jean Jacques, after his essay on the corrupting influence of the arts, waking up among children of nature who had no idea of grilling the raw bone they offered him for breakfast with the primitive flint knife; or Saint Just, after fervidly denouncing all recognition of pre-eminence, receiving a vote of thanks for the unbroken mediocrity of his speech, which warranted the dullest patriots in delivering themselves at equal length. Something of the same sort befell the authoress of "Tasso," when what she had safely demanded of the dead Leonora was enacted by her own Catherine. It is hard for us to live up to our own eloquence, and keep peace with our winged words, while we are treading the solid earth and are liable to heavy dining. Besides, it has long been understood that the proprieties of literature are not those of practical life. Mrs. Arrowpoint naturally wished for the best of everything. She not only liked to feel herself at a higher level of literary sentiment than the ladies with whom she associated; she wished not to be below them in any point of social consideration. While Klesmer was seen in the light of a patronized musician, his peculiarities were picturesque and acceptable; but to see him by a sudden flash in the light of her son-in-law gave her a burning sense of what the world would say. And the poor lady had been used to represent her Catherine as a model of excellence.

Under the first shock she forgot everything but her anger, and snatched at any phrase that would serve as a weapon.

"If Klesmer has presumed to offer himself to you, your father shall horsewhip him off the premises. Pray, speak, Mr. Arrowpoint."

The father took his cigar from his mouth, and rose to the occasion by saying: "This will never do, Cath."

"Do!" cried Mrs. Arrowpoint; "who in their senses ever thought it would do? You might as well say poisoning and strangling will not do. It is a comedy you have got up, Catherine. Else you are mad."

"I am quite sane and serious, mamma, and Herr Klesmer is not to blame. He never thought of my marrying him. I found out that he loved me, and loving him, I told him I would marry him."

"Leave that unsaid, Catherine," said Mrs. Arrowpoint, bitterly. "Every one else will say it for you. You will be a public fable. Every one will say that you must have made the offer to a man who has been paid to come to the house—who is nobody knows what—a gypsy, a Jew, a mere bubble of the earth."

"Never mind, mamma," said Catherine, indignant in her turn. "We all know he is a genius—as Tasso was."

"Those times were not these, nor is Klesmer Tasso," said Mrs. Arrowpoint, getting more heated. "There is no sting in *that* sarcasm, except the sting of undutifulness."

"I am sorry to hurt you, mamma. But I will not give up the happiness of my life to ideas that I don't believe in and customs I have no respect for."

"You have lost all sense of duty, then? You have forgotten that you are our only child—that it lies with you to place a great property in the right hands?"

"What are the right hands? My grandfather gained the property in trade."

"Mr. Arrowpoint, *will* you sit by and hear this without speaking?"

"I am a gentleman, Cath. We expect you to marry a gentleman," said the father, exerting himself.

"And a man connected with the institutions of this country," said the mother. "A woman in your position has serious duties. Where duty and inclination clash, she must follow duty."

"I don't deny that," said Catherine, getting colder in proportion to her mother's heat. "But one may say very true things and apply them falsely. People can easily take the sacred word duty as a name for what they desire any one else to do."

"Your parents' desire makes no duty for you, then?"

"Yes, within reason. But before I give up the happiness of my life——"

"Catherine, Catherine, it will not be your happiness," said Mrs. Arrowpoint, in her most raven-like tones.

"Well, what seems to me my happiness—before I give it up, I must see some better reason than the wish that I should marry a nobleman, or a man who votes with a party that he may be turned into a nobleman. I feel at liberty to marry the man I love and think worthy, unless some higher duty forbids."

"And so it does, Catherine, though you are blinded and cannot see it. It is a woman's duty not to lower herself. You are lowering yourself. Mr. Arrowpoint, will you tell your daughter what is her duty?"

"You must see, Catherine, that Klesmer is not the man for you," said Mr. Arrowpoint. "He won't do at the head of estates. He has a deuced foreign look—is an unpractical man."

"I really can't see what that has to do with it, papa. The land of England has often passed into the hands of foreigners —Dutch soldiers, sons of foreign women of bad character:— if our land were sold to-morrow it would very likely pass into the hands of some foreign merchant on 'Change. It is in everybody's mouth that successful swindlers may buy up half the land in the country. How can I stem that tide?"

"It will never do to argue about marriage, Cath," said Mr. Arrowpoint. "It's no use getting up the subject like a parliamentary question. We must do as other people do. We must think of the nation and the public good."

"I can't see any public good concerned here, papa," said Catherine. "Why is it to be expected of an heiress that she should carry the property gained in trade into the hands of a certain class? That seems to me a ridiculous mish-mash of superannuated customs and false ambition. I should call it a public evil. People had better make a new sort of public good by changing their ambitions."

"That is mere sophistry, Catherine," said Mrs. Arrowpoint. "Because you don't wish to marry a nobleman, you are not obliged to marry a mountebank or a charlatan."

"I cannot understand the application of such words, mamma."

"No, I dare say not," rejoined Mrs. Arrowpoint, with significant scorn. "You have got to a pitch at which we are not likely to understand each other."

"It can't be done, Cath," said Mr. Arrowpoint, wishing to

substitute a better-humored reasoning for his wife's impetuosity. "A man like Klesmer can't marry such a property as yours. It can't be done."

"It certainly will not be done," said Mrs. Arrowpoint, imperiously. "Where is the man? Let him be fetched."

"I cannot fetch him to be insulted," said Catherine. "Nothing will be achieved by that."

"I suppose you would wish him to know that in marrying you he will not marry your fortune," said Mrs. Arrowpoint.

"Certainly; if it were so, I should wish him to know it."

"Then you had better fetch him."

Catherine only went into the music-room and said, "Come": she felt no need to prepare Klesmer.

"Herr Klesmer," said Mrs. Arrowpoint, with a rather contemptuous stateliness, "it is unnecessary to repeat what has passed between us and our daughter. Mr. Arrowpoint will tell you our resolution."

"Your marrying is quite out of the question," said Mr. Arrowpoint, rather too heavily weighted with his task, and standing in an embarrassment unrelieved by a cigar. "It is a wild scheme altogether. A man has been called out for less."

"You have taken a base advantage of our confidence," burst in Mrs. Arrowpoint, unable to carry out her purpose and leave the burden of speech to her husband.

Klesmer made a low bow in silent irony.

"The pretension is ridiculous. You had better give it up and leave the house at once," continued Mr. Arrowpoint. He wished to do without mentioning the money.

"I can give up nothing without reference to your daughter's wish," said Klesmer. "My engagement is to her."

"It is useless to discuss the question," said Mrs. Arrowpoint. "We shall never consent to the marriage. If Catherine disobeys us we shall disinherit her. You will not marry her fortune. It is right you should know that."

"Madam, her fortune has been the only thing I have had to regret about her. But I must ask her if she will not think the sacrifice greater than I am worthy of."

"It is no sacrifice to me," said Catherine, "except that I

am sorry to hurt my father and mother. I have always felt my fortune to be a wretched fatality of my life."

"You mean to defy us, then?" said Mrs. Arrowpoint.

"I mean to marry Herr Klesmer," said Catherine, firmly.

"He had better not count on our relenting," said Mrs. Arrowpoint, whose manner suffered from that impunity in insult which has been reckoned among the privileges of women.

"Madam," said Klesmer, "certain reasons forbid me to retort. But understand that I consider it out of the power either of you or of your fortune to confer on me anything that I value. My rank as an artist is of my own winning, and I would not exchange it for any other. I am able to maintain your daughter, and I ask for no change in my life but her companionship."

"You will leave the house, however," said Mrs. Arrowpoint.

"I go at once," said Klesmer, bowing and quitting the room.

"Let there be no misunderstanding, mamma," said Catherine; "I consider myself engaged to Herr Klesmer, and I intend to marry him."

The mother turned her head away and waved her hand in sign of dismissal.

"It's all very fine," said Mr. Arrowpoint, when Catherine was gone; "but what the deuce are we to do with the property?"

"There is Harry Brendall. He can take the name."

"Harry Brendall will get through it all in no time," said Mr. Arrowpoint, relighting his cigar.

And thus, with nothing settled but the determination of the lovers, Klesmer had left Quetcham.

CHAPTER XXIII.

Among the heirs of Art, as at the division of the promised land, each has to win his portion by hard fighting: the bestowal is after the manner of prophecy, and is a title without possession. To carry the map of an ungotten estate in your pocket is a poor sort of copyhold. And in fancy to cast his shoe over Edom is little warrant that a man shall ever set the sole of his foot on an acre of his own there.

The most obstinate beliefs that mortals entertain about themselves are such as they have no evidence for beyond a constant, spontaneous pulsing of their satisfaction — as it were a hidden seed of madness, a confidence that they can move the world without precise notion of standing-place or lever.

"PRAY go to church, mamma," said Gwendolen the next morning. "I prefer seeing Herr Klesmer alone." (He had written in reply to her note that he would be with her at eleven.)

"That is hardly correct, I think," said Mrs. Davilow, anxiously.

"Our affairs are too serious for us to think of such nonsensical rules," said Gwendolen, contemptuously. "They are insulting as well as ridiculous."

"You would not mind Isabel sitting with you? She would be reading in a corner."

"No, she could not: she would bite her nails and stare. It would be too irritating. Trust my judgment, mamma. I must be alone. Take them all to church."

Gwendolen had her way, of course; only that Miss Merry and two of the girls stayed at home, to give the house a look of habitation by sitting at the dining-room windows.

It was a delicious Sunday morning. The melancholy waning sunshine of autumn rested on the leaf-strewn grass and came mildly through the windows in slanting bands of brightness over the old furniture, and the glass panel that reflected the furniture; over the tapestried chairs with their faded flower-wreaths, the dark enigmatic pictures, the superannuated organ at which Gwendolen had pleased herself with acting Saint Cecilia on her first joyous arrival, the crowd of pallid, dusty knick-knacks seen through the open doors of the antechamber where she had achieved the wearing of her Greek dress as Hermione. This last memory was just now very busy in her; for had not Klesmer then been struck with admiration of her pose and expression? Whatever he had said, whatever she imagined him to have thought, was at this moment pointed with keenest interest for her: perhaps she had never before in her life felt so inwardly dependent, so consciously in need of another person's opinion. There was a new fluttering of spirit within her, a new element of deliberation in her self-estimate which had hitherto been a blissful gift of intuition. Still it was the recurrent burden of her inward soliloquy that Klesmer had seen but little of her, and any unfavorable conclusion of his must have too narrow a foundation. She really felt clever enough for anything.

To fill up the time she collected her volumes and pieces of music, and laying them on top of the piano, set herself to classify them. Then catching the reflection of her movements in the glass panel, she was diverted to the contemplation of the image there and walked toward it. Dressed in black, without a single ornament, and with the warm whiteness of her skin set off between her light-brown coronet of hair and her square-cut bodice, she might have tempted an artist to try again the Roman trick of a statue in black, white, and tawny marble. Seeing her image slowly advancing, she thought, "I *am* beautiful"—not exultingly, but with grave decision. Being beautiful was, after all, the condition on which she most needed external testimony. If any one objected to the turn of her nose or the form of her neck and chin, she had not the sense that she could presently show her power of attainment in these branches of feminine perfection.

There was not much time to fill up in this way before the sound of wheels, the loud ring, and the opening doors, assured her that she was not by any accident to be disappointed. This slightly increased her inward flutter. In spite of her self-confidence, she dreaded Klesmer as part of that unmanageable world which was independent of her wishes—something vitriolic that would not cease to burn because you smiled or frowned at it. Poor thing! she was at a higher crisis of her woman's fate than in her past experience with Grandcourt. The questioning then was whether she should take a particular man as a husband. The inmost fold of her questioning now was, whether she need take a husband at all—whether she could not achieve substantiality for herself and know gratified ambition without bondage.

Klesmer made his most deferential bow in the wide doorway of the ante-chamber—showing also the deference of the finset gray kerseymere trousers and perfect gloves (the "masters of those who know" are happily altogether human). Gwendolen met him with unusual gravity, and holding out her hand, said: "It is most kind of you to come, Herr Klesmer. I hope you have not thought me presumptuous."

"I took your wish as a command that did me honor," said Klesmer, with answering gravity. He was really putting by his own affairs in order to give his utmost attention to what Gwendolen might have to say; but his temperament was still in a state of excitation from the events of yesterday, likely enough to give his expressions a more than usually biting edge.

Gwendolen for once was under too great a strain of feeling to remember formalities. She continued standing near the piano, and Klesmer took his stand at the other end of it, with his back to the light and his terribly omniscient eyes upon her. No affectation was of use, and she began without delay.

"I wish to consult you, Herr Klesmer. We have lost all our fortune; we have nothing. I must get my own bread, and I desire to provide for my mamma, so as to save her from any hardship. The only way I can think of—and I should like it better than anything—is to be an actress—to go on the stage. But of course I should like to take a high position, and I thought—if you thought I could,"—here Gwendolen became a little more nervous—"it would be better for me to be a singer—to study singing also."

Klesmer put down his hat on the piano, and folded his arms as if to concentrate himself.

"I know," Gwendolen resumed, turning from pale to pink and back again—"I know that my method of singing is very defective; but I have been ill taught. I could be better taught; I could study. And you will understand my wish:—to sing and act too, like Grisi, is a much higher position. Naturally, I should wish to take as high a rank as I can. And I can rely on your judgment. I am sure you will tell me the truth."

Gwendolen somehow had the conviction that now she made this serious appeal the truth would be favorable.

Still Klesmer did not speak. He drew off his gloves quickly, tossed them into his hat, rested his hands on his hips, and walked to the other end of the room. He was filled with compassion for this girl: he wanted to put a guard on his speech. When he turned again, he looked at her with a mild frown of inquiry, and said with gentle though quick utterance: "You have never seen anything, I think, of artists and their lives?—I mean of musicians, actors, artists of that kind?"

"Oh, no," said Gwendolen, not perturbed by a reference to this obvious fact in the history of a young lady hitherto well provided for.

"You are,—pardon me," said Klesmer, again pausing near the piano—"in coming to a conclusion on such a matter as this, everything must be taken into consideration—you are perhaps twenty?"

"I am twenty-one," said Gwendolen, a slight fear rising in her. "Do you think I am too old?"

Klesmer pouted his under lip and shook his long fingers upward in a manner totally enigmatic.

"Many persons begin later than others," said Gwendolen, betrayed by her habitual consciousness of having valuable information to bestow.

Klesmer took no notice, but said with more studied gentleness than ever: "You have probably not thought of an artistic career until now: you did not entertain the notion, the longing—what shall I say?—you did not wish yourself an actress, or anything of that sort, till the present trouble?"

"Not exactly; but I was fond of acting. I have acted; you saw me, if you remember—you saw me here in charades, and as Hermione," said Gwendolen, really fearing that Klesmer had forgotten.

"Yes, yes," he answered quickly, "I remember—I remember perfectly," and again walked to the other end of the room. It was difficult for him to refrain from this kind of movement when he was in any argument either audible or silent.

Gwendolen felt that she was being weighed. The delay was unpleasant. But she did not yet conceive that the scale

could dip on the wrong side, and it seemed to her only graceful to say: "I shall be very much obliged to you for taking
the trouble to give me your advice, whatever it may be."

"Miss Harleth," said Klesmer, turning toward her and
speaking with a slight increase of accent, "I will veil nothing
from you in this matter. I should reckon myself guilty if I
put a false visage on things—made them too black or too
white. The gods have a curse for him who willingly tells
another the wrong road. And if I misled one who is so
young, so beautiful—who, I trust, will find her happiness
along the right road, I should regard myself as a—*Bösewicht*."
In the last word Klesmer's voice had dropped to a loud whisper.

Gwendolen felt a sinking of heart under this unexpected
solemnity, and kept a sort of fascinated gaze on Klesmer's
face, while he went on.

"You are a beautiful young lady—you have been brought
up in ease—you have done what you would—you have not said
to yourself, 'I must know this exactly,' 'I must understand
this exactly,' 'I must do this exactly'"—in uttering these
three terrible *musts*, Klesmer lifted up three long fingers in
succession. "In sum, you have not been called upon to be
anything but a charming young lady, whom it is an impolite-
ness to find fault with."

He paused an instant; then resting his fingers on his hips
again, and thrusting out his powerful chin, he said:

"Well, then, with that preparation, you wish to try the life
of the artist; you wish to try a life of arduous, unceasing
work, and—uncertain praise. Your praise would have to be
earned, like your bread; and both would come slowly, scantily
—what do I say?—they might hardly come at all."

This tone of discouragement, which Klesmer half hoped
might suffice without anything more unpleasant, roused some
resistance in Gwendolen. With a slight turn of her head
away from him, and an air of pique, she said:

"I thought that you, being an artist, would consider the
life one of the most honorable and delightful. And if I can
do nothing better?—I suppose I can put up with the same
risks as other people do."

"Do nothing better?" said Klesmer, a little fired. "No,

my dear Miss Harleth, you could do nothing better—neither
man nor woman could do anything better—if you could do
what was best or good of its kind. I am not decrying the life
of the true artist. I am exalting it. I say, it is out of the
reach of any but choice organizations—natures framed to love
perfection and to labor for it; ready, like all true lovers, to
endure, to wait, to say, I am not yet worthy, but she—Art,
my mistress—is worthy, and I will live to merit her. An
honorable life? Yes. But the honor comes from the inward
vocation and the hard-won achievement: there is no honor in
donning the life as a livery."

Some excitement of yesterday had revived in Klesmer and
hurried him into speech a little aloof from his immediate
friendly purpose. He had wished as delicately as possible to
rouse in Gwendolen a sense of her unfitness for a perilous,
difficult course; but it was his wont to be angry with the pre-
tensions of incompetence, and he was in danger of getting
chafed. Conscious of this, he paused suddenly. But Gwendolen's chief impression was that he had not yet denied her
the power of doing what would be good of its kind. Klesmer's fervor seemed to be a sort of glamour such as he was
prone to throw over things in general; and what she desired
to assure him of was that she was not afraid of some preliminary hardships. The belief that to present herself in public
on the stage must produce an effect such as she had been used
to feel certain of in private life, was like a bit of her flesh—
it was not to be peeled off readily, but must come with blood
and pain. She said, in a tone of some insistence:

"I am quite prepared to bear hardships at first. Of course
no one can become celebrated all at once. And it is not necessary that every one should be first-rate—either actresses or
singers. If you would be so kind as to tell me what steps I
should take, I shall have the courage to take them. I don't
mind going up-hill. It will be easier than the dead level of
being a governess. I will take any steps you recommend."

Klesmer was more convinced now that he must speak
plainly.

"I will tell you the steps, not that I recommend, but that
will be forced upon you. It is all one, so far, what your goal

may be—excellence, celebrity, second, third rateness—it is all one. You must go to town under the protection of your mother. You must put yourself under training—musical, dramatic, theatrical:—whatever you desire to do you have to learn——" here Gwendolen looked as if she were going to speak, but Klesmer lifted up his hand and said decisively: "I know. You have exercised your talents—you recite—you sing—from the drawing-room *standpunkt*. My dear Fräulein, you must unlearn all that. You have not yet conceived what excellence is: you must unlearn your mistaken admirations. You must know what you have to strive for, and then you must subdue your mind and body to unbroken discipline. Your mind, I say. For you must not be thinking of celebrity:—put that candle out of your eyes, and look only at excellence. You would of course earn nothing—you could get no engagement for a long while. You would need money for yourself and your family. But that "—here Klesmer frowned and shook his fingers as if to dismiss a triviality—"that could perhaps be found."

Gwendolen turned pink and pale during this speech. Her pride had felt a terrible knife-edge, and the last sentence only made the smart keener. She was conscious of appearing moved, and tried to escape from her weakness by suddenly walking to a seat and pointing out a chair to Klesmer. He did not take it, but turned a little in order to face her, and leaned against the piano. At that moment she wished that she had not sent for him: this first experience of being taken on some other ground than that of her social rank and her beauty was becoming bitter to her. Klesmer, preocccupied with a serious purpose, went on without change of tone.

"Now, what sort of issue might be fairly expected from all this self-denial? You would ask that. It is right that your eyes should be open to it. I will tell you truthfully. The issue would be uncertain and—most probably—would not be worth much."

At these relentless words Klesmer put out his lip and looked through his spectacles with the air of a monster impenetrable by beauty.

Gwendolen's eyes began to burn, but the dread of showing

weakness urged her to added self-control. She compelled herself to say in a hard tone:

"You think I want talent, or am too old to begin."

Klesmer made a sort of hum, and then descended on an emphatic "Yes! The desire and the training should have begun seven years ago—or a good deal earlier. A mountebank's child who helps her father to earn shillings when she is six years old—a child that inherits a singing throat from a long line of choristers and learns to sing as it learns to talk, has a likelier beginning. Any great achievement in acting or in music grows with the growth. Whenever an artist has been able to say, 'I came, I saw, I conquered,' it has been at the end of patient practice. Genius at first is little more than a great capacity for receiving discipline. Singing and acting, like the fine dexterity of the juggler with his cups and balls, require a shaping of the organs toward a finer and finer certainty of effect. Your muscles—your whole frame—must go like a watch, true, true, true, to a hair. That is the work of springtime, before habits have been determined."

"I did not pretend to genius," said Gwendolen, still feeling that she might somehow do what Klesmer wanted to represent as impossible. "I only supposed that I might have a little talent—enough to improve."

"I don't deny that," said Klesmer. "If you had been put in the right track some years ago and had worked well, you might now have made a public singer, though I don't think your voice would have counted for much in public. For the stage your personal charms and intelligence might then have told without the present drawback of inexperience—lack of discipline—lack of instruction."

Certainly Klesmer seemed cruel, but his feeling was the reverse of cruel. Our speech, even when we are most single-minded, can never take its line absolutely from one impulse; but Klesmer's was as far as possible directed by compassion for poor Gwendolen's ignorant eagerness to enter on a course of which he saw all the miserable details with a definiteness which he could not if he would have conveyed to her mind.

Gwendolen, however, was not convinced. Her self-opinion rallied, and since the counsellor whom she had called in gave a decision of such severe peremptoriness, she was tempted to think that his judgment was not only fallible, but biassed. It occurred to her that a simpler and wiser step for her to have taken would have been to send a letter through the post to the manager of a London theatre, asking him to make an appointment. She would make no further reference to her singing: Klesmer, she saw, had set himself against her singing. But she felt equal to arguing with him about her going on the stage, and she answered in a resistant tone:

"I understand, of course, that no one can be a finished actress at once. It may be impossible to tell beforehand whether I should succeed; but that seems to me a reason why I should try. I should have thought that I might have taken an engagement at a theatre meanwhile, so as to earn money and study at the same time."

"Can't be done, my dear Miss Harleth—I speak plainly—it can't be done. I must clear your mind of these notions, which have no more resemblance to reality than a pantomime. Ladies and gentlemen think that when they have made their toilet and drawn on their gloves they are as presentable on the stage as in a drawing-room. No manager thinks that. With all your grace and charm, if you were to present yourself as an aspirant to the stage, a manager would either require you to pay as an amateur for being allowed to perform, or he would tell you to go and be taught—trained to bear yourself on the stage, as a horse, however beautiful, must be trained for the circus; to say nothing of that study which would enable you to personate a character consistently, and animate it with the natural language of face, gesture, and tone. For you to get an engagement fit for you straight away is out of the question."

"I really cannot understand that," said Gwendolen, rather haughtily—then, checking herself, she added in another tone: "I shall be obliged to you if you will explain how it is that such poor actresses get engaged. I have been to the theatre several times, and I am sure there were actresses who seemed to me to act not at all well and who were quite plain."

"Ah, my dear Miss Harleth, that is the easy criticism of the buyer. We who buy slippers toss away this pair and the other as clumsy; but there went an apprenticeship to the making of them. Excuse me: you could not at present teach one of those actresses; but there is certainly much that she could teach you. For example, she can pitch her voice so as to be heard: ten to one you could not do it till after many trials. Merely to stand and move on the stage is an art—requires practice. It is understood that we are not now talking of a *comparse* in a petty theatre who earns the wages of a needle-woman. That is out of the question for you."

"Of course I must earn more than that," said Gwendolen, with a sense of wincing rather than of being refuted; "but I think I could soon learn to do tolerably well all those little things you have mentioned. I am not so very stupid. And even in Paris I am sure I saw two actresses playing important ladies' parts who were not at all ladies, and quite ugly. I suppose I have no particular talent, but I *must* think it is an advantage, even on the stage, to be a lady and not a perfect fright."

"Ah, let us understand each other," said Klesmer, with a flash of new meaning. "I was speaking of what you would have to go through if you aimed at becoming a real artist—if you took music and the drama as a higher vocation in which you would strive after excellence. On that head, what I have said stands fast. You would find—after your education in doing things slackly for one-and-twenty years—great difficulties in study: you would find mortifications in the treatment you would get when you presented yourself on the footing of skill. You would be subjected to tests; people would no longer feign not to see your blunders. You would at first only be accepted on trial. You would have to bear what I may call a glaring insignificance: any success must be won by the utmost patience. You would have to keep your place in a crowd, and after all it is likely you would lose it and get out of sight. If you determine to face these hardships and still try, you will have the dignity of a high purpose, even though you may have chosen unfortunately. You will have some merit, though you may win no prize. You have asked my judgment on your chances of winning. I don't pretend to speak absolutely; but measuring probabilities, my judgment is: you will hardly achieve more than mediocrity."

Klesmer had delivered himself with emphatic rapidity, and now paused a moment. Gwendolen was motionless, looking at her hands, which lay over each other on her lap, till the deep-toned, long-drawn "*But*," with which he resumed, had a startling effect, and made her look at him again.

"But—there are certainly other ideas, other dispositions with which a young lady may take up an art that will bring her before the public. She may rely on the unquestioned power of her beauty as a passport. She may desire to exhibit herself to an admiration which dispenses with skill. This goes a certain way on the stage: not in music: but on the stage, beauty is taken when there is nothing more commanding to be had. Not without some drilling, however: as I have said before, technicalities have in any case to be mastered. But these excepted, we have here nothing to do with art. The woman who takes up this career is not an artist: she is usually one who thinks of entering on a luxurious life by a short and easy road—perhaps by marriage—that is her most brilliant chance, and the rarest. Still, her career will not be luxurious to begin with: she can hardly earn her own poor bread independently at once, and the indignities she will be liable to are such as I will not speak of."

"I desire to be independent," said Gwendolen, deeply stung, and confusedly apprehending some scorn for herself in Klesmer's words. "That was my reason for asking whether I could not get an immediate engagement. Of course I cannot know how things go on about theatres. But I thought that I could have made myself independent. I have no money, and I will not accept help from any one."

Her wounded pride could not rest without making this disclaimer. It was intolerable to her that Klesmer should imagine her to have expected other help from him than advice.

"That is a hard saying for your friends," said Klesmer, recovering the gentleness of tone with which he had begun the conversation. "I have given you pain. That was inevitable. I was bound to put the truth, the unvarnished truth, before you. I have not said—I will not say—you will do wrong to choose the hard, climbing path of an endeavoring artist. You have to compare its difficulties with those of any less hazardous—any more private course which opens itself to you. If you take that more courageous resolve I will ask leave to shake hands with you on the strength of our freemasonry, where we are all vowed to the service of Art, and to serve her by helping every fellow-servant."

Gwendolen was silent, again looking at her hands. She felt herself very far away from taking the resolve that would enforce acceptance; and after waiting an instant or two, Klesmer went on with deepened seriousness:

"Where there is the duty of service there must be the duty of accepting it. The question is not one of personal obligation. And in relation to practical matters immediately affecting your future—excuse my permitting myself to mention in confidence an affair of my own. I am expecting an event which would make it easy for me to exert myself on your behalf in furthering your opportunities of instruction and residence in London—under the care, that is, of your family—without need for anxiety on your part. If you resolve to take art as a bread-study, you need only undertake the study at first; the bread will be found without trouble. The event I mean is my marriage,—in fact—you will receive this as a matter of confidence,—my marriage with Miss Arrowpoint, which will more than double such right as I have to be trusted by you as a friend. Your friendship will have greatly risen in value for *her* by your having adopted that generous labor."

Gwendolen's face had begun to burn. That Klesmer was about to marry Miss Arrowpoint caused her no surprise, and at another moment she would have amused herself in quickly imagining the scenes that must have occurred at Quetcham. But what engrossed her feeling, what filled her imagination now, was the panorama of her own immediate future that Klesmer's words seemed to have unfolded. The suggestion of Miss Arrowpoint as a patroness was only another detail added to its repulsiveness: Klesmer's proposal to help her seemed an additional irritation after the humiliating judgment he had passed on her capabilities. His words had really bitten into her self-confidence and turned it into the pain of a bleeding wound; and the idea of presenting herself before other judges was now poisoned with the dread that they also might be harsh: they also would not recognize the talent she was conscious of. But she controlled herself, and rose from her seat before she made any answer. It seemed natural that she should pause. She went to the piano and looked absently at leaves of music, pinching up the corners. At last she turned toward Klesmer, and said, with almost her usual air of proud equality, which in this interview had not been hitherto perceptible:

"I congratulate you sincerely, Herr Klesmer. I think I never saw any one more admirable than Miss Arrowpoint. And I have to thank you for every sort of kindness this morning. But I can't decide now. If I make the resolve you have spoken of, I will use your permission—I will let you know. But I fear the obstacles are too great. In any case, I am deeply obliged to you. It was very bold of me to ask you to take this trouble."

Klesmer's inward remark was, "She will never let me know." But with the most thorough respect in his manner, he said: "Command me at any time. There is an address on this card which will always find me with little delay."

When he had taken up his hat and was going to make his bow, Gwendolen's better self, conscious of an ingratitude which the clear-seeing Klesmer must have penetrated, made a desperate effort to find its way above the stifling layers of egoistic disappointment and irritation. Looking at him with a glance of the old gayety, she put out her hand, and said with a smile: "If I take the wrong road, it will not be because of your flattery."

"God forbid that you should take any road but one where you will find and give happiness!" said Klesmer fervently. Then, in foreign fashion, he touched her fingers lightly with his lips, and in another minute she heard the sound of his departing wheels getting more distant on the gravel.

Gwendolen had never in her life felt so miserable. No sob came, no passion of tears, to relieve her. Her eyes were burning; and the noonday only brought into more dreary clearness the absence of interest from her life. All memories, all objects, the pieces of music displayed, the open piano—the very reflection of herself in the glass—seemed no better than the packed-up shows of a departing fair. For the first time since her consciousness began, she was having a vision of herself on the common level, and had lost the innate sense that there were reasons why she should not be slighted, elbowed, jostled—treated like a passenger with a third-class ticket, in spite of private objections on her own part. She did not move about; the prospects begotten by disappointment were too oppressively preoccupying; she threw herself into the shadiest corner of the settee, and pressed her fingers over her burning eyelids. Every word that Klesmer had said seemed to have been branded into her memory, as most words are which bring with them a new set of impressions and make an epoch for us. Only a few hours before, the dawning smile of self-contentment rested on her lips as she vaguely imagined a future suited to her wishes: it seemed but the affair of a year or so for her to become the most approved Juliet of the time; or, if Klesmer encouraged her idea of being a singer, to proceed by more gradual steps to her place in the opera, while she won money and applause by occasional performances. Why not? At home, at school, among acquaintances, she had been used to have her conscious superiority admitted; and she had moved in a society where everything, from low arithmetic to high art, is of the amateur kind politely supposed to fall short of perfection only because gentlemen and ladies are not obliged to do more than they like—otherwise they would probably give forth abler writings and show themselves more commanding artists than any the world is at present obliged to put up with. The self-confident visions that had beguiled her were not of a highly exceptional kind; and she had at least shown some rationality in consulting the person who knew the most and had flattered her the least. In asking Klesmer's advice, however, she had rather been borne up by a belief in his latent admiration than bent on knowing anything more unfavorable that might have lain behind his slight objections to her singing; and the truth she had asked for with an expectation that it would be agreeable, had come like a lacerating thong.

"Too old—should have begun seven years ago — you will not, at best, achieve more than mediocrity—hard, incessant

work, uncertain praise—bread coming slowly, scantily, perhaps not at all—mortifications, people no longer feigning not
to see your blunders—glaring insignificance "—all these phrases
rankled in her; and even more galling was the hint that she
could only be accepted on the stage as a beauty who hoped to
get a husband. The "indignities" that she might be visited
with had no very definite form for her, but the mere association of anything called "indignity" with herself roused a
resentful alarm. And along with the vaguer images which
were raised by those biting words, came the more precise conception of disagreeables which her experience enabled her to
imagine. How could she take her mamma and the four sisters to London, if it were not possible for her to earn money
at once? And as for submitting to be a *protégée* and asking
her mamma to submit with her to the humiliation of being
supported by Miss Arrowpoint—that was as bad as being a
governess; nay, worse; for suppose the end of all her study
be as worthless as Klesmer clearly expected it to be, the sense
of favors received and never repaid would embitter the miseries of disappointment. Klesmer doubtless had magnificent
ideas about helping artists; but how could he know the feelings of ladies in such matters? It was all over: she had
entertained a mistaken hope; and there was an end of it.

"An end of it!" said Gwendolen, aloud, starting from her
seat as she heard the steps and voices of her mamma and sisters coming in from church. She hurried to the piano and
began gathering together her pieces of music with assumed dili-
gence, while the expression of her pale face and in her burning eyes was what would have suited a woman enduring a
wrong which she might not resent, but would probably revenge.

"Well, my darling," said gentle Mrs. Davilow, entering,
"I see by the wheel-marks that Klesmer has been here.
Have you been satisfied with the interview?" She had some
guesses as to its object, but felt timid about implying them.

"Satisfied, mamma? oh, yes," said Gwendolen, in a high,
hard tone, for which she must be excused, because she dreaded
a scene of emotion. If she did not set herself resolutely to
feign proud indifference, she felt that she must fall into a

passionate outburst of despair, which would cut her mamma more deeply than all the rest of their calamities.

"Your uncle and aunt were disappointed at not seeing you," said Mrs. Davilow, coming near the piano, and watching Gwendolen's movements. "I only said that you wanted rest."

"Quite right, mamma," said Gwendolen, in the same tone, turning to put away some music.

"Am I not to know anything now, Gwendolen? Am I always to be in the dark?" said Mrs. Davilow, too keenly sensitive to her daughter's manner and expression not to fear that something painful had occurred.

"There is really nothing to tell now, mamma," said Gwendolen, in a still higher voice. "I had a mistaken idea about something I could do. Herr Klesmer has undeceived me. That is all."

"Don't look and speak in that way, my dear child: I cannot bear it," said Mrs. Davilow, breaking down. She felt an undefinable terror.

Gwendolen looked at her a moment in silence, biting her inner lip; then she went up to her, and putting her hands on her mamma's shoulders, said, with a drop of her voice to the lowest undertone: "Mamma, don't speak to me now. It is useless to cry and waste our strength over what can't be altered. You will live at Sawyer's Cottage, and I am going to the bishop's daughters. There is no more to be said. Things cannot be altered, and who cares? It makes no difference to any one else what we do. We must try not to care ourselves. We must not give way. I dread giving way. Help me to be quiet."

Mrs. Davilow was like a frightened child under her daughter's face and voice: her tears were arrested, and she went away in silence.

CHAPTER XXIV.

"I question things and do not find
One that will answer to my mind ;
And all the world appears unkind. "
— WORDSWORTH.

GWENDOLEN was glad that she had got through her interview with Klesmer before meeting her uncle and aunt. She had made up her mind now that there were only disagreeables before her, and she felt able to maintain a dogged calm in the face of any humiliation that might be proposed.

The meeting did not happen until the Monday, when Gwendolen went to the Rectory with her mamma. They had called at Sawyer's Cottage by the way, and had seen every cranny of the narrow rooms in a mid-day light, unsoftened by blinds and curtains; for the furnishing to be done by gleanings from the Rectory had not yet begun.

" How *shall* you endure it, mamma? " said Gwendolen, as they walked away. She had not opened her lips while they were looking round at the bare walls and floors, and the little garden with the cabbage-stalks, and the yew arbor all dust and cobwebs within. " You and the four girls all in that closet of a room, with the green and yellow paper pressing on your eyes? And without me? "

" It will be some comfort that you have not to bear it too, dear. "

" If it were not that I must get some money, I would rather be there than go to be a governess. "

" Don't set yourself against it beforehand, Gwendolen. If you go to the palace you will have every luxury about you. And you know how much you have always cared for that. You will not find it so hard as going up and down those steep narrow stairs, and hearing the crockery rattle through the house, and the dear girls talking. "

" It is like a bad dream, " said Gwendolen, impetuously. " I cannot believe that my uncle will let you go to such a place. He ought to have taken some other steps. "

" Don't be unreasonable, dear child. What could he have done? "

"That was for him to find out. It seems to me a very extraordinary world if people in our position must sink in this way all at once," said Gwendolen, the other worlds with which she was conversant being constructed with a sense of fitness that arranged her own future agreeably.

It was her temper that framed her sentences under this entirely new pressure of evils: she could have spoken more suitably on the vicissitudes in other people's lives, though it was never her aspiration to express herself virtuously so much as cleverly—a point to be remembered in extenuation of her words, which were usually worse than she was.

And, notwithstanding the keen sense of her own bruises, she was capable of some compunction when her uncle and aunt received her with a more affectionate kindness than they had ever shown before. She could not but be struck by the dignified cheerfulness with which they talked of the necessary economies in their way of living, and in the education of the boys. Mr. Gascoigne's worth of character, a little obscured by worldly opportunities—as the poetic beauty of women is obscured by the demands of fashionable dressing—showed itself to great advantage under this sudden reduction of fortune. Prompt and methodical, he had set himself not only to put down his carriage, but to reconsider his worn suits of clothes, to leave off meat for breakfast, to do without periodicals, to get Edwy from school and arrange hours of study for all the boys under himself, and to order the whole establishment on the sparest footing possible. For all healthy people economy has its pleasures; and the Rector's spirit had spread through the household. Mrs. Gascoigne and Anna, who always made papa their model, really did not miss anything they cared about for themselves, and in all sincerity felt that the saddest part of the family losses was the change for Mrs. Davilow and her children.

Anna for the first time could merge her resentment on behalf of Rex in her sympathy with Gwendolen; and Mrs. Gascoigne was disposed to hope that trouble would have a salutary effect on her niece, without thinking it her duty to add any bitters by way of increasing the salutariness. They had both been busy devising how to get blinds and curtains for the cottage out of the household stores; but with delicate feeling they left these matters in the background, and talked at first of Gwendolen's journey, and the comfort it was to her mamma to have her at home again.

In fact there was nothing for Gwendolen to take as a justification for extending her discontent with events to the persons immediately around her, and she felt shaken into a more alert attention, as if by a call to drill that everybody else was obeying, when her uncle began in a voice of firm kindness to talk to her of the efforts he had been making to get her a situation which would offer her as many advantages as possible. Mr. Gascoigne had not forgotten Grandcourt, but the possibility of further advances from that quarter was something too vague for a man of his good sense to be determined by it: uncertainties of that kind must not now slacken his action in doing the best he could for his niece under actual conditions.

"I felt that there was no time to be lost, Gwendolen;—for a position in a good family where you will have some consideration is not to be had at a moment's notice. And however long we waited we could hardly find one where you would be better off than at Bishop Mompert's. I am known to both him and Mrs. Mompert, and that of course is an advantage for you. Our correspondence has gone on favorably; but I cannot be surprised that Mrs. Mompert wishes to see you before making an absolute engagement. She thinks of arranging for you to meet her at Wanchester when she is on her way to town. I dare say you will feel the interview rather trying for you, my dear; but you will have a little time to prepare your mind."

"Do you know *why* she wants to see me, uncle?" said Gwendolen, whose mind had quickly gone over various reasons that an imaginary Mrs. Mompert with three daughters might be supposed to entertain—reasons all of a disagreeable kind to the person presenting herself for inspection.

The Rector smiled. "Don't be alarmed, my dear. She would like to have a more precise idea of you than my report can give. And a mother is naturally scrupulous about a companion for her daughters. I have told her you are very young. But she herself exercises a close supervision over her daughters' education, and that makes her less anxious as to age. She is a woman of taste and also of strict principle, and objects to having a French person in the house. I feel sure that she will think your manners and accomplishments as good as she is likely to find; and over the religious and moral tone of the education she, and indeed the bishop himself, will preside."

Gwendolen dared not answer, but the repression of her decided dislike to the whole prospect sent an unusually deep flush over her face and neck, subsiding as quickly as it came. Anna, full of tender fears, put her little hand into her cousin's, and Mr. Gascoigne was too kind a man not to conceive something of the trial which this sudden change must be for a girl like Gwendolen. Bent on giving a cheerful view of things, he went on in an easy tone of remark, not as if answering supposed objections:

"I think so highly of the position, that I should have been tempted to try and get it for Anna, if she had been at all likely to meet Mrs. Mompert's wants. It is really a home, with a continuance of education in the highest sense: 'governess' is a misnomer. The bishop's views are of a more decidedly Low Church color than my own—he is a close friend of Lord Grampian's; but though privately strict, he is not by any means narrow in public matters. Indeed, he has created as little dislike in his diocese as any bishop on the bench. He has always remained friendly to me, though before his promotion, when he was an incumbent of this diocese, we had a little controversy about the Bible Society."

The Rector's words were too pregnant with satisfactory meaning to himself for him to imagine the effect they produced on the mind of his niece. "Continuance of education" —"bishop's views"—"privately strict"—"Bible Society,"— it was as if he had introduced a few snakes at large for the instruction of ladies who regarded them as all alike furnished with poison-bags, and biting or stinging according to convenience. To Gwendolen, already shrinking from the prospect opened to her, such phrases came like the growing heat of a burning-glass—not at all as the links of persuasive reflection

which they formed for the good uncle.   She began desperately
to seek an alternative.

"There was another situation, I think, mamma spoke of?"
she said, with determined self-mastery.

"Yes," said the Rector, in rather a depreciatory tone; "but
that is in a school.   I should not have the same satisfaction in
your taking that.   It would be much harder work, you are
aware, and not so good in any other respect.   Besides, you
have not an equal chance of getting it."

"Oh, dear, no," said Mrs. Gascoigne, "it would be much
harder for you, my dear—much less appropriate.   You might
not have a bedroom to yourself."   And Gwendolen's memories of school suggested other particulars which forced her to
admit to herself that this alternative would be no relief.   She
turned to her uncle again, and said, apparently in acceptance
of his ideas:

"When is Mrs. Mompert likely to send for me?"

"That is rather uncertain, but she has promised not to entertain any other proposal till she has seen you.   She has
entered with much feeling into your position.   It will be within
the next fortnight, probably.   But I must be off now.   I am
going to let part of my glebe uncommonly well."

The Rector ended very cheerfully, leaving the room with
the satisfactory conviction that Gwendolen was going to adapt
herself to circumstances like a girl of good sense.   Having
spoken appropriately, he naturally supposed that the effects
would be appropriate; being accustomed as a household and
parish authority to be asked to "speak to" refractory persons,
with the understanding that the measure was morally coercive.

"What a stay Henry is to us all!" said Mrs. Gascoigne,
when her husband had left the room.

"He is indeed," said Mrs. Davilow, cordially.   "I think
cheerfulness is a fortune in itself.   I wish I had it."

"And Rex is just like him," said Mrs. Gascoigne.   "I
must tell you the comfort we have had in a letter from him.
I must read you a little bit," she added, taking the letter from
her pocket, while Anna looked rather frightened—she did not
know why, except that it had been a rule with her not to mention Rex before Gwendolen.

The proud mother ran her eyes over the letter, seeking for sentences to read aloud. But apparently she had found it sown with what might seem to be closer allusions than she desired to the recent past, for she looked up, folding the letter, and saying:

"However, he tells us that our trouble has made a man of him; he sees a reason for any amount of work: he means to get a fellowship, to take pupils, to set one of his brothers going, to be everything that is most remarkable. The letter is full of fun—just like him. He says, ' Tell mother she has put out an advertisement for a jolly good hard-working son, in time to hinder me from taking ship; and I offer myself for the place.' The letter came on Friday. I never saw my husband so much moved by anything since Rex was born. It seemed a gain to balance our loss."

This letter, in fact, was what had helped both Mrs. Gascoigne and Anna to show Gwendolen an unmixed kindliness; and she herself felt very amiably about it, smiling at Anna and pinching her chin as much as to say, "Nothing is wrong with you now, is it?" She had no gratuitously ill-natured feeling, or egoistic pleasure in making men miserable. She only had an intense objection to their making her miserable.

But when the talk turned on furniture for the cottage, Gwendolen was not roused to show even a languid interest. She thought that she had done as much as could be expected of her this morning, and indeed felt at an heroic pitch in keeping to herself the struggle that was going on within her. The recoil of her mind from the only definite prospect allowed her was stronger than even she had imagined beforehand. The idea of presenting herself before Mrs. Mompert in the first instance, to be approved or disapproved, came as pressure on an already painful bruise: even as a governess, it appeared she was to be tested and was liable to rejection. After she had done herself the violence to accept the bishop and his wife, they were still to consider whether they would accept her; it was at her peril that she was to look, speak, or be silent. And even when she had entered on her dismal task of self-constraint in the society of three girls whom she was bound incessantly to edify, the same process of inspection was to go on: there was always to be Mrs. Mompert's supervision; always something or other would be expected of her to which she had not the slightest inclination; and perhaps the bishop would examine her on serious topics. Gwendolen, lately used to the social successes of a handsome girl, whose lively venturesomeness of talk has the effect of wit, and who six weeks before would have pitied the dulness of the bishop rather than have been embarrassed by him, saw the life before her as an entrance into a penitentiary. Wild thoughts of running away to be an actress, in spite of Klesmer, came to her with the lure of freedom; but his words still hung heavily on her soul; they had alarmed her pride and even her maidenly dignity: dimly she conceived herself getting amongst vulgar people who would treat her with rude familiarity—odious men, whose grins and smirks would not be seen through the strong grating of polite society. Gwendolen's daring was not in the least that of the adventuress; the demand to be held a lady was in her very marrow; and when she had dreamed that she might be the heroine of the gaming-table, it was with the understanding that no one should treat her with the less consideration, or presume to look at her with irony as Deronda had done. To be protected and petted, and to have her susceptibilities consulted in every detail, had gone along with her food and clothing as matters of course in her life: even without any such warning as Klesmer's she could not have thought it an attractive freedom to be thrown in solitary dependence on the doubtful civility of strangers. The endurance of the episcopal penitentiary was less repulsive than that; though here too she would certainly never be petted or have her susceptibilities consulted. Her rebellion against this hard necessity which had come just to her of all people in the world—to her whom all circumstances had concurred in preparing for something quite different—was exaggerated instead of diminished as one hour followed another, filled with the imagination of what she might have expected in her lot and what it was actually to be. The family troubles, she thought, were easier for every one than for her—even for poor dear mamma, because she had always used herself to not enjoying. As to hoping that if she went to the Momperts' and was patient a little while, things might get better—it would be stupid to entertain hopes for herself after all that had happened: her talents, it appeared, would never be recognized as anything remarkable, and there was not a single direction in which probability seemed to flatter her wishes. Some beautiful girls who, like her, had read romances where even plain governesses are centres of attraction and are sought in marriage, might have solaced themselves a little by transporting such pictures into their own future; but even if Gwendolen's experience had led her to dwell on love-making and marriage as her elysium, her heart was too much oppressed by what was near to her, in both the past and the future, for her to project her anticipations very far off. She had a world-nausea upon her, and saw no reason all through her life why she should wish to live. No religious view of trouble helped her: her troubles had in her opinion all been caused by other people's disagreeable or wicked conduct; and there was really nothing pleasant to be counted on in the world: that was her feeling; everything else she had heard said about trouble was mere phrase-making not attractive enough for her to have caught it up and repeated it. As to the sweetness of labor and fulfilled claims; the interest of inward and outward activity; the impersonal delights of life as a perpetual discovery; the dues of courage, fortitude, industry, which it is mere baseness not to pay toward the common burden; the supreme worth of the teacher's vocation;—these, even if they had been eloquently preached to her, could have been no more than faintly apprehended doctrines: the fact which wrought upon her was her invariable observation that for a lady to become a governess—to "take a situation"—was to descend in life and to be treated at best with a compassionate patronage. And poor Gwendolen had never dissociated happiness from personal pre-eminence and *éclat*. That where these threatened to forsake her, she should take life to be hardly worth the having, cannot make her so unlike the rest of us, men or women, that we should cast her out of our compassion; our moments of temptation to a mean opinion of things in general being usually dependent on some susceptibility about ourselves and some dulness to subjects which every one else would consider more important.

Surely a young creature is pitiable who has the labyrinth of life before her and no clew—to whom distrust in herself and her good fortune has come as a sudden shock, like a rent across the path that she was treading carelessly.

In spite of her healthy frame, her irreconcilable repugnance affected her even physically: she felt a sort of numbness and could set about nothing; the least urgency, even that she should take her meals, was an irritation to her; the speech of others on any subject seemed unreasonable, because it did not include her feeling and was an ignorant claim on her. It was not in her nature to busy herself with the fancies of suicide to which disappointed young people are prone: what occupied and exasperated her was the sense that there was nothing for her but to live in a way she hated. She avoided going to the Rectory again: it was too intolerable to have to look and talk as if she were compliant; and she could not exert herself to show interest about the furniture of that horrible cottage. Miss Merry was staying on purpose to help, and such people as Jocosa liked that sort of thing. Her mother had to make excuses for her not appearing, even when Anna came to see her. For that calm which Gwendolen had promised herself to maintain had changed into sick motivelessness: she thought, "I suppose I shall begin to pretend by and by, but why should I do it now?"

Her mother watched her with silent distress; and, lapsing into the habit of indulgent tenderness, she began to think what she imagined that Gwendolen was thinking, and to wish that everything should give way to the possibility of making her darling less miserable.

One day when she was in the black and yellow bedroom, and her mother was lingering there under the pretext of considering and arranging Gwendolen's articles of dress, she suddenly roused herself to fetch the casket which contained her ornaments.

"Mamma," she began, glancing over the upper layer, "I had forgotten these things. Why didn't you remind me of them? Do see about getting them sold. You will not mind about parting with them. You gave them all to me long ago."

She lifted the upper tray and looked below.

"If we can do without them, darling, I would rather keep them for you," said Mrs. Davilow, seating herself beside Gwendolen with a feeling of relief that she was beginning to talk about something. The usual relation between them had become reversed. It was now the mother who tried to cheer the daughter. "Why, how came you to put that pocket-handkerchief in here?"

It was the handkerchief with the corner torn off which Gwendolen had thrust in with the turquoise necklace.

"It happened to be with the necklace—I was in a hurry," said Gwendolen, taking the handkerchief away and putting it in her pocket. "Don't sell the necklace, mamma," she added, a new feeling having come over her about that rescue of it which had formerly been so offensive.

"No, dear, no; it was made out of your dear father's chain. And I should prefer not selling the other things. None of them are of any great value. All my best ornaments were taken from me long ago."

Mrs. Davilow colored. She usually avoided any reference to such facts about Gwendolen's step-father as that he had carried off his wife's jewelry and disposed of it. After a moment's pause she went on:

"And these things have not been reckoned on for any expenses. Carry them with you."

"That would be quite useless, mamma," said Gwendolen, coldly. "Governesses don't wear ornaments. You had better get me a gray frieze livery and a straw poke, such as my aunt's charity children wear."

"No, dear, no; don't take that view of it. I feel sure the Momperts will like you the better for being graceful and elegant."

"I am not at all sure what the Momperts will like me to be. It is enough that I am expected to be what they like," said Gwendolen, bitterly.

"If there is anything you would object to less—anything that could be done—instead of your going to the bishop's, do say so, Gwendolen. Tell me what is in your heart. I will try for anything you wish," said the mother, beseechingly. "Don't keep things away from me. Let us bear them together."

"Oh, mamma, there is nothing to tell. I can't do anything better. I must think myself fortunate if they will have me. I shall get some money for you. That is the only thing I have to think of. I shall not spend any money this year: you will have all the eighty pounds. I don't know how far that will go in housekeeping; but you need not stitch your poor fingers to the bone, and stare away all the sight that the tears have left in your dear eyes."

Gwendolen did not give any caresses with her words as she had been used to do. She did not even look at her mother, but was looking at the turquoise necklace as she turned it over her fingers.

"Bless you for your tenderness, my good darling!" said Mrs. Davilow, with tears in her eyes. "Don't despair because there are clouds now. You are so young. There may be great happiness in store for you yet."

"I don't see any reason for expecting it, mamma," said Gwendolen, in a hard tone; and Mrs. Davilow was silent, thinking as she had often thought before: "What did happen between her and Mr. Grandcourt?"

"I *will* keep this necklace, mamma," said Gwendolen, laying it apart and then closing the casket. "But do get the other things sold, even if they will not bring much. Ask my uncle what to do with them. I shall certainly not use them again. I am going to take the veil. I wonder if all the poor wretches who have ever taken it felt as I do."

"Don't exaggerate evils, dear."

"How can any one know that I exaggerate, when I am speaking of my own feeling? I did not say what any one else felt."

She took out the torn handkerchief from her pocket again, and wrapt it deliberately round the necklace. Mrs. Davilow observed the action with some surprise, but the tone of the last words discouraged her from asking any question.

The "feeling" Gwendolen spoke of with an air of tragedy was not to be explained by the mere fact that she was going to be a governess: she was possessed by a spirit of general disappointment. It was not simply that she had a distaste for what she was called on to do: the distaste spread itself over the world outside her penitentiary, since she saw nothing very pleasant in it that seemed attainable by her even if she were free.   Naturally her grievances did not seem to her smaller than some of her male contemporaries held theirs to be when they felt a profession too narrow for their powers, and had an *à priori* conviction that it was not worth while to put forth their latent abilities.   Because her education had been less expensive than theirs, it did not follow that she should have wider emotions or a keener intellectual vision.   Her griefs were feminine; but to her as a woman they were not the less hard to bear, and she felt an equal right to the Promethean tone.

But the movement of mind which led her to keep the necklace, to fold it up in the handkerchief, and rise to put it in her *nécessaire,* where she had first placed it when it had been returned to her, was more peculiar, and what would be called less reasonable.   It came from that streak of superstition in her which attached itself both to her confidence and her terror—a superstition which lingers in an intense personality even in spite of theory and science; any dread or hope for self being stronger than all reasons for or against it.   Why she should suddenly determine not to part with the necklace was not much clearer to her than why she should sometimes have been frightened to find herself in the fields alone: she had a confused state of emotion about Deronda—was it wounded pride and resentment, or a certain awe and exceptional trust? It was something vague, and yet mastering, which impelled her to this action about the necklace.   There is a great deal of unmapped country within us which would have to be taken into account in an explanation of our gusts and storms.

CHAPTER XXV.

How trace the why and wherefore in a mind reduced to the barrenness of a fastidious egoism, in which all direct desires are dulled, and have dwindled from motives into a vacillating expectation of motives: a mind made up of moods, where a fitful impulse springs here and there conspicuously rank amid the general weediness? 'Tis a condition apt to befall a life too much at large, unmoulded by the pressure of obligation. *Nam deteriores omnes sumus licentiæ*, saith Terence; or, as a more familiar tongue might deliver it, '*As you like*' *is a bad finger-post.*

POTENTATES make known their intentions and affect the funds at a small expense of words. So, when Grandcourt, after learning that Gwendolen had left Leubronn, incidentally pronounced that resort of fashion a beastly hole worse than Baden, the remark was conclusive to Mr. Lush that his patron intended straightway to return to Diplow. The execution was sure to be slower than the intention, and in fact Grandcourt did loiter through the next day without giving any distinct orders about departure—perhaps because he discerned that Lush was expecting them: he lingered over his toilet, and certainly came down with a faded aspect of perfect distinction which made fresh complexions, and hands with the blood in them, seem signs of raw vulgarity; he lingered on the terrace, in the gambling-rooms, in the reading-room, occupying himself in being indifferent to everybody and everything around him. When he met Lady Mallinger, however, he took some trouble—raised his hat, paused, and proved that he listened to her recommendation of the waters by replying: "Yes; I heard somebody say how providential it was that there always happened to be springs at gambling-places."

"Oh, that was a joke," said innocent Lady Mallinger, misled by Grandcourt's languid seriousness, "in imitation of the old one about the towns and the rivers, you know."

"Ah, perhaps," said Grandcourt, without change of expression. Lady Mallinger thought this worth telling to Sir Hugo, who said: "Oh, my dear, he is not a fool. You must not suppose that he can't see a joke. He can play his cards as well as most of us."

"He has never seemed to me a very sensible man," said Lady Mallinger, in excuse of herself. She had a secret objec-

tion to meeting Grandcourt, who was little else to her than a
large living sign of what she felt to be her failure as a wife—
the not having presented Sir Hugo with a son. Her constant
reflection was that her husband might fairly regret his choice,
and if he had not been very good might have treated her with
some roughness in consequence, gentlemen naturally disliking
to be disappointed.

Deronda, too, had a recognition from Grandcourt, for which
he was not grateful, though he took care to return it with perfect civility. No reasoning as to the foundations of custom
could do away with the early rooted feeling that his birth had
been attended with injury for which his father was to blame;
and seeing that but for this injury Grandcourt's prospect
might have been his, he was proudly resolute not to behave
in any way that might be interpreted into irritation on that
score. He saw a very easy descent into mean, unreasoning
rancor and triumph in others' frustration; and being determined not to go down that ugly pit, he turned his back on it,
clinging to the kindlier affections within him as a possession.
Pride certainly helped him well—the pride of not recognizing a
disadvantage for one's self which vulgar minds are disposed to
exaggerate, such as the shabby equipage of poverty: he would
not have a man like Grandcourt suppose himself envied by him.
But there is no guarding against interpretation. Grandcourt
did believe that Deronda, poor devil, who he had no doubt was
his cousin by the father's side, inwardly winced under their
mutual position; wherefore the presence of that less lucky
person was more agreeable to him than it would otherwise
have been. An imaginary envy, the idea that others feel
their comparative deficiency, is the ordinary *cortège* of egoism; and his pet dogs were not the only beings that Grandcourt liked to feel his power over in making them jealous.
Hence he was civil enough to exchange several words with
Deronda on the terrace about the hunting round Diplow, and
even said: "You had better come over for a run or two when
the season begins."

Lush, not displeased with delay, amused himself very well,
partly in gossiping with Sir Hugo and in answering his questions about Grandcourt's affairs so far as they might affect his

willingness to part with his interest in Diplow. Also about Grandcourt's personal entanglements, the baronet knew enough already for Lush to feel released from silence on a sunny autumn day, when there was nothing more agreeable to do in lounging promenades than to speak freely of a tyrannous patron behind his back. Sir Hugo willingly inclined his ear to a little good-humored scandal, which he was fond of calling *traits de mœurs;* but he was strict in keeping such communications from hearers who might take them too seriously. Whatever knowledge he had of his nephew's secrets, he had never spoken of it to Deronda, who considered Grandcourt a pale-blooded mortal, but was far from wishing to hear how the red corpuscles had been washed out of him. It was Lush's policy and inclination to gratify everybody when he had no reason to the contrary; and the baronet always treated him well, as one of those easy-handled personages who, frequenting the society of gentlemen, without being exactly gentlemen themselves, can be the more serviceable, like the second-best articles of our wardrobe, which we use with a comfortable freedom from anxiety.

"Well, you will let me know the turn of events," said Sir Hugo, "if this marriage seems likely to come off after all, or if anything else happens to make the want of money more pressing. My plan would be much better for him than burdening Ryelands."

"That's true," said Lush, "only it must not be urged on him—just placed in his way that the scent may tickle him. Grandcourt is not a man to be always led by what makes for his own interest; especially if you let him see that it makes for your interest too. I'm attached to him, of course. I've given up everything else for the sake of keeping by him, and it has lasted a good fifteen years now. He would not easily get any one else to fill my place. He's a peculiar character, is Henleigh Grandcourt, and it has been growing on him of late years. However, I'm of a constant disposition, and I've been a sort of guardian to him since he was twenty; an uncommonly fascinating fellow he was then, to be sure—and could be now, if he liked. I'm attached to him; and it would be a good deal worse for him if he missed me at his elbow."

Sir Hugo did not think it needful to express his sympathy or even assent, and perhaps Lush himself did not expect this sketch of his motives to be taken as exact. But how can a man avoid himself as a subject in conversation? And he must make some sort of decent toilet in words, as in cloth and linen. Lush's listener was not severe: a member of Parliament could allow for the necessities of verbal toilet; and the dialogue went on without any change of mutual estimate.

However, Lush's easy prospect of indefinite procrastination was cut off the next morning by Grandcourt's saluting him with the question:

"Are you making all the arrangements for our starting by the Paris train?"

"I didn't know you meant to start," said Lush, not exactly taken by surprise.

"You might have known," said Grandcourt, looking at the burnt length of his cigar, and speaking in that lowered tone which was usual with him when he meant to express disgust and be peremptory. "Just see to everything, will you? and mind no brute gets into the same carriage with us. And leave my P. P. C. at the Mallingers."

In consequence they were at Paris the next day; but here Lush was gratified by the proposal or command that he should go straight on to Diplow and see that everything was right, while Grandcourt and the valet remained behind; and it was not until several days later that Lush received the telegram ordering the carriage to the Wanchester station.

He had used the interim actively, not only in carrying out Grandcourt's orders about the stud and household, but in learning all he could of Gwendolen, and how things were going on at Offendene. What was the probable effect that the news of the family misfortunes would have on Grandcourt's fitful obstinacy he felt to be quite incalculable. So far as the girl's poverty might be an argument that she would accept an offer from him now in spite of any previous coyness, it might remove that bitter objection to risk a repulse which Lush divined to be one of Grandcourt's deterring motives; on the other hand, the certainty of acceptance was just "the sort of thing" to make him lapse hither and thither with no more

apparent will than a moth. Lush had had his patron under
close observation for many years, and knew him perhaps better than he knew any other subject; but to know Grandcourt
was to doubt what he would do in any particular case. It
might happen that he would behave with an apparent mag-
nanimity, like the hero of a modern French drama, whose
sudden start into moral splendor, after much lying and mean-
ness, leaves you little confidence as to any part of his career
that may follow the fall of the curtain. Indeed, what attitude
would have been more honorable for a final scene than that of
declining to seek an heiress for her money, and determining
to marry the attractive girl who had none? But Lush had
some general certainties about Grandcourt, and one was, that
of all inward movements, those of generosity were the least
likely to occur in him. Of what use, however, is a general
certainty that an insect will not walk with his head hindmost,
when what you need to know is the play of inward stimulus
that sends him hither and thither in a network of possible
paths? Thus Lush was much at fault as to the probable issue
between Grandcourt and Gwendolen, when what he desired
was a perfect confidence that they would never be married.
He would have consented willingly that Grandcourt should
marry an heiress, or that he should marry Mrs. Glasher: in
the one match there would have been the immediate abundance
that prospective heirship could not supply, in the other there
would have been the security of the wife's gratitude, for Lush
had always been Mrs. Glasher's friend; and that the future
Mrs. Grandcourt should not be socially received could not
affect his private comfort. He would not have minded, either,
that there should be no marriage in question at all; but he
felt himself justified in doing his utmost to hinder a marriage
with a girl who was likely to bring nothing but trouble to her
husband—not to speak of annoyance if not ultimate injury to
her husband's old companion, whose future Mr. Lush earnestly wished to make as easy as possible, considering that he
had well deserved such compensation for leading a dog's life,
though that of a dog who enjoyed many tastes undisturbed,
and who profited by a large establishment. He wished for
himself what he felt to be good, and was not conscious of

wisning harm to any one else; unless perhaps it were just
now a little harm to the inconvenient and impertinent Gwendolen. But the easiest-humored amateur of luxury and music,
the toad-eater the least liable to nausea, must be expected to
have his susceptibilities. And Mr. Lush was accustomed to
be treated by the world in general as an apt, agreeable fellow:
he had not made up his mind to be insulted by more than one
person.

With this imperfect preparation of a war policy, Lush was
awaiting Grandcourt's arrival, doing little more than wondering how the campaign would begin. The first day Grandcourt
was much occupied with the stables, and amongst other things
he ordered a groom to put a side-saddle on Criterion and let
him review the horse's paces. This marked indication of purpose set Lush on considering over again whether he should
incur the ticklish consequences of speaking first, while he was
still sure that no compromising step had been taken; and he
rose the next morning almost resolved that if Grandcourt
seemed in as good a humor as yesterday, and entered at all
into talk, he would let drop the interesting facts about Gwendolen and her family, just to see how they would work, and
to get some guidance. But Grandcourt did not enter into
talk, and in answer to a question even about his own convenience, no fish could have maintained a more unwinking silence. After he had read his letters he gave various orders
to be executed or transmitted by Lush, and then thrust his
shoulders toward that useful person, who accordingly rose to
leave the room. But before he was out of the door, Grandcourt turned his head slightly and gave a broken languid
"Oh."

"What is it?" said Lush, who, it must have been observed,
did not take his dusty puddings with a respectful air.

"Shut the door, will you? I can't speak into the cor-
ridor."

Lush closed the door, came forward, and chose to sit down.

After a little pause, Grandcourt said: "Is Miss Harleth at
Offendene?" He was quite certain that Lush had made it
his business to inquire about her, and he had some pleasure
in thinking that Lush did not want *him* to inquire.

"Well, I hardly know," said Lush, carelessly. "The family's utterly done up. They and the Gascoignes too have lost all their money. It's owing to some rascally banking business. The poor mother hasn't a *sou*, it seems. She and the girls have to huddle themselves into a little cottage like a laborer's."

"Don't lie to me, if you please," said Grandcourt, in his lowest audible tone. "It's not amusing, and it answers no other purpose."

"What do you mean?" said Lush, more nettled than was common with him—the prospect before him being more than commonly disturbing.

"Just tell me the truth, will you?"

"It's no invention of mine. I have heard the story from several—Bazley, Brackenshaw's man, for one. He is getting a new tenant for Offendene."

"I don't mean that. Is Miss Harleth there, or is she not?" said Grandcourt, in his former tone.

"Upon my soul, I can't tell," said Lush, rather sulkily. "She may have left yesterday. I heard she had taken a situation as governess; she may be gone to it for what I know. But if you wanted to see her, no doubt the mother would send for her back." This sneer slipped off his tongue without strict intention.

"Send Hutchins to inquire whether she will be there to-morrow."

Lush did not move. Like many persons who have thought over beforehand what they shall say in given cases, he was impelled by an unexpected irritation to say some of those pre-arranged things before the cases were given. Grandcourt, in fact, was likely to get into a scrape so tremendous, that it was impossible to let him take the first step toward it without remonstrance. Lush retained enough caution to use a tone of rational friendliness; still he felt his own value to his patron, and was prepared to be daring.

"It would be as well for you to remember, Grandcourt, that you are coming under closer fire now. There can be none of the ordinary flirting done, which may mean everything or nothing. You must make up your mind whether you wish to be accepted; and more than that, how you would like being refused. Either one or the other. You can't be philandering after her again for six weeks."

Grandcourt said nothing, but pressed the newspaper down on his knees and began to light another cigar. Lush took this as a sign that he was willing to listen, and was the more bent on using the opportunity; he wanted if possible to find out which would be the more potent cause of hesitation— probable acceptance or probable refusal.

"Everything has a more serious look now than it had before. There is her family to be provided for. You could not let your wife's mother live in beggary. It will be a confoundedly hampering affair. Marriage will pin you down in a way you haven't been used to; and in point of money you have not too much elbow-room. And after all, what will you get by it? You are master over your estates, present or future, as far as choosing your heir goes; it's a pity to go on encumbering them for a mere whim, which you may repent of in a twelvemonth. I should be sorry to see you making a mess of your life in that way. If there were anything solid to be gained by the marriage, that would be a different affair."

Lush's tone had gradually become more and more unctuous in its friendliness of remonstrance, and he was almost in danger of forgetting that he was merely gambling in argument. When he left off, Grandcourt took his cigar out of his mouth, and looking steadily at the moist end while he adjusted the leaf with his delicate finger-tips, said:

"I knew before that you had an objection to my marrying Miss Harleth." Here he made a little pause, before he continued: "But I never considered that a reason against it."

"I never supposed you did," answered Lush, not unctuously, but dryly. "It was not *that* I urged as a reason. I should have thought it might have been a reason against it, after all your experience, that you would be acting like the hero of a ballad, and making yourself absurd—and all for what? You know you couldn't make up your mind before. It's impossible you can care much about her. And as for the tricks she is likely to play, you may judge of that from what you heard at Leubronn. However, what I wished to point out to you was, that there can be no shilly-shally now."

"Perfectly," said Grandcourt, looking round at Lush and fixing him with narrow eyes; "I don't intend that there should be. I dare say it's disagreeable to you. But if you suppose I care a damn for that, you are most stupendously mistaken."

"Oh, well," said Lush, rising with his hands in his pockets, and feeling some latent venom still within him, "if you have made up your mind!—only there's another aspect of the affair. I have been speaking on the supposition that it was absolutely certain she would accept you, and that destitution would have no choice. But I am not so sure that the young lady is to be counted on. She is kittle cattle to shoe, I think. And she had her reasons for running away before." Lush had moved a step or two till he stood nearly in front of Grandcourt, though at some distance from him. He did not feel himself much restrained by consequences, being aware that the only strong hold he had on his present position was his serviceableness; and even after a quarrel, the want of him was likely sooner or later to recur. He foresaw that Gwendolen would cause him to be ousted for a time, and his temper at this moment urged him to risk a quarrel.

"She had her reasons," he repeated, more significantly.

"I had come to that conclusion before," said Grandcourt, with contemptuous irony.

"Yes, but I hardly think you know what her reasons were."

"You do, apparently," said Grandcourt, not betraying by so much as an eyelash that he cared for the reasons.

"Yes, and you had better know, too, that you may judge of the influence you have over her if she swallows her reasons and accepts you. For my own part, I would take odds against it. She saw Lydia in Cardell Chase and heard the whole story."

Grandcourt made no immediate answer, and only went on smoking. He was so long before he spoke, that Lush moved about and looked out of the windows, unwilling to go away without seeing some effect of his daring move. He had ex-

pected that Grandcourt would tax him with having contrived
the affair, since Mrs. Glasher was then living at Gadsmere a
hundred miles off, and he was prepared to admit the fact:
what he cared about was that Grandcourt should be staggered
by the sense that his intended advances must be made to a
girl who had that knowledge in her mind and had been scared
by it. At length Grandcourt, seeing Lush turn toward him,
looked at him again, and said, contemptuously: "What follows?"

Here certainly was a "mate" in answer to Lush's "check";
and though his exasperation with Grandcourt was perhaps
stronger than it had ever been before, it would have been mere
idiocy to act as if any further move could be useful. He gave
a slight shrug with one shoulder, and was going to walk away,
when Grandcourt, turning on his seat toward the table, said,
as quietly as if nothing had occurred: "Oblige me by pushing
that pen and paper here, will you?"

No thunderous, bullying superior could have exercised the
imperious spell that Grandcourt did. Why, instead of being
obeyed, he had never been told to go to a warmer place, was
perhaps a mystery to several who found themselves obeying
him. The pen and paper were pushed to him, and as he took
them he said: "Just wait for this letter."

He scrawled with ease, and the brief note was quickly addressed. "Let Hutchins go with it at once, will you?" said
Grandcourt, pushing the letter away from him.

As Lush had expected, it was addressed to Miss Harleth,
Offendene. When his irritation had cooled down he was glad
there had been no explosive quarrel; but he felt sure that
there was a notch made against him, and that somehow or
other he was intended to pay. It was also clear to him that
the immediate effect of his revelation had been to harden
Grandcourt's previous determination. But as to the particular movements which made this process in his baffling mind,
Lush could only toss up his chin in despair of a theory.

CHAPTER XXVI.

He brings white asses laden with the freight
Of Tyrian vessels, purple, gold, and balm,
To bribe my will : I'll bid them chase him forth,
Nor let him breathe the taint of his surmise
On my secure resolve.
                    Ay, 'tis secure ;
And therefore let him come to spread his freight.
For firmness hath its appetite and craves
The stronger lure, more strongly to resist ;
Would know the touch of gold to fling it off ;
Scent wine to feel its lip the soberer ;
Behold soft byssus, ivory, and plumes
To say, " They're fair, but I will none of them,"
And flout Enticement in the very face.

Mr. Gascoigne one day came to Offendene with what he felt to be the satisfactory news that Mrs. Mompert had fixed Tuesday in the following week for her interview with Gwendolen at Wanchester. He said nothing of his having incidentally heard that Mr. Grandcourt had returned to Diplow; knowing no more than she did that Leubronn had been the goal of her admirer's journeying, and feeling that it would be unkind uselessly to revive the memory of a brilliant prospect under the present reverses. In his secret soul he thought of his niece's unintelligible caprice with regret, but he vindicated her to himself by considering that Grandcourt had been the first to behave oddly, in suddenly walking away when there had been the best opportunity for crowning his marked attentions. The Rector's practical judgment told him that his chief duty to his niece now was to encourage her resolutely to face the change in her lot, since there was no manifest promise of any event that would avert it.

"You will find an interest in varied experience, my dear, and I have no doubt you will be a more valuable woman for having sustained such a part as you are called to."

"I cannot pretend to believe that I shall like it," said Gwendolen, for the first time showing her uncle some petulance. "But I am quite aware that I am obliged to bear it."

She remembered having submitted to his admonition on a different occasion, when she was expected to like a very different prospect.

"And your good sense will teach you to behave suitably under it," said Mr. Gascoigne, with a shade more gravity. "I feel sure that Mrs. Mompert will be pleased with you. You will know how to conduct yourself to a woman who holds in all senses the relation of superior to you. This trouble has come on you young, but that makes it in some respects easier, and there is benefit in all chastisement if we adjust our minds to it."

This was precisely what Gwendolen was unable to do; and after her uncle was gone, the bitter tears, which had rarely come during the late trouble, rose and fell slowly as she sat alone. Her heart denied that the trouble was easier because she was young. When was she to have any happiness, if it did not come while she was young? Not that her visions of possible happiness for herself were unmixed with necessary evil as they used to be—not that she could still imagine herself plucking the fruits of life without suspicion of their core. But this general disenchantment with the world—nay, with herself, since it appeared that she was not made for easy pre-eminence—only intensified her sense of forlornness: it was a visibly sterile distance enclosing the dreary path at her feet, in which she had no courage to tread. She was in that first crisis of passionate youthful rebellion against what is not fitly called pain, but rather the absence of joy—that first rage of disappointment in life's morning, which we whom the years have subdued are apt to remember but dimly as part of our own experience, and so to be intolerant of its self-enclosed unreasonableness and impiety. What passion seems more absurd, when we have got outside it and looked at calamity as a collective risk, than this amazed anguish that I and not Thou, He, or She, should be just the smitten one? Yet perhaps some who have afterward made themselves a willing fence before the breast of another, and have carried their own heart-wound in heroic silence—some who have made their latter deeds great, nevertheless began with this angry amazement at their own smart, and on the mere denial of their fantastic desires raged as if under the sting of wasps which reduced the universe for them to an unjust infliction of pain. This was nearly poor Gwendolen's condition. What though such a reverse as hers had often happened to other girls? The one point she had been all her life learning to care for was, that it had happened to *her*: it was what *she* felt under Klesmer's demonstration that she was not remarkable enough to command fortune by force of will and merit; it was what *she* would feel under the rigors of Mrs. Mompert's constant expectation, under the dull demand that she should be cheerful with three Miss Momperts, under the necessity of showing herself entirely submissive, and keeping her thoughts to herself. To be a queen disthroned is not so hard as some other down-stepping: imagine one who had been made to believe in his own divinity finding all homage withdrawn, and himself unable to perform a miracle that would recall the homage and restore his own confidence. Something akin to this illusion and this helplessness had befallen the poor spoiled child, with the lovely lips and eyes and the majestic figure—which seemed now to have no magic in them.

She rose from the low ottoman where she had been sitting purposeless, and walked up and down the drawing-room, resting her elbow on one palm while she leaned down her cheek on the other, and a slow tear fell. She thought: "I have always, ever since I was little, felt that mamma was not a happy woman; and now I dare say I shall be more unhappy than she has been." Her mind dwelt for a few moments on the picture of herself losing her youth and ceasing to enjoy—not minding whether she did this or that: but such picturing inevitably brought back the image of her mother. "Poor mamma! it will be still worse for her now. I can get a little money for her—that is all I shall care about now." And then with an entirely new movement of her imagination, she saw her mother getting quite old and white, and herself no longer young but faded, and their two faces meeting still with memory and love, and she knowing what was in her mother's mind—"Poor Gwen too is sad and faded now"—and then for the first time she sobbed—not in anger, but with a sort of tender misery.

Her face was toward the door, and she saw her mother enter. She barely saw that; for her eyes were large with tears, and she pressed her handkerchief against them hurriedly. Before she took it away she felt her mother's arms round her, and this sensation, which seemed a prolongation of her inward vision, overcame her will to be reticent: she sobbed anew in spite of herself, as they pressed their cheeks together.

Mrs. Davilow had brought something in her hand which had already caused her an agitating anxiety, and she dared not speak until her darling had become calmer. But Gwendolen, with whom weeping had always been a painful manifestation to be resisted if possible, again pressed her handkerchief against her eyes, and with a deep breath drew her head backward and looked at her mother, who was pale and tremulous.

"It was nothing, mamma," said Gwendolen, thinking that her mother had been moved in this way simply by finding her in distress. "It is all over now."

But Mrs. Davilow had withdrawn her arms, and Gwendolen perceived a letter in her hand.

"What is that letter?—worse news still?" she asked, with a touch of bitterness.

"I don't know what you will think it, dear," said Mrs. Davilow, keeping the letter in her hand. "You will hardly guess where it comes from."

"Don't ask me to guess anything," said Gwendolen, rather impatiently, as if a bruise were being pressed.

"It is addressed to you, dear."

Gwendolen gave the slightest perceptible toss of the head.

"It comes from Diplow," said Mrs. Davilow, giving her the letter.

She knew Grandcourt's indistinct handwriting, and her mother was not surprised to see her blush deeply; but watching her as she read, and wondering much what was the purport of the letter, she saw the color die out. Gwendolen's lips even were pale as she turned the open note toward her mother. The words were few and formal.

"Mr. Grandcourt presents his compliments to Miss Harleth, and begs to know whether he may be permitted to call at Offendene tomorrow after two, and to see her alone. Mr. Grandcourt has just returned from Leubronn, where he had hoped to find Miss Harleth."

Mrs. Davilow read, and then looked at her daughter inquiringly, leaving the note in her hand. Gwendolen let it fall on the floor, and turned away.

"It must be answered, darling," said Mrs. Davilow, timidly. "The man waits."

"Gwendolen sank on the settee, clasped her hands, and looked straight before her, not at her mother. She had the expression of one who had been startled by a sound and was listening to know what would come of it. The sudden change of the situation was bewildering. A few minutes before she was looking along an inescapable path of repulsive monotony, with hopeless inward rebellion against the imperious lot which left her no choice: and lo, now, a moment of choice was come. Yet—was it triumph she felt most, or terror? Impossible for Gwendolen not to feel some triumph in a tribute to her power at a time when she was first tasting the bitterness of insignificance: again she seemed to be getting a sort of empire over her own life. But how to use it? Here came the terror. Quick, quick, like pictures in a book beaten open with a sense of hurry, came back vividly, yet in fragments, all that she had gone through in relation to Grandcourt—the allurements, the vacillations, the resolve to accede, the final repulsion; the incisive face of that dark-eyed lady with the lovely boy; her own pledge (was it a pledge not to marry him?)—the new disbelief in the worth of men and things for which that scene of disclosure had become a symbol. That unalterable experience made a vision at which, in the first agitated moment, before tempering reflections could suggest themselves, her native terror shrank.

Where was the good of choice coming again? What did she wish? Anything different? No! and yet in the dark seed-growths of consciousness a new wish was forming itself— "I wish I had never known it!" Something, anything she wished for that would have saved her from the dread to let Grandcourt come.

It was no long while—yet it seemed long to Mrs. Davilow, before she thought it well to say, gently:

"It will be necessary for you to write, dear. Or shall I write an answer for you—which you will dictate?"

"No, mamma," said Gwendolen, drawing a deep breath. "But please lay me out the pen and paper."

That was gaining time. Was she to decline Grandcourt's visit—close the shutters—not even look out on what would happen?—though with the assurance that she should remain just where she was? The young activity within her made a warm current through her terror and stirred toward something that would be an event—toward an opportunity in which she could look and speak with the former effectiveness. The interest of the morrow was no longer at a deadlock.

"There is really no reason on earth why you should be so alarmed at the man's waiting a few minutes, mamma," said Gwendolen, remonstrantly, as Mrs. Davilow, having prepared the writing materials, looked toward her expectantly. "Servants expect nothing else than to wait. It is not to be supposed that I must write on the instant."

"No, dear," said Mrs. Davilow, in the tone of one corrected, turning to sit down and take up a bit of work that lay at hand; "he can wait another quarter of an hour, if you like."

It was very simple speech and action on her part, but it was what might have been subtly calculated. Gwendolen felt a contradictory desire to be hastened: hurry would save her from deliberate choice.

"I did not mean him to wait long enough for that needle-work to be finished," she said, lifting her hands to stroke the backward curves of her hair, while she rose from her seat and stood still.

"But if you don't feel able to decide?" said Mrs. Davilow, sympathizingly.

"I *must* decide," said Gwendolen, walking to the writing-table and seating herself. All the while there was a busy undercurrent in her, like the thought of a man who keeps up a dialogue while he is considering how he can slip away. Why should she not let him come? It bound her to nothing. He had been to Leubronn after her: of course he meant a direct unmistakable renewal of the suit which before had been only implied. What then? She could reject him. Why was she to deny herself the freedom of doing this—which she would like to do?

"If Mr. Grandcourt has only just returned from Leubronn," said Mrs. Davilow, observing that Gwendolen leaned back in her chair after taking the pen in her hand—"I wonder whether he has heard of our misfortunes."

"That could make no difference to a man in his position," said Gwendolen, rather contemptuously.

"It would, to some men," said Mrs. Davilow. "They would not like to take a wife from a family in a state of beggary almost, as we are. Here we are at Offendene with a great shell over us as usual. But just imagine his finding us at Sawyer's Cottage. Most men are afraid of being bored or taxed by a wife's family. If Mr. Grandcourt did know, I think it a strong proof of his attachment to you."

Mrs. Davilow spoke with unusual emphasis: it was the first time she had ventured to say anything about Grandcourt which would necessarily seem intended as an argument in favor of him, her habitual impression being that such arguments would certainly be useless and might be worse. The effect of her words now was stronger than she could imagine: they raised a new set of possibilities in Gwendolen's mind—a vision of what Grandcourt might do for her mother if she, Gwendolen, did—what she was not going to do. She was so moved by a new rush of ideas, that like one conscious of being urgently called away, she felt that the immediate task must be hastened: the letter must be written, else it might be endlessly deferred. After all, she acted in a hurry as she had wished to do. To act in a hurry was to have a reason for keeping away from an absolute decision, and to leave open as many issues as possible.

She wrote: "Miss Harleth presents her compliments to Mr. Grandcourt. She will be at home after two o'clock tomorrow."

"Before addressing the note she said: "Pray ring the bell, mamma, if there is any one to answer it." She really did not know who did the work of the house.

It was not till after the letter had been taken away and Gwendolen had risen again, stretching out one arm and then resting it on her head, with a long moan which had a sound of relief in it, that Mrs. Davilow ventured to ask:

"What did you say, Gwen?"

"I said that I should be at home," answered Gwendolen, rather loftily.   Then, after a pause: "You must not expect, because Mr. Grandcourt is coming, that anything is going to happen, mamma."

"I don't allow myself to expect anything, dear.   I desire you to follow your own feeling.   You have never told me what that was."

"What is the use of telling?" said Gwendolen, hearing a reproach in that true statement.   "When I have anything pleasant to tell, you may be sure I will tell you."

"But Mr. Grandcourt will consider that you have already accepted him, in allowing him to come.   His note tells you plainly enough that he is coming to make you an offer."

"Very well; and I wish to have the pleasure of refusing him."

Mrs. Davilow looked up in wonderment, but Gwendolen implied her wish not to be questioned further by saying:

"Put down that detestable needlework, and let us walk in the avenue.   I am stifled."

------◆------

CHAPTER XXVII.

Desire has trimmed the sails, and Circumstance
Brings but the breeze to fill them.

WHILE Grandcourt on his beautiful black Yarico, the groom behind him on Criterion, was taking the pleasant ride from Diplow to Offendene, Gwendolen was seated before the mirror while her mother gathered up the lengthy mass of light-brown hair which she had been carefully brushing.

"Only gather it up easily and make a coil, mamma," said Gwendolen.

"Let me bring you some ear-rings, Gwen," said Mrs. Davilow, when the hair was adjusted, and they were both looking at the reflection in the glass.   It was impossible for them not to notice that the eyes looked brighter than they had done of late, that there seemed to be a shadow lifted from the face,

leaving all the lines once more in their placid youthfulness.
The mother drew some inferences that made her voice rather
cheerful. "You do want your ear-rings?"

"No, mamma; I shall not wear any ornaments, and I shall
put on my black silk. Black is the only wear when one is
going to refuse an offer," said Gwendolen, with one of her old
smiles at her mother, while she rose to throw off her dressing-
gown.

"Suppose the offer is not made after all," said Mrs. Davilow, not without a sly intention.

"Then that will be because I refuse it beforehand," said
Gwendolen. "It comes to the same thing."

There was a proud little toss of her head as she said this;
and when she walked downstairs in her long black robes,
there was just that firm poise of head and elasticity of form
which had lately been missing, as in a parched plant. Her
mother thought: "She is quite herself again. It must be
pleasure in his coming. Can her mind be really made up
against him?"

Gwendolen would have been rather angry if that thought
had been uttered; perhaps all the more because through the
last twenty hours, with a brief interruption of sleep, she had
been so occupied with perpetually alternating images and arguments for and against the possibility of her marrying Grandcourt, that the conclusion which she had determined on beforehand ceased to have any hold on her consciousness: the
alternate dip of counterbalancing thoughts begotten of counterbalancing desires had brought her into a state in which no
conclusion could look fixed to her. She would have expressed
her resolve as before; but it was a form out of which the
blood had been sucked—no more a part of quivering life than
the "God's will be done" of one who is eagerly watching
chances. She did not mean to accept Grandcourt; from the
first moment of receiving his letter she had meant to refuse
him; still, that could not but prompt her to look the unwelcome reasons full in the face until she had a little less awe of
them, could not hinder her imagination from filling out her
knowledge in various ways, some of which seemed to change
the aspect of what she knew. By dint of looking at a dubious

object with a constructive imagination, one can give it twenty different shapes. Her indistinct grounds of hesitation before the interview at the Whispering Stones at present counted for nothing; they were all merged in the final repulsion. If it had not been for that day in Cardell Chase, she said to herself now, there would have been no obstacle to her marrying Grandcourt. On that day and after it, she had not reasoned and balanced: she had acted with a force of impulse against which all questioning was no more than a voice against a torrent. The impulse had come—not only from her maidenly pride and jealousy, not only from the shock of another woman's calamity thrust close on her vision, but—from her dread of wrong-doing, which was vague, it is true, and aloof from the daily details of her life, but not the less strong. Whatever was accepted as consistent with being a lady she had no scruple about; but from the dim region of what was called disgraceful, wrong, guilty, she shrank with mingled pride and terror; and even apart from shame, her feeling would have made her place any deliberate injury of another in the region of guilt.

But now—did she know exactly what was the state of the case with regard to Mrs. Glasher and her children? She had given a sort of promise—had said: "I will not interfere with your wishes." But would another woman who married Grandcourt be in fact the decisive obstacle to her wishes, or be doing her and her boy any real injury? Might it not be just as well, nay, better, that Grandcourt should marry? For what could not a woman do when she was married, if she knew how to assert herself? Here all was constructive imagination. Gwendolen had about as accurate a conception of marriage—that is to say, of the mutual influences, demands, duties of man and woman in the state of matrimony—as she had of magnetic currents and the law of storms.

"Mamma managed badly," was her way of summing up what she had seen of her mother's experience: she herself would manage quite differently. And the trials of matrimony were the last theme into which Mrs. Davilow could choose to enter fully with this daughter.

"I wonder what mamma and my uncle would say if they

knew about Mrs. Glasher!" thought Gwendolen, in her inward debating; not that she could imagine herself telling
them, even if she had not felt bound to silence. "I wonder
what anybody would say; or what they would say to Mr.
Grandcourt's marrying some one else and having other children!" To consider what "anybody" would say was to be
released from the difficulty of judging where everything was
obscure to her when feeling had ceased to be decisive. She
had only to collect her memories, which proved to her that
"anybody" regarded illegitimate children as more rightfully
to be looked shy on and deprived of social advantages than
illegitimate fathers. The verdict of "anybody" seemed to be
that she had no reason to concern herself greatly on behalf of
Mrs. Glasher and her children.

But there was another way in which they had caused her
concern. What others might think could not do away with
a feeling which, in the first instance, would hardly be too
strongly described as indignation and loathing that she should
have been expected to unite herself with an outworn life, full
of backward secrets which must have been more keenly felt
than any associations with *her*. True, the question of love
on her own part had occupied her scarcely at all in relation to
Grandcourt. The desirability of marriage for her had always
seemed due to other feelings than love; and to be enamored
was the part of the man, on whom the advances depended.
Gwendolen had found no objection to Grandcourt's way
of being enamored before she had had that glimpse of his
past, which she resented as if it had been a deliberate
offence against her. His advances to *her* were deliberate, and she felt a retrospective disgust for them. Perhaps other men's lives were of the same kind—full of secrets
which made the ignorant suppositions of the woman they
wanted to marry a farce at which they were laughing in
their sleeves.

These feelings of disgust and indignation had sunk deep;
and though other troublous experience in the last weeks had
dulled them from passion into remembrance, it was chiefly
their reverberating activity which kept her firm to the understanding with herself that she was not going to accept Grand-

court. She had never meant to form a new determination; she had only been considering what might be thought or said. If anything could have induced her to change, it would have been the prospect of making all things easy for "poor mamma": that, she admitted, was a temptation. But no! she was going to refuse him. Meanwhile, the thought that he was coming to be refused was inspiriting: she had the white reins in her hands again; there was a new current in her frame, reviving her from the beaten-down consciousness in which she had been left by the interview with Klesmer. She was not now going to crave an opinion of her capabilities; she was going to exercise her power.

Was this what made her heart palpitate annoyingly when she heard the horse's footsteps on the gravel?—when Miss Merry, who opened the door to Grandcourt, came to tell her that he was in the drawing-room? The hours of preparation and the triumph of the situation were apparently of no use; she might as well have seen Grandcourt coming suddenly on her in the midst of her despondency. While walking into the drawing-room she had to concentrate all her energy in that self-control which made her appear gravely gracious as she gave her hand to him, and answered his hope that she was quite well in a voice as low and languid as his own. A moment afterward, when they were both of them seated on two of the wreath-painted chairs—Gwendolen upright with downcast eyelids, Grandcourt about two yards distant, leaning one arm over the back of his chair and looking at her, while he held his hat in his left hand—any one seeing them as a picture would have concluded that they were in some stage of love-making suspense. And certainly the love-making had begun: she already felt herself being wooed by this silent man seated at an agreeable distance, with the subtlest atmosphere of attar of roses and an attention bent wholly on her. And he also considered himself to be wooing: he was not a man to suppose that his presence carried no consequences: and he was exactly the man to feel the utmost piquancy in a girl whom he had not found quite calculable.

"I was disappointed not to find you at Leubronn," he began, his usual broken drawl having just a shade of amorous languor in it. "The place was intolerable without you. A mere kennel of a place. Don't you think so?"

"I can't judge what it would be without myself," said Gwendolen, turning her eyes on him, with some recovered sense of mischief. "*With* myself I liked it well enough to have stayed longer, if I could. But I was obliged to come home on account of family troubles."

"It was very cruel of you to go to Leubronn," said Grand-court, taking no notice of the troubles, on which Gwendolen—she hardly knew why—wished that there should be a clear understanding at once. "You must have known that it would spoil everything: you knew you were the heart and soul of everything that went on. Are you quite reckless about me?"

It was impossible to say "yes" in a tone that would be taken seriously; equally impossible to say "no"; but what else could she say? In her difficulty, she turned down her eyelids again and blushed over face and neck. Grandcourt saw her in a new phase, and believed that she was showing her inclination. But he was determined that she should show it more decidedly.

"Perhaps there is some deeper interest? Some attraction —some engagement—which it would have been only fair to make me aware of? Is there any man who stands between us?"

Inwardly the answer framed itself: "No; but there is a woman." Yet how could she utter this? Even if she had not promised that woman to be silent, it would have been im-possible for her to enter on the subject with Grandcourt. But how could she arrest this wooing by beginning to make a for-mal speech—"I perceive your intention—it is most flattering, etc."? A fish honestly invited to come and be eaten has a clear course in declining, but how if it finds itself swimming against a net? And apart from the network, would she have dared at once to say anything decisive? Gwendolen had not time to be clear on that point. As it was, she felt com-pelled to silence, and after a pause, Grandcourt said:

"Am I to understand that some one else is preferred?"

Gwendolen, now impatient of her own embarrassment, de-termined to rush at the difficulty and free herself. She raised her eyes again, and said with something of her former clearness and defiance, "No"—wishing him to understand: "What then? I may not be ready to take *you*." There was nothing that Grandcourt could not understand which he perceived likely to affect his *amour propre*.

"The last thing I would do is to importune you. I should not hope to win you by making myself a bore. If there were no hope for me, I would ask you to tell me so at once, that I might just ride away to—no matter where."

Almost to her own astonishment, Gwendolen felt a sudden alarm at the image of Grandcourt finally riding away. What would be left her then? Nothing but the former dreariness. She liked him to be there. She snatched at the subject that would defer any decisive answer.

"I fear you are not aware of what has happened to us. I have lately had to think so much of my mamma's troubles, that other subjects have been quite thrown into the background. She has lost all her fortune, and we are going to leave this place. I must ask you to excuse my seeming preoccupied."

In eluding a direct appeal, Gwendolen recovered some of her self-possession. She spoke with dignity and looked straight at Grandcourt, whose long, narrow, impenetrable eyes met hers, and mysteriously arrested them: mysteriously; for the subtly varied drama between man and woman is often such as can hardly be rendered in words put together like dominoes, according to obvious fixed marks. The word of all work Love will no more express the myriad modes of mutual attraction, than the word Thought can inform you what is passing through your neighbor's mind. It would be hard to tell on which side—Gwendolen's or Grandcourt's—the influence was more fixed. At that moment his strongest wish was to be completely master of this creature—this piquant combination of maidenliness and mischief: that she knew things which had made her start away from him spurred him to triumph over that repugnance; and he was believing that he should triumph. And she—ah, piteous equality in the need to dominate!—she was overcome like the thirsty one who is drawn toward the seeming water in the desert, overcome by the suffused sense that here in this man's homage to her lay the rescue from helpless subjection to an oppressive lot.

All the while they were looking at each other; and Grand-court said, slowly and languidly, as if it were of no impor-tance, other things having been settled:

"You will tell me now, I hope, that Mrs. Davilow's loss of fortune will not trouble you further. You will trust me to prevent it from weighing upon her. You will give me the claim to provide against that."

The little pauses and refined drawlings with which this speech was uttered gave time for Gwendolen to go through the dream of a life. As the words penetrated her, they had the effect of a draught of wine, which suddenly makes all things easier, desirable things not so wrong, and people in general less disagreeable. She had a momentary phantasmal love for this man who chose his words so well, and who was a mere incarnation of delicate homage. Repugnance, dread, scruples —these were dim as remembered pains, while she was already tasting relief under the immediate pain of hopelessness. She imagined herself already springing to her mother, and being playful again. Yet when Grandcourt had ceased to speak, there was an instant in which she was conscious of being at the turning of the ways.

"You are very generous," she said, not moving her eyes, and speaking with a gentle intonation.

"You accept what will make such things a matter of course?" said Grandcourt, without any new eagerness. "You consent to become my wife?"

This time Gwendolen remained quite pale. Something made her rise from her seat in spite of herself and walk to a little distance. Then she turned, and with her hands folded before her stood in silence.

Grandcourt immediately rose too, resting his hat on the chair, but still keeping hold of it. The evident hesitation of this destitute girl to take his splendid offer stung him into a keenness of interest such as he had not known for years. None the less because he attributed her hesitation entirely to her knowledge about Mrs. Glasher. In that attitude of prepa-ration, he said:

"Do you command me to go?" No familiar spirit could have suggested to him more effective words.

"No," said Gwendolen. She could not let him go: that negative was a clutch. She seemed to herself to be, after all, only drifted toward the tremendous decision:—but drifting depends on something besides the currents, when the sails have been set beforehand.

"You accept my devotion?" said Grandcourt, holding his hat by his side and looking straight into her eyes, without other movement. Their eyes meeting in that way seemed to allow any length of pause; but wait as long as she would, how could she contradict herself? What had she detained him for? He had shut out any explanation.

"Yes," came as gravely from Gwendolen's lips as if she had been answering to her name in a court of justice. He received it gravely, and they still looked at each other in the same attitude. Was there ever before such a way of accepting the bliss-giving "Yes"? Grandcourt liked better to be at that distance from her, and to feel under a ceremony imposed by an indefinable prohibition that breathed from Gwendolen's bearing.

But he did at length lay down his hat and advance to take her hand, just pressing his lips upon it and letting it go again. She thought his behavior perfect, and gained a sense of freedom which made her almost ready to be mischievous. Her "Yes" entailed so little at this moment, that there was nothing to screen the reversal of her gloomy prospects: her vision was filled by her own release from the Momperts, and her mother's release from Sawyer's Cottage. With a happy curl of the lips, she said:

"Will you not see mamma? I will fetch her."

"Let us wait a little," said Grandcourt, in his favorite attitude, having his left forefinger and thumb in his waistcoat-pocket, and with his right caressing his whisker, while he stood near Gwendolen and looked at her—not unlike a gentleman who has a felicitous introduction at an evening party.

"Have you anything else to say to me?" said Gwendolen, playfully.

"Yes—I know having things said to you is a great bore," said Grandcourt, rather sympathetically.

"Not when they are things I like to hear."

"Will it bother you to be asked how soon we can be married?"

"I think it will, to-day," said Gwendolen, putting up her chin saucily.

"Not to-day, then, but to-morrow. Think of it before I come to-morrow. In a fortnight—or three weeks—as soon as possible."

"Ah, you think you will be tired of my company," said Gwendolen. "I notice when people are married the husband is not so much with his wife as when they were engaged. But perhaps I shall like that better too."

She laughed charmingly.

"You shall have whatever you like," said Grandcourt.

"And nothing that I don't like?—please say that; because I think I dislike what I don't like more than I like what I like," said Gwendolen, finding herself in the woman's paradise where all her nonsense is adorable.

Grandcourt paused: these were subtleties in which he had much experience of his own. "I don't know—this is such a brute of a world, things are always turning up that one doesn't like. I can't always hinder your being bored. If you like to hunt Criterion, I can't hinder his coming down by some chance or other."

"Ah, my friend Criterion, how is he?"

"He is outside: I made the groom ride him, that you might see him. He had the side-saddle on for an hour or two yesterday. Come to the window and look at him."

They could see the two horses being taken slowly round the sweep, and the beautiful creatures, in their fine grooming, sent a thrill of exultation through Gwendolen. They were the symbols of command and luxury, in delightful contrast with the ugliness of poverty and humiliation at which she had lately been looking close.

"Will you ride Criterion to-morrow?" said Grandcourt. "If you will, everything shall be arranged."

"I should like it of all things," said Gwendolen. "I want

to lose myself in a gallop again. But now I must go and fetch mamma."

"Take my arm to the door, then," said Grandcourt; and she accepted. Their faces were very near each other, being almost on a level, and he was looking at her. She thought his manners as a lover more agreeable than any she had seen described. She had no alarm lest he meant to kiss her, and was so much at her ease that she suddenly paused in the middle of the room and said, half archly, half earnestly:

"Oh, while I think of it—there is something I dislike that you can save me from. I do *not* like Mr. Lush's company."

"You shall not have it. I'll get rid of him."

"You are not fond of him yourself?"

"Not in the least. I let him hang on me because he has always been a poor devil," said Grandcourt, in an *adagio* of utter indifference. "They got him to travel with me when I was a lad. He was always that coarse-haired kind of brute—a sort of cross between a hog and a *dilettante*."

Gwendolen laughed. All that seemed kind and natural enough: Grandcourt's fastidiousness enhanced the kindness. And when they reached the door, his way of opening it for her was the perfection of easy homage. Really, she thought, he was likely to be the least disagreeable of husbands.

Mrs. Davilow was waiting anxiously in her bedroom when Gwendolen entered, stepped toward her quickly, and kissing her on both cheeks, said in a low tone: "Come down, mamma, and see Mr. Grandcourt. I am engaged to him."

"My darling child!" said Mrs. Davilow, with a surprise that was rather solemn than glad.

"Yes," said Gwendolen, in the same tone, and with a quickness which implied that it was needless to ask questions. "Everything is settled. You are not going to Sawyer's Cottage, I am not going to be inspected by Mrs. Mompert, and everything is to be as I like. So come down with me immediately."

BOOK IV.—GWENDOLEN GETS HER CHOICE.

CHAPTER XXVIII.

"Il est plus aisé de connoître l'homme en général que de connoître un homme en particulier."—LA ROCHEFOUCAULD.

AN hour after Grandcourt had left, the important news of Gwendolen's engagement was known at the Rectory, and Mr. and Mrs. Gascoigne, with Anna, spent the evening at Offendene.

My dear, let me congratulate you on having created a strong attachment," said the Rector. "You look serious, and I don't wonder at it: a lifelong union is a solemn thing. But from the way Mr. Grandcourt has acted and spoken I think we may already see some good arising out of our adversity. It has given you an opportunity of observing your future husband's delicate liberality."

Mr. Gascoigne referred to Grandcourt's mode of implying that he would provide for Mrs. Davilow—a part of the love-making which Gwendolen had remembered to cite to her mother with perfect accuracy.

"But I have no doubt that Mr. Grandcourt would have behaved quite as handsomely if you had not gone away to Germany, Gwendolen, and had been engaged to him, as you no doubt might have been, more than a month ago," said Mrs. Gascoigne, feeling that she had to discharge a duty on this occasion. "But now there is no more room for caprice; indeed, I trust you have no inclination to any. A woman has a great debt of gratitude to a man who perseveres in making her such an offer. But no doubt you feel properly."

"I am not at all sure that I do, aunt," said Gwendolen, with saucy gravity. "I don't know everything it is proper to feel on being engaged."

The Rector patted her shoulder and smiled as at a bit of innocent naughtiness, and his wife took his behavior as an indication that she was not to be displeased. As for Anna, she
kissed Gwendolen, and said, "I do hope you will be happy,"
but then sank into the background and tried to keep the tears
back too. In the late days she had been imagining a little
romance about Rex—how if he still longed for Gwendolen her
heart might be softened by trouble into love, so that they could
by and by be married. And the romance had turned to a
prayer that she, Anna, might be able to rejoice like a good sister, and only think of being useful in working for Gwendolen,
as long as Rex was not rich. But now she wanted grace to
rejoice in something else. Miss Merry and the four girls,
Alice with the high shoulders, Bertha and Fanny the whisper-
ers, and Isabel the listener, were all present on this family
occasion, when everything seemed appropriately turning to the
honor and glory of Gwendolen, and real life was as interesting
as "Sir Charles Grandison." The evening passed chiefly in
decisive remarks from the Rector, in answer to conjectures
from the two elder ladies. According to him, the case was
not one in which he could think it his duty to mention settlements: everything must, and doubtless would, safely be left
to Mr. Grandcourt.

"I should like to know exactly what sort of places Ryelands
and Gadsmere are," said Mrs. Davilow.

"Gadsmere, I believe, is a secondary place," said Mr. Gascoigne; "but Ryelands I know to be one of our finest seats.
The park is extensive and the woods of a very valuable order.
The house was built by Inigo Jones, and the ceilings are
painted in the Italian style. The estate is said to be worth
twelve thousand a year, and there are two livings, one a rectory, in the gift of the Grandcourts. There may be some bur-
dens on the land. Still, Mr. Grandcourt was an only child."

"It would be most remarkable," said Mrs. Gascoigne, "if
he were to become Lord Stannery in addition to everything
else. Only think: there is the Grandcourt estate, the Mallinger estate, *and* the baronetcy, *and* the peerage,"—she was
marking off the items on her fingers, and paused on the fourth
while she added—"but they say there will be no land coming

to him with the peerage." It seemed a pity there was nothing for the fifth finger.

"The peerage," said the Rector, judiciously, "must be regarded as a remote chance. There are two cousins between the present peer and Mr. Grandcourt. It is certainly a serious reflection how death and other causes do sometimes concentrate inheritances on one man. But an excess of that kind is to be deprecated. To be Sir Mallinger Grandcourt Mallinger— I suppose that will be his style—with the corresponding properties, is a valuable talent enough for any man to have committed to him. Let us hope it will be well used."

"And what a position for the wife, Gwendolen!" said Mrs. Gascoigne; "a great responsibility indeed. But you must lose no time in writing to Mrs. Mompert, Henry. It is a good thing that you have an engagement of marriage to offer as an excuse, else she might feel offended. She is rather a high woman."

"I am rid of that horror," thought Gwendolen, to whom the name of Mompert had become a sort of Mumbo-jumbo. She was very silent through the evening, and that night could hardly sleep at all in her little white bed. It was a rarity in her strong youth to be wakeful; and perhaps a still greater rarity for her to be careful that her mother should not know of her restlessness. But her state of mind was altogether new: she who had been used to feel sure of herself, and ready to manage others, had just taken a decisive step which she had beforehand thought that she would not take—nay, perhaps, was bound not to take. She could not go backward now; she liked a great deal of what lay before her; and there was nothing for her to like if she went back. But her resolution was dogged by the shadow of that previous resolve which had at first come as the undoubting movement of her whole being. While she lay on her pillow with wide-open eyes, "looking on darkness which the blind do see," she was appalled by the idea that she was going to do what she had once started away from with repugnance. It was new to her that a question of right or wrong in her conduct should rouse her terror; she had known no compunction that atoning caresses and presents could not lay to rest. But here had come a moment when something like a new consciousness was awaked. She seemed on the edge of adopting deliberately, as a notion for all the rest of her life, what she had rashly said in her bitterness, when her discovery had driven her away to Leubronn:—that it did not signify what she did; she had only to amuse herself as best she could. That lawlessness, that casting away of all care for justification, suddenly frightened her: it came to her with the shadowy array of possible calamity behind it—calamity which had ceased to be a mere name for her; and all the infiltrated influences of disregarded religious teaching, as well as the deeper impressions of something awful and inexorable enveloping her, seemed to concentrate themselves in the vague conception of avenging power. The brilliant position she had longed for, the imagined freedom she would create for herself in marriage, the deliverance from the dull insignificance of her girlhood—all were immediately before her; and yet they had come to her hunger like food with the taint of sacrilege upon it, which she must snatch with terror. In the darkness and loneliness of her little bed, her more resistant self could not act against the first onslaught of dread after her irrevocable decision. That unhappy-faced woman and her children —Grandcourt and his relations with her—kept repeating themselves in her imagination like the clinging memory of a disgrace, and gradually obliterated all other thought, leaving only the consciousness that she had taken those scenes into her life. Her long wakefulness seemed a delirium; a faint, faint light penetrated beside the window-curtain; the chillness increased. She could bear it no longer, and cried "Mamma!"

"Yes, dear," said Mrs. Davilow, immediately, in a wakeful voice.

"Let me come to you."

She soon went to sleep on her mother's shoulder, and slept on till late, when, dreaming of a lit-up ball-room, she opened her eyes on her mother standing by the bedside with a small packet in her hand.

"I am sorry to wake you, darling, but I thought it better to give you this at once. The groom has brought Criterion; he has come on another horse, and says he is to stay here."

Gwendolen sat up in bed and opened the packet. It was a

delicate little enamelled casket, and inside was a splendid diamond ring with a letter which contained a folded bit of colored paper and these words:

"Pray wear this ring when I come at twelve in sign of our betrothal. I enclose a check drawn in the name of Mr. Gascoigne, for immediate expenses. Of course Mrs. Davilow will remain at Offendene, at least for some time. I hope, when I come, you will have granted me an early day, when you may begin to command me at a shorter distance.— Yours devotedly, H. M. GRANDCOURT."

The check was for five hundred pounds, and Gwendolen turned it toward her mother, with the letter.

"How very kind and delicate!" said Mrs. Davilow, with much feeling. "But I really should like better not to be dependent on a son-in-law. I and the girls could get along very well."

"Mamma, if you say that again, I will not marry him," said Gwendolen, angrily.

"My dear child, I trust you are not going to marry only for my sake," said Mrs. Davilow, deprecatingly.

Gwendolen tossed her head on the pillow away from her mother, and let the ring lie. She was irritated at this attempt to take away a motive. Perhaps the deeper cause of her irritation was the consciousness that she was not going to marry solely for her mamma's sake—that she was drawn toward the marriage in ways against which stronger reasons than her mother's renunciation were yet not strong enough to hinder her. She had waked up to the signs that she was irrevocably engaged, and all the ugly visions, the alarms, the arguments of the night, must be met by daylight, in which probably they would show themselves weak.

"What I long for is your happiness, dear," continued Mrs. Davilow, pleadingly. "I will not say anything to vex you. Will you not put on the ring?"

For a few moments Gwendolen did not answer, but her thoughts were active. At last she raised herself with a determination to do as she would do if she had started on horseback, and go on with spirit, whatever ideas might be running in her head.

"I thought the lover always put on the betrothal ring himself," she said, laughingly, slipping the ring on her finger, and looking at it with a charming movement of her head. "I know why he has sent it," she added, nodding at her mamma.

"Why?"

"He would rather make me put it on than ask me to let him do it. Aha! he is very proud. But so am I. We shall match each other. I should hate a man who went down on his knees, and came fawning on me. He really is not disgusting."

"That is very moderate praise, Gwen."

"No, it is not, for a man," said Gwendolen, gayly. "But, now I must get up and dress. Will you come and do my hair, mamma, dear," she went on, drawing down her mamma's face to caress it with her own cheeks, "and not be so naughty any more as to talk of living in poverty? You must bear to be made comfortable, even if you don't like it. And Mr. Grandcourt behaves perfectly, now, does he not?"

"Certainly he does," said Mrs. Davilow, encouraged, and persuaded that after all Gwendolen was fond of her betrothed. She herself thought him a man whose attentions were likely to tell on a girl's feeling. Suitors must often be judged as words are, by the standing and the figure they make in polite society : it is difficult to know much else of them. And all the mother's anxiety turned, not on Grandcourt's character, but on Gwendolen's mood in accepting him.

The mood was necessarily passing through a new phase this morning. Even in the hour of making her toilet, she had drawn on all the knowledge she had for grounds to justify her marriage. And what she most dwelt on was the determination, that when she was Grandcourt's wife, she would urge him to the most liberal conduct toward Mrs. Glasher's children.

"Of what use would it be to her that I should not marry him? He could have married her if he had liked; but he did *not* like. Perhaps she is to blame for that. There must be a great deal about her that I know nothing of. And he must have been good to her in many ways, else she would not have wanted to marry him."

But that last argument at once began to appear doubtful. Mrs. Glasher naturally wished to exclude other children who would stand between Grandcourt and her own; and Gwendolen's comprehension of this feeling prompted another way of reconciling claims.

"Perhaps we shall have no children. I hope we shall not. And he might leave the estate to the pretty little boy. My uncle said that Mr. Grandcourt could do as he liked with the estates. Only when Sir Hugo Mallinger dies there will be enough for two."

This made Mrs. Glasher appear quite unreasonable in demanding that her boy should be sole heir; and the double property was a security that Grandcourt's marriage would do her no wrong, when the wife was Gwendolen Harleth with all her proud resolution not to be fairly accused. This maiden had been accustomed to think herself blameless; other persons only were faulty.

It was striking, that in the hold which this argument of her doing no wrong to Mrs. Glasher had taken on her mind, her repugnance to the idea of Grandcourt's past had sunk into a subordinate feeling. The terror she had felt in the night-watches at overstepping the border of wickedness by doing what she had at first felt to be wrong, had dulled any emotions about his conduct. She was thinking of him, whatever he might be, as a man over whom she was going to have indefinite power; and her loving him having never been a question with her, any agreeableness he had was so much gain. Poor Gwendolen had no awe of unmanageable forces in the state of matrimony, but regarded it as altogether a matter of management, in which she would know how to act. In relation to Grandcourt's past she encouraged new doubts whether he were likely to have differed much from other men; and she devised little schemes for learning what was expected of men in general.

But whatever else might be true in the world, her hair was dressed suitably for riding, and she went down in her riding-habit, to avoid delay before getting on horseback. She wanted to have her blood stirred once more with the intoxication of youth, and to recover the daring with which she had been used to think of her course in life. Already a load was lifted off her; for in daylight and activity it was less oppressive to have

doubts about her choice than to feel that she had no choice
but to endure insignificance and servitude.

"Go back and make yourself look like a duchess, mamma,"
she said, turning suddenly as she was going downstairs.
"Put your point-lace over your head. I must have you look
like a duchess. You must not take things humbly."

When Grandcourt raised her left hand gently and looked at
the ring, she said gravely: "It was very good of you to think
of everything and send me that packet."

"You will tell me if there is anything I forget?" he said,
keeping the hand softly within his own. "I will do anything
you wish."

"But I am very unreasonable in my wishes," said Gwendolen, smiling.

"Yes, I expect that. Women always are."

"Then I will not be unreasonable," said Gwendolen, taking
away her hand and tossing her head saucily. "I will not be
told that I am what women always are."

"I did not say that," said Grandcourt, looking at her with
his usual gravity. "You are what no other woman is."

"And what is that, pray?" said Gwendolen, moving to a
distance with a little air of menace.

Grandcourt made his pause before he answered. "You are
the woman I love."

"Oh, what nice speeches!" said Gwendolen, laughing.
The sense of that love which he must once have given to
another woman under strange circumstances was getting familiar.

"Give me a nice speech in return. Say when we are to be
married."

"Not yet. Not till we have had a gallop over the downs.
I am so thirsty for that, I can think of nothing else. I wish
the hunting had begun. Sunday the twentieth, twenty-sev-
enth, Monday, Tuesday." Gwendolen was counting on her
fingers with the prettiest nod while she looked at Grandcourt,
and at last swept one palm over the other while she said tri-
umphantly: "It will begin in ten days!"

"Let us be married in ten days, then," said Grandcourt,
"and we shall not be bored about the stables."

"What do women always say in answer to that?" said Gwendolen, mischievously.

"They agree to it," said the lover, rather off his guard.

"Then I will not!" said Gwendolen, taking up her gauntlets and putting them on, while she kept her eyes on him with gathering fun in them.

The scene was pleasant on both sides. A cruder lover would have lost the view of her pretty ways and attitudes, and spoiled all by stupid attempts at caresses, utterly destructive of drama. Grandcourt preferred the drama; and Gwendolen, left at ease, found her spirits rising continually as she played at reigning. Perhaps if Klesmer had seen more of her in this unconscious kind of acting, instead of when she was trying to be theatrical, he might have rated her chance higher.

When they had had a glorious gallop, however, she was in a state of exhilaration that disposed her to think well of hastening the marriage which would make her life all of a piece with this splendid kind of enjoyment. She would not debate any more about an act to which she had committed herself; and she consented to fix the wedding on that day three weeks, notwithstanding the difficulty of fulfilling the customary laws of the *trousseau*.

Lush, of course, was made aware of the engagement by abundant signs, without being formally told. But he expected some communication as a consequence of it, and after a few days he became rather impatient under Grandcourt's silence, feeling sure that the change would affect his personal prospects, and wishing to know exactly how. His tactics no longer included any opposition—which he did not love for its own sake. He might easily cause Grandcourt a great deal of annoyance, but it would be to his own injury, and to create annoyance was not a motive with him. Miss Gwendolen he would certainly not have been sorry to frustrate a little, but— after all there was no knowing what would come. It was nothing new that Grandcourt should show a perverse wilfulness; yet in his freak about this girl he struck Lush rather newly as something like a man who was *fey*—led on by an ominous fatality; and that one born to his fortune should make a worse business of his life than was necessary, seemed really pitiable. Having protested against the marriage, Lush had a second-sight for its evil consequences. Grandcourt had been taking the pains to write letters and give orders himself instead of employing Lush; and appeared to be ignoring his usefulness, even choosing, against the habit of years, to break-fast alone in his dressing-room. But a *tête-à-tête* was not to be avoided in a house empty of guests; and Lush hastened to use an opportunity of saying—it was one day after dinner, for there were difficulties in Grandcourt's dining at Offendene:

"And when is the marriage to take place?"

Grandcourt, who drank little wine, had left the table and was lounging, while he smoked, in an easy-chair near the hearth, where a fire of oak boughs was gaping to its glowing depths, and edging them with a delicate tint of ashes delight-ful to behold. The chair of red-brown velvet brocade was a becoming background for his pale-tinted, well-cut features and exquisite long hands: omitting the cigar, you might have im-agined him a portrait by Moroni, who would have rendered wonderfully the impenetrable gaze and air of distinction; and a portrait by that great master would have been quite as lively a companion as Grandcourt was disposed to be. But he an-swered without unusual delay:

"On the tenth."

"I suppose you intend to remain here."

"We shall go to Ryelands for a little while; but we shall return here for the sake of the hunting."

After this word there was the languid inarticulate sound frequent with Grandcourt when he meant to continue speak-ing, and Lush waited for something more. Nothing came, and he was going to put another question, when the inarticu-late sound began again and introduced the mildly uttered sug-gestion:

"You had better make some new arrangement for your-self."

"What! I am to cut and run?" said Lush, prepared to be good-tempered on the occasion.

"Something of that kind."

"The bride objects to me. I hope she will make up to you for the want of my services."

"I can't help your being so damnably disagreeable to women," said Grandcourt, in soothing apology.

"To one woman, if you please."

"It makes no difference, since she is the one in question."

"I suppose I am not to be turned adrift after fifteen years without some provision."

"You must have saved something out of me."

"Deuced little. I have often saved something for you."

"You can have three hundred a year. But you must live in town and be ready to look after things for me when I want you. I shall be rather hard up."

"If you are not going to be at Ryelands this winter, I might run down there and let you know how Swinton goes on."

"If you like. I don't care a toss where you are, so that you keep out of sight."

"Much obliged," said Lush, able to take the affair more easily than he had expected. He was supported by the secret belief that he should by and by be wanted as much as ever.

"Perhaps you will not object to packing up as soon as possible," said Grandcourt. "The Torringtons are coming, and Miss Harleth will be riding over here."

"With all my heart. Can't I be of use in going to Gadsmere?"

"No. I am going myself."

"About your being rather hard up. Have you thought of that plan——"

"Just leave me alone, will you?" said Grandcourt, in his lowest audible tone, tossing his cigar into the fire, and rising to walk away.

He spent the evening in the solitude of the smaller drawing-room, where, with various new publications on the table, of the kind a gentleman may like to have at hand without touching, he employed himself (as a philosopher might have done) in sitting meditatively on a sofa and abstaining from literature—political, comic, cynical, or romantic. In this way hours may pass surprisingly soon, without the arduous invisible chase of philosophy; not from love of thought, but from hatred of effort—from a state of the inward world, something like premature age, where the need for action lapses into a

mere image of what has been, is, and may or might be; where
impulse is born and dies in a phantasmal world, pausing in
rejection even of a shadowy fulfilment.   That is a condition
which often comes with whitening hair; and sometimes, too,
an intense obstinacy and tenacity of rule, like the main trunk
of an exorbitant egoism, conspicuous in proportion as the varied
susceptibilities of younger years are stripped away.

But Grandcourt's hair, though he had not much of it, was
of a fine sunny blond, and his moods were not entirely to be
explained as ebbing energy.   We mortals have a strange spiritual chemistry going on within us, so that a lazy stagnation
or even a cottony milkiness may be preparing one knows not
what biting or explosive material.   The navvy waking from
sleep and without malice heaving a stone to crush the life out
of his still sleeping comrade, is understood to lack the trained
motive which makes a character fairly calculable in its actions;
but by a roundabout course even a gentleman may make of
himself a chancy personage, raising an uncertainty as to what
he may do next, which sadly spoils companionship.

Grandcourt's thoughts this evening were like the circlets
one sees in a dark pool continually dying out and continually
started again by some impulse from below the surface.   The
deeper central impulse came from the image of Gwendolen;
but the thoughts it stirred would be imperfectly illustrated by
a reference to the amatory poets of all ages.   It was characteristic that he got none of his satisfaction from the belief that
Gwendolen was in love with him; and that love had overcome
the jealous resentment which had made her run away from
him.   On the contrary, he believed that this girl was rather
exceptional in the fact that, in spite of his assiduous attention
to her, she was not in love with him; and it seemed to him
very likely that if it had not been for the sudden poverty
which had come over her family, she would not have accepted
him.   From the very first there had been an exasperating fascination in the tricksiness with which she had—not met his
advances, but—wheeled away from them.   She had been
brought to accept him in spite of everything—brought to
kneel down like a horse under training for the arena, though
she might have an objection to it all the while.   On the

whole, Grandcourt got more pleasure out of this notion than he could have done out of winning a girl of whom he was sure that she had a strong inclination for him personally. And yet this pleasure in mastering reluctance flourished along with the habitual persuasion that no woman whom he favored could be quite indifferent to his personal influence; and it seemed to him not unlikely that by and by Gwendolen might be more enamored of him than he of her. In any case she would have to submit; and he enjoyed thinking of her as his future wife, whose pride and spirit were suited to command every one but himself. He had no taste for a woman who was all tenderness to him, full of petitioning solicitude and willing obedience. He meant to be master of a woman who would have liked to master him, and who perhaps would have been capable of mastering another man.

Lush, having failed in his attempted reminder to Grandcourt, thought it well to communicate with Sir Hugo, in whom, as a man having perhaps interest enough to command the bestowal of some place where the work was light, gentlemanly, and not ill-paid, he was anxious to cultivate a sense of friendly obligation, not feeling at all secure against the future need of such a place. He wrote the following letter, and addressed it to Park Lane, whither he knew the family had returned from Leubronn:

My dear Sir Hugo:—Since we came home the marriage has been absolutely decided on, and is to take place in less than three weeks. It is so far the worse for him that her mother has lately lost all her fortune, and he will have to find supplies. Grandcourt, I know, is feeling the want of cash ; and unless some other plan is resorted to, he will be raising money in a foolish way. I am going to leave Diplow immediately, and I shall not be able to start the topic. What I should advise is, that Mr. Deronda, who I know has your confidence, should propose to come and pay a short visit here, according to invitation (there are going to be other people in the house), and that you should put him fully in possession of your wishes and the possible extent of your offer. Then, that he should introduce the subject to Grandcourt so as not to imply that you suspect any particular want of money on his part, but only that there is a strong wish on yours. What I have formerly said to him has been in the way of a conjecture that you might be willing to give a good sum for his chance of Diplow ; but if Mr. Deronda came armed with a definite offer that would take another

sort of hold.   Ten to one he will not close for some time to come ; but
the proposal will have got a stronger lodgment in his mind ; and though
at present he has a great notion of the hunting here, I see a likelihood,
under the circumstances, that he will get a distaste for the neighborhood, and there will be the notion of the money sticking by him without being urged.   I would bet on your ultimate success.   As I am not
to be exiled to Siberia, but am to be within call, it is possible that, by
and by, I may be of more service to you.   But at present I can think
of no medium so good as Mr. Deronda.   Nothing puts Grandcourt in
worse humor than having the lawyers thrust their paper under his nose
uninvited.

Trusting that your visit to Leubronn has put you in excellent condition for the winter, I remain, my dear Sir Hugo, yours very faith-
fully,   Thomas Cranmer Lush.

Sir Hugo, having received this letter at breakfast, handed
it to Deronda, who, though he had chambers in town, was
somehow hardly ever in them, Sir Hugo not being contented
without him.   The chatty baronet would have liked a young
companion even if there had been no peculiar reasons for
attachment between them: one with a fine harmonious un-
spoiled face fitted to keep up a cheerful view of posterity and
inheritance generally, notwithstanding particular disappoint-
ments; and his affection for Deronda was not diminished by
the deep-lying though not obtrusive difference in their notions
and tastes.   Perhaps it was all the stronger; acting as the
same sort of difference does between a man and a woman in
giving a piquancy to the attachment which subsists in spite of
it.   Sir Hugo did not think unapprovingly of himself; but he
looked at men and society from a liberal-menagerie point of
view, and he had a certain pride in Deronda's differing from
him which, if it had found voice, might have said: "You see
this fine young fellow—not such as you see every day, is he?
—he belongs to me in a sort of way, I brought him up from a
child; but you would not ticket him off easily, he has notions
of his own, and he's as far as the poles asunder from what I
was at his age."   This state of feeling was kept up by the
mental balance in Deronda, who was moved by an affectionateness such as we are apt to call feminine, disposing him to
yield in ordinary details, while he had a certain inflexibility
of judgment, and independence of opinion, held to be rightfully masculine.

When he had read the letter, he returned it without speaking, inwardly wincing under Lush's mode of attributing a neutral usefulness to him in the family affairs.

"What do you say, Dan? It would be pleasant enough for you. You have not seen the place for a good many years now, and you might have a famous run with the harriers if you went down next week," said Sir Hugo.

"I should not go on that account," said Deronda, buttering his bread attentively. He had an objection to this transparent kind of persuasiveness, which all intelligent animals are seen to treat with indifference. If he went to Diplow, he should be doing something disagreeable to oblige Sir Hugo.

"I think Lush's notion is a good one. And it would be a pity to lose the occasion."

"That is a different matter—if you think my going of importance to your object," said Deronda, still with that aloofness of manner which implied some suppression. He knew that the baronet had set his heart on the affair.

"Why, you will see the fair gambler, the Leubronn Diana, I shouldn't wonder," said Sir Hugo, gayly. "We shall have to invite her to the Abbey, when they are married, Louisa," he added, turning to Lady Mallinger, as if she too had read the letter.

"I cannot conceive whom you mean," said Lady Mallinger, who in fact had not been listening, her mind having been taken up with her first sips of coffee, the objectionable cuff of her sleeve, and the necessity of carrying Theresa to the dentist—innocent and partly laudable preoccupations, as the gentle lady's usually were. Should her appearance be inquired after, let it be said that she had reddish blond hair (the hair of the period), a small Roman nose, rather prominent blue eyes and delicate eyelids, with a figure which her thinner friends called fat, her hands showing curves and dimples like a magnified baby's.

"I mean that Grandcourt is going to marry the girl you saw at Leubronn—don't you remember her?—the Miss Harleth who used to play at roulette."

"Dear me! Is that a good match for him?"

"That depends on the sort of goodness he wants," said Sir

Hugo, smiling. "However, she and her friends have nothing, and she will bring him expenses. It's a good match for my purposes, because if I am willing to fork out a sum of money, he may be willing to give up his chance of Diplow, so that we shall have it out and out, and when I die you will have the consolation of going to the place you would like to go to—wherever I may go."

"I wish you would not talk of dying in that light way, dear."

"It's rather a heavy way, Lou, for I shall have to pay a heavy sum—forty thousand, at least."

"But why are we to invite them to the Abbey?" said Lady Mallinger. "I do *not* like women who gamble, like Lady Cragstone."

"Oh, you will not mind her for a week. Besides, she is not like Lady Cragstone because she gambled a little, any more than I am like a broker because I'm a Whig. I want to keep Grandcourt in good humor, and to let him see plenty of this place, that he may think the less of Diplow. I don't know yet whether I shall get him to meet me in this matter. And if Dan were to go over on a visit there, he might hold out the bait to him. It would be doing me a great service." This was meant for Deronda.

"Daniel is not fond of Mr. Grandcourt, I think, is he?" said Lady Mallinger, looking at Deronda inquiringly.

"There is no avoiding everybody one doesn't happen to be fond of," said Deronda. "I will go to Diplow—I don't know that I have anything better to do—since Sir Hugo wishes it."

"That's a trump!" said Sir Hugo, well pleased. "And if you don't find it very pleasant, it's so much experience. Nothing used to come amiss to me when I was young. You must see men and manners."

"Yes; but I have seen that man, and something of his manners too," said Deronda.

"Not nice manners, I think," said Lady Mallinger.

"Well, you see they succeed with your sex," said Sir Hugo, provokingly. "And he was an uncommonly good-looking fellow when he was two or three and twenty—like his father,

He doesn't take after his father in marrying the heiress, though. If he had got Miss Arrowpoint and my land, too, confound him, he would have had a fine principality."

Deronda, in anticipating the projected visit, felt less disinclination than when consenting to it. The story of that girl's marriage did interest him: what he had heard through Lush of her having run away from the suit of the man she was now going to take as a husband had thrown a new sort of light on her gambling; and it was probably the transition from that fevered worldliness into poverty which had urged her acceptance where she must in some way have felt repulsion. All this implied a nature liable to difficulty and struggle—elements of life which had a predominant attraction for his sympathy, due perhaps to his early pain in dwelling on the conjectured story of his own existence. Persons attracted him, as Hans Meyrick had done, in proportion to the possibility of his defending them, rescuing them, telling upon their lives with some sort of redeeming influence; and he had to resist an inclination, easily accounted for, to withdraw coldly from the fortunate. But in the movement which had led him to repurchase Gwendolen's necklace for her, and which was at work in him still, there was something beyond his habitual compassionate fervor—something due to the fascination of her womanhood. He was very open to that sort of charm, and mingled it with the consciously Utopian pictures of his own future; yet any one able to trace the folds of his character might have conceived that he would be more likely than many less passionate men to love a woman without telling her of it. Sprinkle food before a delicate-eared bird: there is nothing he would more willingly take, yet he keeps aloof, because of his sensibility to checks which to you are imperceptible. And one man differs from another, as we all differ from the Bosjesman, in a sensibility to checks, that come from variety of needs, spiritual or other. It seemed to foreshadow that capability of reticence in Deronda that his imagination was much occupied with two women, to neither of whom would he have held it possible that he should ever make love. Hans Meyrick had laughed at him for having something of the knight-errant in his disposition; and he would have found his proof if he had known what was just now going on in Deronda's mind about Mirah and Gwendolen.

Deronda wrote without delay to announce the visit to Diplow, and received in reply a polite assurance that his coming would give great pleasure. That was not altogether untrue. Grandcourt thought it probable that the visit was prompted by Sir Hugo's desire to court him for a purpose which he did not make up his mind to resist; and it was not a disagreeable idea to him that this fine fellow, whom he believed to be his cousin under the rose, would witness, perhaps with some jealousy, Henleigh Mallinger Grandcourt play the commanding part of betrothed lover to a splendid girl whom the cousin had already looked at with admiration.

Grandcourt himself was not jealous of anything unless it threatened his mastery—which he did not think himself likely to lose.

CHAPTER XXIX.

"Surely whoever speaks to me in the right voice,
   him or her I shall follow,
As the water follows the moon, silently,
   with fluid steps anywhere around the globe."
                                        — WALT WHITMAN.

"Now my cousins are at Diplow," said Grandcourt, "will you go there?—to-morrow? The carriage shall come for Mrs. Davilow. You can tell me what you would like done in the rooms. Things must be put in decent order while we are away at Ryelands. And to-morrow is the only day."

He was sitting sideways on a sofa in the drawing-room at Offendene, one hand and elbow resting on the back, and the other hand thrust between his crossed knees—in the attitude of a man who is much interested in watching the person next to him. Gwendolen, who had always disliked needlework, had taken to it with apparent zeal since her engagement, and now held a piece of white embroidery which on examination would have shown many false stitches. During the last eight or nine days their hours had been chiefly spent on horseback, but some margin had always been left for this more difficult sort of companionship, which, however, Gwendolen had not

found disagreeable. She was very well satisfied with Grandcourt. His answers to her lively questions about what he had
seen and done in his life bore drawling very well. From the
first she had noticed that he knew what to say; and she was
constantly feeling not only that he had nothing of the fool in
his composition, but that by some subtle means he communi-
cated to her the impression that all the folly lay with other
people, who did what he did not care to do. A man who
seems to have been able to command the best has a sovereign
power of depreciation. Then Grandcourt's behavior as a lover
had hardly at all passed the limit of an amorous homage which
was inobtrusive as a wafted odor of roses, and spent all its
effect in a gratified vanity. One day, indeed, he had kissed
not her cheek, but her neck a little below her ear; and Gwendolen, taken by surprise, had started up with a marked agitation which made him rise, too, and say: "I beg your pardon
—did I annoy you?"—"Oh, it was nothing," said Gwendolen,
rather afraid of herself, "only I cannot bear—to be kissed
under my ear." She sat down again with a little playful
laugh, but all the while she felt her heart beating with a
vague fear: she was no longer at liberty to flout him as she
had flouted poor Rex. Her agitation seemed not uncomplimentary, and he had been contented not to transgress again.

To-day a slight rain hindered riding; but to compensate, a
package had come from London, and Mrs. Davilow had just
left the room after bringing in for admiration the beautiful
things (of Grandcourt's ordering) which lay scattered about on
the tables. Gwendolen was just then enjoying the scenery of
her life. She let her hands fall on her lap, and said with a
pretty air of perversity:

"Why is to-morrow the only day?"

"Because the next day is the first with the hounds," said
Grandcourt.

"And after that?"

"After that I must go away for a couple of days—it's a
bore—but I shall go one day and come back the next."
Grandcourt noticed a change in her face, and releasing his
hand from under his knees, he laid it on hers, and said: "You
object to my going away?"

"It is no use objecting," said Gwendolen, coldly. She was resisting to the utmost her temptation to tell him that she suspected to whom he was going—and the temptation to make a clean breast, speaking without restraint.

"Yes, it is," said Grandcourt, enfolding her hand. "I will put off going. And I will travel at night, so as only to be away one day." He thought that he knew the reason of what he inwardly called this bit of temper, and she was particularly fascinating to him at this moment.

"Then don't put off going, but travel at night," said Gwendolen, feeling that she could command him, and finding in this peremptoriness a small outlet for her irritation.

"Then you will go to Diplow to-morrow?"

"Oh, yes, if you wish it," said Gwendolen, in a high tone of careless assent. Her concentration in other feelings had really hindered her from taking notice that her hand was being held.

"How you treat us poor devils of men!" said Grandcourt, lowering his tone. "We are always getting the worst of it."

"*Are* you?" said Gwendolen, in a tone of inquiry, looking at him more naïvely than usual. She longed to believe this commonplace *badinage* as the serious truth about her lover: in that case, she, too, was justified. If she knew everything, Mrs. Glasher would appear more blamable than Grandcourt. "*Are* you always getting the worst?"

"Yes. Are you as kind to me as I am to you?" said Grandcourt, looking into her eyes with his narrow gaze.

Gwendolen felt herself stricken. She was conscious of having received so much, that her sense of command was checked, and sank away in the perception that, look around her as she might, she could not turn back: it was as if she had consented to mount a chariot where another held the reins; and it was not in her nature to leap out in the eyes of the world. She had not consented in ignorance, and all she could say now would be a confession that she had not been ignorant. Her right to explanation was gone. All she had to do now was to adjust herself, so that the spikes of that unwilling penance which conscience imposed should not gall her. With a sort of mental shiver, she resolutely changed her mental attitude. There had been a little pause, during which she had not turned away her eyes; and with a sudden break into a smile, she said:

"If I were as kind to you as you are to me, that would spoil your generosity: it would no longer be as great as it could be—and it is that now."

"Then I am not to ask for one kiss," said Grandcourt, contented to pay a large price for this new kind of love-making, which introduced marriage by the finest contrast.

"Not one!" said Gwendolen, getting saucy, and nodding at him defiantly.

He lifted her little left hand to his lips, and then released it respectfully. Clearly it was faint praise to say of him that he was not disgusting: he was almost charming; and she felt at this moment that it was not likely she could ever have loved another man better than this one. His reticence gave her some inexplicable, delightful consciousness.

"Apropos," she said, taking up her work again, "is there any one besides Captain and Mrs. Torrington at Diplow?—or do you leave them *tête-à-tête?* I suppose he converses in cigars, and she answers with her chignon."

"She has a sister with her," said Grandcourt, with his shadow of a smile, "and there are two men besides—one of them you know, I believe."

"Ah, then, I have a poor opinion of him," said Gwendolen, shaking her head.

"You saw him at Leubronn—young Deronda—a young fellow with the Mallingers."

Gwendolen felt as if her heart were making a sudden gambol, and her fingers, which tried to keep a firm hold on her work, got cold.

"I never spoke to him," she said, dreading any discernible change in herself. "Is he not disagreeable?"

"No, not particularly," said Grandcourt, in his most languid way. "He thinks a little too much of himself. I thought he had been introduced to you."

"No. Some one told me his name the evening before I came away; that was all. What is he?"

"A sort of ward of Sir Hugo Mallinger's. Nothing of any consequence."

"Oh, poor creature! How very unpleasant for him!" said Gwendolen, speaking from the lip, and not meaning any sarcasm. "I wonder if it has left off raining?" she added, rising and going to look out of the window.

Happily it did not rain the next day, and Gwendolen rode to Diplow on Criterion as she had done on that former day when she returned with her mother in the carriage. She always felt the more daring for being in her riding-dress; besides having the agreeable belief that she looked as well as possible in it—a sustaining consciousness in any meeting which seems formidable. Her anger toward Deronda had changed into a superstitious dread—due, perhaps, to the coercion he had exercised over her thought—lest that first interference of his in her life might foreshadow some future influence. It is of such stuff that superstitions are commonly made: an intense feeling about ourselves which makes the evening star shine at us with a threat, and the blessing of a beggar encourage us. And superstitions carry consequences which often verify their hope or their foreboding.

The time before luncheon was taken up for Gwendolen by going over the rooms with Mrs. Torrington and Mrs. Davilow; and she thought it likely that if she saw Deronda, there would hardly be need for more than a bow between them. She meant to notice him as little as possible.

And after all she found herself under an inward compulsion too strong for her pride. From the first moment of their being in the room together, she seemed to herself to be doing nothing but notice him; everything else was automatic performance of an habitual part.

When he took his place at lunch, Grandcourt had said: "Deronda, Miss Harleth tells me you were not introduced to her at Leubronn?"

"Miss Harleth hardly remembers me, I imagine," said Deronda, looking at her quite simply, as they bowed. "She was intensely occupied when I saw her."

Now, did he suppose that she had not suspected him of being the person who redeemed her necklace?

"On the contrary. I remember you very well," said Gwendolen, feeling rather nervous, but governing herself and looking at him in return with new examination. "You did not approve of my playing at roulette."

"How did you come to that conclusion?" said Deronda, gravely.

"Oh, you cast an evil eye on my play," said Gwendolen, with a turn of her head and a smile. "I began to lose as soon as you came to look on. I had always been winning till then."

"Roulette in such a kennel as Leubronn is a horrid bore," said Grandcourt.

"*I* found it a bore when I began to lose," said Gwendolen. Her face was turned toward Grandcourt as she smiled and spoke, but she gave a sidelong glance at Deronda, and saw his eyes fixed on her with a look so gravely penetrating that it had a keener edge for her than his ironical smile at her losses —a keener edge than Klesmer's judgment. She wheeled her neck round as if she wanted to listen to what was being said by the rest, while she was only thinking of Deronda. His face had that disturbing kind of form and expression which threatens to affect opinion—as if one's standard were somehow wrong. (Who has not seen men with faces of this corrective power till they frustrated it by speech or action?) His voice, heard now for the first time, was to Grandcourt's toneless drawl, which had been in her ears every day, as the deep notes of a violoncello to the broken discourse of poultry and other lazy gentry in the afternoon sunshine. Grandcourt, she inwardly conjectured, was perhaps right in saying that Deronda thought too much of himself:—a favorite way of explaining a superiority that humiliates. However, the talk turned on the rinderpest and Jamaica, and no more was said about roulette. Grandcourt held that the Jamaican negro was a beastly sort of Baptist Caliban; Deronda said he had always felt a little with Caliban, who naturally had his own point of view and could sing a good song; Mrs. Davilow observed that her father had an estate in Barbadoes, but that she herself had never been in the West Indies; Mrs. Torrington was sure she should never sleep in her bed if she lived among blacks; her husband corrected her by saying that the blacks would be manageable enough if it were not for the half-breeds; and Deronda remarked that the whites had to thank themselves for the half-breeds.

While this polite pea-shooting was going on, Gwendolen trifled with her jelly, and looked at every speaker in turn that she might feel at ease in looking at Deronda.

"I wonder what he thinks of me really? He must have felt interested in me, else he would not have sent me my necklace. I wonder what he thinks of my marriage? What notions has he to make him so grave about things? Why is he come to Diplow?"

These questions ran in her mind as the voice of an uneasy longing to be judged by Deronda with unmixed admiration—a longing which had had its seed in her first resentment at his critical glance. Why did she care so much about the opinion of this man who was "nothing of any consequence"? She had no time to find the reason—she was too much engaged in caring. In the drawing-room, when something had called Grandcourt away, she went quite unpremeditatedly up to Deronda, who was standing at a table apart, turning over some prints, and said to him:

"Shall you hunt to-morrow, Mr. Deronda?"

"Yes, I believe so."

"You don't object to hunting, then?"

"I find excuses for it. It is a sin I am inclined to—when I can't get boating or cricketing."

"Do you object to my hunting?" said Gwendolen, with a saucy movement of the chin.

"I have no right to object to anything you choose to do."

"You thought you had a right to object to my gambling," persisted Gwendolen.

"I was sorry for it. I am not aware that I told you of my objection," said Deronda, with his usual directness of gaze—a large-eyed gravity, innocent of any intention. His eyes had a peculiarity which has drawn many men into trouble; they were of a dark yet mild intensity, which seemed to express a special interest in every one on whom he fixed them, and might easily help to bring on him those claims which ardently sympathetic people are often creating in the minds of those who need help. In mendicant fashion, we make the goodness of others a reason for exorbitant demands on them. That sort of effect was penetrating Gwendolen.

"You hindered me from gambling again," she answered. But she had no sooner spoken than she blushed over face and neck; and Deronda blushed, too, conscious that in the little affair of the necklace he had taken a questionable freedom.

It was impossible to speak further; and she turned away to a window, feeling that she had stupidly said what she had not meant to say, and yet being rather happy that she had plunged into this mutual understanding. Deronda also did not dislike it. Gwendolen seemed more decidedly attractive than before; and certainly there had been changes going on within her since that time at Leubronn: the struggle of mind attending a conscious error had wakened something like a new soul, which had better, but also worse, possibilities than her former poise of crude self-confidence: among the forces she had come to dread was something within her that troubled satisfaction.

That evening Mrs. Davilow said: "Was it really so, or only a joke of yours, about Mr. Deronda's spoiling your play, Gwen?"

Her curiosity had been excited, and she could venture to ask a question that did not concern Mr. Grandcourt.

"Oh, it merely happened that he was looking on when I began to lose," said Gwendolen, carelessly. "I noticed him."

"I don't wonder at that: he is a striking young man. He puts me in mind of Italian paintings. One would guess, without being told, that there was foreign blood in his veins."

"Is there?" said Gwendolen.

"Mrs. Torrington says so. I asked particularly who he was, and she told me that his mother was some foreigner of high rank."

"His mother?" said Gwendolen, rather sharply. "Then who was his father?"

"Well—every one says he is the son of Sir Hugo Mallinger, who brought him up; though he passes for a ward. She says, if Sir Hugo Mallinger could have done as he liked with his estates, he would have left them to this Mr. Deronda, since he has no legitimate son."

Gwendolen was silent; but her mother observed so marked an effect in her face that she was angry with herself for having repeated Mrs. Torrington's gossip. It seemed, on reflection, unsuited to the ear of her daughter, for whom Mrs. Davilow disliked what is called knowledge of the world; and indeed she wished that she herself had not had any of it thrust upon her.

An image which had immediately arisen in Gwendolen's mind was that of the unknown mother—no doubt a dark-eyed woman—probably sad. Hardly any face could be less like Deronda's than that represented as Sir Hugo's in a crayon portrait at Diplow. A dark-eyed beautiful woman, no longer young, had become "stuff o' the conscience" to Gwendolen.

That night when she had got into her little bed, and only a dim light was burning, she said:

"Mamma, have men generally children before they are married?"

"No, dear, no," said Mrs. Davilow. "Why do you ask such a question?" (But she began to think that she saw the why.)

"If it were so, I ought to know," said Gwendolen, with some indignation.

"You are thinking of what I said about Mr. Deronda and Sir Hugo Mallinger. That is a very unusual case, dear."

"Does Lady Mallinger know?"

"She knows enough to satisfy her. That is quite clear, because Mr. Deronda has lived with them."

"And people think no worse of him?"

"Well, of course he is under some disadvantage: it is not as if he were Lady Mallinger's son. He does not inherit the property, and he is not of any consequence in the world. But people are not obliged to know anything about his birth; you see, he is very well received."

"I wonder whether he knows about it; and whether he is angry with his father?"

"My dear child, why should you think of that?"

"Why?" said Gwendolen, impetuously, sitting up in her

bed. "Haven't children reason to be angry with their parents? How can they help their parents marrying or not marrying?"

But a consciousness rushed upon her, which made her fall back again on her pillow. It was not only what she would have felt months before—that she might seem to be reproaching her mother for that second marriage of hers;—what she chiefly felt now was, that she had been led on to a condemnation which seemed to make her own marriage a forbidden thing.

There was no further talk, and till sleep came over her, Gwendolen lay struggling with the reasons against that marriage—reasons which pressed upon her newly now that they were unexpectedly mirrored in the story of a man whose slight relations with her had, by some hidden affinity, bitten themselves into the most permanent layers of feeling. It was characteristic that, with all her debating, she was never troubled by the question whether the indefensibleness of her marriage did not include the fact that she had accepted Grandcourt solely as the man whom it was convenient for her to marry, not in the least as one to whom she would be binding herself in duty. Gwendolen's ideas were pitiably crude; but many grand difficulties of life are apt to force themselves on us in our crudity. And to judge wisely I suppose we must know how things appear to the unwise; that kind of appearance making the larger part of the world's history.

In the morning, there was a double excitement for her. She was going to hunt, from which scruples about propriety had threatened to hinder her, until it was found that Mrs. Torrington was horsewoman enough to accompany her:—going to hunt for the first time since her escapade with Rex; and she was going again to see Deronda, in whom, since last night, her interest had so gathered that she expected, as people do about revealed celebrities, to see something in his appearance which she had missed before. What was he going to be? What sort of life had he before him—he being nothing of any consequence? And with only a little difference in events he might have been as important as Grandcourt, nay—her imagination inevitably went in that direction—might have held the very estates which Grandcourt was to have. But now Deronda would probably some day see her mistress of the Abbey at

Topping, see her bearing the title which would have been his own wife's. These obvious, futile thoughts of what might have been made a new epoch for Gwendolen. She, whose unquestioning habit it had been to take the best that came to her for less than her own claim, had now to see the position which tempted her in a new light, as a hard, unfair exclusion of others. What she had now heard about Deronda seemed to her imagination to throw him into one group with Mrs. Glasher and her children; before whom she felt herself in an attitude of apology—she who had hitherto been surrounded by a group that in her opinion had need be apologetic to her. Perhaps Deronda himself was thinking of these things. Could he know of Mrs. Glasher? If he knew that she knew, he would despise her; but he could have no such knowledge. Would he, without that, despise her for marrying Grandcourt? His possible judgment of her actions was telling on her as importunately as Klesmer's judgment of her powers; but she found larger room for resistance to a disapproval of her marriage, because it is easier to make our conduct seem justifiable to ourselves than to make our ability strike others. "How can I help it?" is not our favorite apology for incompetence. But Gwendolen felt some strength in saying:

"How can I help what other people have done? Things would not come right if I were to turn round now and declare that I would not marry Mr. Grandcourt." And such turning round was out of the question. The horses in the chariot she had mounted were going at full speed.

This mood of youthful, elated desperation had a tidal recurrence. She could dare anything that lay before her sooner than she could choose to go backward into humiliation; and it was even soothing to think that there would now be as much ill-doing in the one as in the other. But the immediate delightful fact was the hunt, where she would see Deronda, and where he would see her; for always lurking ready to obtrude before other thoughts about him was the impression that he was very much interested in her. But to-day she was resolved not to repeat her folly of yesterday, as if she were anxious to say anything to him. Indeed, the hunt would be too absorbing.

And so it was for a long while. Deronda was there, and

within her sight very often; but this only added to the stimulus of a pleasure which Gwendolen had only once before tasted, and which seemed likely always to give a delight independent of any crosses, except such as took away the chance of riding. No accident happened to throw them together; the run took them within convenient reach of home, and in the agreeable sombreness of the gray November afternoon, with a long stratum of yellow light in the west, Gwendolen was returning with the company from Diplow, who were attending her on the way to Offendene. Now that the sense of glorious excitement was over and gone, she was getting irritably disappointed that she had had no opportunity of speaking to Deronda, whom she would not see again, since he was to go away in a couple of days. What was she going to say? That was not quite certain. She wanted to speak to him. Grandcourt was by her side; Mrs. Torrington, her husband, and another gentleman in advance; and Deronda's horse she could hear behind. The wish to speak to him and have him speaking to her was becoming imperious; and there was no chance of it unless she simply asserted her will and defied everything. Where the order of things could give way to Miss Gwendolen, it must be made to do so. They had lately emerged from a wood of pines and beeches, where the twilight stillness had a repressing effect, which increased her impatience. The horse-hoofs again heard behind at some little distance were a growing irritation. She reined in her horse and looked behind her; Grandcourt, after a few paces, also paused; but she, waving her whip and nodding sideways with playful imperiousness, said: "Go on! I want to speak to Mr. Deronda."

Grandcourt hesitated; but that he would have done after any proposition. It was an awkward situation for him. No gentleman, before marriage, could give the emphasis of refusal to a command delivered in this playful way. He rode on slowly, and she waited till Deronda came up. He looked at her with tacit inquiry, and she said at once, letting her horse go alongside of his:

"Mr. Deronda, you must enlighten my ignorance. I want to know why you thought it wrong for me to gamble. Is it because I am a woman?"

"Not altogether; but I regretted it the more because you were a woman," said Deronda, with an irrepressible smile. Apparently it must be understood between them now that it was he who sent the necklace. "I think it would be better for men not to gamble. It is a besotting kind of taste, likely to turn into a disease. And, besides, there is something revolting to me in raking a heap of money together, and internally chuckling over it, when others are feeling the loss of it. I should even call it base, if it were more than an exceptional lapse. There are enough inevitable turns of fortune which force us to see that our gain is another's loss:— that is one of the ugly aspects of life. One would like to reduce it as much as one could, not get amusement out of exaggerating it." Deronda's voice had gathered some indignation while he was speaking.

"But you do admit that we can't help things," said Gwendolen, with a drop in her tone. The answer had not been anything like what she had expected. "I mean that things are so in spite of us; we can't always help it that our gain is another's loss."

"Clearly. Because of that, we should help it where we can."

Gwendolen, biting her lip inside, paused a moment, and then forcing herself to speak with an air of playfulness again, said:

"But why should you regret it more because I am a woman?"

"Perhaps because we need that you should be better than we are."

"But suppose we need that men should be better than we are," said Gwendolen, with a little air of a "check!"

"That is rather a difficulty," said Deronda, smiling. "I suppose I should have said, we each of us think it would be better for the other to be good."

"You see, I needed you to be better than I was—and you thought so," said Gwendolen, nodding and laughing, while she put her horse forward and joined Grandcourt, who made no observation.

"Don't you want to know what I had to say to Mr. Deronda?'' said Gwendolen, whose own pride required her to account for her conduct.

"A—no," said Grandcourt, coldly.

"Now that is the first impolite word you have spoken—that you don't wish to hear what I had to say," said Gwendolen, playing at a pout.

" I wish to hear what you say to me—not to other men," said Grandcourt.

"Then you wish to hear this. I wanted to make him tell me why he objected to my gambling, and he gave me a little sermon."

"Yes—but excuse me the sermon." If Gwendolen imagined that Grandcourt cared about her speaking to Deronda, he wished her to understand that she was mistaken. But he was not fond of being told to ride on. She saw he was piqued, but did not mind. She had accomplished her object of speaking again to Deronda before he raised his hat and turned with the rest toward Diplow, while her lover attended her to Offendene, where he was to bid farewell before a whole day's absence on the unspecified journey. Grandcourt had spoken truth in calling the journey a bore: he was going by train to Gadsmere.

CHAPTER XXX.

No penitence and no confessional:
No priest ordains it, yet they're forced to sit
Amid deep ashes of their vanished years.

IMAGINE a rambling, patchy house, the best part built of gray stone, and red-tiled, a round tower jutting at one of the corners, the mellow darkness of its conical roof surmounted by a weather-cock making an agreeable object either amidst the gleams and greenth of summer or the low-hanging clouds and snowy branches of winter: the ground shady with spreading trees: a great cedar flourishing on one side, backward some Scotch firs on a broken bank where the roots hung naked, and beyond, a rookery: on the other side a pool overhung with bushes, where the water-fowl fluttered and screamed: all

around, a vast meadow which might be called a park, bordered
by an old plantation and guarded by stone lodges which looked
like little prisons. Outside the gate the country, once entirely
rural and lovely, now black with coal-mines, was chiefly peo-
pled by men and brethren with candles stuck in their hats, and
with a diabolic complexion which laid them peculiarly open
to suspicion in the eyes of the children at Gadsmere—Mrs.
Glasher's four beautiful children, who had dwelt there for
about three years. Now, in November, when the flower-beds
were empty, the trees leafless, and the pool blackly shivering,
one might have said that the place was sombrely in keeping
with the black roads and black mounds which seemed to put
the district in mourning;—except when the children were
playing on the gravel with the dogs for their companions.
But Mrs. Glasher under her present circumstances liked Gadsmere as well as she would have liked any other abode. The
complete seclusion of the place, which the unattractiveness
of the country secured, was exactly to her taste. When she
drove her two ponies with a wagonet full of children, there
were no gentry in carriages to be met, only men of business
in gigs; at church there were no eyes she cared to avoid, for
the curate's wife and the curate himself were either ignorant
of anything to her disadvantage, or ignored it: to them she
was simply a widow lady, the tenant of Gadsmere; and the
name of Grandcourt was of little interest in that district compared with the names of Fletcher and Gawcome, the lessees
of the collieries.

It was full ten years since the elopement of an Irish officer's
beautiful wife with young Grandcourt, and a consequent duel
where the bullets wounded the air only, had made some little
noise. Most of those who remembered the affair now wondered what had become of that Mrs. Glasher whose beauty
and brilliancy had made her rather conspicuous to them in
foreign places, where she was known to be living with young
Grandcourt.

That he should have disentangled himself from that connection seemed only natural and desirable. As to her, it was
thought that a woman who was understood to have forsaken
her child along with her husband had probably sunk lower.

Grandcourt had of course got weary of her. He was much given to the pursuit of women: but a man in his position would by this time desire to make a suitable marriage with the fair young daughter of a noble house. No one talked of Mrs. Glasher now, any more than they talked of a victim in a trial for manslaughter ten years before: she was a lost vessel after whom nobody would send out an expedition of search; but Grandcourt was seen in harbor with his colors flying, registered as seaworthy as ever.

Yet in fact Grandcourt had never disentangled himself from Mrs. Glasher. His passion for her had been the strongest and most lasting he had ever known; and though it was now as dead as the music of a cracked flute, it had left a certain dull disposedness, which on the death of her husband three years before had prompted in him a vacillating notion of marrying her, in accordance with the understanding often expressed between them during the days of his first ardor. At that early time Grandcourt would willingly have paid for the freedom to be won by a divorce; but the husband would not oblige him, not wanting to be married again himself, and not wishing to have his domestic habits printed in evidence.

The altered poise which the years had brought in Mrs. Glasher was just the reverse. At first she was comparatively careless about the possibility of marriage. It was enough that she had escaped from a disagreeable husband and found a sort of bliss with a lover who had completely fascinated her— young, handsome, amorous, and living in the best style, with equipage and conversation of the kind to be expected in young men of fortune who have seen everything. She was an impassioned, vivacious woman, fond of adoration, exasperated by five years of marital rudeness; and the sense of release was so strong upon her that it stilled anxiety for more than she actually enjoyed. An equivocal position was of no importance to her then; she had no envy for the honors of a dull, disregarded wife: the one spot which spoiled her vision of her new pleasant world was the sense that she had left her three-year-old boy, who died two years afterward, and whose first tones saying "mamma" retained a difference from those of the children that came after. But now the years had brought many changes besides those in the contour of her cheek and throat; and that Grandcourt should marry her had become her dominant desire. The equivocal position which she had not minded about for herself was now telling upon her through her children, whom she loved with a devotion charged with the added passion of atonement. She had no repentance except in this direction. If Grandcourt married her, the children would be none the worse off for what had passed: they would see their mother in a dignified position, and they would be at no disadvantage with the world: her son could be made his father's heir. It was the yearning for this result which gave the supreme importance to Grandcourt's feeling for her; her love for him had long resolved itself into anxiety that he should give her the unique, permanent claim of a wife, and she expected no other happiness in marriage than the satisfaction of her maternal love and pride—including her pride for herself in the presence of her children. For the sake of that result she was prepared even with a tragic firmness to endure anything quietly in marriage; and she had had acuteness enough to cherish Grandcourt's flickering purpose negatively, by not molesting him with passionate appeals and with scene-making. In her, as in every one else who wanted anything of him, his incalculable turns, and his tendency to harden under beseeching, had created a reasonable dread:—a slow discovery, of which no presentiment had been given in the bearing of a youthful lover with a fine line of face and the softest manners. But reticence had necessarily cost something to this impassioned woman, and she was the bitterer for it. There is no quailing—even that forced on the helpless and injured—which has not an ugly obverse: the withheld sting was gathering venom. She was absolutely dependent on Grandcourt; for though he had been always liberal in expenses for her, he had kept everything voluntary on his part; and with the goal of marriage before her, she would ask for nothing less. He had said that he would never settle anything except by will; and when she was thinking of alternatives for the future it often occurred to her that, even if she did not become Grandcourt's wife, he might never have a son who would have a legitimate claim on him, and the end might be that her son would be made heir to the best part of his estates. No son at that early age could promise to have more of his father's *physique*. But her becoming Grandcourt's wife was so far from being an extravagant notion of possibility, that even Lush had entertained it, and had said that he would as soon bet on it as on any other likelihood with regard to his familiar companion. Lush, indeed, on inferring that Grandcourt had a preconception of using his residence at Diplow in order to win Miss Arrowpoint, had thought it well to fan that project, taking it as a tacit renunciation of the marriage with Mrs. Glasher, which had long been a mark for the hovering and wheeling of Grandcourt's caprice. But both prospects had been negatived by Gwendolen's appearance on the scene; and it was natural enough for Mrs. Glasher to enter with eagerness into Lush's plan of hindering that new danger by setting up a barrier in the mind of the girl who was being sought as a bride. She entered into it with an eagerness which had passion in it as well as purpose, some of the stored-up venom delivering itself in that way.

After that, she had heard from Lush of Gwendolen's departure, and the probability that all danger from her was got ride of; but there had been no letter to tell her that the danger had returned and had become a certainty. She had since then written to Grandcourt as she did habitually, and he had been longer than usual in answering. She was inferring that he might intend coming to Gadsmere at the time when he was actually on 'the way; and she was not without hope—what construction of another's mind is not strong wishing equal to?—that a certain sickening from that frustrated courtship might dispose him to slip the more easily into the old track of intention.

Grandcourt had two grave purposes in coming to Gadsmere: to convey the news of his approaching marriage in person, in order to make this first difficulty final; and to get from Lydia his mother's diamonds, which long ago he had confided to her and wished her to wear. Her person suited diamonds, and made them look as if they were worth some of the money given for them. These particular diamonds were not mountains of light—they were mere peas and haricots for the ears,

neck, and hair; but they were worth some thousands, and
Grandcourt necessarily wished to have them for his wife.
Formerly when he had asked Lydia to put them into his keeping again, simply on the ground that they would be safer and
ought to be deposited at the bank, she had quietly but absolutely refused, declaring that they were quite safe; and at
last had said: "If you ever marry another woman I will give
them up to her: are you going to marry another woman?"
At that time Grandcourt had no motive which urged him to
persist, and he had this grace in him, that the disposition to
exercise power either by cowing or disappointing others, or
exciting in them a rage which they dared not express—a disposition which was active in him as other propensities became
languid—had always been in abeyance before Lydia. A severe interpreter might say that the mere facts of their relation
to each other, the melancholy position of this woman who depended on his will, made a standing banquet for his delight
in dominating. But there was something else than this in his
forbearance toward her: there was the surviving though
metamorphosed effect of the power she had had over him; and
it was this effect, the fitful dull lapse toward solicitations that
once had the zest now missing from life, which had again and
again inclined him to espouse a familiar past rather than rouse
himself to the expectation of novelty. But now novelty had
taken hold of him and urged him to make the most of it.

Mrs. Glasher was seated in the pleasant room where she
habitually passed her mornings with her children round her.
It had a square projecting window and looked on broad gravel
and grass, sloping toward a little brook that entered the pool.
The top of a low black cabinet, the old oak table, the chairs
in tawny leather, were littered with the children's toys, books,
and garden garments, at which a maternal lady in pastel looked
down from the walls with smiling indulgence. The children
were all there. The three girls, seated round their mother
near the window, were miniature portraits of her—dark-eyed,
delicate-featured brunettes with a rich bloom on their cheeks,
their little nostrils and eyebrows singularly finished as if they
were tiny women, the eldest being barely nine. The boy was
seated on the carpet at some distance, bending his blond head

over the animals from a Noah's ark, admonishing them sep-
arately in a voice of threatening command, and occasionally licking the spotted ones to see if the colors would hold.
Josephine, the eldest, was having her French lesson; and the
others, with their dolls on their laps, sat demurely enough for
images of the Madonna.   Mrs. Glasher's toilet had been made
very carefully—each day now she said to herself that Grandcourt might come in.   Her head, which, spite of emaciation,
had an ineffaceable beauty in the fine profile, crisp curves of
hair, and clearly marked eyebrows, rose impressively above
her bronze-colored silk and velvet, and the gold necklace
which Grandcourt had first clasped round her neck years ago.
Not that she had any pleasure in her toilet; her chief thought
of herself seen in the glass was "How changed!"—but such
good in life as remained to her she would keep.   If her chief
wish were fulfilled, she could imagine herself getting the
comeliness of a matron fit for the highest rank.   The little
faces beside her, almost exact reductions of her own, seemed
to tell of the blooming curves which had once been where now
was sunken pallor.   But the children kissed the pale cheeks
and never found them deficient.   That love was now the one
end of her life.

Suddenly Mrs. Glasher turned away her head from Josephine's book and listened.   "Hush, dear!   I think some one is
coming."

Henleigh the boy jumped up and said: "Mamma, is it the
miller with my donkey?"

He got no answer, and going up to his mamma's knee repeated his question in an insistent tone.   But the door opened,
and the servant announced Mr. Grandcourt.   Mrs. Glasher
rose in some agitation.   Henleigh frowned at him in disgust
at his not being the miller, and the three little girls lifted up
their dark eyes to him timidly.   They had none of them any
particular liking for this friend of mamma's—in fact, when he
had taken Mrs. Glasher's hand and then turned to put his
other hand on Henleigh's head, that energetic scion began to
beat the friend's arm away with his fists.   The little girls
submitted bashfully to be patted under the chin and kissed,
but on the whole it seemed better to send them into the garden,

where they were presently dancing and chatting with the dogs on the gravel.

"How far are you come?" said Mrs. Glasher, as Grandcourt put away his hat and overcoat.

"From Diplow," he answered slowly, seating himself opposite her and looking at her with an unnoting gaze which she noted.

"You are tired, then."

"No, I rested at the Junction—a hideous hole. These railway journeys are always a confounded bore. But I had coffee and smoked."

Grandcourt drew out his handkerchief, rubbed his face, and in returning the handkerchief to his pocket looked at his crossed knee and blameless boot, as if any stranger were opposite to him, instead of a woman quivering with a suspense which every word and look of his was to incline toward hope or dread. But he was really occupied with their interview and what it was likely to include. Imagine the difference in rate of emotion between this woman whom the years had worn to a more conscious dependence and sharper eagerness, and this man whom they were dulling into a more and more neutral obstinacy.

"I expected to see you—it was so long since I had heard from you. I suppose the weeks seem longer at Gadsmere than they do at Diplow," said Mrs. Glasher. She had a quick, incisive way of speaking that seemed to go with her features, as the tone and *timbre* of a violin go with its form.

"Yes," drawled Grandcourt. "But you found the money paid into the bank."

"Oh, yes," said Mrs. Glasher, curtly, tingling with impatience. Always before—at least she fancied so—Grandcourt had taken more notice of her and the children than he did to-day.

"Yes," he resumed, playing with his whisker, and at first not looking at her, "the time has gone on at rather a rattling pace with me; generally it is slow enough. But there has been a good deal happening, as you know"—here he turned his eyes upon her.

"What do I know?" said she, sharply.

He left a pause before he said, without change of manner: "That I was thinking of marrying. You saw Miss Harleth?"

"*She* told you that?"

The pale cheeks looked even paler, perhaps from the fierce brightness in the eyes above them.

"No. Lush told me," was the slow answer. It was as if the thumb-screw and the iron boot were being placed by creeping hands within sight of the expectant victim.

"Good God! say at once that you are going to marry her," she burst out passionately, her knee shaking and her hands tightly clasped.

"Of course, this kind of thing must happen some time or other, Lydia," said he; really, now the thumb-screw was on, not wishing to make the pain worse.

"You didn't always see the necessity."

"Perhaps not. I see it now."

In those few undertoned words of Grandcourt's she felt as absolute a resistance as if her thin fingers had been pushing at a fast-shut iron door. She knew her helplessness, and shrank from testing it by any appeal—shrank from crying in a dead ear and clinging to dead knees, only to see the immovable face and feel the rigid limbs. She did not weep nor speak: she was too hard pressed by the sudden certainty which had as much of chill sickness in it as of thought and emotion. The defeated clutch of struggling hope gave her in these first moments a horrible sensation. At last she rose with a spasmodic effort, and, unconscious of everything but her wretchedness, pressed her forehead against the hard cold glass of the window. The children, playing on the gravel, took this as a sign that she wanted them, and running forward stood in front of her with their sweet faces upturned expectantly. This roused her: she shook her head at them, waved them off, and overcome with this painful exertion sank back in the nearest chair.

Grandcourt had risen too. He was doubly annoyed—at the scene itself, and at the sense that no imperiousness of his could save him from it; but the task had to be gone through, and there was the administrative necessity of arranging things so that there should be as little annoyance as possible in future. He was leaning against the corner of the fireplace. She looked up at him, and said bitterly:

"All this is of no consequence to you. I and the children are importunate creatures. You wish to get away again and be with Miss Harleth."

"Don't make the affair more disagreeable than it need be, Lydia. It is of no use to harp on things that can't be altered. Of course it's deucedly disagreeable to me to see you making yourself miserable. I've taken this journey to tell you what you must make up your mind to;—you and the children will be provided for as usual;—and there's an end of it."

Silence. She dared not answer. This woman with the intense eager look had had the iron of the mother's anguish in her soul, and it had made her sometimes capable of a repression harder than shrieking and struggle. But underneath the silence there was an outlash of hatred and vindictiveness: she wished that the marriage might make two others wretched, besides herself. Presently he went on:

"It will be better for you. You may go on living here. But I think of by and by settling a good sum on you and the children, and you can live where you like. There will be nothing for you to complain of then. Whatever happens, you will feel secure. Nothing could be done beforehand. Everything has gone on in a hurry."

Grandcourt ceased his slow delivery of sentences. He did not expect her to thank him, but he considered that she might reasonably be contented; if it were possible for Lydia to be contented. She showed no change, and after a minute he said:

"You have never had any reason to fear that I should be illiberal. I don't care a curse about the money."

"If you did care about it, I suppose you would not give it us," said Lydia. The sarcasm was irrepressible.

"That's a devilishly unfair thing to say," Grandcourt replied, in a lower tone; "and I advise you not to say that sort of thing again."

"Should you punish me by leaving the children in beggary?" In spite of herself, the one outlet of venom had brought the other.

"There is no question about leaving the children in beggary," said Grandcourt, still in his low voice. "I advise you not to say things that you will repent of."

I am used to repenting," said she, bitterly. "Perhaps *you* will repent. You have already repented of loving me."

"All this will only make it uncommonly difficult for us to meet again. What friend have you besides me?"

"Quite true."

The words came like a low moan. At the same moment there flashed through her the wish that after promising himself a better happiness than that he had had with her, he might feel a misery and loneliness which would drive him back to her to find some memory of a time when he was young, glad, and hopeful. But, no! he would go scathless; it was she who had to suffer.

With this the scorching words were ended. Grandcourt had meant to stay till evening; he wished to curtail his visit, but there was no suitable train earlier than the one he had arranged to go by, and he had still to speak to Lydia on the second object of his visit, which like a second surgical operation seemed to require an interval. The hours had to go by; there was eating to be done; the children came in again—all this mechanism of life had to be gone through with the dreary sense of constraint which is often felt in domestic quarrels of a commoner kind. To Lydia it was some slight relief for her stifled fury to have the children present: she felt a savage glory in their loveliness, as if it would taunt Grandcourt with his indifference to her and them—a secret darting of venom which was strongly imaginative. He acquitted himself with all the advantage of a man whose grace of bearing has long been moulded on an experience of boredom—nursed the little Antonia, who sat with her hands crossed and eyes upturned to his bald head, which struck her as worthy of observation—and propitiated Henleigh by promising him a beautiful saddle and bridle. It was only the two eldest girls who had known him as a continual presence; and the intervening years had overlaid their infantine memories with a bashfulness which Grandcourt's bearing was not likely to dissipate. He and Lydia occasionally, in the presence of the servants, made a conventional remark; otherwise they never spoke; and the stagnant thought in Grandcourt's mind all the while was of his own infatuation in having given her those diamonds, which obliged him to incur the nuisance of speaking about them. He had an ingrained care for what he held to belong to his caste, and about property he liked to be lordly; also he had a consciousness of indignity to himself in having to ask for anything in the world. But however he might assert his independence of Mrs. Glasher's past, he had made a past for himself which was a stronger yoke than any he could impose. He must ask for the diamonds which he had promised to Gwendolen.

At last they were alone again, with the candles above them, face to face with each other. Grandcourt looked at his watch, and then said, in an apparently indifferent drawl: "There is one thing I had to mention, Lydia. My diamonds—you have them."

"Yes, I have them," she answered promptly, rising and standing with her arms thrust down and her fingers threaded, while Grandcourt sat still. She had expected the topic, and made her resolve about it. But she meant to carry out her resolve, if possible, without exasperating him. During the hours of silence she had longed to recall the words which had only widened the breach between them.

"They are in this house, I suppose?"

"No; not in this house."

"I thought you said you kept them by you."

"When I said so it was true. They are in the bank at Dudley."

"Get them away, will you? I must make an arrangement for your delivering them to some one."

"Make no arrangement. They shall be delivered to the person you intended them for. *I* will make the arrangement."

"What do you mean?"

"What I say. I have always told you that I would give them up to your wife. I shall keep my word. She is not your wife yet."

"This is foolery," said Grandcourt, with undertoned disgust. It was too irritating that his indulgence of Lydia had given her a sort of mastery over him in spite of her dependent condition.

She did not speak. He also rose now, but stood leaning against the mantelpiece with his side-face toward her.

"The diamonds must be delivered to me before my marriage," he began again.

"What is your wedding day?"

"The tenth. There is no time to be lost."

"And where do you go after the marriage?"

He did not reply except by looking more sullen. Presently he said: "You must appoint a day before then, to get them from the bank and meet me—or somebody else I will commission:—it's a great nuisance. Mention a day."

"No; I shall not do that. They shall be delivered to her safely. I shall keep my word."

"Do you mean to say," said Grandcourt, just audibly, turning to face her, "that you will not do as I tell you?"

"Yes, I mean that," was the answer that leaped out, while her eyes flashed close to him. The poor creature was immediately conscious that if her words had any effect on her own lot, the effect must be mischievous, and might nullify all the remaining advantage of her long patience. But the word had been spoken.

He was in a position the most irritating to him. He could not shake her nor touch her hostilely; and if he could, the process would not bring the diamonds. He shrank from the only sort of threat that would frighten her—if she believed it. And in general, there was nothing he hated more than to be forced into anything like violence even in words: his will must impose itself without trouble. After looking at her for a moment, he turned his side-face toward her again, leaning as before, and said:

"Infernal idiots that women are!"

"Why will you not tell me where you are going after the marriage? I could be at the wedding if I liked, and learn in that way," said Lydia, not shrinking from the one suicidal form of threat within her power.

"Of course, if you like, you can play the mad woman," said

Grandcourt, with *sotto voce* scorn. "It is not to be supposed that you will wait to think what good will come of it—or what you owe to me."

He was in a state of disgust and imbitterment quite new in the history of their relation to each other. It was undeniable that this woman whose life he had allowed to send such deep suckers into his had a terrible power of annoyance in her; and the rash hurry of his proceedings had left her opportunities open. His pride saw very ugly possibilities threatening it, and he stood for several minutes in silence reviewing the situation—considering how he could act upon her. Unlike himself, she was of a direct nature, with certain simple, strongly colored tendencies, and there was one often-experienced effect which he thought he could count upon now. As Sir Hugo had said of him, Grandcourt knew how to play his cards upon occasion.

He did not speak again, but looked at his watch, rang the bell, and ordered the vehicle to be brought round immediately. Then he removed farther from her, walked as if in expectation of a summons, and remained silent without turning his eyes upon her.

She was suffering the horrible conflict of self-reproach and tenacity. She saw beforehand Grandcourt leaving her without even looking at her again—herself left behind in lonely uncertainty—hearing nothing from him—not knowing whether she had done her children harm—feeling that she had perhaps made him hate her:—all the wretchedness of a creature who had defeated her own motives. And yet she could not bear to give up a purpose which was a sweet morsel to her vindictiveness. If she had not been a mother she would willingly have sacrificed herself to her revenge—to what she felt to be the justice of hindering another from getting happiness by willingly giving her over to misery. The two dominant passions were at struggle. She must satisfy them both.

"Don't let us part in anger, Henleigh," she began, without changing her place or attitude; "it is a very little thing I ask. If I were refusing to give anything up that you call yours, it would be different: that would be a reason for treating me as if you hated me. But I ask such a little thing. If you will tell me where you are going on the wedding day, I will take care that the diamonds shall be delivered to her without scandal. Without scandal," she repeated entreatingly.

"Such preposterous whims make a woman odious," said Grandcourt, not giving way in look or movement. "What is the use of talking to mad people?"

"Yes, I am foolish—loneliness has made me foolish—indulge me." Sobs rose as she spoke. "If you will indulge me in this one folly, I will be very meek—I will never trouble you." She burst into hysterical crying, and said again almost with a scream: "I will be very meek after that."

There was a strange mixture of acting and reality in this passion. She kept hold of her purpose as a child might tighten its hand over a small stolen thing, crying and denying all the while. Even Grandcourt was wrought upon by surprise: this capricious wish, this childish violence, was as unlike Lydia's bearing as it was incongruous with her person. Both had always had a stamp of dignity on them. Yet she seemed more manageable in this state than in her former attitude of defiance. He came close up to her again, and said, in his low, imperious tone: "Be quiet, and hear what I tell you. I will never forgive you if you present yourself again and make a scene."

She pressed her handkerchief against her face, and when she could speak, firmly said, in the muffled voice that follows sobbing: "I will not—if you will let me have my way—I promise you not to thrust myself forward again. I have never broken my word to you—how many have you broken to me? When you gave me the diamonds to wear, you were not thinking of having another wife. And I now give them up— I don't reproach you—I only ask you to let me give them up in my own way. Have I not borne it well? Everything is to be taken away from me, and when I ask for a straw, a chip— you deny it me." She had spoken rapidly, but after a little pause she said more slowly, her voice freed from its muffled tone: "I will not bear to have it denied me."

Grandcourt had a baffling sense that he had to deal with something like madness; he could only govern by giving way. The servant came to say the fly was ready. When the door was shut again, Grandcourt said, sullenly: "We are going to Ryelands, then."

"They shall be delivered to her there," said Lydia, with decision.

"Very well, I am going." He felt no inclination even to take her hand: she had annoyed him too sorely. But now that she had gained her point, she was prepared to humble herself that she might propitiate him.

"Forgive me; I will never vex you again," she said with beseeching looks. Her inward voice said distinctly: "It is only I who have to forgive." Yet she was obliged to ask forgiveness.

"You had better keep that promise. You have made me feel uncommonly ill with your folly," said Grandcourt, apparently choosing this statement as the strongest possible use of language.

"Poor thing!" said Lydia, with a faint smile:—was he aware of the minor fact that he had made her feel ill this morning?

But with the quick transition natural to her, she was now ready to coax him if he would let her, that they might part in some degree reconciled. She ventured to lay her hand on his shoulder, and he did not move away from her: she had so far succeeded in alarming him that he was not sorry for these proofs of returned subjection.

"Light a cigar," she said, soothingly, taking the case from his breast-pocket and opening it.

Amidst such caressing signs of mutual fear they parted. The effect that clung and gnawed within Grandcourt was a sense of imperfect mastery.

-------♦-------

CHAPTER XXXI.

"A wild dedication of yourselves
To unpath'd waters, undream'd shores."
—SHAKESPEARE.

ON the day when Gwendolen Harleth was married and became Mrs. Grandcourt, the morning was clear and bright, and while the sun was low a slight frost crisped the leaves. The

bridal party was worth seeing, and half Pennicote turned out
to see it, lining the pathway up to the church. An old friend
of the Rector's performed the marriage ceremony, the Rector
himself acting as father, to the great advantage of the procession. Only two faces, it was remarked, showed signs of sadness—Mrs. Davilow's and Anna's. The mother's delicate
eyelids were pink, as if she had been crying half the night;
and no one was surprised that, splendid as the match was, she
should feel the parting from a daughter who was the flower of
her children and of her own life. It was less understood why
Anna should be troubled when she was being so well set off
by the bridesmaid's dress. Every one else seemed to reflect
the brilliancy of the occasion—the bride most of all. Of her
it was agreed that as to figure and carriage she was worthy to
be a "lady o' title": as to face, perhaps it might be thought
that a title required something more rosy; but the bridegroom
himself not being fresh-colored—being indeed, as the miller's
wife observed, very much of her own husband's complexion—
the match was the more complete. Anyhow he must be very
fond of her; and it was to be hoped that he would never cast
it up to her that she had been going out to service as a governess, and her mother to live at Sawyer's Cottage—vicissitudes
which had been much spoken of in the village. The miller's
daughter of fourteen could not believe that high gentry behaved badly to their wives, but her mother instructed her:
"Oh, child, men's men: gentle or simple, they're much of a
muchness. I've heard my mother say Squire Pelton used to
take his dogs and a long whip into his wife's room, and flog
'em there to frighten her; and my mother was lady's maid
there at the very time."

"That's unlucky talk for a wedding, Mrs. Girdle," said the
tailor. "A quarrel may end wi' the whip, but it begins wi'
the tongue, and it's the women have got the most o' that."

"The Lord gave it 'em to use, I suppose," said Mrs. Girdle; " *He* never meant you to have it all your own way."

"By what I can make out from the gentleman as attends to
the grooming at Offendene," said the tailor, "this Mr. Grandcourt has wonderful little tongue. Everything must be done
dummy-like without his ordering."

"Then he's the more whip, I doubt," said Mrs. Girdle. "*She's* got tongue enough, I warrant her. See, there they come out together!"

"What wonderful long corners she's got to her eyes!" said the tailor. "She makes you feel comical when she looks at you."

Gwendolen, in fact, never showed more elasticity in her bearing, more lustre in her long brown glance: she had the brilliancy of strong excitment, which will sometimes come even from pain. It was not pain, however, that she was feeling: she had wrought herself up to much the same condition as that in which she stood at the gambling-table when Deronda was looking at her, and she began to lose. There was enjoyment in it: whatever uneasiness a growing conscience had created, was disregarded as an ailment might have been, amidst the gratification of that ambitious vanity and desire for luxury within her which it would take a great deal of slow poisoning to kill. This morning she could not have said truly that she repented her acceptance of Grandcourt, or that any fears in hazy perspective could hinder the glowing effects of the immediate scene in which she was the central object. That she was doing something wrong—that a punishment might be hanging over her—that the woman to whom she had given a promise and broken it, was thinking of her in bitterness and misery with a just reproach—that Deronda with his way of looking into things very likely despised her for marrying Grandcourt, as he had despised her for gambling—above all, that the cord which united her with this lover and which she had hitherto held by the hand, was now being flung over her neck,—all this yeasty mingling of dimly understood facts with vague but deep impressions, and with images half real, half fantastic, had been disturbing her during the weeks of her engagement. Was that agitating experience nullified this morning? No: it was surmounted and thrust down with a sort of exulting defiance as she felt herself standing at the game of life with many eyes upon her, daring everything to win much—or if to lose, still with *éclat* and a sense of importance. But this morning a losing destiny for herself did not press upon her as a fear: she thought that she was entering on a fuller power of managing circumstance—with all the official strength of marriage, which some women made so poor a use of. That intoxication of youthful egoism out of which she had been shaken by trouble, humiliation, and a new sense of culpability, had returned upon her under the newly fed strength of the old fumes. She did not in the least present the ideal of the tearful, tremulous bride. Poor Gwendolen, whom some had judged much too forward and instructed in the world's ways!—with her erect head and elastic footstep she was walking amid illusions; and yet, too, there was an under-consciousness in her that she was a little intoxicated.

"Thank God you bear it so well, my darling!" said Mrs. Davilow, when she had helped Gwendolen to doff her bridal white and put on her travelling dress. All the trembling had been done by the poor mother, and her agitation urged Gwendolen doubly to take the morning as if it were a triumph.

"Why, you might have said that if I had been going to Mrs. Mompert's, you dear, sad, incorrigible mamma!" said Gwendolen, just putting her hands to her mother's cheeks with laughing tenderness—then retreating a little and spreading out her arms as if to exhibit herself. "Here am I—Mrs. Grandcourt! What else would you have me, but what I am sure to be? You know you were ready to die with vexation when you thought that I would not be Mrs. Grandcourt."

"Hush, hush, my child, for heaven's sake!" said Mrs. Davilow, almost in a whisper. "How can I help feeling it when I am parting from you. But I can bear anything gladly if you are happy."

"Not gladly, mamma, no!" said Gwendolen, shaking her head, with a bright smile. "Willingly you would bear it, but always sorrowfully. Sorrowing is your sauce; you can take nothing without it." Then, clasping her mother's shoulders and raining kisses first on one cheek and then on the other between her words, she said, gayly: "And you shall sorrow over my having everything at my beck—and enjoying everything gloriously—splendid houses—and horses—and diamonds, I shall have diamonds—and going to court—and being Lady Certainly—and Lady Perhaps—and grand here—and tantivy there—and always loving you better than anybody else in the world."

"My sweet child!—But I shall not be jealous if you love your husband better; and he will expect to be first."

Gwendolen thrust out her lips and chin with a pretty grimace, saying: "Rather a ridiculous expectation. However, I don't mean to treat him ill, unless he deserves it."

Then the two fell into a clinging embrace, and Gwendolen could not hinder a rising sob when she said: "I wish you were going with me, mamma."

But the slight dew on her long eyelashes only made her the more charming when she gave her hand to Grandcourt to be led to the carriage.

The Rector looked in on her to give a final "Good-by; God bless you; we shall see you again before long," and then returned to Mrs. Davilow, saying half cheerfully, half solemnly:

"Let us be thankful, Fanny. She is in a position well suited to her, and beyond what I should have dared to hope for. And few women can have been chosen more entirely for their own sake. You should feel yourself a happy mother."

There was a railway journey of some fifty miles before the new husband and wife reached the station near Ryelands. The sky had veiled itself since the morning, and it was hardly more than twilight when they entered the park-gates, but still Gwendolen, looking out of the carriage-window as they drove rapidly along, could see the grand outlines and the nearer beauties of the scene—the long winding drive bordered with evergreens backed by huge gray stems; then the opening of wide grassy spaces and undulations studded with dark clumps; till at last came a wide level where the white house could be seen, with a hanging wood for a background, and the rising and sinking balustrade of a terrace in front.

Gwendolen had been at her liveliest during the journey, chatting incessantly, ignoring any change in their mutual position since yesterday; and Grandcourt had been rather ecstatically quiescent, while she turned his gentle seizure of her hand into a grasp of his hand by both hers, with an increased vivacity as of a kitten that will not sit quiet to be petted. She

was really getting somewhat febrile in her excitement; and
now in this drive through the park her usual susceptibility to
changes of light and scenery helped to make her heart palpitate newly. Was it at the novelty simply, or the almost incredible fulfilment about to be given to her girlish dreams of
being "somebody"—walking through her own furlong of cor-
ridors and under her own ceilings of an out-of-sight loftiness,
where her own painted Spring was shedding painted flowers,
and her own fore-shortened Zephyrs were blowing their trum-
pets over her; while her own servants, lackeys in clothing
but men in bulk and shape, were as nought in her presence, and
revered the propriety of her insolence to them:—being in short
the heroine of an admired play without the pains of art? Was
it alone the closeness of this fulfilment which made her heart
flutter? or was it some dim forecast, the insistent penetration
of suppressed experience, mixing the expectation of a triumph
with the dread of a crisis? Hers was one of the natures in
which exultation inevitably carries an infusion of dread ready
to curdle and declare itself.

She felt silent in spite of herself as they approached the
gates, and when her husband said, "Here we are at home!"
and for the first time kissed her on the lips, she hardly knew
of it: it was no more than the passive acceptance of a greeting in the midst of an absorbing show. Was not all her hurrying life of the last three months a show, in which her consciousness was a wondering spectator? After the half-wilful
excitement of the day, a numbness had come over her personality.

But there was a brilliant light in the hall—warmth, mat-
ting, carpets, full-length portraits, Olympian statues, assiduous servants. Not many servants, however: only a few from
Diplow in addition to those constantly in charge of the house;
and Gwendolen's new maid, who had come with her, was
taken under guidance by the housekeeper. Gwendolen felt
herself being led by Grandcourt along a subtly scented corri-
dor, then into an ante-room where she saw an open doorway
sending out a rich glow of light and color.

"These are our dens," said Grandcourt. "You will like to
be quiet here till dinner. We shall dine early."

He pressed her hand to his lips and moved away, more in love than he had ever expected to be.

Gwendolen, yielding up her hat and mantle, threw herself into a chair by the glowing hearth, and saw herself repeated in glass panels with all her faint-green satin surroundings. The housekeeper had passed into this boudoir from the adjoining dressing-room and seemed disposed to linger, Gwendolen thought, in order to look at the new mistress of Ryelands, who, however, being impatient for solitude, said to her: "Will you tell Hudson when she has put out my dress to leave everything? I shall not want her again, unless I ring."

The housekeeper, coming forward, said: "Here is a packet, madam, which I was ordered to give into nobody's hands but yours, when you were alone. The person who brought it said it was a present particularly ordered by Mr. Grandcourt; but he was not to know of its arrival till he saw you wear it. Excuse me, madam; I felt it right to obey orders."

Gwendolen took the packet, and let it lie on her lap till she heard the doors close. It came into her mind that the packet might contain the diamonds which Grandcourt had spoken of as being deposited somewhere and to be given to her on her marriage. In this moment of confused feeling and creeping luxurious languor she was glad of this diversion—glad of such an event as having her own diamonds to try on.

Within all the sealed paper coverings was a box, but within the box there *was* a jewel-case; and now she felt no doubt that she had the diamonds. But on opening the case, in the same instant that she saw their gleam she saw a letter lying above them. She knew the handwriting of the address. It was as if an adder had lain on them. Her heart gave a leap which seemed to have spent all her strength; and as she opened the bit of thin paper, it shook with the trembling of her hands. But it was legible as print, and thrust its words upon her.

"These diamonds which were once given with ardent love to Lydia Glasher, she passes on to you. You have broken your word to her, that you might possess what was hers. Perhaps you think of being happy, as she once was, and of having beautiful children such as hers, who will thrust hers aside. God is too just for that. The man you have married has a withered heart. His best young love was mine; you could not take that from me when you took the rest. It is dead; but I am the grave in which your chance of happiness is buried as well as mine. You had your warning. You have chosen to injure me and my children. He had meant to marry me. He would have married me at last, if you had not broken your word. You will have your punishment. I desire it with all my soul.

"Will you give him this letter to set him against me and ruin us more—me and my children? Shall you like to stand before your husband with these diamonds on you, and these words of mine in his thoughts and yours? Will he think you have any right to complain when he has made you miserable? You took him with your eyes open. The willing wrong you have done me will be your curse. "

It seemed at first as if Gwendolen's eyes were spellbound in reading the horrible words of the letter over and over again as a doom of penance; but suddenly a new spasm of terror made her lean forward and stretch out the paper toward the fire, lest accusation and proof at once should meet all eyes. It flew like a feather from her trembling fingers and was caught up in the great draught of flame. In her movement the casket fell on the floor and the diamonds rolled out. She took no notice, but fell back in her chair again, helpless. She could not see the reflections of herself then: they were like so many women petrified white; but coming near herself you might have seen the tremor in her lips and hands. She sat so for a long while, knowing little more than that she was feeling ill, and that those written words kept repeating themselves in her.

Truly here were poisoned gems, and the poison had entered into this poor young creature.

After that long while, there was a tap at the door and Grandcourt entered, dressed for dinner. The sight of him brought a new nervous shock, and Gwendolen screamed again and again with hysterical violence. He had expected to see her dressed and smiling, ready to be led down. He saw her pallid, shrieking as it seemed with terror, the jewels scattered around her on the floor. Was it a fit of madness?

In some form or other the Furies had crossed his threshold.

CHAPTER XXXII.

In all ages it hath been a favorite text that a potent love hath the nature of an isolated fatality, whereto the mind's opinions and wonted resolves are altogether alien; as, for example, Daphnis his frenzy, wherein it had little availed him to have been convinced of Heraclitus his doctrine; or the philtre-bred passion of Tristan, who, though he had been as deep as Duns Scotus, would have had his reasoning marred by that cup too much; or Romeo in his sudden taking for Juliet, wherein any objections he might have held against Ptolemy had made little difference to his discourse under the balcony. Yet all love is not such, even though potent; nay, this passion hath as large scope as any for allying itself with every operation of the soul: so that it shall acknowledge an effect from the imagined light of unproven firmaments, and have its scale set to the grander orbits of what hath been and shall be.

DERONDA, on his return to town, could assure Sir Hugo of his having lodged in Grandcourt's mind a distinct understanding that he could get fifty thousand pounds by giving up a prospect which was probably distant, and not absolutely certain; but he had no further sign of Grandcourt's disposition in the matter than that he was evidently inclined to keep up friendly communications.

"And what did you think of the future bride on a nearer survey?" said Sir Hugo.

"I thought better of her than I did at Leubronn. Roulette was not a good setting for her; it brought out something of the demon. At Diplow she seemed much more womanly and attractive—less hard and self-possessed. I thought her mouth and eyes had quite a different expression."

"Don't flirt with her too much, Dan," said Sir Hugo, meaning to be agreeably playful. "If you make Grandcourt savage when they come to the Abbey at Christmas, it will interfere with my affairs."

"I can stay in town, sir."

"No, no. Lady Mallinger and the children can't do without you at Christmas. Only don't make mischief—unless you can get up a duel, and manage to shoot Grandcourt, which might be worth a little inconvenience."

"I don't think you ever saw me flirt," said Deronda, not amused.

"Oh, haven't I, though?" said Sir Hugo, provokingly. "You are always looking tenderly at the women, and talking to them in a Jesuitical way. You are a dangerous young fel-

low—a kind of Lovelace who will make the Clarissas run after
you instead of your running after them."

What was the use of being exasperated at a tasteless joke?
—only the exasperation comes before the reflection on utility.
Few friendly remarks are more annoying than the information
that we are always seeming to do what we never mean to do.
Sir Hugo's notion of flirting, it was to be hoped, was rather
peculiar; for his own part, Deronda was sure that he had
never flirted. But he was glad that the baronet had no knowledge about the repurchase of Gwendolen's necklace to feed his
taste for this kind of rallying.

He would be on his guard in future; for example, in his
behavior at Mrs. Meyrick's, where he was about to pay his
first visit since his arrival from Leubronn. For Mirah was
certainly a creature in whom it was difficult not to show a
tender kind of interest both by looks and speech.

Mrs. Meyrick had not failed to send Deronda a report of
Mirah's well-being in her family. "We are getting fonder
of her every day," she had written. "At breakfast-time we
all look toward the door with expectation to see her come
in; and we watch her and listen to her as if she were a native
from a new country. I have not heard a word from her lips
that gives me a doubt about her. She is quite contented and
full of gratitude. My daughters are learning from her, and
they hope to get her other pupils; for she is anxious not to
eat the bread of idleness, but to work, like my girls. Mab
says our life has become like a fairy tale, and all she is afraid
of is that Mirah will turn into a nightingale again and fly
away from us. Her voice is just perfect: not loud and strong,
but searching and melting, like the thoughts of what has been.
That is the way old people like me feel a beautiful voice."

But Mrs. Meyrick did not enter into particulars which
would have required her to say that Amy and Mab, who had
accompanied Mirah to the synagogue, found the Jewish faith
less reconcilable with their wishes in her case than in that of
Scott's Rebecca. They kept silence out of delicacy to Mirah,
with whom her religion was too tender a subject to be touched
lightly; but after a while, Amy, who was much of a practical
reformer, could not restrain a question.

"Excuse me, Mirah, but *does* it seem quite right to you that the women should sit behind rails in a gallery apart?"

"Yes, I never thought of anything else," said Mirah, with mild surprise.

"And you like better to see the men with their hats on?" said Mab, cautiously proposing the smallest item of difference.

"Oh, yes. I like what I have always seen there, because it brings back to me the same feelings—the feelings I would not part with for anything else in the world."

After this, any criticism, whether of doctrine or of practice, would have seemed to these generous little people an inhospitable cruelty. Mirah's religion was of one fibre with her affections, and had never presented itself to her as a set of propositions.

"She says herself she is a very bad Jewess, and does not half know her people's religion," said Amy, when Mirah was gone to bed. "Perhaps it would gradually melt away from her, and she would pass into Christianity like the rest of the world, if she got to love us very much, and never found her mother. It is so strange to be of the Jews' religion now."

"Oh, oh, oh!" cried Mab. "I wish I were not such a hideous Christian. How can an ugly Christian, who is always dropping her work, convert a beautiful Jewess, who has not a fault?"

"It may be wicked of me," said shrewd Kate, "but I cannot help wishing that her mother may not be found. There might be something unpleasant."

"I don't think it, my dear," said Mrs. Meyrick. "I believe Mirah is cut out after the pattern of her mother. And what a joy it would be to her to have such a daughter brought back again! But a mother's feelings are not worth reckoning, I suppose" (she shot a mischievous glance at her own daughters), "and a dead mother is worth more than a living one?"

"Well, and so she may be, little mother," said Kate; "but we would rather hold you cheaper, and have you alive."

Not only the Meyricks, whose various knowledge had been acquired by the irregular foraging to which clever girls have usually been reduced, but Deronda himself, with all his masculine instruction, had been roused by this apparition of Mirah to the consciousness of knowing hardly anything about modern Judaism or the inner Jewish history. The Chosen People have been commonly treated as a people chosen for the sake of somebody else; and their thinking as something (no matter exactly what) that ought to have been entirely otherwise; and Deronda, like his neighbors, had regarded Judaism as a sort of eccentric fossilized form which an accomplished man might dispense with studying, and leave to specialists. But Mirah, with her terrified flight from one parent, and her yearning after the other, had flashed on him the hitherto neglected reality that Judaism was something still throbbing in human lives, still making for them the only conceivable vesture of the world; and in the idling excursion on which he immediately afterward set out with Sir Hugo he began to look for the outsides of synagogues, and the titles of books about the Jews. This wakening of a new interest—this passing from the supposition that we hold the right opinions on a subject we are careless about, to a sudden care for it, and a sense that our opinions were ignorance—is an effectual remedy for *ennui*, which unhappily cannot be secured on a physician's prescription; but Deronda had carried it with him, and endured his weeks of lounging all the better. It was on this journey that he first entered a Jewish synagogue—at Frankfort—where his party rested on a Friday. In exploring the Juden-gasse, which he had seen long before, he remembered well enough its picturesque old houses; what his eyes chiefly dwelt on now were the human types there; and his thought, busily connecting them with the past phases of their race, stirred that fibre of historic sympathy which had helped to determine in him certain traits worth mentioning for those who are interested in his future. True, when a young man has a fine person, no eccentricity of manners, the education of a gentleman, and a present income, it is not customary to feel a prying curiosity about his way of thinking, or his peculiar tastes. He may very well be settled in life as an agreeable, clever young fellow without passing a special examination on those heads. Later, when he is getting rather slovenly and portly, his peculiarities are more distinctly discerned, and it is taken as a mercy if

they are not highly objectionable. But any one wishing to
understand the effect of after-events on Deronda should know
a little more of what he was at five-and-twenty than was evident in ordinary intercourse.

It happened that the very vividness of his impressions had
often made him the more enigmatic to his friends, and had
contributed to an apparent indefiniteness in his sentiments.
His early wakened sensibility and reflectiveness had developed
into a many-sided sympathy, which threatened to hinder any
persistent course of action: as soon as he took up any antagonism, though only in thought, he seemed to himself like the
Sabine warriors in the memorable story—with nothing to meet
his spear but flesh of his flesh, and objects that he loved. His
imagination had so wrought itself to the habit of seeing things
as they probably appeared to others, that a strong partisan-
ship, unless it were against an immediate oppression, had become an insincerity for him. His plenteous, flexible sympathy had ended by falling into one current with that reflective
analysis which tends to neutralize sympathy. Few men were
able to keep themselves clearer of vices than he; yet he hated
vices mildly, being used to think of them less in the abstract
than as a part of mixed human natures having an individual
history, which it was the bent of his mind to trace with understanding and pity. With the same innate balance he was fervidly democratic in his feeling for the multitude, and yet,
through his affections and imagination, intensely conservative;
voracious of speculations on government and religion, yet loath
to part with long-sanctioned forms which, for him, were quick
with memories and sentiments that no argument could lay
dead. We fall on the leaning side; and Deronda suspected
himself of loving too well the losing causes of the world.
Martyrdom changes sides, and he was in danger of changing
with it, having a strong repugnance to taking up that clew of
success which the order of the world often forces upon us and
makes it treason against the common weal to reject. And yet
his fear of falling into an unreasoning narrow hatred made a
check for him: he apologized for the heirs of privilege; he
shrank with dislike from the loser's bitterness and the denun-
ciatory tone of the unaccepted innovator. A too reflective and

diffusive sympathy was in danger of paralyzing in him that indignation against wrong and that selectness of fellowship which are the conditions of moral force; and in the last few years of confirmed manhood he had become so keenly aware of this that what he most longed for was either some external event, or some inward light, that would urge him into a definite line of action, and compress his wandering energy. He was ceasing to care for knowledge—he had no ambition for practice—unless they could both be gathered up into one current with his emotions; and he dreaded, as if it were a dwelling-place of lost souls, that dead anatomy of culture which turns the universe into a mere ceaseless answer to queries, and knows, not everything, but everything else about everything—as if one should be ignorant of nothing concerning the scent of violets except the scent itself for which one had no nostril. But how and whence was the needed event to come?—the influence that would justify partiality, and make him what he longed to be yet was unable to make himself—an organic part of social life, instead of roaming in it like a yearning disembodied spirit, stirred with a vague social passion, but without fixed local habitation to render fellowship real? To make a little difference for the better was what he was not contented to live without; but how make it? It is one thing to see your road, another to cut it. He found some of the fault in his birth and the way he had been brought up, which had laid no special demands on him and given him no fixed relationship except one of a doubtful kind; but he did not attempt to hide from himself that he had fallen into a meditative numbness, and was gliding farther and farther from that life of practically energetic sentiment which he would have proclaimed (if he had been inclined to proclaim anything) to be the best of all life, and for himself the only life worth living. He wanted some way of keeping emotion and its progeny of sentiments—which make the savors of life—substantial and strong in the face of a reflectiveness that threatened to nullify all differences. To pound the objects of sentiment into small dust, yet keep sentiment alive and active, was something like the famous recipe for making cannon : to first take a round hole and then enclose it with iron; whatever you do keeping fast hold of your round hole. Yet how distinguish what our will may wisely save in its completeness from the heaping of cat-mummies and the expensive cult of enshrined putrefactions?

Something like this was the common undercurrent in Deronda's mind, while he was reading law, or imperfectly attending to polite conversation. Meanwhile he had not set about one function in particular with zeal and steadiness. Not an admirable experience, to be proposed as an ideal; but a form of struggle before break of day which some young men since the patriarch have had to pass through, with more or less of bruising if not laming.

I have said that under his calm exterior he had a fervor which made him easily feel the presence of poetry in everyday events; and the forms of the Juden-gasse, rousing the sense of union with what is remote, set him musing on two elements of our historic life which that sense raises into the same region of poetry: the faint beginnings of faiths and institutions, and their obscure lingering decay; the dust and withered remnants with which they are apt to be covered only enhancing for the awakened perception the impressiveness either of a sublimely penetrating life, as in the twin green leaves that will become the sheltering tree, or of a pathetic inheritance in which all the grandeur and the glory have become a sorrowing memory.

This imaginative stirring, as he turned out of the Juden-gasse, and continued to saunter in the warm evening air, meaning to find his way to the synagogue, neutralized the repellent effect of certain ugly little incidents on his way. Turning into an old book-shop to ask the exact time of service at the synagogue, he was affectionately directed by a precocious Jewish youth, who entered cordially into his wanting not the fine new building of the Reformed but the old Rabbinical school of the orthodox; and then cheated him like a pure Teuton, only with more amenity, in his charge for a book quite out of request as one "nicht so leicht zu bekommen." Meanwhile at the opposite counter a deaf and grisly tradesman was casting a flinty look at certain cards, apparently combining advantages of business with religion, and shoutingly proposed to him in Jew-dialect by a dingy man in a tall coat hanging from neck to heel, a bag in hand, and a broad low hat surmounting his chosen nose—who had no sooner disappeared than another dingy man of the same pattern issued from the backward glooms of the shop and also shouted in the same dialect. In fact, Deronda saw various queer-looking Israelites not altogether without guile, and just distinguishable from queer-looking Christians of the same mixed *morale*. In his anxiety about Mirah's relatives, he had lately been thinking of vulgar Jews with a sort of personal alarm. But a little comparison will often diminish our surprise and disgust at the aberrations of Jews and other dissidents whose lives do not offer a consistent or lovely pattern of their creed; and this evening Deronda, becoming more conscious that he was falling into unfairness and ridiculous exaggeration, began to use that corrective comparison: he paid his thaler too much, without prejudice to his interests in the Hebrew destiny, or his wish to find the *Rabbinische Schule*, which he arrived at by sunset, and entered with a good congregation of men.

He happened to take his seat in a line with an elderly man from whom he was distant enough to glance at him more than once as rather a noticeable figure—his ample white beard and felt hat framing a profile of that fine contour which may as easily be Italian as Hebrew. He returned Deronda's notice till at last their eyes met: an undesirable chance with unknown persons, and a reason to Deronda for not looking again; but he immediately found an open prayer-book pushed toward him and had to bow his thanks. However, the congregation had mustered, the reader had mounted to the *almemor* or platform, and the service began. Deronda, having looked enough at the German translation of the Hebrew in the book before him to know that he was chiefly hearing Psalms and Old Testament passages or phrases, gave himself up to that strongest effect of chanted liturgies which is independent of detailed verbal meaning—like the effect of an Allegri's *Miserere* or a Palestrina's *Magnificat*. The most powerful movement of feeling with a liturgy is the prayer which seeks for nothing special, but is a yearning to escape from the limitations of our own weakness and an invocation of all Good to enter and abide with us; or else a self-oblivious lifting up

of gladness, a *Gloria in excelsis* that such Good exists; both
the yearning and the exultation gathering their utmost force
from the sense of communion in a form which has expressed
them both for long generations of struggling fellow-men.
The Hebrew liturgy, like others, has its transitions of litany,
lyric, proclamation, dry statement, and blessing; but this
evening all were one for Deronda: the chant of the *Chazan's*
or Reader's grand wide-ranging voice, with its passage from
monotony to sudden cries, the outburst of sweet boys' voices
from the little choir, the devotional swaying of men's bodies
backward and forward, the very commonness of the building and shabbiness of the scene where a national faith, which
had penetrated the thinking of half the world, and moulded
the splendid forms of that world's religion, was finding a remote, obscure echo—all were blent for him as one expression
of a binding history, tragic and yet glorious. He wondered
at the strength of his own feeling; it seemed beyond the occasion—what one might imagine to be a divine influx in the
darkness, before there was any vision to interpret. The whole
scene was a coherent strain, its burden a passionate regret,
which, if he had known the liturgy for the Day of Reconcilia-
tion, he might have clad in its antithetic burden: "Happy
the eye which saw all these things; but verily to hear only of
them afflicts our soul. Happy the eye that saw our temple
and the joy of our congregation; but verily to hear only of
them afflicts our soul. Happy the eye that saw the fingers
when tuning every kind of song; but verily to hear only of
them afflicts our soul."

But with the cessation of the devotional sounds and the
movement of many indifferent faces and vulgar figures before
him there darted into his mind the frigid idea that he had
probably been alone in his feeling, and perhaps the only person in the congregation for whom the service was more than
a dull routine. There was just time for this chilling thought
before he had bowed to his civil neighbor and was moving
away with the rest—when he felt a hand on his arm, and
turning with the rather unpleasant sensation which this abrupt
sort of claim is apt to bring, he saw close to him the white-
bearded face of that neighbor, who said to him in German:

"Excuse me, young gentleman—allow me—what is your parentage—your mother's family—her maiden name?"

Deronda had a strongly resistant feeling: he was inclined to shake off hastily the touch on his arm; but he managed to slip it away, and said coldly: "I am an Englishman."

The questioner looked at him dubiously still for an instant, then just lifted his hat and turned away—whether under a sense of having made a mistake or of having been repulsed, Deronda was uncertain. In his walk back to the hotel he tried to still any uneasiness on the subject by reflecting that he could not have acted differently. How could he say that he did not know the name of his mother's family to that total stranger?—who indeed had taken an unwarrantable liberty in the abruptness of his question, dictated probably by some fancy of likeness such as often occurs without real significance. The incident, he said to himself, was trivial; but whatever import it might have, his inward shrinking on the occasion was too strong for him to be sorry that he had cut it short. It was a reason, however, for his not mentioning the synagogue to the Mallingers—in addition to his usual inclination to reticence on anything that the baronet would have been likely to call Quixotic enthusiasm. Hardly any man could be more good-natured than Sir Hugo; indeed, in his kindliness, especially to women, he did actions which others would have called romantic; but he never took a romantic view of them, and in general smiled at the introduction of motives on a grand scale, or of reasons that lay very far off. This was the point of strongest difference between him and Deronda, who rarely ate his breakfast without some silent discursive flight after grounds for filling up his day according to the practice of his contemporaries.

This halt at Frankfort was taken on their way home, and its impressions were kept the more actively vibrating in him by the duty of caring for Mirah's welfare. That question about his parentage, which if he had not both inwardly and outwardly shaken it off as trivial, would have seemed a threat rather than a promise of revelation, had re-enforced his anxiety as to the effect of finding Mirah's relatives and his resolve to proceed with caution. If he made any unpleasant discovery, was he bound to a disclosure that might cast a new net of trouble around her?

He had written to Mrs. Meyrick to announce his visit at four o'clock, and he found Mirah seated at work with only Mrs. Meyrick and Mab, the open piano, and all the glorious company of engravings. The dainty neatness of her hair and dress, the glow of tranquil happiness in a face where a painter need have changed nothing if he had wanted to put it in front of the host singing "peace on earth and good-will to men," made a contrast to his first vision of her that was delightful to Deronda's eyes. Mirah herself was thinking of it, and immediately on their greeting said:

"See how different I am from that miserable creature by the river!—all because you found me and brought me to the very best."

"It was my good chance to find you," said Deronda. "Any other man would have been glad to do what I did."

"That is not the right way of thinking about it," said Mirah, shaking her head with decisive gravity. "I think of what really was. It was you, and not another, who found me, and were good to me."

"I agree with Mirah," said Mrs. Meyrick. "Saint Anybody is a bad saint to pray to."

"Besides, Anybody could not have brought me to you," said Mirah, smiling at Mrs. Meyrick. "And I would rather be with you than with any one else in the world except my mother. I wonder if ever a poor little bird, that was lost and could not fly, was taken and put into a warm nest where there was a mother and sisters who took to it so that everything came naturally, as if it had been always there. I hardly thought before that the world could ever be as happy and without fear as it is to me now." She looked meditative a moment, and then said: "Sometimes I am a *little* afraid."

"What is it your are afraid of?" said Deronda, with anxiety.

"That when I am turning at the corner of a street I may meet my father. It seems dreadful that I should be afraid of meeting him. That is my only sorrow," said Mirah, plaintively.

"It is surely not very probable," said Deronda, wishing that it were less so; then, not to let the opportunity escape: "Would it be a great grief to you now, if you were never to meet your mother?"

She did not answer immediately, but meditated again, with her eyes fixed on the opposite wall. Then she turned them on Deronda, and said firmly, as if she had arrived at the exact truth: "I want her to know that I have always loved her, and if she is alive I want to comfort her. She may be dead. If she were, I should long to know where she was buried; and to know whether my brother lives, so that we can remember her together. But I will try not to grieve. I have thought much for so many years of her being dead. And I shall have her with me in my mind, as I have always had. We can never be really parted. I think I have never sinned against her. I have always tried not to do what would hurt her. Only she might be sorry that I was not a good Jewess."

"In what way are you not a good Jewess?" said Deronda.

"I am ignorant, and we never observed the laws, but lived among Christians just as they did. But I have heard my father laugh at the strictness of the Jews about their food and all customs, and their not liking Christians. I think my mother was strict; but she could never want me not to like those who are better to me than any of my own people I have ever known. I think I could obey in other things that she wished, but not in that. It is so much easier to me to share in love than in hatred. I remember a play I read in German —since I have been here, it has come into my mind—where the heroine says something like that."

"Antigone," said Deronda.

"Ah, you know it. But I do not believe that my mother would wish me not to love my best friends. She would be grateful to them." Here Mirah had turned to Mrs. Meyrick, and with a sudden lighting up of her whole countenance she said: "Oh, if we ever do meet, and know each other as we are now, so that I could tell what would comfort her—I should be so full of blessedness, my soul would know no want but to love her!"

"God bless you, child!" said Mrs. Meyrick, the words escaping involuntarily from her motherly heart. But to relieve the strain of feeling she looked at Deronda and said: "It is curious that Mirah, who remembers her mother so well, it is as if she saw her, cannot recall her brother the least bit—except the feeling of having been carried by him when she was tired, and of his being near her when she was in her mother's lap. It must be that he was rarely at home. He was already grown up. It is a pity her brother should be quite a stranger to her."

"He is good; I feel sure Ezra is good," said Mirah, eagerly. He loved my mother—he would take care of her. I remember more of him than that. I remember my mother's voice once calling, 'Ezra!' and then his answering from the distance, 'Mother!'"—Mirah had changed her voice a little in each of these words, and had given them a loving intonation—"and then he came close to us. I feel sure he is good. I have always taken comfort from that."

It was impossible to answer this either with agreement or doubt. Mrs. Meyrick and Deronda exchanged a quick glance: about this brother she felt as painfully dubious as he did. But Mirah went on, absorbed in her memories:

"Is it not wonderful how I remember the voices better than anything else? I think they must go deeper into us than other things. I have often fancied heaven might be made of voices."

"Like your singing—yes," said Mab, who had hitherto kept a modest silence, and now spoke bashfully, as was her wont in the presence of Prince Camaralzaman.—"Ma, do ask Mirah to sing. Mr. Deronda has not heard her."

"Would it be disagreeable to you to sing now?" said Deronda, with a more deferential gentleness than he had ever been conscious of before.

"Oh, I shall like it," said Mirah. "My voice has come back a little with rest."

Perhaps her ease of manner was due to something more than the simplicity of her nature. The circumstances of her life had made her think of everything she did as work demanded from her, in which affectation had nothing to do; and she had begun her work before self-consciousness was born.

She immediately rose and went to the piano—a somewhat worn instrument that seemed to get the better of its infirmities under the firm touch of her small fingers as she preluded. Deronda placed himself where he could see her while she sang; and she took everything as quietly as if she had been a child going to breakfast.

Imagine her—it is always good to imagine a human creature in whom bodily loveliness seems as properly one with the entire being as the bodily loveliness of those wondrous transparent orbs of life that we find in the sea—imagine her with her dark hair brushed from her temples, but yet showing certain tiny rings there which had cunningly found their own way back, the mass of it hanging behind just to the nape of the little neck in curly fibres, such as renew themselves at their own will after being bathed into straightness like that of water-grasses. Then see the perfect cameo her profile makes, cut in a duskish shell where by some happy fortune there pierced a gem-like darkness for the eye and eyebrow; the delicate nostrils defined enough to be ready for sensitive movements, the finished ear, the firm curves of the chin and neck entering into the expression of a refinement which was not feebleness.

She sang Beethoven's "Per pietà non dirmi addio," with a subdued but searching pathos which had that essential of perfect singing, the making one oblivious of art or manner, and only possessing one with the song. It was the sort of voice that gives the impression of being meant like a bird's wooing for an audience near and beloved. Deronda began by looking at her, but felt himself presently covering his eyes with his hand, wanting to seclude the melody in darkness; then he refrained from what might seem oddity, and was ready to meet the look of mute appeal which she turned toward him at the end.

"I think I never enjoyed a song more than that," he said, gratefully.

"You like my singing? I am so glad," she said, with a smile of delight. "It has been a great pain to me, because it failed in what it was wanted for. But now we think I can use it to get my bread. I have really been taught well. And

now I have two pupils, that Miss Meyrick found for me.
They pay me nearly two crowns for their two lessons."

"I think I know some ladies who would find you many
pupils after Christmas," said Deronda. "You would not
mind singing before any one who wished to hear you?"

"Oh, no, I want to do something to get money. I could
teach reading and speaking, Mrs. Meyrick thinks. But if no
one would learn of me, that is difficult." Mirah smiled with
a touch of merriment he had not seen in her before. "I dare
say I should find her poor—I mean my mother. I should
want to get money for her. And I cannot always live on
charity; though"—here she turned so as to take all three of
her companions in one glance—"it is the sweetest charity in
all the world."

"I should think you can get rich," said Deronda, smiling.
"Great ladies will perhaps like you to teach their daughters.
We shall see. But now do sing again to us."

She went on willingly, singing with ready memory various
things by Gordigiani and Schubert; then, when she had left
the piano, Mab said, entreatingly: "Oh Mirah, if you would
not mind singing the little hymn."

"It is too childish," said Mirah. "It is like lisping."

"What is the hymn?" said Deronda.

"It is the Hebrew hymn she remembers her mother singing
over her when she lay in her cot," said Mrs. Meyrick.

"I should like very much to hear it," said Deronda, "if you
think I am worthy to hear what is so sacred."

"I will sing it if you like," said Mirah, "but I don't sing
real words—only here and there a syllable like hers—the rest
is lisping. Do you know Hebrew? because if you do, my
singing will seem childish nonsense."

Deronda shook his head. "It will be quite good Hebrew
to me."

Mirah crossed her little feet and hands in her easiest attitude, and then lifted up her head at an angle which seemed
to be directed to some invisible face bent over her, while she
sang a little hymn of quaint melancholy intervals, with syllables that really seemed childish lisping to her audience; but
the voice in which she gave it forth had gathered even a

sweeter, more cooing tenderness than was heard in her other songs.

"If I were ever to know the real words, I should still go on in my old way with them," said Mirah, when she had repeated the hymn several times.

"Why not?" said Deronda. "The lisped syllables are very full of meaning."

"Yes, indeed," said Mrs. Meyrick; "a mother hears something like a lisp in her children's talk to the very last. Their words are not just what everybody else says, though they may be spelt the same. If I were to live till my Hans got old, I should still see the boy in him. A mother's love, I often say, is like a tree that has got all the wood in it, from the very first it made."

"Is not that the way with friendship, too?" said Deronda, smiling. "We must not let mothers be too arrogant."

The bright little woman shook her head over her darning.

"It is easier to find an old mother than an old friend. Friendships begin with liking or gratitude—roots that can be pulled up. Mother's love begins deeper down."

"Like what you were saying about the influence of voices," said Deronda, looking at Mirah. "I don't think your hymn would have had more expression for me if I had known the words. I went to the synagogue at Frankfort before I came home, and the service impressed me just as much as if I had followed the words—perhaps more."

"Oh, was it great to you? Did it go to your heart?" said Mirah, eagerly. "I thought none but our people would feel that. I thought it was all shut away like a river in a deep valley, where only heaven saw—I mean——" she hesitated, feeling that she could not disentangle her thought from imagery.

"I understand," said Deronda. "But there is not really such a separation—deeper down, as Mrs. Meyrick says. Our religion is chiefly a Hebrew religion; and since Jews are men, their religious feelings must have much in common with those of other men—just as their poetry, though in one sense peculiar, has a great deal in common with the poetry of other nations. Still it is to be expected that a Jew would feel the

forms of his people's religion more than one of another race—
and yet"—here Deronda hesitated in his turn—"that is perhaps not always so."

"Ah, no," said Mirah, sadly. "I have seen that. I have
seen them mock. Is it not like mocking your parents?—like
rejoicing in your parents' shame?"

"Some minds naturally rebel against whatever they were
brought up in, and like the opposite: they see the faults in
what is nearest to them," said Deronda, apologetically.

"But you are not like that," said Mirah, looking at him
with unconscious fixedness.

"No, I think not," said Deronda; "but you know I was not
brought up as a Jew."

"Ah, I am always forgetting," said Mirah, with a look of
disappointed recollection, and slightly blushing.

Deronda also felt rather embarrassed, and there was an
awkward pause, which he put an end to by saying playfully:

"Whichever way we take it, we have to tolerate each other;
for if we all went in opposition to our teaching, we must end
in difference, just the same."

"To be sure. We should go on forever in zigzags," said
Mrs. Meyrick. "I think it is very weak-minded to make
your creed up by the rule of contrary. Still one may honor
one's parents, without following their notions exactly, any
more than the exact cut of their clothing. My father was a
Scotch Calvinist and my mother was a French Calvinist: I am
neither quite Scotch nor quite French, nor two Calvinists rolled
into one, yet I honor my parents' memory."

"But I could not make myself not a Jewess," said Mirah,
insistently, "even if I changed my belief."

"No, my dear. But if Jews and Jewesses went on changing their religion, and making no difference between themselves and Christians, there would come a time when there
would be no Jews to be seen," said Mrs. Meyrick, taking that
consummation very cheerfully.

"Oh, please not to say that," said Mirah, the tears gathering. "It is the first unkind thing you ever said. I will not
begin that. I will never separate myself from my mother's
people. I was forced to fly from my father; but if he came

back in age and weakness and want, and needed me, should I say, 'This is not my father'? If he had shame, I must share it. It was he who was given to me for my father, and not another. And so it is with my people. I will always be a Jewess. I will love Christians when they are good, like you. But I will always cling to my people. I will always worship with them."

As Mirah had gone on speaking she had become possessed with a sorrowful passion—fervent, not violent. Holding her little hands tightly clasped and looking at Mrs. Meyrick with beseeching, she seemed to Deronda a personification of that spirit which impelled men after a long inheritance of professed Catholicism to leave wealth and high place, and risk their lives in fight, that they might join their own people and say, "I am a Jew."

"Mirah, Mirah, my dear child, you mistake me!" said Mrs. Meyrick, alarmed. "God forbid I should want you to do anything against your conscience. I was only saying what might be if the world went on. But I had better have left the world alone, and not wanted to be over-wise. Forgive me! Come! we will not try to take you from anybody you feel has more right to you."

"I would do anything else for you. I owe you my life," said Mirah, not yet quite calm.

"Hush, hush, now," said Mrs. Meyrick. "I have been punished enough for wagging my tongue foolishly—making an almanac for the Millennium, as my husband used to say."

"But everything in the world must come to an end some time. We must bear to think of that," said Mab, unable to hold her peace on this point. She had already suffered from a bondage of tongue which threatened to become severe if Mirah were to be too much indulged in this inconvenient susceptibility to innocent remarks.

Deronda smiled at the irregular, blond face, brought into strange contrast by the side of Mirah's—smiled, Mab thought, rather sarcastically as he said: "That prospect of everything coming to an end will not guide us far in practice. Mirah's feelings, she tells us, are concerned with what is."

Mab was confused, and wished she had not spoken, since

Mr. Deronda seemed to think that she had found fault with
Mirah; but to have spoken once is a tyrannous reason for
speaking again, and she said:

"I only meant that we must have courage to hear things,
else there is hardly anything we can talk about." Mab felt
herself unanswerable here, inclining to the opinion of Socrates:
"What motive has a man to live, if not for the pleasures of
discourse?"

Deronda took his leave soon after; and when Mrs. Meyrick
went outside with him to exchange a few words about Mirah,
he said: "Hans is to share my chambers when he comes at
Christmas."

"You have written to Rome about that?" said Mrs. Meyrick, her face lighting up. "How very good and thoughtful
of you! You mentioned Mirah, then?"

"Yes, I referred to her. I concluded he knew everything
from you."

"I must confess my folly. I have not yet written a word
about her. I have always been meaning to do it, and yet
have ended my letter without saying a word. And I told the
girls to leave it to me. However!—Thank you a thousand
times."

Deronda divined something of what was in the mother's
mind, and his divination re-enforced a certain anxiety already
present in him. His inward colloquy was not soothing. He
said to himself that no man could see this exquisite creature
without feeling it possible to fall in love with her; but all the
fervor of his nature was engaged on the side of precaution.
There are personages who feel themselves tragic because they
march into a palpable morass, dragging another with them,
and then cry out against all the gods. Deronda's mind was
strongly set against imitating them.

"I have my hands on the reins now," he thought, "and I
will not drop them. I shall go there as little as possible."

He saw the reasons acting themselves out before him. How
could he be Mirah's guardian and claim to unite with Mrs.
Meyrick, to whose charge he had committed her, if he showed
himself as a lover—whom she did not love—whom she would
not marry? And if he encouraged any germ of lover's feel-

ing in himself it would lead up to that issue. Mirah's was not a nature that would bear dividing against itself; and even if love won her consent to marry a man who was not of her race and religion, she would never be happy in acting against that strong native bias which would still reign in her conscience as remorse.

Deronda saw these consequences as we see any danger of marring our own work well begun. It was a delight to have rescued this child acquainted with sorrow, and to think of having placed her little feet in protected paths. The creature we help to save, though only a half-reared linnet, bruised and lost by the wayside—how we watch and fence it, and dote on its signs of recovery! Our pride becomes loving, our self is a not-self for whose sake we become virtuous, when we set to some hidden work of reclaiming a life from misery and look for our triumph in the secret joy: "This one is the better for me."

"I would as soon hold out my finger to be bitten off as set about spoiling her peace," said Deronda. "It was one of the rarest bits of fortune that I should have had friends like the Meyricks to place her with—generous, delicate friends without any loftiness in their ways, so that her dependence on them is not only safety, but happiness. There could be no refuge to replace that, if it were broken up. But what is the use of my taking the vows and settling everything as it should be, if that marplot Hans comes and upsets it all?"

Few things were more likely. Hans was made for mishaps: his very limbs seemed more breakable than other people's—his eyes more of a resort for uninvited flies and other irritating guests. But it was impossible to forbid Hans's coming to London. He was intending to get a studio there and make it his chief home; and to propose that he should defer coming on some ostensible ground, concealing the real motive of winning time for Mirah's position to become more confirmed and independent, was impracticable. Having no other resource, Deronda tried to believe that both he and Mrs. Meyrick were foolishly troubling themselves about one of those endless things called probabilities, which never occur; but he did not quite succeed in his trying; on the contrary, he found

himself going inwardly through a scene where, on the first discovery of Hans's inclination, he gave him a very energetic
warning—suddenly checked, however, by the suspicion of personal feeling that his warmth might be creating in Hans. He
could come to no result but that the position was peculiar, and
that he could make no further provision against dangers until
they came nearer. To save an unhappy Jewess from drowning herself, would not have seemed a startling variation among
police reports; but to discover in her so rare a creature as
Mirah was an exceptional event which might well bring exceptional consequences. Deronda would not let himself for a
moment dwell on any supposition that the consequences might
enter deeply into his own life. The image of Mirah had never
yet had that penetrating radiation which would have been
given to it by the idea of her loving him. When this sort of
affluence is absent from the fancy (whether from the fact or
not) a man may go far in devotedness without perturbation.

As to the search for Mirah's mother and brother, Deronda
took what she had said to-day as a warrant for deferring any
immediate measures. His conscience was not quite easy in
this desire for delay, any more than it was quite easy in his
not attempting to learn the truth about his own mother: in
both cases he felt that there might be an unfulfilled duty to a
parent, but in both cases there was an overpowering repugnance to the possible truth, which threw a turning weight into
the scale of argument.

"At least, I will look about," was his final determination.
"I may find some special Jewish machinery. I will wait till
after Christmas."

What should we all do without the calendar, when we want
to put off a disagreeable duty? The admirable arrangements
of the solar system, by which our time is measured, always
supply us with a term before which it is hardly worth while
to set about anything we are disinclined to.

CHAPTER XXXIII.

"No man," says a Rabbi, by way of indisputable instance, "may turn the bones of his father and mother into spoons"—sure that his hearers felt the checks against that form of economy. The market for spoons has never expanded enough for any one to say, "Why not?" and to argue that human progress lies in such an application of material. The only check to be alleged is a sentiment, which will coerce none who do not hold that sentiments are the better part of the world's wealth.

DERONDA meanwhile took to a less fashionable form of exercise than riding in Rotten Row. He went often rambling in those parts of London which are most inhabited by common Jews: he walked to the synagogues at times of service, he looked into shops, he observed faces—a process not very promising of particular discovery. Why did he not address himself to an influential Rabbi or other member of a Jewish community, to consult on the chances of finding a mother named Cohen, with a son named Ezra, and a lost daughter named Mirah? He thought of doing so—after Christmas. The fact was, notwithstanding all his sense of poetry in common things, Deronda, where a keen personal interest was aroused, could not, more than the rest of us, continuously escape suffering from the pressure of that hard, unaccommodating Actual, which has never consulted our taste and is entirely unselect. Enthusiasm, we know, dwells at ease among ideas, tolerates garlic breathed in the middle ages, and sees no shabbiness in the official trappings of classic processions: it gets squeamish when ideals press upon it as something warmly incarnate, and can hardly face them without fainting. Lying dreamily in a boat, imagining one's self in quest of a beautiful maiden's relatives in Cordova elbowed by Jews in the time of Ibn-Gebirol, all the physical incidents can be borne without shock. Or if the scenery of St. Mary Axe and Whitechapel were imaginatively transported to the borders of the Rhine at the end of the eleventh century, when, in the ears listening for the signals of the Messiah, the Hep! Hep! Hep! of the Crusaders came like the bay of bloodhounds; and in the presence of those devilish missionaries with sword and firebrand the crouching figure of the reviled Jew turned round erect, heroic,

flashing with sublime constancy in the face of torture and
death—what would the dingy shops and unbeautiful faces
signify to the thrill of contemplative emotion? But the fervor of sympathy with which we contemplate a grandiose martyrdom is feeble compared with the enthusiasm that keeps un-
slacked where there is no danger, no challenge—nothing but
impartial mid-day falling on commonplace, perhaps half-repul-
sive, objects which are really the beloved ideas made flesh.
Here undoubtedly lies the chief poetic energy:—in the force
of imagination that pierces or exalts the solid fact, instead of
floating among cloud-pictures. To glory in a prophetic vision
of knowledge covering the earth is an easier exercise of believing imagination than to see its beginning in newspaper
placards, staring at you from a bridge beyond the corn-fields;
and it might well happen to most of us dainty people that we
were in the thick of the battle of Armageddon without being
aware of anything more than the annoyance of a little explosive smoke and struggling on the ground immediately about us.

It lay in Deronda's nature usually to contemn the feeble,
fastidious sympathy which shrinks from the broad life of
mankind; but now, with Mirah before him as a living reality
whose experience he had to care for, he saw every common
Jew and Jewess in the light of comparison with her, and had
a presentiment of the collision between her idea of the unknown mother and brother and the discovered fact—a presentiment all the keener in him because of a suppressed consciousness that a not unlike possibility of collision might lie hidden
in his own lot. Not that he would have looked with more
complacency of expectation at wealthy Jews, outdoing the
lords of the Philistines in their sports; but since there was no
likelihood of Mirah's friends being found among that class,
their habits did not immediately affect him. In this mood he
rambled, without expectation of a more pregnant result than
a little preparation of his own mind, perhaps for future theo-
rizing as well as practice—very much as if, Mirah being related to Welsh miners, he had gone to look more closely at the
ways of those people, not without wishing at the same time
to get a little light of detail on the history of Strikes.

He really did not long to find anybody in particular; and

when, as his habit was, he looked at the name over a shop-door, he was well content that it was not Ezra Cohen. I confess, he particularly desired that Ezra Cohen should not keep a shop. Wishes are held to be ominous; according to which belief the order of the world is so arranged that if you have an impious objection to a squint, your offspring is the more likely to be born with one; also, that if you happened to desire a squint, you would not get it. This desponding view of probability the hopeful entirely reject, taking their wishes as good and sufficient security for all kinds of fulfilment. Who is absolutely neutral? Deronda happening one morning to turn into a little side street out of the noise and obstructions of Holborn, felt the scale dip on the desponding side.

He was rather tired of the streets, and had paused to hail a hansom cab which he saw coming, when his attention was caught by some fine old clasps in chased silver displayed in the window at his right hand. His first thought was that Lady Mallinger, who had a strictly Protestant taste for such Catholic spoils, might like to have these missal-clasps turned into a bracelet; then his eyes travelled over the other contents of the window, and he saw that the shop was that kind of pawnbroker's where the lead is given to jewelry, lace, and all equivocal objects introduced as *bric-à-brac*. A placard in one corner announced—*Watches and Jewelry exchanged and repaired*. But his survey had been noticed from within, and a figure appeared at the door, looking round at him, and saying in a tone of cordial encouragement, "Good-day, sir." The instant was enough for Deronda to see that the face, unmistakably Jewish, belonged to a young man about thirty; and wincing from the shopkeeper's persuasiveness that would probably follow, he had no sooner returned the "Good-day," than he passed to the other side of the street and beckoned to the cabman to draw up there. From that station he saw the name over the shop-window—*Ezra Cohen*.

There might be a hundred Ezra Cohens lettered above shop-windows, but Deronda had not seen them. Probably the young man interested in a possible customer was Ezra himself; and he was about the age to be expected in Mirah's brother, who was grown up while she was still a little child.

But Deronda's first endeavor as he drove homeward was to convince himself that there was not the slightest warrantable presumption of this Ezra being Mirah's brother; and next, that even if, in spite of good reasoning, he turned out to be that brother, while on inquiry the mother was found to be dead, it was not his—Deronda's—duty to make known the discovery to Mirah. In inconvenient disturbance of this conclusion there came his lately acquired knowledge that Mirah would have a religious desire to know of her mother's death, and also to learn whether her brother were living. How far was he justified in determining another life by his own notions? Was it not his secret complaint against the way in which others had ordered his own life that he had not open daylight on all its relations, so that he had not, like other men, the full guidance of primary duties?

The immediate relief from this inward debate was the reflection that he had not yet made any real discovery, and that by looking into the facts more closely he should be certified that there was no demand on him for any decision whatever. He intended to return to that shop as soon as he could conveniently, and buy the clasps for Lady Mallinger. But he was hindered for several days by Sir Hugo, who, about to make an after-dinner speech on a burning topic, wanted Deronda to forage for him on the legal part of the question, besides wasting time every day on argument which always ended in a drawn battle. As on many other questions, they held different sides; but Sir Hugo did not mind this, and when Deronda put his point well, said, with a mixture of satisfaction and regret:

"Confound it, Dan! why don't you make an opportunity of saying these things in public? You're wrong, you know. You won't succeed. You've got the massive sentiment—the heavy artillery of the country against you. But it's all the better ground for a young man to display himself on. When I was your age, I should have taken it. And it would be quite as well for you to be in opposition to me here and there. It would throw you more into relief. If you would seize an occasion of this sort to make an impression, you might be in Parliament in no time. And you know that would gratify me."

"I am sorry not to do what would gratify you, sir," said Deronda. "But I cannot persuade myself to look at politics as a profession."

"Why not? If a man is not born into public life by his position in the country, there's no way for him but to embrace it by his own efforts. The business of the country must be done—her Majesty's Government carried on, as the old Duke said. And it never could be, my boy, if everybody looked at politics as if they were prophecy, and demanded an inspired vocation. If you are to get into Parliament, it won't do to sit still and wait for a call either from heaven or constituents."

"I don't want to make a living out of opinions," said Deronda; "especially out of borrowed opinions. Not that I mean to blame other men. I dare say many better fellows than I don't mind getting on to a platform to praise themselves, and giving their word of honor for a party."

"I'll tell you what, Dan," said Sir Hugo, "a man who sets his face against every sort of humbug is simply a three-cornered, impractical fellow. There's a bad style of humbug, but there is also a good style—one that oils the wheels and makes progress possible. If you are to rule men, you must rule them through their own ideas; and I agree with the Archbishop at Naples who had a St. Januarius procession against the plague. It's no use having an Order in Council against popular shallowness. There is no action possible without a little acting."

"One may be obliged to give way to an occasional necessity," said Deronda. "But it is one thing to say, ' In this particular case I am forced to put on this foolscap and grin,' and another to buy a pocket foolscap and practise myself in grinning. I can't see any real public expediency that does not keep an ideal before it which makes a limit of deviation from the direct path. But if I were to set up for a public man I might mistake my own success for public expediency."

It was after this dialogue, which was rather jarring to him, that Deronda set out on his meditated second visit to Ezra Cohen's. He entered the street at the end opposite to the Holborn entrance, and an inward reluctance slackened his pace while his thoughts were transferring what he had just

been saying about public expediency to the entirely private
difficulty which brought him back again into this unattractive
thoroughfare. It might soon become an immediate practical
question with him how far he could call it a wise expediency
to conceal the fact of close kindred. Such questions turning
up constantly in life are often decided in a rough and ready
way; and to many it will appear an over-refinement in Deronda that he should make any great point of a matter con-
fined to his own knowledge. But we have seen the reasons
why he had come to regard concealment as a bane of life, and
the necessity of concealment as a mark by which lines of action
were to be avoided. The prospect of being urged against the
confirmed habit of his mind was naturally grating. He even
paused here and there before the most plausible shop-windows
for a gentleman to look into, half inclined to decide that he
would not increase his knowledge about that modern Ezra,
who was certainly not a leader among his people—a hesitation
which proved how, in a man much given to reasoning, a bare
possibility may weigh more than the best-clad likelihood; for
Deronda's reasoning had decided that all likelihood was against
this man's being Mirah's brother.

One of the shop-windows he paused before was that of a
second-hand book-shop, where, on a narrow table outside, the
literature of the ages was represented in judicious mixture,
from the immortal verse of Homer to the mortal prose of the
railway novel. That the mixture was judicious, was apparent
from Deronda's finding in it something that he wanted—
namely, that wonderful bit of autobiography, the life of the
Polish Jew, Salomon Maimon; which, as he could easily slip
it into his pocket, he took from its place, and entered the
shop to pay for, expecting to see behind the counter a grimy
personage showing that nonchalance about sales which seems
to belong universally to the second-hand book-business. In
most other trades you find generous men who are anxious to
sell you their wares for your own welfare; but even a Jew
will not urge Simson's Euclid on you with an affectionate assurance that you will have pleasure in reading it, and that he
wishes he had twenty more of the article, so much is it in request. One is led to fear that a second-hand bookseller may

belong to that unhappy class of men who have no belief in the good of what they get their living by, yet keep conscience enough to be morose rather than unctuous in their vocation.

But instead of the ordinary tradesman, he saw, on the dark background of books in the long narrow shop, a figure that was somewhat startling in its unusualness. A man in thread-bare clothing, whose age was difficult to guess—from the dead yellowish flatness of the flesh, something like an old ivory carving—was seated on a stool against some book-shelves that projected beyond the short counter, doing nothing more remarkable than reading the yesterday's *Times;* but when he let the paper rest on his lap and looked at the incoming customer, the thought glanced through Deronda that precisely such a physiognomy as that might possibly have been seen in a prophet of the Exile, or in some New Hebrew poet of the mediæval time. It was a finely typical Jewish face, wrought into intensity of expression apparently by a strenuous eager experience in which all the satisfaction had been indirect and far off, and perhaps by some bodily suffering also, which involved that absence of ease in the present. The features were clear-cut, not large; the brow not high, but broad, and fully defined by the crisp black hair. It might never have been a particularly handsome face, but it must always have been forcible; and now with its dark, far-off gaze, and yellow pallor in relief on the gloom of the backward shop, one might have imagined one's self coming upon it in some past prison of the Inquisition, which a mob had suddenly burst open: while the look fixed on an incidental customer seemed eager and questioning enough to have been turned on one who might have been a messenger either of delivery or of death. The figure was probably familiar and unexciting enough to the inhabitants of this street; but to Deronda's mind it brought so strange a blending of the unwonted with the common, that there was a perceptible interval of mutual observation before he asked his question: " What is the price of this book? "

After taking the book and examining the fly-leaves without rising, the supposed bookseller said: " There is no mark, and Mr. Ram is not in now. I am keeping the shop while he is gone to dinner. What are you disposed to give for it? " He held the book closed on his lap with his hand on it, and looked examiningly at Deronda, over whom there came the disagreeable idea that possibly this striking personage wanted to see how much could be got out of a customer's ignorance of prices. But without further reflection he said: "Don't you know how much it is worth?"

"Not its market-price. May I ask, have you read it?"

"No. I have read an account of it, which makes me want to buy it."

"You are a man of learning—you are interested in Jewish history?" This was said in a deepened tone of eager inquiry.

"I am certainly interested in Jewish history," said Deronda, quietly, curiosity overcoming his dislike to the sort of inspection as well as questioning he was under.

But immediately the strange Jew rose from his sitting posture, and Deronda felt a thin hand pressing his arm tightly, while a hoarse, excited voice, not much above a loud whisper, said:

"You are perhaps of our race?"

Deronda colored deeply, not liking the grasp, and then answered with a slight shake of the head, "No." The grasp was relaxed, the hand withdrawn, the eagerness of the face collapsed into uninterested melancholy, as if some possessing spirit which had leaped into the eyes and gestures had sunk back again to the inmost recesses of the frame; and moving further off as he held out the little book, the stranger said in a tone of distant civility: "I believe Mr. Ram will be satisfied with half-a-crown, sir."

The effect of this change on Deronda—he afterward smiled when he recalled it—was oddly embarrassing and humiliating, as if some high dignitary had found him deficient and given him his *congé*. There was nothing further to be said, however: he paid his half-crown and carried off his *Salomon Maimon's Lebensgeschichte* with a mere "Good-morning."

He felt some vexation at the sudden arrest of the interview, and the apparent prohibition that he should know more of this man, who was certainly something out of the common way—as different probably as a Jew could well be from Ezra Cohen, through whose door Deronda was presently entering, and whose flourishing face glistening on the way to fatness was hanging over the counter in negotiation with some one on the other side of the partition, concerning two plated stoppers and three teaspoons, which lay spread before him. Seeing Deronda enter, he called out "Mother! Mother!" and then with a familiar nod and smile, said: "Coming, sir—coming directly."

Deronda could not help looking toward the door from the back with some anxiety, which was not soothed when he saw a vigorous woman beyond fifty enter and approach to serve him. Not that there was anything very repulsive about her: the worst that could be said was that she had that look of having made her toilet with little water, and by twilight, which is common to unyouthful people of her class, and of having presumably slept in her large ear-rings, if not in her rings and necklace. In fact, what caused a sinking of heart in Deronda was her not being so coarse and ugly as to exclude the idea of her being Mirah's mother. Any one who has looked at a face to try and discern signs of known kinship in it will understand his process of conjecture—how he tried to think away the fat which had generally disguised the outlines of youth, and to discern what one may call the elementary expressions of the face. He was sorry to see no absolute negative to his fears. Just as it was conceivable that this Ezra, brought up to trade, might resemble the scapegrace father in everything but his knowledge and talent, so it was not impossible that this mother might have had a lovely refined daughter whose type of feature and expression was like Mirah's. The eyebrows had a vexatious similarity of line; and who shall decide how far a face may be masked when the uncherishing years have thrust it far onward in the ever-new procession of youth and age? The good-humor of the glance remained and shone out in a motherly way at Deronda, as she said, in a mild, guttural tone:

"How can I serve you, sir?"

"I should like to look at the silver clasps in the window," said Deronda; "the larger ones, please, in the corner there."

They were not quite easy to get at from the mother's station, and the son seeing this called out: " I'll reach 'em, mother; I'll

reach 'em,"—running forward with alacrity, and then handing
the clasps to Deronda with the smiling remark:

"Mother's too proud: she wants to do everything herself.
That's why I called her to wait on you, sir. When there's a
particular gentleman customer, sir, I daren't do any other
than call her. But I can't let her do herself a mischief with
stretching."

Here Mr. Cohen made way again for his parent, who gave
a little guttural amiable laugh while she looked at Deronda,
as much as to say: "This boy will be at his jokes, but you
see he's the best son in the world"; and evidently the son
enjoyed pleasing her, though he also wished to convey an apology to his distinguished customer for not giving him the
advantage of his own exclusive attention.

Deronda began to examine the clasps as if he had many
points to observe before he could come to a decision.

"They are only three guineas, sir," said the mother, encouragingly.

"First-rate workmanship, sir—worth twice the money;
only got 'em a bargain from Cologne," said the son, paren-
thetically, from a distance.

Meanwhile two new customers entered, and the repeated
call, "Addy!" brought from the back of the shop a group
that Deronda turned frankly to stare at, feeling sure that the
stare would be held complimentary. The group consisted of
a black-eyed young woman who carried a black-eyed little
one, its head already well covered with black curls, and deposited it on the counter, from which station it looked round
with even more than the usual intelligence of babies; also a
robust boy of six, and a younger girl, both with black eyes
and black-ringed hair—looking more Semitic than their parents, as the puppy lions show the spots of far-off progenitors.
The young woman answering to "Addy"—a sort of paroquet
in a bright blue dress, with coral necklace and ear-rings, her
hair set up in a huge bush—looked as complacently lively and
unrefined as her husband; and by a certain difference from
the mother deepened in Deronda the unwelcome impression
that the latter was not so utterly common a Jewess as to exclude her being the mother of Mirah. While that thought

was glancing through his mind, the boy had run forward into
the shop with an energetic stamp, and setting himself about
four feet from Deronda, with his hands in the pockets of his
miniature knickerbockers, looked at him with a precocious air
of survey. Perhaps it was chiefly with a diplomatic design
to linger and ingratiate himself that Deronda patted the boy's
head, saying:

"What is your name, sirrah?"

"Jacob Alexander Cohen," said the small man, with much
ease and distinctness.

"You are not named after your father, then?"

"No; after my grandfather. He sells knives and razors
and scissors—my grandfather does," said Jacob, wishing to
impress the stranger with that high connection. "He gave
me this knife." Here a pocket-knife was drawn forth, and
the small fingers, both naturally and artificially dark, opened
two blades and a cork-screw with much quickness.

"Is not that a dangerous plaything?" said Deronda, turning to the grandmother.

"He'll never hurt himself, bless you!" said she, contem-
plating her grandson with placid rapture.

"Have you got a knife?" says Jacob, coming closer. His
small voice was hoarse in its glibness, as if it belonged to an
aged commercial soul, fatigued with bargaining through many
generations.

"Yes. Do you want to see it?" said Deronda, taking a
small penknife from his waistcoat pocket.

Jacob seized it immediately and retreated a little, holding
the two knives in his palms and bending over them in meditative comparison. By this time the other clients were gone,
and the whole family had gathered to the spot, centring their
attention on the marvellous Jacob: the father, mother, and
grandmother behind the counter, with baby held staggering
thereon, and the little girl in front leaning at her brother's
elbow to assist him in looking at the knives.

"Mine's the best," said Jacob, at last, returning Deronda's
knife as if he had been entertaining the idea of exchange and
had rejected it.

Father and mother laughed aloud with delight. "You

won't find Jacob choosing the worst," said Mr. Cohen, wink-ing, with much confidence in the customer's admiration.   De-ronda, looking at the grandmother, who had only an inward silent laugh, said:

"Are these the only grandchildren you have?"

"All.   This is my only son," she answered, in a communi-cative tone, Deronda's glance and manner as usual conveying the impression of sympathetic interest—which on this occa-sion answered his purpose well.   It seemed to come naturally enough that he should say:

"And you have no daughter?"

There was an instantaneous change in the mother's face. Her lips closed more firmly, she looked down, swept her hands outward on the counter, and finally turned her back on De-ronda to examine some Indian handkerchiefs that hung in pawn behind her.   Her son gave a significant glance, set up his shoulders an instant, and just put his fingers to his lips,— then said quickly: "I think you're a first-rate gentleman in the city, sir, if I may be allowed to guess."

"No," said Deronda, with a preoccupied air, "I have noth-ing to do with the city."

"That's a bad job.   I thought you might be the young principal of a first-rate firm," said Mr. Cohen, wishing to make amends for the check on his customer's natural desire to know more of him and his.   "But you understand silver-work, I see."

"A little," said Deronda, taking up the clasps a moment and laying them down again.   That unwelcome bit of circum-stantial evidence had made his mind busy with a plan which was certainly more like acting than anything he had been aware of in his own conduct before.   But the bare possibility that more knowledge might nullify the evidence now over-powered the inclination to rest in uncertainty.

"To tell you the truth," he went on, "my errand is not so much to buy as to borrow.   I dare say you go into rather heavy transactions occasionally."

"Well, sir, I've accommodated gentlemen of distinction— I'm proud to say it.   I wouldn't exchange my business with any in the world.   There's none more honorable, nor more charitable, nor more necessary for all classes, from the good lady who wants a little of the ready for the baker, to a gentleman like yourself, sir, who may want it for amusement. I like my business, I like my street, and I like my shop. I wouldn't have it a door further down. And I wouldn't be without a pawn-shop, sir, to be the Lord Mayor. It puts you in connection with the world at large. I say it's like the Government revenue—it embraces the brass as well as the gold of the country. And a man who doesn't get money, sir, can't accommodate. Now what can I do for *you*, sir?"

If an amiable self-satisfaction is the mark of earthly bliss, Solomon in all his glory was a pitiable mortal compared with Mr. Cohen—clearly one of those persons who, being in excellent spirits about themselves, are willing to cheer strangers by letting them know it. While he was delivering himself with lively rapidity, he took the baby from his wife, and holding it on his arm, presented his features to be explored by its small fists. Deronda, not in a cheerful mood, was rashly pronouncing this Ezra Cohen to be the most unpoetic Jew he had ever met with in books or life: his phraseology was as little as possible like that of the Old Testament; and no shadow of a Suffering Race distinguished his vulgarity of soul from that of a prosperous pink-and-white huckster of the purest English lineage. It is naturally a Christian feeling that a Jew ought not to be conceited. However, this was no reason for not persevering in his project, and he answered at once in adventurous ignorance of technicalities:

"I have a fine diamond ring to offer as security—not with me at this moment, unfortunately, for I am not in the habit of wearing it. But I will come again this evening and bring it with me. Fifty pounds at once would be a convenience to me."

"Well, you know, this evening is the Sabbath, young gentleman," said Cohen, "and I go to the *Shool*. The shop will be closed. But accommodation is a work of charity; if you can't get here before, and are any ways pressed—why, I'll look at your diamond. You're perhaps from the West End—a longish drive?"

"Yes; and your Sabbath begins early at this season. I

could be here by five—will that do?" Deronda had not been
without hope that by asking to come on a Friday evening he
might get a better opportunity of observing points in the family character, and might even be able to put some decisive
question.

Cohen assented; but here the marvellous Jacob, whose
physique supported a precocity that would have shattered a
Gentile of his years, showed that he had been listening with
much comprehension by saying: "You are coming again.
Have you got any more knives at home?"

"I think I have one," said Deronda, smiling down at
him.

"Has it two blades and a hook—and a white handle like
that?" said Jacob, pointing to the waistcoat pocket.

"I dare say it has."

"Do you like a cork-screw?" said Jacob, exhibiting that
article in his own knife again, and looking up with serious
inquiry.

"Yes," said Deronda, experimentally.

"Bring your knife, then, and we'll shwop," said Jacob, returning the knife to his pocket, and stamping about with the
sense that he had concluded a good transaction.

The grandmother had now recovered her usual manners,
and the whole family watched Deronda radiantly when he
caressingly lifted the little girl, to whom he had not hitherto
given attention, and seating her on the counter, asked for her
name also. She looked at him in silence, and put her fingers
to her gold ear-rings, which he did not seem to have noticed.

Adelaide Rebekah is her name," said her mother, proudly.
"Speak to the gentleman, lovey."

"Shlav'm Shabbes fyock on," said Adelaide Rebekah.

"Her Sabbath frock, she means," said the father, in explanation. "She'll have her Sabbath frock on this evening."

"And will you let me see you in it, Adelaide?" said Deronda, with that gentle intonation which came very easily
to him.

"Say yes, lovey—yes, if you please, sir," said her mother,
enchanted with this handsome young gentleman, who appre-
ciated remarkable children.

"And will you give me a kiss this evening?" said Deronda, with a hand on each of her little brown shoulders.

Adelaide Rebekah (her miniature crinoline and monumental
features corresponded with the combination of her names) immediately put up her lips to pay the kiss in advance; whereupon her father, rising into still more glowing satisfaction
with the general meritoriousness of his circumstances, and
with the stranger who was an admiring witness, said cordially:

"You see there's somebody will be disappointed if you
don't come this evening, sir. You won't mind sitting down
in our family place and waiting a bit for me, if I'm not in
when you come, sir? I'll stretch a point to accommodate a
gent of your sort. Bring the diamond, and I'll see what I
can do for you."

Deronda thus left the most favorable impression behind
him, as a preparation for more easy intercourse. But for his
own part those amenities had been carried on under the heavi-
est spirits. If these were really Mirah's relatives, he could
not imagine that even her fervid filial piety could give the
reunion with them any sweetness beyond such as could be
found in the strict fulfilment of a painful duty. What did
this vaunting brother need? And with the most favorable supposition about the hypothetic mother, Deronda shrank from the
image of a first meeting between her and Mirah, and still more
from the idea of Mirah's domestication with this family. He
took refuge in disbelief. To find an Ezra Cohen when the
name was running in your head was no more extraordinary
than to find a Josiah Smith under like circumstances; and as
to the coincidence about the daughter, it would probably turn
out to be a difference. If, however, further knowledge confirmed the more undesirable conclusion, what would be wise
expediency—to try and determine the best consequences by
concealment, or to brave other consequences for the sake of
that openness which is the fresh air of our moral life?

CHAPTER XXXIV.

" Er ist geheissen
Israel. Ihn hat verwandelt
Hexenspruch in einen Hund.

. . . .

Aber jeden Freitag Abend,
In der Dämmrungstunde, plötzlich
Weicht der Zauber, und der Hund
Wird aufs Neu' ein menschlich Wesen. "
       —HEINE: *Prinzessin Sabbath.*

WHEN Deronda arrived at five o'clock, the shop was closed
and the door was opened for him by the Christian servant.
When she showed him into the room behind the shop he was
surprised at the prettiness of the scene. The house was old,
and rather extensive at the back: probably the large room he
now entered was gloomy by daylight, but now it was agreeably lit by a fine old brass lamp with seven oil-lights hanging
above the snow-white cloth spread on the central table. The
ceiling and walls were smoky, and all the surroundings were
dark enough to throw into relief the human figures, which had
a Venetian glow of coloring. The grandmother was arrayed
in yellowish brown with a large gold chain in lieu of the necklace, and by this light her yellow face with its darkly marked
eyebrows and framing roll of gray hair looked as handsome as
was necessary for picturesque effect. Young Mrs. Cohen was
clad in red and black, with a string of large artificial pearls
wound round and round her neck: the baby lay asleep in the
cradle under a scarlet counterpane; Adelaide Rebekah was in
braided amber; and Jacob Alexander was in black velveteen
with scarlet stockings. As the four pairs of black eyes all
glistened a welcome at Deronda, he was almost ashamed of
the supercilious dislike these happy-looking creatures had
raised in him by daylight. Nothing could be more cordial
than the greeting he received, and both mother and grandmother seemed to gather more dignity from being seen on the
private hearth, showing hospitality. He looked round with
some wonder at the old furniture: the oaken bureau and high
side-table must surely be mere matters of chance and econ-

omy, and not due to the family taste.   A large dish of blue-
and-yellow ware was set up on the side-table, and flanking it
were two old silver vessels; in front of them a large volume
in darkened vellum with a deep-ribbed back.   In the corner
at the farther end was an open door into an inner room, where
there was also a light.

Deronda took in these details by parenthetic glances while
he met Jacob's pressing solicitude about the knife.   He had
taken the pains to buy one with the requisites of the hook and
white handle, and produced it on demand, saying:

"Is that the sort of thing you want, Jacob?"

It was subjected to a severe scrutiny, the hook and blades
were opened, and the article of barter with the cork-screw was
drawn forth for comparison.

"Why do you like a hook better than a cork-screw?" said
Deronda.

"'Caush I can get hold of things with a hook.   A cork-
screw won't go into anything but corks.   But it's better for
you, you can draw corks."

"You agree to change, then?" said Deronda, observing that
the grandmother was listening with delight.

"What else have you got in your pockets?" said Jacob, with
deliberative seriousness.

"Hush, hush, Jacob, love," said the grandmother.   And
Deronda, mindful of discipline, answered:

"I think I must not tell you that.   Our business was with
the knives."

Jacob looked up into his face scanningly for a moment or
two, and apparently arriving at his conclusions, said gravely:

"I'll shwop," handing the cork-screw knife to Deronda,
who pocketed it with corresponding gravity.

Immediately the small son of Shem ran off into the next
room, whence his voice was heard in rapid chat; and then ran
back again—when, seeing his father enter, he seized a little
velveteen hat which lay on a chair and put it on to approach
him.   Cohen kept on his own hat, and took no notice of the
visitor, but stood still while the two children went up to him
and clasped his knees: then he laid his hands on each in turn
and uttered his Hebrew benediction; whereupon the wife, who

had lately taken baby from the cradle, brought it up to her
husband and held it under his outstretched hands, to be
blessed in its sleep.   For the moment Deronda thought that
this pawnbroker proud of his vocation was not utterly prosaic.

"Well, sir, you found your welcome in my family, I
think," said Cohen, putting down his hat and becoming his
former self.   "And you've been punctual.   Nothing like a
little stress here," he added, tapping his side pocket as he
sat down.   "It's good for us all in our turn.   I've felt it
when I've had to make up payments.   I began early—had to
turn myself about and put myself into shapes to fit every sort
of box.   It's bracing to the mind.   Now, then! let us see, let
us see."

"That is the ring I spoke of," said Deronda, taking it from
his finger.   "I believe it cost a hundred pounds.   It will be
a sufficient pledge to you for fifty, I think.   I shall probably
redeem it in a month or so."

Cohen's glistening eyes seemed to get a little nearer together as he met the ingenuous look of this crude young gentleman, who apparently supposed that redemption was a satisfaction to pawnbrokers.   He took the ring, examined and
returned it, saying with indifference: "Good, good.   We'll
talk of it after our meal.   Perhaps you'll join us, if you've
no objection.   Me and my wife'll feel honored, and so will
mother; won't you, mother?"

The invitation was doubly echoed, and Deronda glady accepted it.   All now turned and stood round the table.   No
dish was at present seen except one covered with a napkin;
and Mrs. Cohen had placed a china bowl near her husband
that he might wash his hands in it.   But after putting on his
hat again, he paused, and called in a loud voice: "Mordecai!"

Can this be part of the religious ceremony? thought Deronda, not knowing what might be expected of the ancient
hero.   But he heard a "Yes" from the next room, which
made him look toward the open door; and there, to his astonishment, he saw the figure of the enigmatic Jew whom he
had this morning met with in the book-shop.   Their eyes met,
and Mordecai looked as much surprised as Deronda—neither
in his surprise making any sign of recognition.   But when

Mordecai was seating himself at the end of the table, he just bent his head to the guest in a cold and distant manner, as if the disappointment of the morning remained a disagreeable association with this new acquaintance.

Cohen now washed his hands, pronouncing Hebrew words the while: afterward he took off the napkin covering the dish and disclosed the two long flat loaves besprinkled with seed— the memorial of the manna that fed the wandering forefathers —and breaking off small pieces gave one to each of the family, including Adelaide Rebekah, who stood on the chair with her whole length exhibited in her amber-colored garment, her little Jewish nose lengthened by compression of the lip in the effort to make a suitable appearance. Cohen then uttered another Hebrew blessing, and after that, the male heads were uncovered, all seated themselves, and the meal went on without any peculiarity that interested Deronda. He was not very conscious of what dishes he ate from, being preoccupied with a desire to turn the conversation in a way that would enable him to ask some leading question; and also with thinking of Mordecai, between whom and himself there was an exchange of fascinated, half-furtive glances. Mordecai had no handsome Sabbath garment, but instead of the threadbare rusty black coat of the morning he wore one of light drab, which looked as if it had once been a handsome loose paletot now shrunk with washing; and this change of clothing gave a still stronger accentuation to his dark-haired, eager face, which might have belonged to the prophet Ezekiel—also probably not modish in the eyes of contemporaries. It was noticeable that the thin tails of the fried fish were given to Mordecai; and in general the sort of share assigned to a poor relation— no doubt a "survival" of pre-historic practice, not yet generally admitted to be superstitious.

Mr. Cohen kept up the conversation with much liveliness, introducing as subjects always in taste (the Jew is proud of his loyalty) the Queen and the Royal Family, the Emperor and Empress of the French—into which both grandmother and wife entered with zest. Mrs. Cohen the younger showed an accurate memory of distinguished birthdays; and the elder assisted her son in informing the guest of what occurred when the Emperor and Empress were in England and visited the city, ten years before.

"I dare say you know all about it better than we do, sir," said Cohen, repeatedly, by way of preface to full information; and the interesting statements were kept up in a trio.

"Our baby is named *Eu*genie Esther," said young Mrs. Cohen, vivaciously.

"It's wonderful how the Emperor's like a cousin of mine in the face," said the grandmother; "it struck me like lightning when I caught sight of him. I couldn't have thought it."

"Mother and me went to see the Emperor and Empress at the Crystal Palace," said Mr. Cohen. "I had a fine piece of work to take care of mother; she might have been squeezed flat—though she was pretty near as lusty then as she is now. I said if I had a hundred mothers I'd never take one of 'em to see the Emperor and Empress at the Crystal Palace again; and you may think a man can't afford it when he's got but one mother—not if he'd ever so big an insurance on her." He stroked his mother's shoulder affectionately, and chuckled a little at his own humor.

"Your mother has been a widow a long while, perhaps," said Deronda, seizing his opportunity. "That has made your care for her the more needful."

"Ay, ay, it's good many *yore-zeit* since I had to manage for her and myself," said Cohen, quickly. "I went early to it. It's that makes you a sharp knife."

"What does—what makes a sharp knife, father?" said Jacob, his cheek very much swollen with sweet-cake.

The father winked at his guest, and said: "Having your nose put on the grindstone."

Jacob slipped from his chair with the piece of sweet-cake in his hand, and going close up to Mordecai, who had been totally silent hitherto, said: "What does that mean—putting my nose to the grindstone?"

"It means that you are to bear being hurt without making a noise," said Mordecai, turning his eyes benignantly on the small face close to his. Jacob put the corner of the cake into Mordecai's mouth as an invitation to bite, saying meanwhile, "I sha'n't, though," and keeping his eyes on the cake to observe how much of it went in this act of generosity. Mordecai took a bite and smiled, evidently meaning to please the lad, and the little incident made them both look more lovable. Deronda, however, felt with some vexation that he had taken little by his question.

"I fancy that is the right quarter for learning," said he, carrying on the subject that he might have an excuse for addressing Mordecai, to whom he turned and said: "You have been a great student, I imagine."

"I have studied," was the quiet answer. "And you?—You know German, by the book you were buying."

"Yes, I have studied in Germany. Are you generally engaged in bookselling?" said Deronda.

"No; I only go to Mr. Ram's shop every day to keep it while he goes to meals," said Mordecai, who was now looking at Deronda with what seemed a revival of his original interest: it seemed as if the face had some attractive indication for him which now neutralized the former disappointment. After a slight pause, he said: "Perhaps you know Hebrew?"

"I am sorry to say, not at all."

Mordecai's countenance fell: he cast down his eyelids, looking at his hands which lay crossed before him, and said no more. Deronda had now noticed more decisively than in their former interview a difficulty of breathing which he thought must be a sign of consumption.

"I've had something else to do than to get book-learning," said Mr. Cohen,—"I've had to make myself knowing about useful things. I know stones well,"—here he pointed to Deronda's ring. I'm not afraid of taking that ring of yours at my own valuation. "But now," he added, with a certain drop in his voice to a lower, more familiar nasal, "what do you want for it?"

"Fifty or sixty pounds," Deronda answered, rather too carelessly.

Cohen paused a little, thrust his hands into his pockets, fixed on Deronda a pair of glistening eyes that suggested a miraculous guinea-pig, and said: "Couldn't do you that. Happy to oblige, but couldn't go that length. Forty pounds—say forty—I'll let you have forty on it."

Deronda was aware that Mordecai had looked up again at
the words implying a monetary affair, and was now examining him again, while he said: "Very well; I shall redeem it
in a month or so."

"Good. I'll make you out a ticket by and by," said Cohen,
indifferently. Then he held up his finger as a sign that conversation must be deferred. He, Mordecai, and Jacob put on
their hats, and Cohen opened a thanksgiving which was carried on by responses, till Mordecai delivered himself alone at
some length, in a solemn chanting tone, with his chin slightly
uplifted and his thin hands clasped easily before him. Not
only in his accent and tone, but in his freedom from the self-
consciousness which has reference to others' approbation, there
could hardly have been a stronger contrast to the Jew at the
other end of the table. It was an unaccountable conjunction
—the presence among these common, prosperous, shopkeeping
types, of a man who, in an emaciated threadbare condition,
imposed a certain awe on Deronda, and an embarrassment at
not meeting his expectations.

No sooner had Mordecai finished his devotional strain, than
rising, with a slight bend of his head to the stranger, he walked
back into his room, and shut the door behind him.

"That seems to be rather a remarkable man," said Deronda, turning to Cohen, who immediately set up his shoulders, put out his tongue slightly, and tapped his own brow.
It was clearly to be understood that Mordecai did not come
up to the standard of sanity which was set by Mr. Cohen's
view of men and things.

"Does he belong to your family?" said Deronda.

This idea appeared to be rather ludicrous to the ladies as
well as to Cohen, and the family interchanged looks of amusement.

"No, no," said Cohen. "Charity! charity! He worked
for me, and when he got weaker and weaker I took him in.
He's an encumbrance; but he brings a blessing down, and he
teaches the boy. Besides, he does the repairing at the watches
and jewelry."

Deronda hardly abstained from smiling at this mixture of
kindliness and the desire to justify it in the light of a calcula-

tion; but his willingness to speak further of Mordecai, whose character was made the more enigmatically striking by these new details, was baffled. Mr. Cohen immediately dismissed the subject by reverting to the "accommodation," which was also an act of charity, and proceeded to make out the ticket, get the forty pounds, and present them both in exchange for the diamond ring. Deronda, feeling that it would be hardly delicate to protract his visit beyond the settlement of the business which was its pretext, had to take his leave, with no more decided result than the advance of forty pounds and the pawn-ticket in his breast pocket, to make a reason for returning when he came up to town after Christmas. He was resolved that he would then endeavor to gain a little more insight into the character and history of Mordecai; from whom also he might gather something decisive about the Cohens—for example, the reason why it was forbidden to ask Mrs. Cohen the elder whether she had a daughter. .